Jack buzzed three t... crackled from the spea...

"This is Federal Deli... delivery to the Chamberlain Auditorium was refused. We're returning the package to the sender."

"I'll be right there."

Jack moved close to the door, drew his Tactical. He heard the lock click. The knob turned and the door opened a crack. Jack kicked it open. It crashed against a blonde woman who flew backward, striking her head against the wall. Jack moved through the doorway, weapon ready as he scanned the office for threats. The blonde woman was lying still. Jack leveled his weapon at her, kicked the gun out of her hand.

He noticed the computer on the desk, printouts stacked up around it. On the monitor he saw a schematic similar to the one they'd printed out at architect Nawaf Sanjore's home. He caught movement out of the corner of his eye, saw the woman on the floor shifting, heard her groan.

"What are these plans on the screen?" he called to her. "What are you up to?"

The woman wiped a trickle of blood off her cheek, saw her gun was gone.

"What are these plans for?" Jack repeated.

The woman simply smirked. "You can kill me, but you're too late to stop us."

Jack saw her jaw move, heard the crunch of the capsule in her mouth. With a gasp, she began jerking spastically, legs kicking wildly, foam flecking her mouth . . .

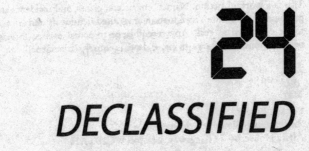

24

DECLASSIFIED

TROJAN HORSE

M A R C   C E R A S I N I

Based on the series by Joel Surnow & Robert Cochran

POCKET
BOOKS

LONDON • SYDNEY • NEW YORK • TORONTO

POCKET BOOKS
An Imprint of Simon & Schuster Ltd.
Africa House, 64–78 Kingsway, London WC2B 6AH

ISBN: 1-4165-1171-7
EAN: 9781416511717

Pocket Books and related logo are trademarks of Simon & Schuster, Ltd.

First Pocket Books paperback printing: February 2006

Printed and bound in Great Britain

10 9 8 7 6 5 4 3 2 1

A CIP catalogue record for this book is available from the British Library

This novel is dedicated to my mother,
Evelyn May Cerasini

ACKNOWLEDGMENTS

The author sends out a hearty "w00t" of thanks to Sharon K. Wheeler, software engineer (and mainframe maven), for her helpful guidance in all things digital. If there are any errors, or if literary license was taken in the depiction of computer technology in this book, the responsibility falls entirely with the author.

Special thanks to Hope Innelli and Josh Behar of HarperCollins for their vision, guidance, and personal encouragement. Thanks also to Virginia King of 20th Century Fox for her continued support.

Without the groundbreaking, Emmy Award-winning "24" creators, Joel Surnow and Robert Cochran, and their talented writing team, this novel would not exist. Special thanks to them and also to Kiefer Sutherland for breathing life into the memorable character of Jack Bauer.

Finally, a personal thank you to my literary agent, John Talbot, for his ongoing support. And a very special thank you to my wife, Alice Alfonsi. A guy couldn't ask for a better partner—in writing or in life.

Tro•jan horse

noun

1: the large, hollow wooden horse filled with Greek soldiers and introduced within the walls of Troy by a stratagem
2: a seemingly innocent computer program that is willingly downloaded by the user without suspicion, but when executed, activates hidden programming that performs malicious or unwanted actions

After the 1993 World Trade Center attack, a division of the Central Intelligence Agency established a domestic unit tasked with protecting America from the threat of terrorism. Headquartered in Washington, D.C., the Counter Terrorist Unit established field offices in several American cities. From its inception, CTU faced hostility and skepticism from other Federal law enforcement agencies. Despite bureaucratic resistance, within a few years CTU had become a major force. After the war against terror began, a number of early CTU missions were declassified. The following is one of them . . .

24
DECLASSIFIED

TROJAN HORSE

PROLOGUE

He found Jack Bauer hunched over the conference room table, head cradled in his arms. It took Administrative Director Richard Walsh only a moment to realize his agent was fast asleep. Setting the digital audio recorder on the table, Walsh wondered how Jack could find peace amid the chaos that still reigned on the other side of the wall, in CTU's war room, hours after the crisis had presumably passed.

Walsh unbuttoned the suit jacket that seemed to stretch too tightly across his broad shoulders. He would have preferred to leave Jack to his dreams. *God knows, the man earned his rest.* But with his bosses at Langley demanding answers—probably because *their* bosses in the House and Senate Intelligence Committees were demanding same—Walsh had no choice but to gather all the statements as soon as possible, and deliver his findings. The Administrative Director of CTU shut the door, sat down in a steel chair across from the sleeping man.

Jack awoke at the sound, instantly alert. He sat up, arrow-straight, fully aware of his surroundings. Jack self-consciously rubbed the stubble on his jaw, combed his sandy-blond hair back with his fingers, embarrassed to appear before his superior in such a disheveled state.

" 'Morning Jack. Have a nice nap?"

Bauer shrugged off the gentle jibe as his superior tossed him a sympathetic smile. It vanished a moment later when Walsh keyed his digital recorder.

"Log number 32452, subheading IAC. Debriefing Special Agent Jack Bauer," said Walsh, adding Jack's service tag, the day, date, and time. Then Walsh scratched his closely shaved chin and fixed his pale-blue gaze on the man across the table.

"Ryan Chappelle tells me that a raid on a major movie studio triggered this unpleasantness. What the hell were you and Blackburn's tactical team doing in Hollywood?"

"Utopia Studios is not a major movie studio and it's not in Hollywood," Jack replied. "Utopia *was* a marginal direct-to-video production company until they fell on hard times—a combination of rising production costs and diminishing interest in the soft-core porn and low-rent horror films they were peddling did them in."

"So Utopia Studios became a threat to national security?"

"Utopia Studios doesn't exist. Not anymore," said Jack. "Its CEO declared bankruptcy, incorporated a brand new firm with a new financial partner and shifted production facilities to Montreal. The move saved him a bundle but left his old studio on the ass-end of Glendale's industrial zone vacant, its proprietorship a matter of ongoing litigation. In the meantime, narco-terrorists moved in and set up shop—or at least, that was the intel we had at the time."

Walsh studied the sheaf of papers in front of him.

"According to the DEA this was primarily a drug raid."

"That's true. Chet Blackburn and I were members of a joint task force working with the DEA—part of District Director Ryan Chappelle's interagency initiative."

"Yeah. I think I got the memo on that," Walsh said dryly.

"The initiative was launched because the CIA and the DEA unearthed intelligence indicating a new level of cooperation between international terrorists and certain drug cartels. Chappelle thought it best to team up with the Drug Enforcement Agency in order to better manage the problem—"

"And spread some of the responsibility around in case things went south."

Jack nodded. "That too."

"So beyond some faulty intelligence, what was the rationale for this *interagency initiative*?"

"Things are heating up. In the past twenty months, the DEA has captured military-grade weapons in several raids along the U.S.–Mexican border. And you recall that CTU recently thwarted a plot to use smuggled North Korean Long Tooth shoulder-fired missiles to down U.S. commercial airliners."

Walsh smoothed his walrus moustache with his thumb and index finger. "You're talking about Hell Gate."

It wasn't a question so Jack didn't reply.

Walsh shifted in the steel chair, which seemed too small for the brawny man.

"Chappelle also tells me that despite the obvious threat to national security, you initially resisted this assignment. Now why would you do that, Special Agent Bauer?"

Walsh was staring at Jack now, waiting.

"Permission to speak freely, sir."

Walsh turned off the audio recorder. "Talk."

"When it comes to the Counter Terrorist Unit, interagency cooperation has always been a one-way street," Jack began. "CTU *gave*, the FBI, the DOD, the DEA *took*. Period."

"It's gotten better," said Walsh. His lined face was impassive, unreadable.

"I'll concede that the situation has improved in recent months. But CTU is still getting squeezed out of the big picture—by some of the same people Chappelle ordered me to work alongside."

"You could have refused the assignment. You could have come to me and I would have handled things with Chappelle. You had to make a choice here." Walsh paused. "So what changed your mind, Jack?"

"Karma."

Richard Walsh activated the recorder. "Tell me everything that happened to you and members of the Los Angeles unit in the past twenty-four hours, Special Agent Bauer. Start at the beginning . . ."

1 2 3 4 5 6 7 8 9
10 11 12 13 14 15 16 17
18 19 20 21 22 23 24

....

**THE FOLLOWING TAKES PLACE
BETWEEN THE HOURS OF
5 A.M. AND 6 A.M.
PACIFIC DAYLIGHT TIME**

....

5:01:01 A.M. PDT
Atwater Village, Los Angeles

Jack Bauer gazed at Utopia, or so the sign proclaimed.
But beyond the vacant security gate and tattered chain
link fence, Bauer saw only an expanse of pitted asphalt abutting an interconnected cluster of ugly,
graffiti-stained concrete block buildings.

Squinting through a telescopic imager, Jack
scanned the shuttered loading docks and steel doors,
the windows boarded up tight. He double-checked
one particular entrance, with the number 9 painted
on its flat steel door. Then he tucked the tiny device
into a sheath on his night-black assault suit. Now that
the sun was creeping above the horizon, he no longer

required the imager's thermal or light-enhancing capabilities to pierce the gloom.

Sprawled on his belly atop a rocky brown rise that separated Utopia from another dusty industrial park, Jack lowered his head behind a clump of scrub-grass and adjusted the assault rifle in the Velcro zip holster strapped across his back. He had arrived at his position hours before, moving into place along with five members of Chet Blackburn's CTU assault team, now scattered and invisible among the rocks and low hills around him. Though Jack could not see them, he knew another tactical squad from the Drug Enforcement Agency lurked in the bluffs on the opposite side of the complex. When the signal came, the two assault teams would converge on the buildings in a coordinated two-pronged attack.

In the dead of the hot dry night, the tactical units had converged to surround the supposedly abandoned production studio, unseen and undetected by those inside. Then they waited until the sun was a hot yellow ball surrounded by hazy dust, until the arrival of the big fish both agencies were hoping to scoop up in their net.

Jack shifted position, clenching and unclenching his sweaty hands, stretching his sleepy arms and legs, always careful not to expose his position. He moved a stone that had been chafing him, rubbed his sore neck. Compared to his days as a member of Delta Force, this was not a particularly unpleasant mission. In the line of duty Jack had experienced far worse things than watching the Southern California sun rise from a quiet bluff. Perhaps it was merely his age that made his joints ache, his muscles stiff from inactivity. Perhaps creeping old age also explained why, as zero hour approached, Jack felt an uncharacteristic edginess, an impatience as he waited for the signal to move.

Or perhaps it was the fact that Jack Bauer had to wait for that command, just like everyone else. Working in tandem with the DEA was not part of Bauer's job description, nor did he appreciate taking orders from others. That's why, when Ryan first handed him this assignment weeks ago, Jack refused it. Chappelle didn't seemed surprised by Bauer's reaction; rather he advised Jack to look first, then decide.

"Go to the briefing this afternoon," Ryan said. "Listen to what the DEA has to say. It may change your mind."

To Jack's surprise, his mind *was* changed after the DEA briefed him and other select members of the intelligence community about the dangers of Karma, a potent new drug poised to hit the streets of America, a narcotic that had the potential to make the crack epidemic of the 1980s look like an ice cream party.

According to researchers who studied a sample of this substance, Karma was a type of super methamphetamine. But Karma wasn't merely a powerful stimulant. The drug also induced a sense of invulnerability and euphoria in the user, sometimes accompanied by mild hallucinogenic reactions. The pharmacological experts who studied the new compound and its effects on the brain believed Karma to be more addictive than crack cocaine or even heroin.

Karma was ingested orally—dissolved under the tongue like a lozenge or simply swallowed—and the drug's ease of consumption was an element of its appeal. Virtually undetectable, it could be dissolved in a flavored or alcoholic beverage, which made it the perfect date-rape drug.

No one knew what criminal or narco-terrorist group initially synthesized Karma, but the drug had first appeared in the streets of Eastern Europe, Russia, and the Chechen Republic nearly a year before. Karma was not available in America or Western Europe as yet, because it was difficult to manufacture. It required real laboratory conditions to be synthesized properly. Even after synthesis, the compound broke down rapidly, making for a relatively short shelf life. Complicated, well-equipped labs for churning out the stuff had to be established locally.

The upside for criminal producers was that once the network was up and running, labs would be difficult to find. No illegal smuggling was involved in the manufacturing process. Karma's ingredients were not controlled substances; they were common chemicals available commercially. Already, at least one overseas crime lord was bankrolling the establishment of Karma labs in Los Angeles, San Francisco, Seattle, Montreal.

According to the DEA's best intelligence, the illegal manufacturing facility inside of the Utopia Studios complex was the first of the U.S. labs to go on line. The DEA wanted to shut it down and capture its operators before their poison ever reached the street.

His musings were interrupted when Jack's earbud chirped.

"This is Angel Three. A car's just come off North San Fernando Road. It's moving east along Andrita."

"This is Angel Two. Roger," Jack replied, voice calm.

Angel Three—Agent Miguel Avilla—was a twenty-year veteran of the DEA. Thin, wiry and acerbic, Avilla was positioned in plain sight, right outside the studio gate and across Andrita Street from the abandoned movie studio. Unwashed and unshaven, shuffling around wrapped in a dirty blanket, Agent Avilla had posed as a homeless man for the past nine days while he'd observed the activities at the old studio.

To better reconnoiter the facility, Avilla had taken up residence among a copse of twisted trees in an empty lot, where he swilled booze openly, urinated in the gutter, and generally elicited no notice from those who worked along the lightly traveled street. He also made hourly reports to his superiors at the Los Angeles DEA office—relating the number of trucks arriving at and leaving the supposedly deserted studio, and observing several visits by a well-known representative of a Midwest narcotics distributor.

On his third day living on Andrita Street, several *cholos* emerged from Utopia Studios and dished Avilla a pretty severe beating. They punched and kicked him while going through his filthy clothes. Not satisfied, the punks tore up the rickety shopping basket Avilla pushed around, scattering its contents across the empty lot. Fortunately Avilla was careful and the punks found nothing but a half-bottle of cheap wine, which they poured in the gutter. After that, Avilla had established his authenticity in their minds, and the punks working at the studio pretty much ignored the homeless man just like everyone else. As a precaution, Agent Avilla continued to bury his radio and weapon in a shallow grave at the base of a scrub oak.

"This is Angel Three. The car has stopped outside the gate. Repeat, the car has stopped."

"This is Angel One. Roger that. Probably waiting for someone to unlock the gate . . . These goons don't have a clue what's coming for them. Over and out."

Even over the headphones, Jack could hear the tension in the other man's voice, tension masked by too many words, too much bravado. It was obvious to Jack that DEA Agent Brian McConnell—Angel One— was not yet ready to make command decisions or lead an assault team in a raid of this scope and importance.

So why was he put in charge of the tactical teams?

"This is Angel Three. Someone's coming out to open the gate."

"This is it," cried Angel One, voice tight with tension. "Get ready to move."

Breaking protocol, Jack spoke. "This is Angel Two, hold your positions. Hold your positions."

But no one was listening. No one from the DEA anyway. Jack could see men in black assault gear and lumpy body armor rising from cover on the opposite side of the studio compound.

"Get your men down before they're observed, Angel One," Jack commanded. As he spoke, Jack slipped the Heckler & Koch G36 Commando short carbine from its sheath across his back, chambered a 5.56mm armor-piercing round.

Another voice broke into the net. "This is Archangel. Stand down, Angel One. Wait for a positive ID on the men in the car."

Jack was relieved to see the men on the opposite bluff melt back into the terrain.

Archangel was DEA chief Jason Peltz, the overall commander of this operation. Late forties, stoop-shouldered with salt and pepper hair balding in the middle, Peltz more resembled a high school history teacher than a major force in the Drug Enforcement Agency with two decades of experience. Last year Peltz had moved into the top spot at the DEA's Los Angeles office. Since then, he'd become more of a bureaucrat than a front line operative. But Peltz was savvy enough to surround himself with dedicated, competent and incorruptible veterans of the drug wars like Miguel Avilla, so his pension was secure.

If Jack had an issue with Peltz's management style, it was that the man chose to issue orders from a portable command center hidden inside a dirty van parked a block and a half away. As Jack saw it, Peltz should have been here, on the ground, among his troops. It troubled Jack that Peltz left the heavy lifting to an inexperienced assault team leader like Brian McConnell, who was clearly not up to the task.

No harm done, but the snafu should not have occurred.

"Angel Three, this is Angel One. Do you have a positive ID on the car, the passengers?"

"It's a different car, Angel One," Avilla replied. "I think it's the same driver, though. There are three other men in the vehicle but I can't get a good look at them through the tinted glass."

"Listen to me, Avilla. I need a positive ID, pronto, or we can pack up and go home right now."

"I'm trying, McConnell. Give me a fucking minute."

Jack chafed at the breach of radio discipline. Communications were breaking down and Agent McConnell was making the situation worse by badgering Avilla.

"Angel One, this is Angel Two," said Jack. "I observe movement on the northeast corner of the second building. Can you confirm."

Jack had seen a bird fluttering on the roof and recognized what he'd seen. But he wanted to divert McConnell's focus away from Avilla long enough for the man on the street to do his job.

"This is Angel One. I see no activity in the northeast. You probably saw a bird."

"Roger that," Jack replied.

"This is Angel Three. I have a positive ID on the passenger. The target is in the car. Repeat, the target is in the car."

"This is Angel One. Let's move. Go, go, go."

Jack burst from cover, his chukkas kicking up dust as he sprinted across the bluff and descended the rocky slope, balancing with one arm, the other gripping his assault rifle. Behind him, three more figures emerged from cover—Chet Blackburn and members of his CTU tactical team.

Jack's feet hit the asphalt before anyone else. He flicked off the safety, then aimed the muzzle of the G36 at the steel door marked with the number 9. Feet pounded the pavement at his shoulder. It was Chet Blackburn, covering his back.

They hit the wall simultaneously three seconds later, flattening themselves on either side of the door. Already, Blackburn had sculpted a wad of C-4 plastic explosives into a donut to encircle the doorknob. He draped it around the metal lock, plugged in the detonator.

"Five seconds," Chet Blackburn warned.

It seemed longer. Jack had pressed closer to the wall, waiting. When the blast finally came, he felt the shock ripple along his spine. The door blew off its hinges, spun away. Jack heard the clang as it landed somewhere inside the studio. The noise of the blast quickly faded. Bauer and Blackburn moved cautiously but quickly through the door. The other two men remained outside, guarding their backs and making sure no one escaped the net.

Then, from the opposite side of the studio com-

pound, and near the front gate, the CTU agents heard
shots.

Squinting against the glare, Tony Almeida slipped
heavy-framed sunglasses over his eyes. Already the
Southern California sun was over the horizon and
burning too bright, too hot. The L.A. basin was expe-
riencing the most severe drought in fifteen years.
Down here near the border it was even worse. A haze
hung over the hills from the brushfires.

But this was nothing new. Since Tony had moved to
the City of Angels after his stint in the Marine Corps,
Southern California seemed to be in one crisis mode
after another. Droughts and the resulting wildfires.
Mudslides. Riots. And the ubiquitous earthquakes.

He glanced at the TAG Heuer steel chronograph on
his wrist. Nearly 5:30 with six miles to go, and traffic
so thick he might not make it in time. Tony cursed,
swerved the late-model Dodge truck to get around a
meandering driver, nearly adding to the dents and
scrapes that covered the vehicle's exterior. The woman
in the seat next to him squealed. She'd spilled some of
her steaming hot coffee on her low-riders.

"Slow down, Tony. What's the rush?"

Tony downshifted, applied the brake—not to ap-
pease Fay Hubley, but because traffic had once again
slowed to a crawl in all four lanes. When they rolled
to a complete stop a moment later, Tony lowered the
window. Dust and hot dry air filled the cabin. Fay,
dabbing at the brown stains on her faded denims,

coughed theatrically. Tony ignored her, stuck his head out in a futile effort to see around a lumbering truck that filled his windshield. An aircraft heading in to Brown Field Municipal Airport roared overhead, adding to the cacophony.

Tony closed the window, slumped behind the wheel. The rattle of the air conditioner replaced the ear-battering road roar.

"Thank god you didn't get any coffee, you're so tense," said Fay. "Are we late? Is that why you didn't want to stop? I mean, we lost like two minutes at the Starbucks drive-through."

Tony let go of the steering wheel, stroked his black goatee, a larger amount of beard than he was used to beneath his lip. His hair felt strange, too. Long in the back and bunched into a small ponytail at the nape of his neck.

Fay glanced at Tony from under long blond lashes, then looked away. She pursed her glossed lips, brushed dangling strands of curly blond hair away from her tanned face.

"Chill out, will you, boss? It's not like we're on a deadline, right?"

"Actually we *are* on a deadline, Agent Hubley. If we don't cross the border at the right time, with the right border guard on duty, we risk the chance that we might get stopped. And if they found the stuff in the back of this truck we'd have some explaining to do."

"It's not like we're the bad guys. We can tell the border patrol who we are, what we're doing."

"Yeah, let's let some border guard in on classified information," Tony replied, his tone impatient. "Hell, for all we know the guard we talk to could be the same corrupt son of a bitch who let Richard Lesser escape across the Mexican border in the first place."

Fay turned away from Tony, gazed out the passenger side window.

Tony regretted his tone, if not his words, as soon as he said them. It wasn't Fay Hubley's fault that she was inexperienced, that she had never gone undercover before, never even worked in the field. She wouldn't be doing it now if circumstances didn't demand her involvement. Tony needed Agent Hubley's computer expertise to sniff out their prey's cyber trail while Tony ran down the fugitive in the real world.

The man they were hunting, Richard Lesser, was approximately the same age as Fay. A graduate of Stanford, Lesser held a Master's degree in Computer Science. He was also one of the top programmers in his class. Not satisfied making a cool half-million dollars a year creating security protocols or designing computer games, Lesser decided his first career move after university would be to hack the computer of America's top computer security specialists, then hold its entire database hostage. Boscom Systems paid up to protect their reputation—to the tune of five million dollars. Ultimately their own cyber-sleuths managed to identify Lesser from a piece of errant coding his "Hijack" program inadvertently left buried in Boscom's mainframe.

Two weeks ago, Lesser had managed to jump across the border hours before an indictment against him was handed down. Since his crimes were purely economic and limited to a narrow scope of damage, he wasn't the type of malefactor CTU usually hunted. But in the past eight days, persistent and urgent chatter had been detected between two known Central American narco-terrorist groups and an unknown cell led by a shadowy figure named Hasan. All three groups mentioned Richard Lesser by name. One of these cells was located in Colombia, the other was based in Mexico City, and the third somewhere in the United States. All placed the fugitive Lesser somewhere in Tijuana, and analysts believed all three groups were dispatching representatives to snatch him up.

The intercepts set off alarm bells inside of CTU's Cyber-Division—Fay Hubley's unit. After being briefed, Special Agent Larry Hastings, Director of CTU's Cyber-Operations in Washington, told Ryan Chappelle he believed Lesser to be the most dangerous fugitive of his kind in the world because of the knowledge and skills the man possessed. Hastings felt it was imperative Lesser be captured and returned to the United States, or prevented from linking up with the terrorists by whatever means necessary. With Washington's stamp of approval, Tony's and Fay's mission was hastily assembled.

On the road, the traffic began to move again. Tony shifted into first and drove on in silence, still rueful over his sharp rebuke. It didn't help Almeida's mood that he hadn't showered or shaved in nearly twenty-four hours. That it wasn't even 6 A.M. and he could already feel the heat suffocating him, the grit collecting around the collar of his denim jacket, the sweat pooling in his Steve Madden boots.

"I can tell you're not relaxing," Fay Hubley said, trying to break the tension.

"I'll relax when we get to Tijuana," Tony replied, eyes forward.

Tony Almeida would have preferred to leave Fay Hubley safe in front of her computer in L.A. Under normal circumstances, that's just what he would have done. But for this high priority mission to be successful, Tony required the help of someone who could keep constant tabs on the computer activity of the man they were hunting, to monitor Richard Lesser's bank accounts, credit cards, his computer use and Internet activity. No one was better at this type of cyber-detective work than Fay Hubley, CTULA's newest recruit.

Agent Hubley was twenty-five, fresh out of Carnegie Mellon University graduate school and eager to serve her country. Instead of returning to her family in Columbus, Ohio, and taking a job with some dot.com, Fay Hubley was recruited by the Counter Terrorist Unit, where she served first in Washington, D.C., later in the Los Angeles division.

It was Administrative Director Richard Walsh who brought Agent Hubley to the West Coast after he learned she'd created a bloodhound program that could trace a computer user using a phone line to a specific telephone number, or even a Wi Fi zone. Already CTU had used her protocols to trace the activities of a computer hacker who had nearly cracked the CIA database at Langley. The man was currently behind bars and awaiting trial.

For her first undercover mission, Fay Hubley's computer skills required the use of a quarter of a million dollars' worth of hardware and software, now riding in the back of their van along with eye candy—several hundred stolen credit cards and a few magnetic strip detectors—there to mask their true mission.

If Tony or Fay ran afoul of the Mexican authorities, they had a credible cover story and evidence to back it up. And Tony Almeida—a.k.a. Tony Navarro, gringo credit card fraud and identity thief—had enough cash on hand to get him and his girlfriend free of any corrupt Mexican law enforcement officials.

They would face far less danger here if they were

thought to be white-collar criminals than U.S. government agents working undercover. As far as Tony was concerned, DEA Agent Enrique Camarena Salazar was still a valid cautionary tale. Salazar had been snatched off the streets of Guadalajara and tortured to death by drug traffickers, who'd been tipped off by corrupt Mexican police officials.

"Look! We're almost there," Fay cried. "Two miles to the border."

She gestured at the sign, sloshed more coffee on her jeans.

Tony glanced at the woman's attire, finding it hard to reconcile Fay Hubley's quiet, conservative, sometimes drab appearance at CTU with her current undercover persona. At one time in his life, Tony Almeida had been accurately described as a street punk. Growing up in a tough, violent neighborhood in Chicago he became tough and violent, too. Though that period in his life was long gone, Tony could still summon enough of his former self to convince the bad guys that he was one of them. But try as he might, Tony could not imagine what hidden aspect of her personality Fay Hubley mined to create her false identity.

Over sandals and form-fitting low-riders Fay wore a scarlet, belly-baring cotton blouse with dangling, retro-1970s fringe. Sleeveless, the top revealed a tattoo of intertwined vines encircling Fay's upper arm. Another tattoo of an elaborate dragonfly spreading its wings across the small of her back was also on display. Fay's finger and toenails were polished bright purple to match her eye shadow and lipstick.

Last night, after the pre-mission briefing, as the pair was preparing to depart CTU Headquarters for

Tijuana, Jamey Farrell got a look at her co-worker in disguise.

"Whoa," she said, "who knew Fay Hubley was more Bratz than Barbie?"

Tony was not certain if the tattoos were real or temporary, but the mission was assembled so quickly there would have been no time for Fay to get her navel pierced—yet a delicate silver dragonfly now swung on a thin chain that dangled from the woman's navel ring.

Tony looked away before Fay noticed his stare. *Man*, he thought, *the quiet ones can really surprise you.*

5:46:01 A.M. PDT
Utopia Studios

They'd made it inside the abandoned studio, only to be stopped by a hail of gunfire. Now Jack Bauer and Chet Blackburn huddled back to back, between the concrete wall and a dumpster in one of Utopia Studios' large sound stages. Armor-piercing rounds battered the metal container with enough force to pierce the steel and ricochet like mad inside the dumpster.

"They're cornered. They're not going anywhere. Why the hell didn't they just give up?" Blackburn cried over the noise. Under his faceplate, the man's dark skin was shiny with sweat.

"They brought guns," said Jack. "They figured they had to use them."

Jack hunkered down, wiped the stream of blood that leaked from his nose. He yanked off his helmet, wondering why the communicator had stopped working. He discovered that the transmitter inside the liner had been shattered by the same round that had grazed his headpiece a moment before.

"Try to reach Angel One," Jack said, spitting crimson. "Find out what's happening on the other side of that wall."

Cautiously, Jack poked his head out. Across fifty feet of sound stage cluttered with movie props—everything from ornate period furniture to grandfather clocks, fake laboratory machinery, even a suit of armor—Jack saw another steel door that was still sealed. His movement attracted a short crackle of fire. As Jack ducked back behind cover, metal rounds splattered against the wall, spraying the two men with shrapnel and dust. Jack grunted. A shard of hot metal had pierced his battle suit, burning a hole into his left arm at the biceps. Jack swallowed bile, ignored the fiery sting.

"Angel One's team should have been through that door by now," Jack told Blackburn.

"They can't get through," Blackburn replied. "That door's been welded shut to protect the lab from this kind of raid. The DEA has taken the lab, captured the big fish, too. Now they're looking for another way to reach us."

"They better hurry," said Jack.

Blackburn eyed the stain on Bauer's arm. "You know we can't sit here and wait. We move or we die." Then a wry smile appeared. "You know, we could go out the way we came in. These guys are only goons and they aren't getting away. We could wait them out, or come back in with more muscle."

Bauer shook his head. "Let's finish this now, before someone gets hurt. How many shooters did you spot?"

"I counted two," Blackburn replied. "One at three

o'clock. Another one's lurking over there near that suit of armor, or he was a minute ago."

Now the man could be anywhere. They both knew it. Jack shook the shards of broken transmitter out of his Kevlar assault helmet, slipped it on. Jack lowered the cracked visor, then he and Blackburn checked their weapons.

"Let's go," Jack said.

They rolled away from one another, emerging in a sprint on either side of the pockmarked dumpster. Jack aimed the G36—at air. His prey had vanished.

Chet Blackburn was luckier. His man rose up from behind cover and opened up with twin .45s. Hispanic, mid-twenties, the *cholo* wore athletic gear, white sneakers and enough bling to open a jewelry store. He clutched the handguns in a sideways gangsta grip, too—a tactic impressive in a drive-by shooting but hardly effective in this situation.

Blackburn stood his ground as the first two shots warbled past his ears, winced when the third round nicked his body armor and tore away a chunk of battle suit. Then he fired twice. His first shot struck the shooter between the eyes, snapping his head back. The second entered under the man's chin, blew away the top of his skull. The dead man flopped to the ground, the twitching hand pumping off one last shot, which ricocheted off the wall.

Jack spied his quarry racing across the old movie set. He raised his G36 to fire, then lowered the muzzle and slung the weapon over his shoulder. Deciding on a capture, Jack took off in a sprint. He would try to head off the youth at the edge of the set.

Blackburn glanced up from securing the dead man's weapons. He watched Bauer catch up with the

running man, seize the nape of his neck, a handful of long dark hair. Together the two men slammed into the suit of armor, which was actually a sculpture of welded steel. Jack grunted, the wind knocked out of him as the other man's body cushioned the impact.

Chet Blackburn winced. Even from ten meters away he'd heard the sickening crunch when the fugitive's nose flattened, his front teeth shattered against the iron breastplate.

After stumbling to his feet, Jack leaned against the medieval prop. He used plastic zip cuffs to secure the bleeding man's arms behind his back. But before he could haul his prisoner to his feet, the studio was rocked by another explosion. Dust billowed from a far corner of the massive sound stage as a chunk of the wall blew away in a tumble of shattered plaster. Angel One, along with three other members of the DEA assault squad, emerged from the smoke.

Jack turned to face them. A trickle of blood ran down from his nose. More blood stained his battle suit. But Jack Bauer stood tall, still gripping the battered prisoner under the shadow of the medieval armor.

"Well, well," said Chet Blackburn, teeth flashing white against his dark skin. "Here comes the cavalry, right on time."

5:59:56 A.M. PDT
Santa Monica

The sound of the phone on the nightstand shook Teri Bauer out of her sleep. She rolled over, reached across the bed. The sheets were cool, unruffled. She lifted the receiver. "Jack?"

"Teri?" The voice was male, a higher octave than Jack's, with a British accent.

Teri sat up, eyes wide. "*Dennis*? Is that you?"

The man laughed. "I can't believe you recognize my voice after all this time."

"It was the accent that gave you away. And it's only been a year or so."

"Nearly two, and I've been counting the hours."

Teri ran her hand through her short, raven hair, not sure what to say next. The last thing she expected was a call from her former employer, Dennis Winthrop.

"Look, I know it's a crazy time to call, but I just got off the red-eye from London—"

"London, wow. Long trip."

"—and I remembered how you used to wake up at four A.M. and get a couple of hours of design work done before you had to get your daughter ready for school. You always showed up at the production office around noon with really fantastic stuff."

Teri smiled. "Oh, come on."

"No. no, don't sell your work short." The man paused. "You were awake, right? I'd hate to think I got you out of bed."

"Oh, yeah," Teri lied. "Been up for hours now. So what's going on?"

"Well, I'm back in town because of the awards show tonight. You know, the Silver Screen Awards . . ."

"Right, right. The Silver Screen Awards," said Teri, recalling she'd seen something about the awards show on the cover of an entertainment magazine she'd flipped through on line at the supermarket.

"Did you know that *Demon Hunter* is up for three awards, including one for production design?"

"My god, I didn't know. That's great, Dennis. Really great. Congratulations."

"Look, I know it's short notice, but I opened my L.A. office this morning and found sixteen tickets for tonight's show sitting on my desk. My staff is going, the cast is going . . . and I wanted you to come."

"I'm speechless. That's really generous and thoughtful—"

"Not at all. You're as much a part of the design as anyone else. You were involved and I want you to be there to share the glory. I'm calling Chandra and Carla, too. And Nancy is coming."

"Nancy! Oh, I'd love to see Nancy again."

"She's had a baby you know. A son."

"I didn't know."

"And Carla is engaged."

"My god . . ."

"Everyone is getting married or engaged or having babies, it seems." A short silence followed. "You're still with Jack?"

"Oh, yes. You know."

"Well that's great. You can tell me about Jack and Kim tonight. You're coming, right?"

"Well I . . . I . . ."

"Say yes."

"Okay, I'm coming," Teri said, relenting at last. "But this thing is on television, right? What do I wear?"

"I'm sure you'll think of something. You'll look lovely no matter what you choose."

"Okay," said Teri nervously. "What time?"

"I'll send a limousine to pick you up at five o'clock. It's early but the show is broadcast live on the East Coast."

"I don't need a limo, Dennis," Teri said.

"Don't worry about it. The studio is paying for everything. It will be fun. And, Teri . . ." His voice lowered an octave. "It will be great to see you again."

Teri felt her cheeks flushing warm. "It will be really good to see you too, Dennis."

1 2 3 4 5 6 7 8 9
10 11 12 13 14 15 16 17
18 19 20 21 22 23 24

6:01:31 A.M. PDT
Utopia Studios

One ambulance departed with Jack Bauer's prisoner strapped to a stretcher, while two paramedics worked on Jack. He let them strip away his shoulder armor, Kevlar vest, knee and elbow pads. He sat in cooperative silence while they patched up his arm and stanched his bleeding nose. But trouble started when one paramedic tried to put Jack on a stretcher, too. He refused, became argumentative. Finally a female emergency worker stepped forward and tried to reason with him.

"I don't care how hard that helmet is, or how tough

you think you are, Officer Bauer. You most likely have a concussion and you ought to get it checked out."

"Listen . . ." Jack checked the woman's ID tag. "Ms. Besario . . . Inez. I'm fine. Really. I'm not feeling drowsy. I'm not going into shock. My vision's fine and I don't even have a headache."

Her eyes were large and round and very dark. From her set expression Jack could see Inez Besario was as stubborn as he was. "You have a lump on your head and your nose has barely stopped bleeding."

Jack smiled, touched her shoulder. "I'll have the docs check me out after I get back to headquarters. Thank you for your concern."

She stared up at Jack through long lashes. Then she flashed him a sly smile. "You cops are all alike. You think you're supermen."

Jack noticed the wedding band on her finger. "Sounds like you speak from experience."

"Special Agent Bauer. Over here."

Jack turned at the call. Agent Brian McConnell didn't wait for Bauer to follow. He turned on his heels and walked back to the white van parked near the blown-out door to studio nine.

"Excuse me," Jack told the paramedic.

She nodded. "Better go, *Special Agent* Bauer."

Inez Besario joined the other emergency workers administering first aid to Chet Blackburn's leg. Jack hurried across the parking lot. He spied Agent Avilla, tightening the flex-ties on one of the *cholos* who'd worked him over the other day. Finally Jack caught up with Angel One at the door to the battered van. McConnell slapped the dirty side panel twice with the palm of his hand.

"Come," a muffled voice called from inside.

McConnell jerked the handle and slid the door open. Inside the command center, Jason Peltz sat in a chair bolted to the van's floor. The man was surrounded by computers, flickering monitors and banks of communications equipment. There was even a small chemical lab inside. A technician with gloved hands was working with vials, testing a sample of the narcotic found inside Utopia Studios. Peltz powered down his station, yanked off his headset, and stepped out of the cluttered van.

"Good job, Bauer. And you can pass on my thanks to Agent Blackburn and his people. Through intra-agency cooperation, we shut down the largest methamphetamine laboratory on the West Coast and captured those responsible—"

"Wait a minute," Jack interrupted. "Did you say methamphetamine lab? This lab was supposed to be producing Karma."

"It appears our intelligence was faulty," Peltz said. "My forensics people can't find evidence this lab was used for anything more than the production of high quality crystal meth."

Peltz frowned. Like his smile, the mask of expression never reached the man's eyes. "I'm really sorry, Jack."

Bauer was angry, but he couldn't show it. He looked at Brian McConnell, but the man would not meet his gaze. Jack didn't know if Angel One was suffering from disappointment or guilt—which meant that Jack didn't know if this was just another DEA snafu, or if he and CTU were being played.

Reflexively, Jack massaged his throbbing temple. "That's a bad break," he said evenly. "Where does that leave us, Peltz?"

Peltz sighed, slapped his thigh. "Right now, we say goodbye."

"What?"

"This is a pretty big bust, and my bosses in Sacramento wanted to make some hay out it." Peltz paused. "The press is being alerted, Jack, even as we speak. The cameras will be here any minute. I've already ordered my men out. You'd best get your team out of here if you don't want to see the faces of your undercover operatives on the network news."

Seething, Jack turned and crossed the parking lot. He found Chet Blackburn leaning against an ambulance, studying the bandage around his leg.

"Assemble your team and get them out of here. The press is on its way."

Blackburn blinked. "That was fast."

Bauer looked at the white van. "Someone tipped them off. I'll ride back to headquarters with you."

"Don't you want to say hello to your old pal first?"

Jack turned. Chet was grinning. Behind him a man leaned against a blue, late-model Lexus. About the same age as Jack, he wore khaki pants and a polo shirt. His arms and face were deeply tanned under light brown, thinning hair.

"Frank! Frank Castalano." Jack grabbed the man's hand.

"Good to see you, Jack." Castalano slapped his arm and Jack winced. "In the shit again, eh?"

"As I recall, Frank, you were never far from the stink yourself."

Chet sniffed the air. "I don't smell any stink on him, Jack. He sure isn't kicking down doors anymore. All this heat and he hasn't even broken a sweat."

Jack grinned. "That's because he's *Detective* Frank

Castalano of the Los Angeles Homicide Bureau now.
So what are you doing here, partner?"

Frank caught Jack's eye. "Actually, I wish this were
a social call, but it's not."

"Chet, you can go ahead back to headquarters and
file your report," said Jack. "I'll find my own way
back."

Blackburn had caught the exchange. Now he was
feeling the chill. "Okay then," he said "It was nice
seeing you, Frank. Keep in touch."

After Chet and the rest of his tactical assault team
piled into a black CTU tactical van and drove away,
Detective Castalano opened the passenger side door of
his Lexus.

"Let's go for a ride, Jack."

"Am I under arrest?"

Frank laughed, moved to slap Bauer's arm again
then checked himself. "Thirty minutes of your time,
Jack. That's all I ask. Then I'll take you home. You
still live in Santa Monica, right?"

6:23:44 A.M. PDT
Tijuana, Mexico

They'd made it to the border crossing on Route 5 with
seconds to spare. Tony eased the van through the second gate from the right, as per his briefing. The border guard recognized the car and Tony's disguise and
waved the van right through the checkpoint.

The area around the border crossing resembled a
war zone, with layers of chain link fences topped by
curls of barbed wire, blades glinting in the sun. No
plants grew in this no-man's land. The only move-

ment were the tiny tornadoes of dust that swirled over the scorched stretch of rocky desert.

Along the last few miles, they'd seen more and more bilingual signs. Now everything—the road signs, the advertisements, everything—was in Spanish. Tony steered the van to the bridge. They really weren't in Tijuana until they crossed the Tijuana River Canal. Because of the drought, the "river" more resembled a muddy creek, and the entire town seemed to be coated with a fine, powdery dust.

Tony rolled down the window to pass a slow moving truck. Fumes filled the cab and Fay's nose curled. "Somebody ought to Midasize it."

"That's *leaded* gasoline. It's legal down here. Get used to it," said Tony.

On the other side of the river, Tony drove a few blocks through a market area, then turned onto Revolucion. Though early, some of the bars and restaurants were open for business. Already the food carts were filling the hot dry morning with the smell of burned charcoal and seared meat.

"Is the whole town like this?" Fay asked.

"This is the tourist area."

She smiled knowingly. "I get it. This is the sleazy part of town."

"No. This is the *nice* part."

Tony stayed on Revolucion, right through Centro—Tijuana's downtown—until the avenue ended. He turned left at Amacusac, then made another left on winding Murrieta. On Juan Escutia Tony pulled up in front of a three-story brick building with rickety balconies fronting the structure on the second and third floors. The sign above the single door read LA HACIENDA. Tony cut the engine.

"We're here," he said. He released his seatbelt. Fay Hubley reached for the door handle. Tony stopped her.

"Remember your instructions. Use first names only, but remember your cover. I'm Tony Navarro. You're Fay Kelly. Best not to get into any conversations, and don't look anyone in the eye. And remember, if we get separated or if something happens to me—"

"Go directly to the United States Consulate and tell them who I am."

Tony nodded. "All right. Let me activate the security system, and we'll go."

He reached under the dash, to a small laser lens hidden under the upholstery near his left foot. Tony flatted his thumb against the glass eye, pressed. His thumbprint verified, Tony heard a beep resembling a seatbelt warning tone. That sound told him a half-dozen devices had been activated, making the van impenetrable and immobile. The engine was impossible to start, even if the ignition was bypassed, and the wheels locked with a built-in system that worked like a traffic cop's car boot. Even a tow truck would have trouble hauling the van away

While Tony secured the vehicle, Fay stared through the tinted windshield at the neighborhood. The area was mostly composed of ramshackle two- and three-story wooden or brick buildings. Single-story shops were squeezed between more durable buildings, mostly produce markets and food stalls. Laundry waved like banners from dirty ropes strung between the buildings. The few trees Fay could see were brown from the persistent drought.

"God, I can't believe we're staying here."

Tony understood the woman's jitters. This was the first time Fay Hubley was doing field work, and she wasn't technically even a field agent. Her training was limited to several briefings in the past twenty-four hours. And on top of that, Fay Hubley probably had never even walked into a dive like La Hacienda, let alone spent the night there.

"Look. I've stayed at this inn before. It's not as bad as it looks," Tony told her in a tone meant to be reassuring. "I'm recognized here, but not known. No one should mess with us. We'll be fine."

Outside, the heat hit them like a hammer. It was already close to one hundred degrees, and the day would only get hotter. Gas fumes and cooking smells filled the air, mingling with the ever-present dust. As soon as they exited the vehicle, the pair was mobbed by nearly a dozen children—beggars. Tony moved through the horde as if he were wading through the surf. Fay grinned at the children, and Tony shot her a warning look.

"Ignore them," he barked. "And the flower girls over there, too. They're probably pickpockets."

"What is this, *Oliver Twist*?"

"You're not in Kansas anymore."

"I'm from *Ohio*, Tony. I told you I'm from Ohio."

"Forget it."

Tony led the way as they pushed through a fly-specked screen door. Fay heard a persistent and angry buzzing, looked up. Her nose wrinkled in disgust when she saw a long strip of orange flypaper covered with writhing black bodies. The pest strip was dangling above her head. Fay hurried through the door.

It was ten degrees cooler inside La Hacienda's small lobby. The floor consisted of multicolored tiles, some of them chipped and stained. The peeling walls were pale blue, a large ceiling fan turned in lazy circles high above them, and near the door sat several empty chairs, newspapers scattered on the floor around them.

Tony stepped up to a wooden partition covered with scratched green Formica. A door opened, and a young man greeted them in Spanish. Tony replied in kind. Tony booked the room, paid in U.S. dollars, and signed the registry. Then they climbed a flight of shabbily carpeted stairs to the second floor. At the top of the steps, a portrait of Mexican President Vicente Fox grinned at them beneath the flag of Mexico.

"Room six, here we are."

Tony turned the key, pushed the door open.

The room wasn't as bad as Fay feared it would be. Two curtained windows, a dresser, a small battered desk, two rickety-looking beds, a lumpy armchair, and a telephone. A tiny bathroom next to a walk in closet. Enough room for a shower but not a bathtub.

The room was hot and stuffy. Fay opened the heavy curtains to find the windows were barred. She reached around the iron barrier and unlocked the window, but she could only slide it open about six inches before a security bolt stopped her.

Tony dropped his backpack on the bed near the window. The springs squeaked like irritated mice. He opened the curtain blocking the other window, found the air conditioner. It rattled so much when he flipped it on, he thought it might fall out the window. But the unit soon settled down and began pumping out cool air.

"Fay, start setting up. I'm going back down to the truck to bring up the rest of the equipment. When I get back, we'll contact CTU—we're going to need an update on Lesser's activities over the past four hours before we can start our operation here."

Detective Castalano drove southeast on north San Fernando Road, toward Fletcher Drive, then headed south on California Route 2. Traffic was heavy already, and the going was slow. The police radio inside the Lexus crackled once. Frank turned it off.

"It must be nice, living so close to the ocean," Castalano said. "Do much surfing these days?"

Jack Bauer shook his head. "Nah. Too busy with work. The family. Been teaching Kim to surf, though. Sometimes she even pretends to enjoy it."

Castalano chuckled. "Yeah, family time can be far more complicated than the job. How's Teri?"

"Itching to get back to work, full time. That's fine with me, but she's not having much luck finding work that suits her. How's Rachel, and Harry?"

"Rachel's great, still teaching. Harry's twelve now and a holy terror. Second year in Little League—"

"No kidding?"

"The team sucks, they haven't won a game yet but he loves it. Nat Greer is the coach. You remember Nat?"

"Sure. How's he like retirement?"

"Forced retirement due to injuries. He'd be the first to clarify that, which tells you all you need to know about how Nat's enjoying his golden years."

Castalano merged onto U.S. 101, heading north. Traffic was thick, but moving.

"I would ask you if you missed the excitement of

the old days, Jack, but I can see your life is still full of thrills. What was going on back there on Andrita Street?"

"My agency was working with the DEA on a drug bust. It will be all over the evening news, apparently."

"Still kicking down doors."

Jack stared at the road ahead, rubbed his temple. "When I have to."

"I always got the impression the LAPD was holding you back," Castalano said. "Too many drills, too many training sessions, not enough real-time action. The rest of us were humping to keep up with the training, the missions—shortchanging our families and burning our candles at both ends. Meanwhile you were bored."

"I was younger then."

The traffic stopped moving suddenly. Castalano braked and the Lexus rolled to a halt. The detective turned to face Jack.

"Nat Greer told me you were always a thrill seeker. Says you were a biker, a surfer, back in high school. before the military. He said you got into some secret shit, too. Special ops stuff."

"Nat talks too much."

Castalano swerved onto the Sunset Boulevard ramp. Traffic was lighter off the highway, and moving pretty steadily along Sunset. The sun beat through the tinted windows. Jack's head began to throb and he was tired of banalities. "Where are we going?" he asked.

Castalano answered Jack's question with one of his own. "Do you ever work freelance these days, Jack? Private detective or consulting work, maybe? Special work for some corporation?"

"No. That's impossible with the job I do now."

"I knew you guys do spooky stuff at CTU. I didn't

figure there'd be much opportunity for moonlighting."

Jack was unable to mask his impatience any longer. "Look, Frank, what the hell is this about?"

Castalano's face was grim, eyes straight ahead. They were climbing the hills now, on a winding road. "I can tell you what this is about, Jack. But it's better if I show you. And I can do that in another minute or two. We're almost there."

Near the crest of a hill, Frank made a sharp right turn. The Lexus pulled into a narrow driveway fairly well masked by the trees around it. Despite the drought, the lawns, the trees were greener, more lush up here.

"We're in Beverly Hills," said Jack.

Though the driveway continued on, Frank rolled up to circular-stone structure not much larger than a freestanding garage. The Lexus stopped under an arch, where a small wall fountain trickled. In the cool shade, Frank cut the engine while Jack studied his surroundings.

The building had a large glass door behind a cast iron gate. The gate was wide open, the door ajar. Farther along the driveway, Jack spied several other vehicles huddled together under a copse of spreading eucalyptus trees—two unmarked police cars, two ambulances, and a black crime scene van. Jack also noticed a tan Rolls-Royce convertible with the top down. Except for a plainclothes detective loitering around and trying to look nonchalant, no one else was in sight. All of the vehicles were deep enough inside the grounds to be invisible from the road, and Jack thought that was intentional. The authorities were deliberately trying to hide something.

"Have you ever heard of Hugh Vetri?" Frank asked.

The name jogged something in Jack's memory. "Maybe. Should I know him?"

"Let's go," said Frank. "I'll introduce you."

As they climbed out of the car, a member of the LAPD Crime Scene Unit came through the glass door. The man saw Frank with a stranger and frowned. He approached, handed them both latex gloves.

"We're finished in the bedroom and the study. We're working on the nanny's room now," the forensics man told Castalano. "But I still don't want anyone going in there who doesn't have to."

"We'll make it quick," Castalano replied. The other man had more questions so he and the detective huddled for a few minutes. Not wishing to eavesdrop, Jack moved a discreet distance away, pulled on the gloves. The morning sun was already scorching, even in the cool shade. Jack massaged his forehead, squeezed his eyes shut to block out the glare for a moment. Finally, Castalano broke away from the other man, waved Jack through the door.

A moment later, Jack found himself in an air-conditioned glass-enclosed entranceway which housed a wide staircase made of a single steel beam stacked with marble stairs. Hugh Vetri's mansion had been constructed vertically, down the side of the hill. Each of its three glass-fronted stories shared a spectacular view of the valley below, already swathed in haze and smog.

"Down here, Jack."

Castalano led Jack down the curved staircase. Modern art and hanging sculptures dominated the walls, the ceiling. The lamps, the furniture resembled the art; it was all made of cold steel, glass and chrome. When they arrived on the first level, Jack heard many voices. The tone was professional, but their voices muted, respectful, whispered. That's when Jack knew someone had died in this place.

"Who is this Hugh Vetri?" Jack asked, his professional instincts aroused. "A movie star or director?"

"Vetri's an independent producer," Castalano replied. "A couple of years ago he made some fantasy movie that turned into *the* blockbuster of the year. He's about to release the sequel, or he was."

"Was?"

Castalano halted in front of an ornately carved oaken door, pushed it open. "Meet Hugh Vetri."

The smell hit Jack first. Spilled blood, emptied bowels and bladder—the stink of the abattoir. His eyes followed a trail of clotted brown blood that led to a large oak desk. A man was sprawled across it, arms and legs out, like a frog on a dissecting table. Leather belts and silk ties had been used to bind the man's wrists and ankles, and like some biological specimen, the victim had been eviscerated. Ribbons of entrails lay scattered across the room. On the floor, a chunk of the man's liver gleamed dully in the sunlight streaming through the glass wall. The organ lay amid the scattered contents of the desk top—only the corpse and a computer monitor remained on the oak surface. The computer was running, on the monitor a screensaver with an ocean view played in an endless loop.

Jack tamped down his revulsion enough to study the corpse without touching it. Of particular interest was the positioning of the body, the binding wounds on the arms and legs, the bright bruise on the cheek, under the right eye. Most revealing was the expression on the dead man's face—one eye open, the other closed, mouth gaping and blood flecked, tongue black and distended. This man's death was deliberately prolonged. He'd experienced hours of torture before being released.

Detective Castalano broke the silence. "His wife, Sarah, is in the master bedroom. Her throat was cut. Vetri's daughter is in the bathhouse. Whoever did this found her while she was taking a midnight swim. She was the first to die, but it was mercifully quick, unlike this poor bastard."

"Anyone else?" Jack's voice was brittle.

"The live-in nanny and an infant son. They're both in the nursery. Want to see those crime scenes?"

"No."

"That's smart. Their murders were savage enough, Christ knows. But whoever did this saved their real fury for Hugh Vetri."

"How did the murderer get in?"

"That's the funny part," Castalano replied. "The alarm company says the alarm was activated at eight P.M., then turned off again around midnight. The code was used. Whoever did this may have been an insider. We're checking out that angle now, along with some others."

Castalano glanced at the corpse, looked away. "It's like fucking Charles Manson all over again. I thought hippies were extinct."

Jack began to back out of the room. Castalano caught his arm. "Sorry. There's more you have to see, Jack."

The detective crossed the room to the computer still sitting on the corner of the desk. The keyboard had been knocked on the floor, but the wireless mouse was lying on its pad near the dead man's head.

"Hugh Vetri was using his computer when he was

murdered," Castalano said. "He was viewing the information from a CD-ROM."

Using a gloved hand, Castalano reached out and touched the wireless mouse. The screensaver vanished and the computer jumped to the last file on display. Jack stifled a shocked gasp when his own face appeared.

To go with the picture there was an accurate profile of Jack, complete with the names of his family members, his home address, and all of his numbers, including his home phone, his cell, and the office telephone at CTU Headquarters. Jack leaned closer to the monitor. On second glance, it appeared this file came right out of CTU's own database.

"Where did Hugh Vetri get this information?"

Castalano shrugged. "Your guess is as good as mine. Maybe the experts can tell us both, once they data mine the dead man's hard drive."

Jack studied the monitor. "Who found the bodies?"

"We're thinking the killer called it in," Castalano replied. "911 received an anonymous tip five hours ago. We've got some leads; the call came from a pay phone and we traced it. Nothing definitive yet, though."

There was a pause. "Jack. I have to ask you this."

Jack nodded. "Shoot."

"Do you know any reason why Hugh Vetri would be interested in you or any member of your immediate family?"

"Not a clue," Jack replied.

1 2 **3** 4 5 6 7 8 9
10 11 12 13 14 15 16 17
18 19 20 21 22 23 24

....

THE FOLLOWING TAKES PLACE
BETWEEN THE HOURS OF
7 A.M. AND 8 A.M.
PACIFIC DAYLIGHT TIME

....

7:05:11 A.M. PDT
La Hacienda
Tijuana, Mexico

Tony dragged the remaining backpack out of the cargo bay, set it on the hot pavement. Music blared on the street. Not a traditional Mexican ballad or even brassy mariachi music—just raucous urban hiphop chanted in Spanish. Men, old and young, headed to jobs or to look for work. Children traipsed off to school in groups, darting among the cars as they raced across the crowded streets, while stalled traffic continued to pump noxious fumes into an already smog-choked atmosphere.

The back of the van was empty now. This would be

Tony's final trip. Upstairs, Fay Hubley had already gotten the satellite interface up and running. The computer system would be next.

Before he closed the driver's side door, Tony considered pocketing one of the two Glock C18s hidden in a secret compartment in the floor—then changed his mind. Guns were trouble and the fugitive they hunted wasn't prone to violence. Tony hoped he could get through this mission without resorting to weapons.

He was almost finished when he suddenly felt his sweat-dampened skin prickle. Someone was observing him. He could feel it. Without looking up, he reset the van's security system and slammed the door. While adjusting the backpack on his shoulders, Tony casually glanced around. A policeman leaned against a squad car on the opposite side of the street. His gray uniform appeared crisp, despite the melting heat; his face was impassive, unreadable; his eyes hidden behind dark sunglasses.

Tony considered the possibilities. He could be eyeing the van for towing later. Though the vehicle was legally parked, auto extortion was common enough in Tijuana, especially cars with U.S. license plates. Vehicles disappeared only to be returned after a hefty "towing fee" was paid to the *policia*.

On the other hand, the guy could be watching out of natural curiosity, the need to know what's happening on his beat. Tony hoped it was the latter. Among other things, the CTU pre-mission briefing reminded him and Fay that criminal gangs did, on occasion, kidnap Americans and hold them for ransom. Corrupt police had been known to get a piece of that action as well.

With a final yank on the strap, Tony circled the van

and walked through the doors of La Hacienda. With every step he could feel the cop's eyes boring into his spine.

Back in room six, things seemed suddenly cluttered. Several laptop computers, interconnected with a small server to form a network, were now spread out across the small desk and one of the two beds. Lights blinked and disk drives whirred, but Fay was nowhere in sight. Tony saw the closed bathroom door and heard water running. He peeled the pack off his shoulder and set it down next to five others just like it—all empty now.

With a tired groan Tony sank into a lumpy chair and pulled off his boots. Leaning into the seat, Tony crossed his arms, propped his legs on the edge of the laptop-covered bed and closed his eyes. The persistent rattle of the air conditioner had nearly lulled him into sleep when he heard the bathroom door open. Fay bounded out in a cloud of steam, swathed in nothing more than a towel. Her hair was pinned up and she smelled of citrus. Tony shifted position to let her pass, uncomfortable with the woman's choice of attire—or lack thereof.

"Any word on Lesser?" Tony asked.

Fay sat down on the edge of the bed, across from Tony, and crossed her long legs. "He hasn't logged onto the Internet yet, but we're watching for him," she replied. "Of course, Richard Lesser may have some fake identities, servers and accounts we don't know about, but he can't launch any attacks without using his signature protocols, and when he does that we've got him."

As she spoke Fay undid her hair. Blond locks tumbled down around her pale shoulders. Though she clutched the towel to her breasts, the terrycloth had dipped low enough for Tony to see the dragonfly tattoo on her lower back. He looked away, his gaze settling on the computers scattered all over the hotel room.

"Back at CTU, your boss Hastings said you required a half-million dollars worth of stuff to find Lesser," said Tony. "But all I see are a few laptops, a server, a satellite hookup, and some network connections."

Fay laughed. "Most of the expensive stuff is back at CTU," she told him. "I'm sure Hastings was talking about the cost of allocating all of CTU's resources for a single manhunt. This stuff here just interfaces with the systems and protocols running back at CTU's cyber division."

Tony leaned forward, glanced at one of the monitors. Data scrolled along the flat screen. Though he was hardly a novice, Tony could make no sense of the information being displayed.

"What are you doing?" he asked.

"Well," said Fay, sliding across the bed to the largest monitor. "As you know, originally CTU used two separate computer systems to gather intelligence information. One system mined data from unclassified but secure sources—credit card companies, airline logs, banking records, state and federal bureaus, chemical supply stores, stuff like that. Since your average terrorist lives in the real world, they have to do everyday things like eat, buy things, go places, work at jobs and pay the rent. By utilizing an algorithm similar to the mathematical model employed by Able Danger—"

Tony rubbed the black stubble along his jawline, scratched his new goatee. "You're talking about the clandestine DOD project to hunt al-Qaeda?"

"That's the one. By using a similar system, algorithms and protocols, CTU has had some success in locating and capturing terrorists within our borders."

"Using CTU's random sequencer, right?"

Fay nodded. "We also have a second system which mines data, but this one collects its intelligence from closed, or even classified sources. With it CTU can access private accounts, trace secured transactions, search classified CIA and DOD files, the State Department and Commerce Department files, telephone logs, corporate computers, secure medical data—even Interpol files. In the case of Richard Lesser, we're running protocols that will even let us know if he phones his bank for a balance. Any electronic activity at all will show up on our radar."

"That still doesn't tell me what you're up to with this setup."

Fay tossed long blond curls over her shoulder. "Using the random sequencer, I've managed to set up a third system. This one mines data from the World Wide Web, all of it—including a lot of stuff once considered secure."

"What, like a super search engine?"

Fay grinned, her pride evident. "More like a super *bloodhound*. Once I know who I'm looking for, what computer, server or ISP is being used, then my program and CTU's mainframe working in tandem with my magic fingers will hunt them down."

Tony was skeptical. "How close can you get?"

"From this laptop I can trace a subject's activity to a specific server, then on to a specific phone number or Wi Fi zone. If I'm on top of my game—which is, like, *always*—no matter how many times Lesser washes his system or tries to cover his tracks, he's mine. With the warrant we have, I can legally access all kinds of data that the government was barred from collecting before."

Tony folded his arms. "Funny how extending the RICO Act makes some people crazy. But if we can use these laws to prosecute drug dealers, why not apply the same laws to stopping terrorists, too?"

"Yeah, strange how no one complains about the IRS knowing every single financial transaction a citizen makes in a given year, but knowing what book a suspect borrows from the library is suddenly a problem."

"It's the theoretical versus the real world," said Tony. "Most people aren't lying awake at night worrying whether the Feds know what book they borrowed from the library. They're worried red tape is going to prevent the government from failing to stop a terrorist attack like Beslan, or Bali, or London."

Fay fumbled with one of the laptops, almost losing her towel. "Here, check this out."

She rose, tiptoed over to Tony and set the portable PC in his lap. Fay moved behind him, leaned over his shoulder to point at the screen. He could feel her breasts pressing against his shoulder, long hair tickling his nose.

"Richard Lesser has two other identities that we know of, only he doesn't know we know because he thinks he's covered his tracks. Those identities are represented by these two graphs right here. Of course, he might just use his real name—he's not a fugitive down here, so I've covered that with this box right here . . . As you can see, there's no activity yet, from any of the three protocols CTU is running, but it's only a matter of time."

"Time?"

"Remember what I said about living in the real

world," Fay replied. "Sooner or later, Richard Lesser is going to write a check, withdraw cash from one of over a dozen accounts, use a credit card, or turn on his computer. I'll trace the activity back to the point of origin and we'll know where he is—or where he was in the past thirty minutes or so, anyway."

Tony rubbed his stiff neck. "I'm impressed."

Fay brushed Tony's short, newly grown ponytail aside, moved her hands over his neck and shoulders, kneading his aching muscles. He allowed the intimacy for a minute—mainly because it felt so damn good.

Finally, Tony leaned forward, out of Fay's reach, while pretending to study the activity on the monitor. "So how do you know Lesser hasn't launched another worm or some kind of cyber-attack, like the one against Boscom?"

Fay stepped around the chair, sat on the bed and crossed her bare legs. "The folks at Boscom Systems found Richard Lesser because he got lazy and left some errant codes buried in his invader virus. I did a little research and found out he tried a similar stunt on Microsoft when he was still at Stanford. Jamey Farrell got me a copy of Lesser's bug from an old friend at MS security. True to form, that virus has the same code buried inside. It's like his signature, a fingerprint."

"So you think he'll make the same mistake again?"

Fay nodded. "Sure. Richard Lesser is smart, maybe a genius, but he's impatient or he wouldn't be a criminal. He wants results *now*, which means he takes shortcuts. *And* he's a creature of habit."

Fay adjusted the hotel's threadbare towel. "So what do you want to do now, Tony? . . ." She smiled. "I mean, we can't go out because I have to stick around here and monitor these computers, but . . ."

Tony swallowed. The last thing he wanted to do

was hurt Fay Hubley's feelings. For starters, hard feelings might compromise the mission. But then so would having casual sex with her in a Tijuana dive. Bottom line, for the duration of this mission, Tony was her supervisor. Any sort of intimacy would be completely inappropriate.

"I think it's time we got a little sleep, but in shifts," Tony declared. "Once Richard Lesser decides to make a move, we might be busy for hours or even days. Better rest while we can."

"You're the boss," said Fay, trying hard to mask her disappointment.

7:55:34 A.M. PDT
Santa Monica

On his quiet suburban street, Jack Bauer watched Frank Castalano's Lexus swing around the corner and out of sight. The hint of a breeze from the ocean, nearly a mile away, slightly reduced the scorching heat of the day, but not Jack's pounding headache. Bypassing the stone sidewalk, he crossed the lawn and strode toward the front door of his split-level, ranch-style house.

He glanced at his watch and realized he'd missed seeing Kim. Her school bus had come and gone. By now she was already sitting in homeroom. But then, missing his daughter on this particular morning might have been a blessing. Jack touched his wound. Under a thin jacket he was still clad in his black battle suit, the bloodstained bandage wrapped around his arm. Bad enough he kept weapons in the house. He didn't like reminding Kim of the hazards that came with his job.

Looking forward to a cool shower and a few hours of sleep, he fumbled for his keys, felt the CD-ROM in his pocket, packed in an LAPD evidence bag. Though it took plenty of convincing, Detective Castalano allowed a team from CTU's Cyber-Unit to take Hugh Vetri's computer back to headquarters for analysis by Jamey Farrell. Jack's argument—that CTU could do a much better job of mining the data on the hard drive than the LAPD—was logical and accurate. But both men knew the real, unspoken motive for Jack's request.

It was the violation. The fact that Bauer's privacy had been invaded and details about his personal life and the lives of his family had been compromised, perhaps putting them in jeopardy. Jack Bauer needed to know how and why that happened, and what he must do to protect those he loved.

That's why he'd held on to the CD-ROM. He would slip that disk to Jamey later, unofficially and in private, and ask her to deliver her results to him personally.

The thought that his family might be in danger sent a jolt of adrenaline through him, and Jack paused before opening the door, to collect himself. Tamping down his fears, he steadied his hand. It was imperative that his family never see the anxiety, the uncertainty, the dread on his face. For Jack Bauer, bringing home his job, or its dangers, was not an option.

After unlocking the front door, Jack stepped into the foyer and then the living room, which was empty but hardly quiet. Kim had left the television on again—that, or his wife had taken to watching MTV. He slipped off his jacket, hung it in the closet. Then he quickly tore away the stained bandages and rolled the sleeve down to cover the wound. He flexed his arm, moved it from side to side, happy to see the limb still worked and the pain had receded to a dull throb. Jack crossed the living room and switched off the television.

In the kitchen he stuffed the bandages deep into the garbage can. A fresh pot of coffee had just been brewed. The aroma was tempting, but Jack resisted it, knowing he needed a few hours' sleep.

"Honey?" he called, walking toward the bathroom.

"In here," came a muffled voice from farther down the hall.

Jack found his wife in the bedroom, still in her pajamas. She had pretty much emptied her closet, the clothes spread out across their queen-sized bed, the chair, desk and dresser, the shoes scattered across the floor.

"What's going on?" Jack asked, leaning against the doorframe.

"What's going on is I don't have a thing to wear." Teri crossed the room, pecked her husband on the cheek. If she noticed his attire, she didn't comment. Nor did she mention the lump on his head, though Jack wasn't sure it was even visible.

"Are you going somewhere special?"

"I might be," Teri replied. "Depends."

Jack's eyebrows arched. "Depends on what?"

"On whether I have something to wear tonight. Something suitable for television."

"*Oprah*'s taping in L.A.?"

"Not even close."

Jack emptied his pockets, tossed his key, wallet, cell phone on the dresser. "Okay, I give up. What's going on?"

Teri draped a little black dress over herself and examined her reflection. "Do you remember when I had that freelance job with Coventry Productions?"

Jack moved some clothing, sat down on the edge of the bed. "The animation studio? I remember. You worked with that other artist . . . Natalie."

"Nancy."

"That's right. Nancy."

Jack mind raced back to that time, two years before. What sprang to mind first were his CTU missions. Since coming to CTU, his missions had become the measure of Jack's life. Two years ago, Operation Jump Rope was wrapping up and Operation Proteus was just launching. And at home—well, Jack wasn't home enough to know, he remembered that much. Kim was entering her teens and the mother-daughter bond became a pact of mutual destruction.

Jack recalled that Teri was working long hours then, too. With some British animator named Dennis at an office in Century City. Jack never met the man beyond hearing his voice when answering the phone, but Teri seemed impressed with him—Jack remembered that much, too.

"So what's up with Nancy?" he asked.

"Well I heard she just had a baby. A little boy."

"You heard? From Nancy?"

Teri tore through another pile of clothing. "Actually Dennis Winthrop called. He was Nancy's boss. I don't think you ever met him so you wouldn't remember his name."

"No."

"Anyway, *Demon Hunter*—the animated feature Coventry Productions produced—has been nominated for a Silver Screen Award. Since I worked on the art direction, I was invited to the show tonight. It's going to be broadcast live on television."

"That's great," said Jack. "Are you going to get a trophy if you win?"

"Don't be stupid." Teri laughed. "I worked as a freelance assistant for the background artist. I'm lucky to be invited. I can't wait to see Nancy. And Carla and Chandra, too."

Jack stood up, embraced his wife. "Since you might be on television, why don't you go out and buy something brand new to wear?"

"That's silly, Jack. I've already decided on the black dress."

"Good," he smiled. "You look pretty hot in that."

"You don't mind, do you Jack?"

"Of course not. Kim and I can get take out pizza."

"Great. But don't get pepperoni. Kim's a vegetarian again."

Jack snorted skeptically. "Since when?"

"Since I cooked meat loaf last night."

"Well, we'll have a great time trying to spot you during the broadcast."

Teri laughed. "Don't blink then."

Jack sat back down on the bed, yanked off his chukkas, and tossed them into the corner. Teri walked to the mirror, brushed the short locks of dark hair away from her face with her long fingernails and studied her features in the glass.

"One more thing," Jack said, rising and heading for the bathroom and a quick shower. "If you *do* win, don't forget to thank your faithful and supporting husband in your acceptance speech."

Teri smiled, catching Jack's eye in the mirror. "You and Kim are always first on my list, Jack. You know that."

1 2 3 4 5 6 7 8 9
10 11 12 13 14 15 16 17
18 19 20 21 22 23 24

• •

**THE FOLLOWING TAKES PLACE
BETWEEN THE HOURS OF
8 A.M. AND 9 A.M.
PACIFIC DAYLIGHT TIME**

• •

8:03:41 A.M. PDT
Angeles Crest Highway
Angeles National Forest

Although it was not nearly as spectacular as the famous Sierra Nevadas to the north, the San Gabriel Mountains and its surrounding national park had a more distinct advantage for the people of L.A.—it was only a thirty minute drive from the Glendale corridor. The San Gabriels were forested with oak, pine, and cedar and graced with clear streams, small lakes, waterfalls, and steep canyons perfect for fishing, hiking, and camping.

Several roads climbed into the 700,000-acre park, all of them twisting, steep and narrow, but the main

route through the mountains was the Angeles Crest
Highway. It rose steadily from La Canada Flintridge,
eventually peaking at nearly eight thousand feet above
sea level, before descending to an eventual end in the
flat, blasted wasteland of the Mojave Desert.

Veering off a sharp curve in this highway was an
unmarked road. At the end of the short, bumpy dirt
path, flanked by tall pines, sat three wooden buildings, several picnic tables, a flagpole, and a half-dozen
tents. This small no-frills campground had been established by two inner city churches in the late
1980s—the Lion of God Church in South Central,
Los Angeles, and the Baptist Church School of Compton, a small Christian congregation operated out of a
dilapidated storefront.

With a sharp cliff presenting perfect vistas of
higher mountain peaks, they could give urban kids a
few days of escape from the scorching heat of the city
and fulfill their mission statement for all retreats: here
the children could witness the glories of God as reflected in nature, rather than the sins and hubris of
mankind cast in concrete; they could inhale the scents
of plants and trees instead of smog; they could listen
to birdsong, while they received biblical instruction,
instead of the constant assault of subwoofers in gang-
banger SUVs.

Nine of the kids who'd come for this particular retreat session—four boys and five girls between the
ages of twelve and fourteen—were now seated around
a pair of picnic tables. Breakfast had ended, the paper
plates had been gathered up, and Reverend Landers,
tall and reed thin with a hide like brown leather and
white hair bristling over an expansive forehead, was
leading them all in a goodbye prayer.

Fifty feet away, twenty-five-year-old Laney Caulder

emerged from the camp's largest building to stand on its porch. Squinting against the morning glare, the slender young African-American woman with long hair braided into a beautiful cascade of cornrows, looked away from the yellow sun blazing in the sky before covering her head with a baseball cap.

"Sure is gonna be hot down in the city. I almost hate to leave these mountains," Laney said.

Behind her, a heavyset black woman in her late fifties rolled out of the building on an electric wheelchair.

"It's hot all right," Rita Taft observed. "But I can feel a chill in the wind coming off the highlands. Winter's coming. In a couple more weeks the Reverend's gonna have to close this place down till spring."

The older woman scanned the distant mountains with tired eyes. Then, using a chin control to operate the wheelchair, she circled around to face the younger woman.

"Back when this place first opened up, back twenty years ago, you could see snow on the mountains every summer—even in July. But this year's different. With the drought and all, there's been no snow. Not one little flake."

Rita paused, fixed her gaze on the younger woman. "I been thinking that maybe things are better without the white powder, if you know what I mean . . ."

Laney Caulder nodded. "It's better."

"So you're telling me you ain't gonna need that nasty snow no more, not even when you get back to the city? Back to that world and all its evil influences?"

The younger woman shook her head. "I've been off the drugs nine months now, free and clear. Thanks to you and the Reverend, I found me a better way. I'm not gonna backslide . . ."

Rita Taft's grin lit up her round face. "God bless

you girl. Keep it up and next year you can take over my job!"

Laney's brown eyes opened wide. "I could never—"

"You said the same thing six months ago when the Reverend made you a camp counselor. Now you're the kids' favorite."

"I sure do love 'em."

A cloud of dust appeared above the trees at the end of the camp. A moment later the church van arrived to take the kids home. Laney glanced at the bus nervously, hesitant to leave.

Rita cleared her throat. "You have your cell phone. Don't forget to call me when you get back to Compton," she said. "And don't fret. You'll only be gone a few days. I'll see you here next Tuesday when you come up with a fresh batch of kids."

Laney stooped and kissed the old woman on the cheek. "Take care, Miss Taft, and make sure to remind Tyrell to recharge your battery or you're gonna get stuck again."

Rita jerked the chair forward playfully. "Go home, girl."

Laney bounded off the porch and down to the bus—really a large van with four rows for passengers. Already the kids were climbing inside choosing seats. She circled around to the passenger door and climbed aboard. Thelma Layton, a mother of five with cocoa skin and short black curls, greeted her with a wide grin from behind the steering wheel. "Girl, you are gonna regret going back to that city. Hell has got to be cooler than Compton."

"Shhh," hissed Laney. "Watch your language in front of the kids."

Thelma threw her head back and laughed. "Those kids don't scare me, and they ain't listening anyway. I do watch my mouth in front of Miss Taft, however. Once I used the F word and she whacked me in the shins with that damn chair of hers."

Laney shot her friend a shocked look. "You're lucky she didn't have Tyrell wash out your mouth with soap."

Thelma offered Laney a sly smile. "I don't worry about Tyrell nor the Reverend either. They're both too old to catch up with me."

Thelma checked the passengers through the rearview mirror.

"Okay, everyone, buckle up," she called loudly over the laughter and cries of the children. A moment later she started the engine, kicked up the air conditioner. The bus circled the camp one last time, then climbed back up the hill toward the highway.

The wooden gate was closed. Thelma braked and the dust cloud they'd kicked up washed over the bus. "I told Tyrell to leave that gate open. Where was he going, anyway?"

"The Wal-Mart in Verdugo City. Miss Taft needed some stuff," Laney replied. "Don't worry. I'll open the gate."

She popped the door and hopped out, ran to the wooden gate and dragged it open. A few yards beyond the entrance, the concrete ribbon of highway began.

"Get in!" Thelma called.

Laney shook her head. "I don't want to leave the gate open. Go through and wait for me on the highway."

Thelma waved and moved the vehicle forward. Over the rumble of the van's engine, Laney thought she heard another sound—a roar like an airplane.

Just as the church van rolled onto the highway, the muted, unidentified noise Laney heard before was suddenly a deafening roar. Racing full-throttle, a crimson sports car squealed around the corner, rushing toward the packed van for a head-on collision. Tires squealed and the vehicle fishtailed as Thelma tried to get out of the way of the oncoming hot rod. Her quick maneuver avoided a total smash-up, and the two vehicles struck with a glancing blow.

Laney heard the sound of tearing metal, saw sparks. Shards of glass rained down on the highway as the windows blew out of the van. Careening off the sports car, the van slammed into a guardrail that had already been weakened by a minor landslide. Its velocity, and the vehicle's heavy weight, ripped the base of the rail out of the ground and sent the van tumbling down the steep side of the mountain.

Helpless to do more than scream, Laney watched the SUV roll down the steep embankment. Clutching her head in horror, she ignored the sports car as it rolled onto the shoulder of the road and skidded to a halt in a shower of dirt and rocks.

The young woman bolted across the highway, watched as the church van flipped over and tumbled end over end into a deep, tree-lined chasm. Over the crunch of metal and the crash of sliding rocks, Laney heard Thelma's cries and the screams of the children. But when the bus finally struck the bottom of the canyon, all human sounds abruptly ceased.

Laney fell on her knees, sobbing, beating the pavement with her fists. She looked around, hoping for someone to help, for a miracle. Only then did she spot the red Jaguar. The driver had never even gotten out of the car. Now he was trying to back out of the shoulder of the road, onto the roadway. Laney realized the speeder was trying to get away.

"Stop!" Laney screamed. "They need help! You can't just leave them."

The car finally skidded onto the pavement. Laney saw that the driver's side window was gone—shattered—and the car door crushed. Inside, a swarthy man in a white T-shirt with dirty brown stains sat behind the wheel, sunglasses covering his eyes. The tires smoked as the man gunned the engine, trying to speed away. Finally the wheels gained some traction and the swarthy man raced away without a backward glance.

Though she was shaken to the core of her being by the tragedy she'd just witnessed, Laney had the presence of mind to pull the cell phone out of her purse and call the police. She reported the accident, its location, and the license plate of the vehicle that had fled the scene.

It took the LAPD only thirty seconds to positively identify the vehicle involved in the hit and run accident—a cherry-red 1998 Jaguar registered to Mr. Hugh Vetri, film producer, vanity plate number FYLM-BOY. The automobile had been reported stolen from a crime scene in Beverly Hills earlier that day. Within two minutes, an all-points bulletin had been issued, and a statewide manhunt for the fugitive driver had begun.

8:23:06 A.M. PDT
La Hacienda
Tijuana, Mexico

A single rap on the door launched Tony off the rickety bed. On bare feet, he moved silently across the floor and pressed his ear to the scarred wood. Across the room, Fay sat up in the second bed, tense with worry. Tony caught her eye, placed his index finger to his lips.

"Who's there?" he called.

"Hey, Navarro . . . It's me. Ray Dobyns."

Only then did Tony peer through the peephole. He recognized Dobyns at once and cursed silently.

Ray Dobyns was a transplant from Wichita, Kansas. His grifts in his home state, and in Arkansas, Texas, and California, finally caught up with Dobyns a decade ago and he fled south to extradition-free Mexico. Since then, Ray had made a marginal living by pulling off similar grifts to the ones Tony's cover "Navarro" was supposedly running right now— credit card fraud, Internet fraud, passing bad checks.

As Navarro, Tony Almeida had had some dealings with Dobyns two years ago in Ensenada when he'd been working another case. Now Tony tried to recall if he'd given the man any reason to suspect he was more than a petty con man.

"Come on, let me in, man," Dobyns called from the other side of the thin, battered wood.

"Give me a second," Tony called. Then he faced Fay Hubley, "Get dressed," he whispered, "and when I introduce you, talk as little as possible."

Fay crossed to the bathroom, closed the door. Tony stripped off his shirt, tossed it on the bed and rumpled it among the sheets, Clad only in his chinos, he unbolted the door and flung it open.

Dobyns was nearly a head shorter than Tony— around Fay Hubley's height. But his girth more than made up for his lack of stature. If anything, Dobyns had only gotten fatter since the last time Tony had seen him. At five-six, Dobyns had to be tipping the scale at three hundred pounds.

"Hey, Ray, come on in," said Tony, stepping aside.

Dobyn's face was round, florid, and freckled. Sweaty strands of short-cropped red hair protruded from under the brim of a white Panama hat. He was probably forty, but his baby fat made him appear ten years younger. Pudgy arms dangled from the sleeves of a long Hawaiian shirt, and thick, hairy legs stuck out of white linen shorts. On his wide-splayed feet, dirty, ragged toenails thrust out of the tips of his worn leather sandals.

"Did I *interrupt* you?" Dobyns asked with a leering grin. He looked around the room. His eyes instantly settled on the computers scattered on the desk, the floor, the bag of plastic credit cards and magnetic card readers stacked in the corner.

"Ah, I see you're up to your old tricks, Navarro."

Tony closed the door. "The usual thing. I'm using the Internet to fill a warehouse in Pasadena, only the stuff's going in one door and out the other, if you get my drift. In another week I'll disappear with two-hundred thousand dollars' worth of merchandise."

Dobyns nodded, impressed.

"What about you, Ray? What have you been up to?"

Dobyns removed his hat, tossed it on the bed. "A little of this, a little of that. Lately I've been moving Prada knockoffs north—some of the top boutiques in Beverly Hills are my best customers, too. Can't trust anybody these days."

"How did you know I was in town?"

"A little birdy told me. One of those *official*-type birdies."

Tony remembered the Mexican policeman watching him unload. *Dobyns always did have great connections. Then again, a guy like him would need protection to survive down here.*

The bathroom door opened and Fay Hubley

emerged. She'd dressed in a short denim skirt and skimpy purple tank top.

"I *did* interrupt you," said Dobyns with a lewd smirk.

"This is Fay, my new partner," said Tony.

Fay crossed the room, entwined her arm in Tony's. "I'm his girlfriend, too, but he's too afraid of commitment to admit it," she said. Fay nuzzled Tony's neck, gently bit his earlobe.

Dobyns's smirk widened. "I'd say get a room but you already *got* one."

Tony gently pushed Fay away. "Get back to work."

Fay tossed her long, curly blond hair and strolled over to the desk, Dobyns's eyes following her every move. "Lucky man," he said.

"Want to go get a drink?" Dobyns asked.

Tony shook his head. "Anything you have to say to me you can say in front of Fay," he told the man.

"Fair enough," said Dobyns. "Last week I lost a shipment. Prada handbags. Fourteen thousand units—fuckin' Feds snapped them up on the border. The goddamn line wasn't moving anyway—"

Tony cut the conversation short. "What's this to me?"

Dobyns's eyes moved from Tony to Fay, then back again. "I was wondering if you've got room on your score for a third party. Things are getting tough down here. The gangs are muscling in on all the action—MS-13, *Seises Seises*, the Kings—that's one of the things I came here to warn you about."

Tony sighed and rubbed his neck. Fay pretended to study the monitor in front of her.

"This grift is marginal, not much left to go around," said Tony. The man's face fell. Tony figured it was time to throw him a bone. He placed his arm around Dobyns's shoulder. When he spoke again, it was in a conspiratorial whisper. "Hey, listen Ray. Maybe I can cut you in on one piece of action."

Dobyns grinned. "Speak, kemosabe."

"There's a guy down here, showed up in the last two or three days. He's another con man who uses computers, just like me. His name's Richard Lesser and he owes me a lot of money. If you can steer me in Lesser's direction, I can promise you a piece of action."

Dobyns stared at Tony through watery green eyes. "How much cash are we talking here?"

Tony pretended to consider the question. "I guess it's worth a grand up front. Ten more if you lead me to Lesser."

Dobyns blinked. "This guy must be into you big time. You got a deal, Navarro."

Tony reached into his chinos, pulled out a thick wallet. He peeled off ten crisp one-hundred-dollar bills, stuffed them into the man's sweaty hands. Then he pushed Ray Dobyns toward the door.

"I'll be right here, waiting," said Tony. "But only for a couple more days. Locate Richard Lesser and tell me where he's hiding, and there's more bills just like those coming your way."

8:46:18 A.M. PDT
South San Pedro Street
Little Tokyo

Lonnie snapped up the receiver on the first ring. "This is Nobunaga. Speak."

"Up and at 'em, samurai. I can't believe you're still at home. You're burning daylight, dude. This is your big day, and opportunity only knocks once."

Lon greeted his editor by name. Even if hadn't recognized Jake Gollob's voice, he'd have recognize the
man's style of discourse. Gollob spoke fluent cliché.

"Been up for hours, Jake," Lon replied. "Getting
ready to go now." He pulled another delivery uniform
out of the closet—this one from Peter's Pizza—and
tossed it, hanger and all, on top of a pile of shirts and
overalls already on the bed.

He caught sight of his own reflection in the full-
length mirror. At five-eleven he was tall for a Japanese-American. Thin, bordering on scrawny from
lack of sleep and a lousy diet. Black hair askew. By his
own assessment, Lon didn't really look much different than he had during his sophomore year at
UCLA—the year he'd dropped out.

"The cameras are all packed and I'm heading downtown in fifteen minutes," Lon told his boss, "just as
soon as I settle on the appropriate camouflage."

He yanked a pair of overalls out of the closet. The
tag read Pacific Power and Light.

"What do you think?" Lon asked. "Should I go
with the Peter's Pizza delivery man outfit, or stick to
House Dynasty Chinese Restaurant disguise?"

"You got a Singapore Airline uniform in your
closet?"

Lon paused. "What's up?"

"A stringer for Reuters spotted Abigail Heyer
boarding an airplane in Singapore."

"Yeah, so? She's giving out an award at the Silver
Screens tonight. It's on the schedule, man."

"Listen, Lon," Gollob was almost whispering now.
"My guy said she was pregnant. Maybe six months or
more. She was showing, for sure."

Lon dropped the overalls on the floor. "No shit?
Do you think the father's that Tarik Fareed guy, the

Turk she was dating in London? Or that Nikolai Manos guy she was seeing on that last movie shoot in Romania?"

"How the hell should I know?" Gollob shot back. "I just found out the bitch was knocked up five minutes ago. I know something else, though—"

Oh shit.

"I want a picture of Ms. Heyer on next week's cover."

"Jesus, boss. Wait ten hours and you'll have photos from every wire service to choose from."

"If I pay a wire service for my cover photo, why the hell am I paying *you*?" Gollob barked.

"Good point."

"Listen, Lon. Abigail Heyer's flight lands at LAX in an hour and a half, if it isn't delayed. Get out there and get me a photo."

"Come on, boss man—"

But the line was dead. His editor had hung up already. Angrily Lon punched the phone number of *Midnight Confession* magazine on Sunset Strip. Then an idea sprang into his mind and Lon cancelled the call.

Why the hell should I drive all the way out to the airport, get into a shoving match with fifty other paparazzi, all to get essentially the same freaking shot as everyone else? That's just nuts, especially when I have a better way to get a picture . . . an exclusive picture.

Lon snatched up his bag of tricks—a large garment bag stuffed full of clothing collected over the years. Then he draped the camera bag over his shoulder.

For luck, Lon touched an eight-by-ten color glossy on his way out the door.

Lots of folks identified with movie characters. For some it was Batman, others adored tough guys like Humphrey Bogart. Lon's hero was hanging on the wall near the light switch—a photograph of actor Danny DeVito from *L.A. Confidential.*

Detective Frank Castalano could barely hear his partner's transmission. The LAPD helicopter he rode in was cruising at top speed, at less than six hundred feet over the city's northern suburbs. At that low altitude, the roar of the engine and the sound of the beating rotors bounced off the ground, magnifying the deafening clamor inside the aircraft.

"Say again," Castalano roared, clutching the headset tightly to his ears to shut out all other sound.

"I said everyone's in on the manhunt now," Detective Jerry Alder replied. "The uniforms, the State Police, the sheriff's office, even the goddamn Park Rangers. There's a ring around Angeles National Park the Rams couldn't break through, and a chopper is tracking the Jaguar—"

"Hopefully from a discreet distance."

"You know how that goes," Alder replied.

Castalano cursed. It was his case, but he was losing control of it. Bad enough Jack Bauer convinced him to turn over the victim's computer. Though Castalano knew he would get an analysis of the computer's hard drive and history faster from CTU than from his own department, it was a double bind—Jack or his bosses could also withhold information from the LAPD in the name of "national security."

"Christ, Jerry," Castalano moaned, "with so many squad cars and guns around here, the odds for a capture instead of a kill are looking as bad as a Vegas slot machine. And the fucking air dispatcher warned me that word was getting out about the church bus full of kids the perp ran off the road."

"That was bad," Alder replied. "But it gets worse."

"Enlighten me."

"Nina Vandervorn of TV News Nine just phoned the chief," Alder said. "The station has got footage of the police cars in front of Vetri's house, the ambulances coming and going. Says she's running with the footage on the noon news—"

"Shit."

"We can't keep this buried much longer," Alder warned.

"Noon is a couple of hours away," Castalano said, his mind racing. "If we can snatch up this asshole in the Jag, we might solve our case. Go ahead and get permission to schedule a news conference for eleven o'clock. We might have our man by then. Either way, we'll control release of the information—*and* steal Ms. Vandervorn's thunder."

8:59:43 A.M. PDT
Santa Monica

Jack Bauer opened his eyes the instant Teri's hand touched his shoulder. He didn't need to check his watch to know he hadn't slept long. His hair was still damp from the shower, and his head still throbbed.

Teri stood over him, the cordless phone in one hand. "Sorry to wake you, Jack. It's Nina Myers."

Jack sat up, took the phone. He held the receiver to his naked chest until Teri exited the bedroom. Then he put the phone to his ear.

"Nina?"

"What are you doing, Jack?" Nina cried. "Ryan Chappelle flew back from D.C. on the red-eye and hit the roof."

"I don't follow." Jack rubbed his injured arm, now stiff from sleep.

"The raid at Utopia Studios. It was supposed to be a clandestine operation. Now it's on the morning news."

"Jesus," Jack groaned.

"I talked to Chet Blackburn. He told me you took off with some Los Angeles detective. Something personal. Does that computer the Cyber-Unit brought in have something to do with it?"

"Yes."

"Needless to say, I kept those facts from Ryan. He's angry enough as it is."

"Thanks, Nina, I'll explain everything when I get there."

"You'd better fly."

Jack glanced at his watch. "Give me half an hour."

Nina sighed. "I'll do what I can."

"I owe you, Nina."

"Yes, Jack. You do."

....

THE FOLLOWING TAKES PLACE
BETWEEN THE HOURS OF
9 A.M. AND 10 A.M.
PACIFIC DAYLIGHT TIME

....

9:00:35 A.M. PDT
CTU Headquarters, Los Angeles

When CTU's head programmer, Jamey Farrell, arrived at her workstation to start the day, she was surprised to find Milo Pressman at the diagnostics platform. Milo was a network and encryption specialist and head of CTU computer security. Snapped up by CTU just out of Stanford University, he had soulful eyes, black, curly hair, and still wore the earring he'd acquired in graduate school.

Petite, wiry, and Hispanic, Jamey was only two years older than Milo, but as a divorced single mother of a toddler son, she often felt more like a decade older in maturity. Case in point: Milo *never* arrived early for work, yet here he was, downloading the memory from a Dell desktop.

"Welcome home, stranger. Back so soon?" Jamey said, dropping her purse.

Pressmen sat back in his chair. "Miss me?" he teased.

"No," Jamey declared, popping the lid on her Starbucks. "It was nice *not* having a man around the house. When did you get back?"

"I took the red-eye from Washington last night. Flew in with Ryan Chappelle—first class. He gave me a ride back to headquarters with him, too."

"Ohhh, I'm impressed." Jamey's tone implied she wasn't.

"Come on, Jamey. Cut the guy some slack. Chappelle's not so bad. Looks to me like he's stuck between a rock and a hard place."

Jamey waved his comment aside. "You've been in Washington too long. You're talking like a bureaucrat."

"Langley's in Virginia."

Jamey sipped her French Roast—cream, triple sugar—while she eyed Milo's set up. "What's all this?"

Milo shrugged. "Found it wrapped in plastic on the table. The directive clipped to it said Jack sent the PC over for analysis. Arrived this morning, according to the manifest."

"You need any help with that?"

"I got it under control," Milo replied. "Where's Fay?"

"She's in the field with Tony Almeida. Down in Mexico looking for some guy named Lesser."

Milo gaped. "*Richard* Lesser."

Jamey looked up. "How did you know?"

"Let's say I'm not surprised. I knew 'Little Dick' Lesser at Stanford. He was a total asshole then. Called himself the Goddess Silica's gift to programming."

"The Goddess Silica?"

Milo shrugged. "Some gaming shit. Let's backtrack a bit . . . Did you say Fay's looking for Lesser in Mexico?"

"It's all in the daily update. Red file seven."

"Who's got time to read the update? I just got here after two weeks at the Puzzle Palace, and another week spent almost entirely in an emissions-proof and windowless cave at Foggy Bottom. I haven't slept for twenty hours. Anyway, I've—"

Suddenly Milo was on his feet. "What the hell? I just got an unknown virus warning."

Jamey heard the warning tone a moment later, and nearly dropped her coffee. "Where did it come from?"

"I was downloading the memory from this desktop and my security protocols went crazy. How long has it been since the archives were updated?"

CTU's computer security archives stored a copy of every worm, virus, spyware, and adware program released onto the World Wide Web as soon as it made an appearance. The ongoing collection and analysis of computer "mayhem ware" as Milo dubbed it was one of CTU's mandates, and the Cyber-Unit's most important tasks. Jamey was scrupulous about updating the system at least twice a day and Milo knew it.

"Listen, Milo . . . I updated the archives last night at nine o'clock, before I went home. You can see the update log right on the screen."

"Calm down. I'm not accusing you of anything."

"Can you isolate it?"

"W00t!" cheered Milo "I already have."

Milo stroked his keyboard as he quarantined the virus in a secure file, assigned the data a PIN, then dispatched it to the archives. He kept a copy isolated in his own system, too, for analysis.

While Milo was hunched over his computer, typing away, Jamey lifted Jack Bauer's directive from the top of a ball of clear plastic wrap the Dell had been swathed in.

"The virus is in one mother of a file—a Trojan horse. It's hidden inside a movie download," said Milo.

"That makes sense," said Jamey. "This computer belongs to Hugh Vetri. He's a movie producer."

"Cool," said Milo. "How did you know?"

Jamey waved the directive under his nose. "Because I actually read this memo past page one."

Milo blinked. "This download. The file's called *Gates of Heaven*. Isn't that the name of a new movie?"

"If it doesn't star Brad Pitt or Vin Diesel, I don't pay any attention," said Jamey after a gulp of caffeine.

9:18:40 A.M. PDT
Route 39
Near the Morris Reservoir

Detective Castalano popped the door and leaped out of the chopper. His feet hit the rocky ground before the helicopter's skids touched down. Crouching under the whirling rotors, he raced across the roadway toward a cluster of California State Police cars and Parks Department vehicles.

Castalano almost had his man—almost. The tricky part was yet to come. The roadway in front of him consisted of two narrow lanes, pitted and cracked, a faded yellow line down the middle. About two hundred yards before the roadblock, the road vanished around a sharp curve. The shoulder of the road was raised on both sides and topped with thick tangles of trees and brush. The State Troopers had chosen their spot well. It looked perfect.

Across the road, the helicopter lifted off again, kicking up dust and blades of sere scrub grass. Castalano ran a hand through his thinning brown hair, combing it back into place as he approached the phalanx of official vehicles. A California State Policeman stepped forward to greet him.

"Castalano? Frank Castalano? I'm Captain Lang."

They clasped hands. The state policeman was as broad as a linebacker and at least a head taller than the LAPD detective. He had a sunburned hide, iron-gray hair, and deep lines around his eyes. His black boots shined like mirrors, and Castalano would bet the farm the man had scared the bejesus out of more than a few California motorists over the years.

"Can you give me an update, Captain?"

Lang steered Castalano toward an emerald-green Parks Department Hummer. Hanging out the door, a Park Ranger in a dun-colored uniform held a large topographical map of the area around them. Another man standing over his shoulder spoke through the vehicle's radio.

"With the help of a helicopter pilot hovering out there somewhere, these two Rangers are tracking the Jaguar's movements, which you can see on the chart," Lang explained. Castalano studied the map.

"The fugitive was wandering aimlessly for a while," the Captain continued. "Then he managed to find the old access road that connected 39 to the Angeles Crest Highway. Using this service road, he came to this stretch of Route 39. But the road's been closed for years, and he's got himself bottled up. He can't turn around and go back the way he came—it's blocked by a hundred police cars by now. And back this way"—Lang jerked a meaty thumb over his shoulder—"road's blocked by a landslide."

"What's your plan, Captain?"

Lang gestured toward the point on the horizon where the deserted highway vanished around the curve.

"The fugitive can't see the roadblock until he's right on it. We have tire shredders spread out at the base of the curve. Another set fifty yards ahead of the first. One second after he comes around that corner he'll be cruising on rims, I guarantee it." Lang faced the detective. "If the plan's okay with you, that is."

"You're in charge here, Captain Lang. All I ask is that your men do everything they can to take this fugitive alive."

The Captain stared at the vanishing point. "I'm afraid that's not really up to my men, Detective. With all those tire shredders on the road, the suspect's overall health will depend on how fast he comes around that corner."

"He's a suspect in a multiple murder investigation—"

"I heard about those kids in the bus."

"Not only them," said Castalano. "He also killed a family in Los Angeles. And he may not be acting alone. I need to bring him back to L.A. *alive* and interrogate him."

"Is he armed, Detective?"

"No firearms were used in the murders." Castalano knew that wasn't an answer. As far as anyone knew, the perp could have a fifty-caliber machine gun for a hood ornament.

The Ranger on the radio gestured for silence, listened intently. "He's less than two miles away, coming up fast," he said at last. "Ninety seconds, maybe less."

Lang faced his men. "Everyone in position," he bellowed loud enough to be heard without a bullhorn. "Get behind those vehicles. The suspect is probably not armed. Repeat, the suspect is probably *not* armed. Use Tasers to subdue him if you must, but no deadly force. I want this man taken *alive*."

Castalano nodded his thanks to Captain Lang, studied the faces of the other men. The State Troopers were keyed up, ready to go. The Rangers looked worried as they moved behind the steel wall of vehicles.

In less than thirty seconds everyone was in position, listening. For a long moment, the only sound they heard was the winds whistling through the mountains, the rustling of trees.

Far up the road, near the curve, a State Trooper acting as an advance spotter popped out of his camouflaged position near the curve. He waved to Lang, then ducked out of sight.

The Captain touched the handle of the .357 Magnum in its holster. "He's almost here," Lang warned in a voice like muted thunder.

The roar of the Jaguar's high-performance engine rapidly rose in volume and lowered in pitch, a blur of chrome and crimson raced into view. Then came the explosive blast as the two front tires blew at the same instant. Castalano winced, fearing for a moment that some trigger-happy State Trooper had opened fire. Two more sharp pops followed, and the Jag dropped to the cracked concrete. Shredded rubber rolled free, and the engine's rumble was replaced by a terrible scraping squeal. Sparks erupted as the undercarriage hit the pavement. The Jag fishtailed, leaning so far to one side that Castalano thought the hurling steel projectile would flip over. Instead, the vehicle careened into the raised shoulder of the road, to slam to a halt in a cloud of dust and a shower of sparks and rocks.

Feet instantly pounded the ground. Castalano followed the State Troopers as they burst from cover and ran toward the car. The first helmeted trooper who reached the Jag extended his arms, aiming a Taser with both hands.

The passenger side door swung wide. A chunk of chrome clanged to the ground.

"Do *not* move!" the Trooper cried. "Keep both hands on the steering wheel and remain seated or I will shoot."

Castalano was still fifteen feet away when he saw a figure leaping out of the shattered automobile like a wolf vaulting toward its prey. The Trooper fired the Taser. It struck the man squarely in the chest, but the momentum of the driver's attack carried both men to the ground. That's when Castalano saw the driver's teeth buried in the State Trooper's neck, blood rapidly pooling on the weathered roadway.

Detective Castalano drew his service revolver, his vow to capture the man alive forgotten in the savagery of the attack. A wall of State Troopers closed around the thrashing men on the ground, more Tasers flashed. Castalano saw pops and sparks, heard a sharp cry of anguish. The stench of ozone stung his nostrils, mingling with a raw smell of sweat, the metallic stench of blood. Sharp copper tips pierced flesh, electricity crackled and the suspect jerked and howled, yet continued to fight.

Castalano pushed through the wall of muscle and black leather. His foot came down on the pavement and he slipped in a pool of blood—the Trooper's carotid artery had been ripped open. Twitching, eyes wide in astonishment, the man poured his life on the ground while the maniac tore at him. Finally a booted foot crashed down on the back of the attacker's head. The man grunted, went limp. Captain Lang followed with a second kick that sent the blood-soaked fugitive rolling off the Trooper and across the concrete. The other Troopers descended on the struggling man like vultures, punching and kicking.

"No!" Castalano yelled, "take him alive."

More angry cries. Someone jerked the suspect to his feet. Though blood poured from his nose and his head lolled to one side, the man was still conscious. For the first time, Castalano got a good look at the suspect. He was five-nine or ten, maybe twenty-five, Middle Eastern. His clothes, his face were caked with gore. Fresh rivulets of blood rolled down his chin, his neck. Some of it was his. Most belonged to the State Trooper. There was old blood, too. Caked and brown. Hugh Vetri?

The man's eyes remained unfocused. Then he caught Castalano watching him. Helpless, his arms cuffed behind him, a dozen hands restraining his hands and legs, the man spat a mouthful of hot blood in Castalano's face.

"Hasan bin Sabah! The old man on the mountain! He sees all and when he moves his hand, no infidel will be safe."

The man spoke through battered lips and broken teeth, his eyes wild. Yet the words were spoken clearly, precisely, in an Oxford-educated accent.

What followed his pronouncement was an incoherent scream. The man's eyes glazed once again and he struggled anew. His cries were in another language now. Castalano figured it was some form of Arabic because the words *Allah Akbar* were repeated many times—never a good sign.

"Get him into the chopper," said Castalano in disgust. "I'm flying this bastard back to headquarters for interrogation."

As the suspect was hauled away to the clearing to await the helicopter, Detective Castalano stumbled suddenly, leaned against the hood of the smashed Jaguar. Gagging, he yanked a handkerchief out of his pants and wiped the gore off his face.

He peered inside the Jaguar. The tan leather seats were brown with dried blood, but he could see no knife or any kind of murder weapon. He did notice several empty glass vials on the floor of the car. They looked like crack vials. Then Castalano saw a vial that was still full. It contained a blue crystalline substance, definitely not crack cocaine or crystal meth— he'd seen enough of both to know the difference. The crime scene unit from L.A. had not yet arrived and Castalano decided not to wait. He snapped on a pair of latex gloves, reached into the vehicle and fumbled for the vial, which he quickly pocketed.

When he was finished, Castalano looked up to find Captain Lang looming over him.

"Good job," the detective said hoarsely. "How's your man doing?"

A shadow fell across Lang's face. He shook his head.

9:27:14 A.M. PDT
CTU Headquarters, Los Angeles

Jack Bauer entered the conference room, clad in charcoal-gray slacks with a knife-sharp crease, a newly pressed cobalt-blue shirt. Ryan Chappelle, presiding over the hastily assembled meeting, looked up from his chair at the head of the table.

"Good of you to join us, Jack."

Jamey Farrell sat tapping a pencil. Next to her Milo Pressman shuffled the pages of a print out. Nina Myers was there, too. She offered Jack a warning look.

"Sorry about the mix-up Ryan. I should have returned to headquarters after the raid—"

"That would have been nice," Chappelle interrupted. "Then I wouldn't have heard the bad news from the television report."

"We had bad intelligence, that's all—"

"Let's drop this subject, Special Agent Bauer. Jamey Farrell and Milo Pressman brought me up to speed on that other matter."

Jack took a seat opposite Nina. "The other matter?" he said.

"The computer you sent us for analysis this morning," said Jamey. "Your instincts were correct. What we found connects up with another investigation—"

Chappelle stared at Jamey. "Are you saying Jack knew what was on this computer?"

"He reads the daily reports," Jamey replied. "He knows Richard Lesser is a person of interest in an ongoing investigation."

Jack knew Jamey was trying to cover for him, but he wasn't having it. "Wait a minute," he said. "Are you saying this computer ties in with the Richard Lesser investigation?"

This time it was Milo Pressman who spoke. "It sure does, Jack. There was a pirated movie download inside the hard drive, a copy of *Gates of Heaven*. I traced it right back to Lesser's server down in Mexico. If that isn't enough proof, there's more. Inside of that download there was a hidden program—a Trojan horse virus."

"You said it was a pirated copy of *Gates of heaven*," said Jack. "That makes no sense."

Chappelle spoke up. "Enlighten us, Jack. Start with telling us how and where you got this computer."

Jack told them about Detective Frank Castalano's visit, the murders at Hugh Vetri's house—still not public news. He carefully left out the existence of the CD-ROM still in his pocket and the personal information on Bauer and his family the disk contained, hoping no one would ask why an LAPD detective contacted him in the first place.

"I see Jack's point now. Why would Hugh Vetri download his own movie?" Chappelle asked.

"He knew the film was pirated. Maybe he wanted to see what the thieves really had," offered Milo. "If he saw the pirate version, he might be able to trace it backward, to the thief who stole the digital file in the first place."

"Or maybe he knew about the Trojan horse and wanted to stop the virus before it spread," said Jamey.

"Any clue what this virus does?" Jack asked.

Milo shrugged. "We turned it loose inside an isolated computer. So far, nothing's happened. The virus is encrypted too well to crack easily. We might have to reverse-engineer the sucker to figure out what it's designed to do." Milo paused. "That, or we can catch Little Dick Lesser. If I know the guy like I think I do, he'll crack pretty easily."

Jamey closed her eyes and quietly sighed. *How stupid can Milo be*, she wondered. *And instead of shutting up, he just keeps on talking, digging his grave a little deeper with every dumb word out of his stupid mouth.*

"Dick Lesser's fingerprints are all over this program," Milo declared, throwing his hands in the air.

"This is just the kind of crap he used to pull at Stanford!"

Ryan Chappelle looked at Milo and grinned.

Here it comes, thought Jamey.

"Mr. Pressman. Are you saying you know this Richard Lesser?"

Milo, of course, never saw the hammer. "Yeah, sure," he said, nodding. "I went to graduate school with him . . . When I was a TA, I had an office right next to his."

Chappelle placed the palms of his hands on the table, pushed himself to his feet. "Mr. Pressman, I'm authorizing you to take a helicopter to the Mexican border, pick up a car from CTU's safe house and head south. I want you to link up with Almeida in Tijuana as soon as possible."

Milo blinked. "Hey, wait a minute. I don't do espionage. I'm not a field agent."

"Neither is Fay Hubley. You'll join her in Mexico, too. Don't worry. Tony will be there to handle security while you hunt for Lesser."

"Me?" Milo cried, hand over his heart. "How am I gonna hunt Richard Lesser?"

"You know this guy," Ryan replied. "Lesser's psychology, quirks, things not found in any file."

"But—"

"Get on it, Milo. Now."

Chappelle crossed the conference room. He paused at the door. "And Jack—I'll expect your after-action report on this morning's botched raid on my desk within the hour."

When Chappelle was gone, Jamey whirled on Milo. "I told you not to shoot your mouth off in front of Chappelle. You thought Chappelle was your pal. Now he's sending you into harm's way."

Nina rose, waited at the door for Jack. He waved her off, approached Jamey Farrell.

"I need to see you in my office," Jack said softly. "Twenty minutes."

"Okay, boss," Jamey replied with a puzzled expression.

Jack caught up to Nina in the hallway. "Thanks again, Nina."

"What happened this morning, Jack?" she asked.

"You mean the raid? Like I told Chappelle. Bad intel, that's all. It was a meth lab. Nothing more. Still haven't found the Karma lab."

"Well the DEA is making hay over the bust anyway. I saw the district head on the news ten minutes ago."

Jack frowned.

"Stroke of genius bringing in that computer," Nina continued. "Nothing like a diversion to redirect Ryan Chappelle's attention away from a major snafu. I'm impressed. You're starting to play bureaucratic politics like a chess master."

Jack sighed. "I just want to do my job, Nina. That's all."

9:56:52 A.M. PDT
La Hacienda
Tijuana, Mexico

The curtains were drawn, the room was dark, the hum of the air conditioner a constant, white noise. When the knock came, a single rap, Tony rose from the bed and looked through the peephole.

Ray Dobyns stood on the other side of the scarred wood, rocking on his heels. The portly man wore a smug smile that told Tony the informant had found something.

Tony opened the door. Dobyns didn't enter. Instead, he stood on the threshold, gazing past Tony at Fay, her face illuminated by the light from the monitor.

"Hey, old buddy. I was wondering if I might have a word with you. In private." As he spoke, Dobyns's eyes lingered on Fay, who pointedly ignored them both.

Tony slipped into the hallway, closed the door behind him. "What's up?" he asked in a low voice.

"I think I may have a lead on Lesser," Dobyns replied. As he spoke, he dabbed beads of sweat from his upper lip with a stained handkerchief. "Ever hear of a bar called Little Fishes? The address is Cinco Albino, just west of Centro."

Tony shook his head.

"Yeah, well, Little Fishes is more than a bar. There's a brothel upstairs. They deal drugs there, and stolen goods move through the warehouse behind the whorehouse. The whole set up is reputedly run by the SS."

SS was short for *Seises Seises*. A Mexican outfit named after the prison cellblock—66—where the gang originated. The SS was the most recent criminal gang to spring from the corrupt and brutal Mexican penal system. So far their activities had been confined to Northern Mexico and the Baja, but like all cancers, Tony knew their contagion was bound to spread.

"What's this got to do with Lesser?"

Dobyns shifted uneasily. "Word is a gringo came to the Little Fishes about a week ago. Brought a lot of computer shit with him. Been holed up on the third floor of that dump ever since. Sound about right to you, Navarro?"

Tony nodded.

"The bad news is the guy's about to bolt," Dobyns continued. "Been packing all day. He might be gone already."

"Take me there now," Tony commanded.

Dobyns nodded. "I thought that would be your reaction. But messin' with the SS is gonna cost a bit more."

"I'll up the ante to twenty thousand. That's the limit."

Tony could see the war behind the man's eyes, caught the moment when greed won over survival instinct.

"Can I trust you, Navarro?"

Tony met the man's gaze. "If we find Lesser, then we both make out. If he gets away, we both get nothing."

Dobyns nodded. "Okay. But we leave now, before our mark goes underground."

9:59:11 A.M. PDT
CTU Headquarters, Los Angeles

Jack Bauer had just handed over the disk to Jamey Farrell for analysis and sent her on her way—after exacting a promise that she would divulge her findings only to him.

He was about to tackle the after-action report on the morning raid when his phone warbled. "Bauer."

"Special Agent Bauer? This is Detective Jerry Alder, LAPD. I'm Frank Castalano's partner."

Jack sat up. "What can I do for you, Detective?"

"Frank wanted you to know he's captured a suspect in the Beverly Hills murder."

"Where? When?"

"The Angeles National Forest, about fifteen minutes ago. Listen. The man is a Saudi citizen here on an education visa. He's high on some kind of drug and talking jihad against all infidels—"

"Don't say anything more over this line. Where's Frank taking the suspect?"

"Central Facilities between Fifth and Sixth Street, near the bus terminal. We can control access to the prisoner better there than at the Court House."

"That's smart." Jack knew *controlling access to the prisoner* was a euphemism for keeping him away from a lawyer for as long as possible. Jack glanced at his watch.

Chappelle would hit the roof if he didn't see the after-action report on his desk in thirty minutes, but instincts told Jack this was more important than composing a futile exercise in bureaucratic double-speak.

"Tell Frank I'm on my way."

••

**THE FOLLOWING TAKES PLACE
BETWEEN THE HOURS OF
10 A.M. AND 11 A.M.
PACIFIC DAYLIGHT TIME**

••

10:01:01 A.M. PDT
Terrence Alton Chamberlain Auditorium
Los Angeles

The eight-man crew representing the Stage Carpenters and Craftsmen Union, Local 235, had gathered inside the union-mandated break area—in this case a large silver recreational vehicle parked on the street outside the mammoth Chamberlain Auditorium.

Not a hundred yards from the RV's door, the red carpet was being rolled out for the Silver Screen Awards Ceremony. In less than eight hours, celebrities would be strutting down that carpet and into the pavilion. Fans and ranks of paparazzi were already staking claims to the choicest locations—behind well-guarded police barricades.

Inside the air-conditioned RV things were more relaxed. The workers lounged on couches and chairs and some took advantage of the microwave oven and coffee maker. Others smoked—strictly against Los Angeles County regulations—and watched television.

The men had been at it since 6 A.M., putting together the stage props for tonight's awards show. Everything was in place now, except an elaborate replica of the award itself, and a large wooden podium to set it on. These props were to be placed at center stage, and the prefabricated structure was on its way over from a construction contractor in El Monte. This final piece of the set would arrive within the hour, with plenty of time to set it up before the curtain rose on the live broadcast.

Even if the parts had arrived, the union contract stipulated that after four hours of work, a meal break was mandatory. Of course, the team was supposed to stagger their breaks so that someone was always available for carpentry work. But Pat Morganthau—the team's regular foreman—had not shown up for work and could not be found at any of his usual haunts. Meanwhile the instructions issued by the substitute foreman the management company had dispatched to the site—a twenty-something guy named Eddie Sabir—were being pretty much ignored by the union men.

In the middle of a cable sports report, the RV door opened.

"Heads up, the Teamsters have arrived," yelled one of the carpenters. Boos and catcalls followed.

A Middle Eastern man stood in the doorway. He waved a greeting with one hand, the other held a bright blue plastic storage container.

A portly fellow watching ESPN from a lounge chair

slapped his forehead. "Shit, Haroun, why'd you have to show up now?"

The man in the doorway offered the union men a broad smile.

"Good morning, good morning," said Haroun. "The bad news is that the props are in the truck and the truck is here, which means we all have work to do. But the good news is that my wife has made honey cakes again."

A burly carpenter with a long ponytail whistled. "Man, bring 'em on."

The portly man muted the sportscast. "Come on in, Haroun, sit down. We just made a fresh pot of coffee."

Haroun set the plastic container on the table, shook his head. "No, no, I must get the truck into the loading dock. Please be my guest. I shall return in a few minutes and join you."

"Better hurry," said the carpenter with the ponytail. "The last time you brought honey cakes they were gone before the foreman got any! And boy did Morganthau bitch."

Haroun hurried out the door. Ponytail Man helped himself to one of the tiny nutty cakes dripping with sweet honey. He passed the container to the others. "Man, these hit the spot," he gushed after a hearty first bite.

Before he took another, a groan came from the couch, out of the mouth of the youngest man in the room. He was slumped on the couch beside the portly worker. The lanky, twenty-two-year-old had shaggy blond hair and a deep surfer's tan. He groaned again and clutched his stomach.

"What the fuck is wrong with him," the portly man asked before sampling the sticky pastry.

"Dickhead here went to that new strip club out by the airport," Ponytail Man replied. "He drank till three A.M., then came to work."

"He ain't gonna be worth shit," opined a middle-aged, muscle-bound worker with a shaved head. He leaned back in his armchair and licked his gooey fingers.

The sick young man couldn't take it anymore—all the eating, the smacking lips, the smells. He jumped up and raced to the john, slammed the door and locked it behind him. He hung his head over the toilet, waiting.

"Another worshipper of the porcelain god," quipped Ponytail Man. The others laughed.

Inside the cramped head, the young man gagged a few times, but nothing came up despite his nausea, the wracking cramps. He wasn't surprised. He'd lost the contents of his stomach a long time ago, and wondered now when the agony would subside. Vowing never to drink to excess again, he ran water, washed out his mouth, rinsed his face. After he toweled off, he felt a little better, so he took a deep breath and opened the door.

At first he thought the whole thing was a twisted joke.

Ponytail Man was slumped over the table, head lolling to one side, eyes wide and unblinking, lips blue. The portly sports fan's eyes were wide and staring at the television broadcast, but he could no longer see. Another man was sprawled next to him on the couch, mouth gaping, tongue black and distended.

The big, bald dude lay dead on the floor, fingers curled and clutching the carpet. The youth whimpered, felt more than saw movement behind him. Then something hard and cold touched the back of his head. The young man froze, knees suddenly weak.

"You really should have eaten the cakes," said

Haroun. The sound suppressed Colt bucked in his hand. The young man's head burst like a melon; his body jerked and tumbled limply to the floor.

Haroun grunted as blood sprayed across his face. "As Hasan commands, so it shall be," he murmured.

The muffled sound of the shot had hardly faded before eight men in jeans and T-shirts entered the RV. Unlike Haroun, not one of these men was of Middle Eastern origin. All were Caucasians with brown or black hair, three were blond with fair skin and gray or green eyes. Their appearance easily fit the names and identities of the dead men around them.

Silently, the newcomers stripped the tool belts, ID tags, wallets, vests, clothes, keys and watches from the dead men. Meanwhile Haroun gingerly lifted the box of cakes and gathered up the fallen pastries, careful not to touch the tainted confections with his bare flesh. He dumped the poisoned food into a garbage bag, tossed the sound suppressed handgun in with it, then joined the others.

For the past two weeks, Haroun—obeying the instructions of the mysterious Hasan—had worked side-by-side, and socialized with the murdered men who lay at his feet. On three previous occasions Haroun had brought honey cakes baked, he said, by his dutiful and obedient Muslim wife. In truth Haroun had no wife, nor would he ever have one— except perhaps in Paradise where he would have many. Each time, the cakes had been delivered to him by an operative of Hasan, and Haroun was advised to share them with these men.

But not today. This time Haroun was told not to touch the pastries on pain of death. As always, he obeyed his master's instructions to the letter.

It was the least he could do for the man who

showed him the Gate of Paradise, granted him a tantalizingly brief vision of the world beyond this one.

Haroun did not know what deadly poison his master had used to kill these men. Nor did he care. All that mattered was that at last the plan had been set into motion. Nothing could stop the tide of blood to come. The dead men scattered around him were but the first of many who would fall. But unlike the quiet, anonymous deaths of these foolish pawns, the massacre to come would be seen by hundreds of millions all over the world.

10:12:41 A.M. PDT
La Hacienda
Tijuana, Mexico

The pop tune ringtone shook Fay Hubley out of her monitor trance. She saved her work, reached for the cell in her leather bag, dangling off the back of the chair

"Hello."

"Fay? It's Jamey. I tried to reach Tony but—"

"He turned his phone off. He hooked up with some smelly snitch down here and he's following a lead or something."

"He should have passed that information on to Nina."

"Tony told me to make the call," said Fay. "I was just about to—"

"What's the name of this snitch?"

"The guy's last name's Dobyns. His first name is Ray."

"Can you spell his last name?"

"No, but Tony said he knew the guy from before so it's probably in one of his after-action reports."

"And where did Tony go?" asked Jamey.

Fay exhaled with distaste. "Some ho' house. A place called *El Pequeños Pescados* on Albino Street."

Jamey noted the information in the mission log, pumped Fay for more and came up dry. She was concerned about Fay. The girl sounded distracted. "Listen, Fay, I want to give you a heads up. We found a Trojan horse. It's an attractive download for people with the right equipment—a movie that hasn't been released yet. Milo Pressman matched the hidden virus with the protocols you isolated and he says it has Lesser's fingerprints all over it."

Fay chewed her lip. "That's bad. If Lesser's launched something in the last five days, he did it from a server we know nothing about. That means he's at least one step ahead of us."

"Ryan Chappelle is sending Milo Pressman down there to back you up. He should arrive in a few hours. I'll update you when I know more."

"Cool," said Fay. "That will be fun. Milo's cute."

"Listen up, girl. You're not on vacation. Stay alert. Stay wary. Tony's an ex-Marine, and he has good field experience. If he left you with instructions, follow them. This mission is heating up and a lot can go bad down there."

Fay laughed. "Take it easy, Jamey. I'm not in Afghanistan. I'm just across the Mexican border. Really, what can happen to me in the middle of the day?"

Ray and Tony took a cab to the choked streets of Centro, but Tony made them get out in front of Planet Hollywood.

"Why are we switching cabs?" Dobyns asked nervously. "Are we being shadowed or something?"

"We're walking from here, that's all," said Tony.

It was apparent from his girth that Ray Dobyns didn't like walking. All the way to Albino Street the man complained about his sore feet, the uneven pavement, the crowds, the heat, the exhaust fumes.

The neighborhood surrounding the tavern and brothel called *El Pequeños Pescados* had decayed since the last time Tony had been to Tijuana. Perhaps in its heyday Albino Street had aspired to genuine middle class status, but things had obviously gone to seed. Now there were too many bars nestled between ramshackle storefront churches, fortune tellers in street stalls, pawnshops, liquor stores and check cashing businesses. There were also unmistakable signs of criminal activity—gang graffiti, street whores, pickpockets visible to those who knew how to spot them. A battered shell of a car, windows shattered, interior looted, sat next to a crumbling curb.

Ray Dobyns described Number Five Albino Street as a warehouse, but it was obvious to Tony that the building had been an ice house in the 1940s and '50s before it was converted to industrial use. The warehouse was a flat-roofed, windowless rectangle of dingy red brick. A three-story wooden clapboard tavern and inn had been built against the older brick structure sometime in the 1950s. Over the rough wooden porch that fronted the tavern, a faded bill-board for Azteca beer and a neon Cuervo sign in the window were the only indication this place was more than another tenement. A battered Ford van was parked in front of the building, locked tight. No one was visible on the porch, or on either of the narrow wooden balconies fronting the second and third floors.

"Do we go in?" Tony asked.

Dobyns shook his head. "Listen, Navarro. I don't want to blow this deal—I need the money bad. Let me go in first and check the place out. I've been here before. They know me. I'll be back in five minutes or less. You can time me."

Tony considered the man's plan. While he didn't trust Dobyns, Tony knew the con man would gain nothing by double-crossing him. Above all, Dobyns loved money, and he seemed to be in desperate need of some right now.

"Okay," grunted Tony. "I'll meet you right here in five minutes."

Dobyns waddled across the street, pushed through the wooden screen door and into the seedy tavern. Tony watched for a moment, then went into a tiny store and purchased a cold bottle of Jarritos. Sipping the sugary Mexican soda, he waited, glancing at his watch from time to time.

Dobyns reappeared exactly five minutes later. But instead of crossing the street, he motioned to Tony from the porch.

Tony chugged his drink, tossed the empty bottle into a garbage can and crossed the dusty street.

"It's Lesser, all right," said Dobyns. "He's upstairs on the third floor. He's not even hiding. The bartender spilled when I slipped him an Andrew Jackson."

"Is he alone?"

Dobyns nodded. "Come on. The faster you find him, the faster I get my money."

Tony hesitated. As tactical situations went, this whole set up stunk. He was heading into an unknown environment armed with only the Gerber Mark II serrated combat knife in his boot. On the other hand, Lesser was small potatoes and had no clue anyone from the U.S. government was looking for him, and he was not a violent felon. He was, in fact, a computer nerd. Plus Dobyns had nothing to gain and everything to lose if the deal fell apart.

"Lead the way."

Dobyns grinned and pushed through the screen door.

The interior was dim and nearly empty. Behind the bar, a squat bartender nodded at Dobyns, then went back to watching the jai alai match on the television above the bar. At a corner table far from the door, two middle-aged men were partying with two young prostitutes. The men were hang-dog drunk, the women clinging. Two more women sat in the corner, gossiping and polishing their nails. They looked up when the door opened, but when they saw Tony was with Dobyns, they returned to their conversation.

"The stairs are back here."

Dobyns led Tony across the bar to a narrow hallway. Beyond the single rest room another door opened into a stairwell. A trio of leaping silver-gray fish, stuffed and lacquered, were mounted above that door, which gave the brothel its name, *El Pequeños Pescados*—"Little Fishes."

Dobyns, in the lead, squeezed through the narrow doorway and slowly lumbered up the steep staircase to the second, then third floor.

Through another door, another narrow hallway

flanked by peeling wallpaper, a floor of stained, avocado-green linoleum. From somewhere behind a wall, a man grunted, a woman laughed.

They went to the wooden door at the end of the hallway. Dobyns knocked twice. "Come," a muffled voice called from within. Dobyns winked at Tony and opened the door.

The room was dark, the curtains drawn, but Tony could see two computer monitors flickering brightly, a figure seated in a chair facing them, his back turned to the door. Computers and components were scattered about on tables and chairs, even on the floor.

Dobyns opened his mouth to speak; Tony silenced him, stepped over the threshold.

"Richard Lesser? I need to speak—"

Tony never saw the truncheon that came down hard on the back of his head. Mercifully, he never felt the blow, either.

That pain, and more, would come later.

10:34:09 A.M. PDT
LAPD Central Facilities, Los Angeles

Jack Bauer observed the suspect through a one-way mirror. The Middle Eastern youth was locked in an interrogation room in the LAPD's Central Facilities. Routine prisoners were taken to one of the city's jails and booked there. But celebrity criminals—or soon to be celebrity, as was the case with this man—were often brought here because the press had not yet tumbled upon the existence of cells and interrogation rooms in what was basically a garage and repair facility a block away from the Los Angeles bus station.

The interrogation room was dim, the man pinned in a single column of bright white light as he sat immobile on a restraining seat, staring straight ahead, arms and legs shackled. His torn, bloodstained clothing had been collected as evidence. Now the killer wore virgin white overalls, white tube socks sans shoes. He'd been scrubbed clean, too. Blood samples and bits of human flesn had been collected from his skin, from under his fingernails, from between his teeth. His raven-black long hair was still damp.

Detective Frank Castalano stood at Jack's shoulder, his partner Jerry Alder a discreet distance away.

"I might have called you in even if this wasn't personal, Jack," Castalano was saying. "This man's a Saudi national. He's been talking jihad, praising Allah, and claiming he was doing the will of a terrorist named Hasan. When we ran his fingerprints, his education visa gave him away, and his name turned up on a Department of Homeland Security memo as a person of interest."

Jack took the file from Castalano's hand, flipped through it.

"His name is Ibn al Farad, twenty-two years old," Castalano continued. "His father is Omar al Farad, a millionaire vice president of the Royal Saudi Bank of Riyadh and a Deputy Minister in the government. He sent Ibn to America to study at the University of Southern California, but the boy vanished a year ago. The Saudi Arabian Consulate is looking for this kid and they may get word of his capture at any time . . ."

Jack's studied the suspect. "So now Ibn al Farad has resurfaced, this time as the suspect in a heinous multi-murder." Bauer shook his head. "It doesn't make any sense. Has he given any sort of statement?"

Castalano frowned. "He was ranting when we caught him, babbling in the helicopter, and chattering all the way down here to the interrogation room. But as soon as we started asking real questions, taping his words, the suspect stopped talking."

"You say he spoke of a man named Hasan," said Jack, recalling that same name had cropped up in the past twenty-four hours in connection with the fugitive Richard Lesser.

"He kept referring to this Hasan as 'the old man on the mountain.' Claimed that's what he was doing driving like a madman all over the San Gabriels—trying to find the old man."

Bauer frowned. The reference to the old man on a mountain jogged something in Jack's brain, but he could not isolate the memory thread and gave up. "You said he was high on some drug?"

Castalano showed Jack the vial he pulled out of the wrecked Jaguar. "I thought it was methamphetamine, dyed blue for street marketing, maybe a gang marking. But it's not meth, which might explain the color."

Jack held the vial up to the light and his frown deepened. "This is a new drug called Karma," he said hoarsely. "This stuff makes meth look like NoDoz."

Jack handed the vial back to Castalano. "Did he have anything else on him? A murder weapon? A copy of the Koran?"

"He had a note. It's in Ibn al Farad's own handwriting—we matched it with university records. But the note doesn't make much sense, it just seems like ravings scrawled when this guy was under the influence."

Castalano opened another file, showed Jack the handwritten document now sealed in a Mylar evidence bag. The handwriting alternated from tiny and cramped to expansive, the language lapsed between English and his native Arabic.

"Crazy stuff," muttered the detective.

But from what Jack could understand from scanning the man's writings, it was not all that crazy—not to a newly converted Muslim fanatic who claimed to have experienced a powerful vision of the afterlife, as Ibn al Farad did in this document. The man also vowed to purge the Islamic world of the satanic and pervasive influence of American culture.

Could that have been the reason why Hugh Vetri and his family were murdered? Because he made movies?

Much of the document was unreadable and Jack gave up trying. Perhaps CTU's Language and Document Division could make more sense of it.

Bauer turned his back to the prisoner, faced Detective Castalano.

"Frank, I need to move Ibn al Farad to CTU Headquarters for a thorough interrogation. As a suspect in a homicide, there are limits to the means the L.A. police can use to break him. But as the obvious perpetrator of the brutal terrorist act, the assassin of Hugh Vetri, a prominent and influential U.S. citizen, CTU can push his interrogation to the limit using methods you don't want to know about."

He could see the war behind Castalano's eyes. "Believe me, Frank," Jack continued. "I can break this man, but not here. Police methods are inadequate in the face of this man's fanaticism."

Castalano's features darkened. "A couple of years ago, the loss of basic civil liberties you're talking about would have scared the hell out of me . . . But that was before I saw the horrors in Hugh Vetri's home this morning."

The detective paused, thought of that van full of innocent kids, thought of his own. He swallowed hard. "If the Chief of Police signs off on the transfer, then this bastard's yours. But I'm going with you, Jack. I'm going to sit in on this man's interrogation and I'm going to hunt down any accomplices he names, no matter who they are."

10:49:12 A.M. PDT
La Hacienda
Tijuana, Mexico

Fay Hubley heard a sound in the hall outside the door of her hotel room. Heavy footsteps, then whispering. She quietly saved her work, put the computer to sleep and slipped out of her chair. Silently she crept across the room. Remembering Tony's instructions, she placed her ear against the door rather than open the peephole—a move that only served to alert anyone lurking outside that the room was occupied.

Fay held her breath, listened for a long moment. She heard nothing. Relieved, she took a step toward the bathroom. The knock exploded like thunder in the tiny room and the noise made her jump.

What do I do? What do I do?

Tony had told her that if someone knocked, she was to pretend she wasn't there, that the room was empty. With the chain lock in place, even with a key, it would be difficult for someone to get inside without making a whole lot of noise and attracting undue attention.

Fay stifled a gasp when she noticed she'd neglected to fasten the chain lock after Tony left with Dobyns. The knock came again. Louder and more insistent this time.

Fay remembered the gun Tony had given her, telling

her to have it in her hand if anyone tried to gain entry to the room. There'd been two Glocks hidden in their van outside and he'd brought one of them up, shown her how to fire it—but she had told herself the entire time she didn't want to fire it, never intended to, wouldn't have to. So she'd shoved it beneath a pillow on her bed.

Now she'd have to choose—run for the gun or fasten the chain.

The chain. That'll be enough, she told herself.

Practically leaping to the door, she fumbled with the metal links, barely got it fastened into place before the door reverberated from a powerful blow that knocked her backward. The frame splintered, the lock and chain gave way, and the door flew open.

Fay opened her mouth to scream, but the first of three men was too fast. His hand closed over Fay's mouth, even as he dragged her to the bed. Two other men followed the first one into the room, slammed the broken door behind them.

She struggled helplessly, her muffled cries reaching a frenzy when the man's rough hands fumbled under her blouse, groped her soft flesh.

10:57:59 A.M. PDT
CTU Headquarters, Los Angeles

Jamey Farrell had finished updating the Lesser file with information she culled from her conversation with Fay Hubley. Now she was ready to analyze the CD-ROM disk Jack had given her. But when she turned away from the monitor to retrieve it, she found Ryan Chappelle silently hovering over her shoulder.

"Can I help you?" she asked.

"I was looking for Jack Bauer," said Chappelle. "Have you seen him?"

"He was in his office a half an hour ago. I've been busy since."

Chappelle made a sour face. "So you have an analysis of the virus for me?"

Jamey blinked. "Excuse me?"

"An analysis of Lesser's Trojan horse. I promised the Cyber-Division Headquarters in Washington that I'd have something for them today."

"If that's what you wanted, you probably shouldn't have sent Milo—our encryption expert—to Mexico on a wild goose chase."

Ryan's frown intensified. "So you're saying you can't do it?"

"I'm saying I'm the head programmer. Mayhem-ware is not my specialty."

"Well contact Division and get someone—pronto. We need to know what systems and programs the Trojan horse targets, and what it does."

"But—"

"*Now*, Jamey."

Ryan turned and walked away. Jamey cursed under her breath. What was she supposed to do now? Pull an expert out of her butt?

Jamey was about to make what she knew to be a futile call to the Cyber-Unit in D.C. for help, when she suddenly remembered the name of someone who might be available to do the job on short notice. Jamey opened her Filofax and flipped through it. She found the name and phone number she was searching for on the first pass.

Lifting the receiver, Jamey punched up an outside line and dialed the number of Doris Soo Min.

1 2 3 4 5 6 7 8 9
10 11 12 13 14 15 16 17
18 19 20 21 22 23 24

....

**THE FOLLOWING TAKES PLACE
BETWEEN THE HOURS OF
11 A.M. AND 12 P.M.
PACIFIC DAYLIGHT TIME**

....

11:03:17 A.M. PDT
LAPD Central Facilities, Los Angeles

Jack Bauer opened his cell phone, tapped the speed dial with his thumb. Nina Myers answered on the first tone.

"Jack? Ryan was just in my office, he's looking—"

"Listen, Nina, I don't have much time. I just sent you a data dump from the LAPD Central Facilities computer. Cache 32452."

He heard Nina tapping the keyboard. "Got it," she said.

"That file contains everything we know about a Saudi national named Ibn al Farad and the multiple murders he committed last night—"

Nina's breath caught, and Jack knew she'd opened the crime scene folder.

"Listen, Nina. Ibn al Farad claims to be a disciple of Hasan. He may have even had personal contact with the terrorist leader."

"If this is true, this man is our first real lead—"

"There's more. The suspect was under the influence of Karma when he was captured. The LAPD recovered a vial of the substance from the car he'd totaled."

"Then the DEA was right," said Nina. "The drug *is* on the street."

"Maybe. I'm not sure. I think something else might be going on." Jack stroked his temple with his thumb and index finger. His head was beginning to throb again. "I'm bringing the suspect in for interrogation. I should be there in thirty minutes."

"I'll get things ready on this end."

"One more thing." Jack paused, gulped down two Tylenol capsules. "Detective Frank Castalano told me that after Farad was captured, he used an odd phrase several times. The old man on the mountain, or maybe the old man *in* the mountains. Find out what that means, if anything. Check our current databanks. Check MI-5, Interpol. And search the historic databanks, too."

"I'll do that myself," Nina replied. "Do you need Chet Blackburn's tactical squad to escort you back to headquarters?"

"There's no time," said Jack. "The Saudi Arabian Embassy probably knows the police have Ibn al Farad. His father is a powerful and wealthy man. I want to stay one step ahead of his lawyers. We're out of here in two minutes."

"Understood."

11:14:27 A.M. PDT
Ice House
Tijuana, Mexico

Tony tasted metal, smelled cat piss. A persistent roar battered his eardrums as air rushed over him, as if he were trapped inside a wind tunnel.

He opened his eyes and saw a dirty ceiling, faded industrial green paint peeling. The only illumination came from a shaft of sunlight pouring through a small, barred vent in the roof. He moved his head and felt a lance of pain jab the base of his neck. Tony tried to massage the area, discovered his hands were cuffed behind his back. He shifted position—a move that caused sluggish agony as blood slowly returned to his numb arms, wrists and hands. His feet, at least, were not shackled, but his boots were gone. So was his combat knife, the empty sheath still strapped to his calf.

Using his legs and shoulders, Tony sat up, a move which caused black jets of agony to explode behind his eyes. He'd been sprawled on an uneven wooden floor, now he'd propped himself up against a stack of packing crates. In the corner, an ancient box spring, stripped down its metal innards, leaned against the dirty brick wall. The rusty metal was burned black in some places, scorched white in others. Tony realized its purpose and shuddered.

He took a deep breath and found that the stench was worse sitting up. A chemical reek was carried by a blasting hot wind that rippled his long hair, now half freed of its ponytail. A sharp smell like nail polish remover burned his nostrils, mixed with an eye-stinging blast of ammonia. Tony wanted to cover his mouth, but it was impossible. Not only was he bound, but his fingers had swollen like sausages. When he could finally move them a few moments later, he found he'd been shackled with old-fashioned metal handcuffs that were too small, too tight. Recreational cuffs for the kinky set, most likely a prop from the brothel where he'd been snatched.

Tony heard voices speaking Spanish, lolled his head to the side. Peering between boxes, he saw three men working around a bank of identical white kitchen stoves where a dozen clear glass beakers bubbled with fluids. Vapors rose, filling translucent plastic tubes with dark brown sediment. The tubes, the beakers, were connected together with duct tape and wires.

He realized with alarm that he was inside an illegal methamphetamine lab—one of the largest he'd ever seen. Most illicit labs could fit into a large suitcase, and cost only a few hundred dollars up front to obtain the parts. But this lab was churning out the stuff like an assembly line.

Two of the three men were clad in blue plastic Tyvek suits, rubber gloves, oversized galoshes on their feet in lieu of chemical-proof environmental boots. They wore air filters around their noses and mouths, carpentry goggles over their eyes. The third man, thin to the point of emaciation, was wrapped head to toe in black plastic garbage bags, wearing what looked like a beekeeper's hat on his head. Behind the gauze veil he wore a vintage World War II gas mask.

Industrial strength fans on tall metal stands did their best to clear the toxic miasma of cooking chemicals out of the air, but Tony knew every breath he took in this place was deadly. Methamphetamine labs were among the most toxic environments on the planet. The process of cooking pseudoephedrine pills—over-the-counter cold medicine—into a powerfully addictive drug known in the states under street names like crank, crystal, zip or hillbilly heroin produced lethal by-products. For every pound of the manufactured drug, six pounds of toxic waste was created. Tony saw drains in the floor, the concrete bleached white around them, and knew these men were simply dumping their poisonous leftovers like benzene, hydrochloric acid, and sodium cyanide into the sewer system.

Studying his surroundings, he realized he was inside the brick ice house behind the brothel. He wondered why he'd been grabbed. Had he been double-crossed by his "old pal" Ray Dobyns, or was the con man a victim, too? Was Tony just a gringo kidnapping and extortion victim of a Mexican gang? Or was his capture related to CTU's pursuit of Richard Lesser?

Most of all, Tony wondered if Fay Hubley was safe back at the hotel.

11:32:11 A.M. PDT
South Bradbury Boulevard and Clark Street
Los Angeles

There had been an accident on the freeway. A jack-knifed truck was now sprawled across three lanes. All traffic going the same direction as the LAPD prisoner transport vehicle and its escorts was at a standstill.

Fortunately Jack Bauer, in the lead vehicle, received a timely warning from the pilot of the police helicopter providing aerial surveillance. He steered the convoy off the highway at the next ramp, before they got tangled up in the bottleneck. They were only a few miles from CTU Headquarters, so rather than risk the choked main streets, Jack directed the three-vehicle caravan through a lightly traveled industrial area where the traffic consisted mostly of trucks and commercial vehicles.

The streets were congested around the freeway ramp, but as soon as the convoy reached Clark Street they made up for lost time.

Glancing at his watch, Jack cursed the delay. Back at Central Facilities, Detective Castalano insisted Jack ride in the lead vehicle along with a uniformed driver and a fully outfitted member of the LAPD Special Weapons and Tactics team. His logic made sense. Jack would have to get the parade through CTU gate security, and that would be easier if he were at the head of the convoy. But Jack felt he was losing valuable time. If he'd ridden in the same vehicle as the prisoner, he might have gotten an early start on his interrogation.

But at least the LAPD had supplied enough men to get them to CTU safely, even though resources were stretched because of the Silver Screen Awards ceremony scheduled for that evening. Beyond the armored van Jack rode in, there was a second armored vehicle containing two SWAT team members bringing up the rear—both members of the D Platoon of the Metro Division. Sandwiched between the two vans was an LAPD prisoner transport truck containing Detective Castalano, his partner Jerry Alder, two uniformed officers and the prisoner, Ibn al Farad. Above, a police chopper monitored their movement and directed them around obstacles.

But Jack was still not sufficiently satisfied with the

security arrangement. Before they left the Central Facilities, he insisted on tagging the prisoner as an added precaution. While Castalano and Alder located an ankle bracelet and attached it to the young man, Jack removed one of the stems on his wristwatch. Unseen, he rested his hand on the suspect, pinning the tiny transmitter to the collar of Ibn al Farad's white jumpsuit, effectively double-tagging him.

At the time Jack though he might be overcautious—even paranoid—when he double-tagged the Saudi national. But since the sudden traffic jam on the highway, his suspicions had returned. So far they appeared to be unfounded.

As they rolled past the intersection of South Bradbury Boulevard and Clark Street, the convoy moved out of an area of chain link fences and truck parks, entering a two-lane canyon flanked by block-long rows of flat, two- and three-story industrial buildings. Noting their location, Jack opened his cell phone, intending to contact Nina for an update on tracking down a reference for the "old man on the mountain." Instead Jack was thrown against his shoulder harness when the driver slammed on the brakes. A long trailer truck had backed out of a garage, directly in the path of the convoy. Tires squealed, but there was no collision.

"Stupid son of a bitch could have killed us!" cried the policeman at the wheel. While Jack retrieved his fallen cell, the driver rolled down his window to yell at the trucker.

"Once a traffic cop, always a traffic cop," grunted the tactical officer in the backseat.

Still stooped over and fumbling for his phone, Jack heard the voice of the chopper pilot on his headset. "Code Red. Code Red, there are men on the roof. Repeat—"

But Jack wasn't listening. He'd spied the driver's open window and cried out. "No! That glass is bulletproof. Don't expose—"

Almost simultaneously Jack heard the sonic boom and the thwack of the bullet as it struck the driver in the throat. Hot blood sprayed the window, coating it. Two more shots ricocheted through the vehicle. A grunt, and the tactical officer slumped forward in his seat, left eye dripping from its socket. More bullets riddled the vehicle, chipping—but not penetrating—the bulletproof glass. Jack stayed close to the floor, realizing that reaching for his fallen cell phone was the only thing that had saved him.

"Officers down," he shouted into his headset. "We are under fire. Officers down. Repeat, officers down."

A voice crackled in his ear—the chopper pilot, but Jack could not make out his words. Outside, he heard the chatter of automatic weapons and guessed the helicopter was under attack.

Still on the floor of the cab, Jack reached out and closed the passenger side window. More shots bounced off the reinforced windshield. Jack pocketed the cell phone and took a deep breath. Then he leaped into the backseat. More shots struck the window, cracking the windshield down the middle.

Jack landed next to the SWAT team officer. Like the driver, the man was gone, his Heckler & Koch MP5 submachine gun still in his hands. Jack pried the weapon loose, collected a pair of XM84 stun grenades from the dead man's vest, looted clips of gore-soaked ammo from his belt. The voices on the police net had reached panic level, screaming into Jack's ear. Lifting his head above the seat, he scanned the vehicles behind him.

The armored van bringing up the rear sat with its

doors hanging open. Though protected in their bullet-resistant van, the tactical officers had attempted to respond to the attack. Now they both lay in the street, rivers of blood pooling around them on the hot pavement. So far, the prisoner transport vehicle did not seem to have been breached, though the driver was hunched, unmoving, over the steering wheel.

Jack flipped onto his back. Sprawled across the backseat, he scanned the rooftops. He could see armed, masked, black-clad figures on the edge of the buildings. They were on both sides of the street, four on each building, eight in all—then a ninth rose into view. The man held a dull gray tube on his shoulder, aimed the weapon at armored transport.

"Frank!" Jack screamed into his headset. "If you can hear me, get out of there now—"

Trailing fire and hot smoke, the shoulder-fired anti-tank missile slammed into the prisoner transport vehicle. Jack watched helplessly as the blunt tip of the shape-charged projectile punched a hole into the side of the truck, filling the vehicle with a fiery jet of molten plasma. The interior of the cab lit up like a strobe light as the windows and doors blew out. The dead driver was flipped like a rag doll over the steering wheel and into the street.

The echo of the blast had not yet faded when a half-dozen men burst out of the doors of the trailer truck that had veered into their path. Jack heard footsteps pounding as the men ran past his van, heading toward the shattered transport. Jack knew they were after the prisoner—to rescue Ibn al Farad or silence him forever. Either way, Jack had to stop them.

He set the weapon to its sustained fire setting, took

a deep breath and toggled the door. As soon as it opened, Jack tumbled to the street, rolling under the van. He aimed the MP5 at three men clustered around the door to the transport, squeezed the trigger. The weapon would spew bullets as long as the trigger was depressed.

Two figures danced as hot steel shells ripped them apart. Jack saw their weapons clatter to the pavement—an M-16 A2 assault rifle and a Remington M870 shotgun.

Slithering across the hot, oily pavement, Jack moved to the other side of the van. He rolled out from under the vehicle, tossing a non-lethal stun grenade into a second knot of men. The explosion sent the men reeling. One figure turned, aimed a shotgun. The MP5 bucked in Jack's hands and he stitched a bloody path up the man's torso.

Three men emerged from the smoking interior of the shattered transport truck—two attackers dragging a stunned Ibn al Farad between them.

Jack took aim, but before he could squeeze the trigger, a steel-toed boot crashed against his head, knocking him aside. Jack bounced off the van with a hollow thud; the weapon flew from his grip.

Dazed, Jack opened his eyes to see the muzzle of a Remington shotgun just inches from his face. He stared past the gun, into the eyes of the man behind the mask, and he saw his own death.

Then Jerry Alder stumbled out of the wreckage, his service revolver blazing. The man standing over Jack jerked once, twice, then sprawled across him, the shotgun clattering on the pavement. Jack struggled under the dead man's weight, watching helplessly as the assassins tossed Ibn al Farad into another vehicle.

More shots, and Alder was knocked backward in a fountain of blood. Engines roared, tires squealed on hot asphalt and the assassins raced away. In seconds the chaotic battlefield fell silent. Jack threw the corpse aside and stumbled to his feet. Reeling unsteadily, he lurched toward the transport.

Detective Castalano was there, beside the smoking vehicle. Blood oozed from his nose, mouth. He held his partner in his arms. Alder was alive, too, and alert. His jacket was open, white shirt ripped. A sucking chest wound bubbled black arterial blood.

"Frank! Are you okay?"

The man didn't respond, so Jack touched his arm. Frank whirled on him, revolver aimed at his face.

"I called for backup," Jack told him. "Help is on its way."

Frank lowered his weapon. He shook his head. "I can't hear you, Jack . . ."

Jack realized his friend had been deafened by the blast that had torn the vehicle open. Jack realized something else, too. The ankle bracelet with the tracker embedded inside was lying in the truck. It had been cut away by the men who took their prisoner.

In the distance, Jack heard sirens. He swung around. Eyes scanning, he noted the van that had brought up the rear was still in working order. The driver and passenger were dead on the pavement, but the engine was still idling. Jack grabbed Frank's arm, squeezed it until the man looked up again.

"I'm going after them," Jack said slowly, hoping Frank could read his lips. "I'm going to get the men who did this. Do you understand me, Frank?"

Castalano nodded. Beside him, his partner's eyes were etched with pain, his breath came in choking coughs.

"I'll get them, Frank. I promise."

Jerry Alder jerked convulsively, and Frank took his partner's hand. "It'll be okay, Jerry, hang on." His partner settled back, face ghastly white.

When Castalano looked up again, Jack Bauer was gone.

11:46:32 A.M. PDT
CTU Headquarters, Los Angeles

Nina Myers's initial search of United States intelligence service databases yielded little of value. After several false leads and dead ends, she finally located Federal Bureau of Investigation files pertaining to a secret inquiry conducted at the behest of the Governor of New Hampshire.

The FBI was asked to determine if a nationally famous landmark called the Old Man of the Mountain—a stone formation featured on the state seal and the official New Hampshire quarter issued by the U.S. mint—had been destroyed by vandals or terrorists in 2003. The FBI, with the help of geologists, eventually concluded wind and water erosion and the winter/summer freeze and thaw cycle had been the true culprits and the case was quietly closed.

Within fifteen minutes, Nina had completed a search of all current intelligence databases and came up empty. Then she recalled that Jack had requested a search of CTU's historical archives. It was an odd directive, considering the negligible amount of useful information a search of that particular database usually yielded. And yet, in working with Jack for the past several years, Nina had discovered that Special

Agent Bauer's instincts were often on the mark—
another factor that made the man such a dangerous
and unpredictable adversary.

On Jack's cue, Nina called up the link to the historical archives and typed in the phrase "old man in/on
mountain." To her surprise she immediately received
a hit. The phrase "Old Man on the Mountain" turned
up in a scholarly paper published in 1998 by Dr. A. A.
Dhabegeah, Professor of Middle Eastern Studies at
Brown University in Providence, Rhode Island. The title of the dissertation jumped out at Nina: *Hasan bin
Sabah and the Rise of Modern Terror.*

Hasan! A name regularly turning up in terrorist
chatter over the past several months. A shadowy figure CTU had been tracking without success.

Nina called up the PDF file and paged through it.
With each click of the mouse, the loose threads of the
past few months slowly began to come together. Jack
had been correct. Clues to their present mystery lay in
the past.

Minutes later, a three-toned chirp broke Nina's
concentration. She snapped up the receiver. "Myers."

"Nina!" The voice was breathless, excited.

"Jack, what's the matter?"

"The convoy was ambushed, shot to pieces. The attackers grabbed Ibn al Farad."

"Terrorists?"

"I don't think so," Jack replied. "They were using
NATO small arms and equipment. Their tactics were
straight out of the Special Forces training manual."

"Where are you?"

"I'm driving an unmarked LAPD van, in pursuit of
the suspect's vehicle. Before we left Central Facilities, I
planted a locator on Farad. I'm tracking his signal right
now with the GPS device in my watch. The vehicle

Farad's riding in is approximately three blocks ahead of me. I'm giving his kidnappers plenty of space so they think they got away clean."

Jack gave Nina his location, speed, and direction. "In case of trouble, I want the Tactical Unit on alert and ready to move at a moment's notice."

"I'm on it," Nina replied, instantly alerting Blackburn's unit via computer.

"Listen, Jack. I found a reference to the Old Man on the Mountain—in the historical archives, just like you said."

Nina heard tires squeal, Jack curse. "Give me the facts in shorthand. I've got my hands full right now."

"The Old Man on the Mountain was a Muslim holy man in the eleventh century. His name was Hasan bin Sabah—"

"*Hasan.* That can't be a coincidence."

"This Hasan was something of a heretic. He went to war against the whole Muslim world. But he only had a small cadre of followers, so he could never win a battle against the armies of the Persians, the Syrians, the Turks. He needed a force multiplier, so he resorted to terrorism. Hasan was, in fact, the world's first terrorist."

Jack grunted. "If the enemy you oppose outnumbers you, strike terror into their hearts and they will retreat."

"I'm not up on my Sun Tzu," said Nina. "Or is that Machiavelli?"

"Neither," said Jack. "I was quoting a man named Victor Drazen."

"There's more," Nina continued. "The historical Hasan brainwashed his followers by drugging them with hashish, then spiriting them to a garden filled with plants, perfumes, wine and beautiful women who fulfilled their every desire. After hours of bliss, they were drugged again and awoke in Hasan's presence. He told them they had glimpsed Paradise, and if they died for his cause they would spend eternity there. Because hashish was used to brainwash them, these followers came to be known as *Ashishin*—assassins. Using these suicidal fanatics, Hasan bin Sabah carried out a wave of political murders from Syria to Cairo to Baghdad."

"That explains the Karma," said Jack. "Hasan must be using the new drug to brainwash his killers. Ibn al Farad was caught with vials of the stuff. That could mean that Hasan is somewhere in this city right now, winning new converts right under our noses."

"It sounds . . . well it all sounds so crazy," Nina said doubtfully.

"No," Jack replied. "It makes perfect sense."

11:56:43 A.M. PDT
La Hacienda
Tijuana, Mexico

Milo crossed the deserted lobby, tapped the bell on the green Formica countertop. He waited a moment but no one showed so he clanged the bell again. Still the inn was quiet, the only sound the constant swish of the ceiling fan.

"Guess everyone's out to lunch or having a siesta," muttered Milo. He decided booking a room could wait. Better if he hooked up with Tony Almeida and Fay Hubley right away.

Milo headed for the stairs, taking them two at a time. He fully expected to be stopped by the manager at any moment, but Milo reached the second floor without seeing another human. Room six was at the end of the shabby hallway. He knocked once, and the door swung open.

Though it was almost noon on the sun-washed streets outside, the room was dark, the curtains drawn. Milo slowly peeked his head into the darkness. "Hello . . . Tony? Fay? Is anyone here?"

He stepped over the threshold, fumbling for the light switch. He found it, switched it on and off but nothing happened. He cautiously took another step, his eyes slowly becoming accustomed to the dark. Glass crunched under his shoe, and Milo realized he'd stepped on pieces of a smashed light bulb.

"Hello?"

Milo saw the window and yanked the curtains open. A wall a few feet outside the door blocked most of the sunlight, but enough streamed in for Milo to see Fay's computer network had been set up and was still running, though the monitor had been placed in hibernation mode.

Finally, Milo noticed light streaming from around the door to the bathroom. Over the constant hum of the feeble air conditioner, he listened for running water. He walked up to the door, placed his ear against it. "Tony? Fay?" he called.

Milo touched the brass doorknob, turned it. The bathroom door swung open. There was no window in the bathroom, but the tiny space was lit by fluorescent lights on either side of the cracked mirror. There was no bathtub, but the shower curtains were drawn.

He was about to leave the bathroom when Milo noticed brown spots on the white tiled floor . . . Lots of them. The big splotches weren't brown, really. More like a dark red. The trail led to the shower. With trepidation, Milo slowly drew the plastic curtains aside.

Fay Hubley lay in the corner of the shower. Milo knew she was dead. There was no way she could be alive. Not after what had been done to her.

Gagging, Milo whirled, stumbled out of the bathroom and into the powerful grip of a brawny giant in a T-shirt and black leather vest. The man had long sandy-blond hair in a ponytail, a raggedy beard and shoulders as wide as a sports utility vehicle. Milo struggled and the man tightened his grip. Then Milo cursed—only to be silenced when the barrel of a sawed-off shotgun was shoved against the side of his head. When the intruder spoke, his breath stank of stale beer.

"Don't make a sound, kid, or I'll blow your fuckin' head off."

1 2 3 4 5 6 7 **8** 9
10 11 12 13 14 15 16 17
18 19 20 21 22 23 24

....

THE FOLLOWING TAKES PLACE
BETWEEN THE HOURS OF
12 P.M. AND 1 P.M.
PACIFIC DAYLIGHT TIME

....

12:00:01 P.M. PDT
Abigail Heyer's estate
Beverly Hills

The famously wealthy enclave of Beverly Hills was bounded by Robertson Boulevard on the east, Olympic Boulevard to the south, and the communities of Westwood and Century City on the west. Palm-lined streets and palatial mansions dominated the landscape, but all was not glitz and glamour inside this exclusive neighborhood.

An army of housekeepers and service personnel were also a part of this community—albeit a practically invisible part who cooked, made beds, washed clothes, cleaned pools, drove limousines, cut lawns, and nursed the children of the pampered show business elite.

At the moment, Lon Nobunaga was grateful for the service industry's relative obscurity in this realm of the high and mighty. That, and a lack of vigilance by a member of Abigail Heyer's security personnel, had allowed the tabloid photographer to climb a power pole that overlooked the front yard and driveway of the actress's sprawling, Moorish-style mansion. Abandoning his car several blocks away, Lon, clad in his fake Pacific Power and Light overalls and ID tag, lugged a metal case containing his photographic gear to the front gate of Ms. Heyer's estate.

"I'm here to check the power grid," he'd told the guard. Without checking Lon's ID—he had a fake in case—and without searching the toolbox in his hand, the guard simply nodded and swung the steel gate open. It was so easy Lon nearly chuckled. He knew that a second and third line of defense secured the three-story mansion, the patios and pool behind the house. But Lon didn't need to get anywhere near the residence to snap the photo he was after—not when he could plainly see the driveway that led to the front door from atop this power pole. Not when he had his trusty Nikon D2X and fourteen different lenses to go with it.

Like most professional photographers, Lon was a recent convert to the digital realm. He'd chafed at the limitations of early digital cameras and stuck to the tried and true. But the technology slowly improved until Lon could find no fault with the newer models. Now he shot his pictures, selected the best, cropped and edited them, and then sent them via e-mail to the Sunset Strip offices of *Midnight Confes-*

sion magazine. His checks were direct deposit, and cleared in his account in less than twenty-four hours. It was fast, efficient, and best of all Lon didn't have to see his boss Jake Gollob more than two or three days a month.

For the past fifty-five minutes, Lon had pretended to work on the circuit box at the top of the pole. Meanwhile he listened to the all-news radio network, which broadcast Silver Screen pre-show updates every twenty minutes or so. He learned from the broadcast that Abigail Heyer's plane had landed at LAX about an hour before. The newscaster mentioned Ms. Heyer's tireless work on behalf of children trapped in the conflict-torn regions of Bosnia, Croatia, Chechnya, Daghrebistan. He added that her work with the United Nations focused the world's attention on the plight of orphans around the world. But there was no mention of the woman's pregnancy, which meant that no photographers or television crews had gotten anywhere near Abigail Heyer at the airport.

If the rumors of her impending childbirth were true—and his boss Jake Gollob was almost never wrong—then Lon's photograph of the suddenly pregnant movie queen would be a major scoop. It would probably make the wire services, too. That meant money in the bank for Lon, and a happy boss at *Midnight Confession* magazine.

Lon put the pause on his dreams of wealth when he spied a flurry of activity near the front gate. The guard was on the phone, nodding. Another security man rushed to the estate's entrance. A Rolls-Royce with tinted glass windows rolled through the gate, followed by a black sedan with bodyguards.

Lon tore off his headset and fumbled for his Nikon.

Crouching low behind the circuit box, he pointed the lens at the Rolls as it halted near the front door of the three-story mansion. He began snapping photos as soon as the driver climbed out and opened the back door. Though the interior of vehicle was dim, he hoped the digital camera pierced the shadows for a decent shot, but almost immediately the view was blocked by a security man—a tall giant with white-blond, short-cropped hair who looked like a KGB man in a 1980s political thriller. Lon stopped snapping when he knew all he was getting was the guard's broad back.

Finally, after a few long moments, Abigail Heyer climbed out of the backseat with help from the driver and security man, who took her proffered hands. She was very pregnant indeed, almost as big as she was in the movie *Bangor, Maine*, where the star played a working-class single mother struggling to unionize her low-paying workplace. Lon let out a breath, not realizing he'd been holding it. Then he snapped away, getting close to twenty usable shots by his own estimation, before the woman entered the front door and vanished from sight.

Lon quickly closed up the camera, stuffed it into the case meant to hold power tools, and climbed down the pole. He waited until the activity subsided before he walked back to the gate.

"All fixed," he declared.

The gate guard didn't reply. He simply buzzed Lon through, not bothering to open the gate himself.

As he hurried back to his car, Lon again marveled at how much the actually pregnant Abigail Heyer resembled the falsely pregnant character she played in *Bangor, Maine*. Several critics noted that the pregnancy suit she wore in that film was contoured to make her look great no matter what!

Amazing how she looks that good now—maybe better, mused Lon. *I guess some people are just naturally photogenic, which explains why Abigail Heyer is a movie star 'cause her acting is crap on a stick.*

12:06:33 P.M. PDT
La Hacienda
Tijuana, Mexico

Milo ceased struggling when he felt the muzzle of the sawed-off shotgun press against his temple. He looked up into the emotionless gray eyes of the Hell's Angel wannabe.

"Okay, you win," Milo said, raising his hands. Even in surrender, the CTU analyst couldn't hide the fear in his voice. He was convinced this man was the same person who'd murdered Fay Hubley.

"Step back against that wall," the big man said, prodding Milo with the shotgun. Milo backed up until his spine hit the peeling wallpaper. "Now turn around."

When Milo's cheek was flat against the wall, the man stepped around him and through the open bathroom door. Still leveling the shotgun at Milo's head, the man peered into the shower.

"Shit."

He stepped back, gazed at Milo. "You didn't do that, did you?"

"Didn't you?" said Milo. He tried to face the intruder, but the man slammed him flat with a powerful thrust of his tattooed forearm.

"I said don't move. I meant don't move."

"Okay, okay," Milo's hands went up higher. "It's just that you asked me a question."

"And you had to move to answer it?"

The biker lowered the shotgun, whacked Milo in the gut. Air shot out of his lungs and Milo doubled over. The man crossed the room, opened the front door. Through a haze of pain, Milo heard someone else step over the threshold. The door closed behind the newcomer. The man with the shotgun tried the light switch. It didn't work. He moved to a bedside lamp, turned it on, knocked the shade off. Milo stood straight again, blinked against the glare.

"Well, well," said the man who came in. "If it isn't my old pal, Milo De-Pressman."

Despite the scruffy-looking armed man still waving a weapon at him, Milo bristled at the sound of his hated college nickname. "Blow it out your ass, Lesser."

Lesser smirked. "That earring is bad enough. But my God, De-Pressman, what's with the soul patch?"

A head taller than Milo, Richard Lesser was bone thin, with curly brown hair coiled into a crown atop his high forehead, a sallow complexion, crud-brown eyes, and, in Milo's opinion, a chin as weak as ever.

"Look, Lesser . . ." Milo tried to step away from the wall but the big man slammed him back again.

"Down, boy. Heel, Cole," said Lesser. The armed man stepped back, lowered his weapon. "This is my bodyguard, Cole Keegan. Cole, meet my dear old classmate, Milo De-Pressman."

Lesser turned his back on the pair, examining Fay's network configuration. "I believe you or your colleagues were monitoring my Internet activities from here, am I correct? It's a nice setup, and the software is something I've never encountered before. But you have to have a big mainframe somewhere, feeding you this stuff."

Lesser gestured contemptuously at the computers linked to the tiny server in the middle of the room. "This Mickey Mouse set up just won't do. Are you working for a corporation? Boscom perhaps?"

Lesser poked the wireless mouse and the computer came out of hibernation. He blinked when he saw his own Internet accounts, banking records on the screen. "I'd like to meet the individual who invented this search program. Very clever."

"She's in the bathroom," said Milo with contempt. "Why don't you go in and introduce yourself."

Cole Keegan shook his shaggy head. "You don't want to go in there, boss. It's a mess."

"Listen, Richard," said Milo, his tone reasonable. "I was sent down here to bring you back."

"Sent? By whom? To take me back where? To prison?"

"I work for the CIA's Counter Terrorist Unit."

Lesser laughed. "You work for CTU? That's rich. I see the old saying, 'good enough for government work,' still applies if they're hiring *you*."

"And I see you're still as arrogant an asshole as you ever were, Little Dick."

"Watch it, Milo. I've got the bodyguard and Cole has the shotgun."

Cole Keegan touched Lesser's arm. "Remember why we came."

Lesser sighed. "Yes, of course. You're right."

"Why *did* you come, Lesser?" Milo asked. "To gloat over murdering Fay?"

"I murdered no one," said Lesser. "I came here to make a deal because someone named Hasan is trying rather hard to murder *me*."

Milo stared. "Gee, I can't imagine why."

12:11:21 P.M. PDT
Palm Drive
Beverly Hills

Jack Bauer followed Ibn al Farad and his captors to Beverly Hills. As he hoped, the kidnappers assumed they'd made a clean getaway. The farther away they got from the shootout, the more they relaxed their guard. By the time the kidnappers rolled through West Hollywood, Jack was less than a block away.

The vehicle finally swerved into a gated estate on Palm Drive, just a few doors down from Jean Harlow's mansion, and the house Joe DiMaggio and Marilyn Monroe shared during their ill-fated marriage. Jack cruised past the three-story Spanish-style house and down the street.

When he was around a curve and out of sight, Jack rolled to a halt under a knot of palm trees. Here in the hills, he was just five miles from the ocean, yet no cooling breezes reached even this elite enclave. The lawns may have been greener in Beverly Hills, the air conditioners more expensive, but even the wealthy had to step outside sometime and nothing could save them from the punishing heat now scorching all of LA.

Head throbbing, Jack called Jamey Farrell. He reported his position and asked for the property records of the house on Palm Drive. Jamey had an answer for him in less than three minutes.

"The home belongs to Nareesa al-Bustani. She's

the widow of a Saudi billionaire named Mohammed al-Bustani."

"What's his background?"

"He went missing during a recent purge of political dissidents."

Jack chewed on that a moment. In recent months the Royal Saudi intelligence service had begun to investigate citizens suspected of funding terrorism. During the course of their inquest, the secret police rounded up dozens of businessmen, government ministers, imams, and prominent citizens. Most were never seen again. There were no public trials, they just disappeared—tortured to death or shot, or dumped in the desert to perish. Mohammed al-Bustani had been one of them.

"Do the files contain any intelligence to suggest why al-Bustani was arrested?"

"Nothing."

"What about Mohammed's wife?"

"Naressa was living in her Beverly Hills home at the time of her husband's disappearance in Saudi Arabia. The couple's been estranged for decades, according to CIA intelligence."

"If that's true, then why is she helping a known terrorist now? And could Nareesa al-Bustani have a connection to Hasan? Or is there some connection to Ibn al Farad that we don't know about yet? Maybe he's a member of the woman's family—"

Jamey interrupted his verbalized speculations. "Nina's here. She wants to know what you plan to do next."

"Tell her to dispatch Chet Blackburn's team to Olympia Boulevard, but no closer than that. They'll be minutes away. I'll call if I need them."

"Jack? What are you going to do?" It was Nina's voice on the phone this time.

"The al-Bustani mansion has a man at the gate, armed. Otherwise the home security doesn't seem particularly daunting. I'm going to break in."

"But the kidnappers are still in there," Nina countered. "They're trained and armed."

"They think they've won. I'm sure they've let their guard down."

"But—"

"I can't wait, Nina. I've got a feeling time is running out."

12:19:07 P.M. PDT
La Hacienda
Tijuana, Mexico

"At first it sounded pretty good. Rip off the digital files of a yet-to-be-released tent pole film from a secured server at a special effects studio in San Francisco. A piece of cake, and money in the bank for me and Cole here."

Lesser leaned back on his chair, a self-satisfied grin on his narrow face. "Secured server! What a joke. The studio's computer system was easier to crack than that lockout code you put on your computer back in grad school."

The two men spoke in Tony and Fay's darkened hotel room. Milo sat on the edge of one of the two narrow beds, Lesser on the wobbly desk chair. Cole Keegan stood near the only exit, shotgun in hand, ear pressed to the door.

Milo narrowed his eyes. "Let's not relive our old school days, *Dick*. You're still not telling me about the virus you created, and why you chose to stick it in the movie download file."

"Don't be so impatient. Have you no sense of drama?"

Milo folded his arms and waited.

"Well, as I was telling you," Lesser continued, "I had a copy of the film when suddenly I get a knock at my door. Turns out my former associate Guido—"

"Guido?"

"Guido Nardini," Lesser replied. "Some folks would call him a mobster. I, however, prefer to speak of Mr. Nardini as a folk hero comparable to Robin Hood or the Scarecrow of Romney Marsh, immortalized—"

"Cut to the chase," Milo snapped.

"So, anyway, Guido mentioned to certain parties that I had the *Gates of Heaven* download and not so very long after that I had a visit from a representative of an ethnic organization based right here in Tijuana."

"The criminal gang *Seises Seises*?"

Lesser nodded. "The double-six boys had a proposition for me, and since a Federal indictment was being handed down along with a warrant for my arrest, I decided to take them up on their kind offer of asylum south of the border in exchange for pirating more Hollywood blockbusters."

"So why did the Mexicans turn on you?"

"Who said they turned on me? I had no trouble with the banditos. Give them a couple of downloads they can turn into knockoff DVDs, teach them a few computer games and they're happy as clams in a paella. The trouble came when the Chechens arrived."

Milo blinked. "Chechens? Like from Chechnya?"

"*Da*, comrade," said Lesser. "These guys were real self-starters, not like the laid-back Mexicans. Pretty soon the *cholos* were taking orders from the Chechens and their leader, some guy named Hasan."

"Did you meet this Hasan?"

"No. But I took his money. Lots of it. Hasan asked me to develop a Trojan horse program that would target a specific auditing program used by the Hollywood studios."

"Do you know why?"

Lesser shrugged. "I assumed they wanted to rip off the studios with bogus wire transfers of money or something. But the execute file Hasan had me create worked more like a security override program—there were all kinds of protocols to seal or unseal doors, disable alarms and stuff. It seemed more like he was going to knock-off a bank vault than steal currency the easy way—electronically."

"If you created the program he wanted, then why did Hasan turn on you?"

A shadow crossed Lesser's face. "Two days ago, Hasan's agent, a Chechen named Ordog—"

"*Ordog?*"

"That's what he calls himself. It means devil or something like that. Anyway, Ordog comes to me clutching a four-gigabit thumb drive. Says it contains a virus that he wanted me to unleash tonight, at midnight, local time."

"Isn't that your thing, Lesser. Mayhem and anarchy?"

"Listen, Pressman, ripping off movies is one thing, and I've got nothing against ripping off some greedy multinational communications conglomerate, either. But destroying the World Wide Web is where I get off the train. I mean, the Web is my bread and butter, why would I burn my toast?"

"What are you talking about?"

"I took a hard look at Hasan's little virus while the

66 boys were busy playing computer games. This virus is a monster. The most irresponsible hacker in the world wouldn't unleash this bug—not unless he never wanted to hack again in this lifetime."

"What does the virus do?"

"Remember the Rock'em Sock'em Robots'?"

"That kids' toy?"

"Two robots beating each other until one of them gets his block knocked off. That's what Hasan's virus would do—turn every infected computer against every other computer, every infected server against every other server in the Battle of the Network Mainframes."

"How fast does the virus reproduce?" Milo asked.

"This virus propagates like government-subsidized soybeans. The infected networks would attack the healthy ones, then they would attack one another with overwhelming service requests, confounding data loops, on/off protocols, suicide codes, the works. The only cure would be to shut down the entire system, purge it, or rebuild the system from scratch. I doubt eighty percent of the world's data would be retrievable."

"Holy shit, Lesser. Recovery from that would take years—"

"*Decades*, Pressman. Meanwhile all Internet commerce, all electronic mail and business transactions would be history. We'd be back to doing our work on paper. Hello 1960s."

"And this virus is going to be unleashed at midnight?"

Lesser shook his head, drew a length of the hemp necklace draped around his skinny throat. A shiny black plastic oval dangled on the end.

"I've got the thumb drive right here. According to

Ordog, it contains the only copy of the virus. That's why Hasan and his crew are out to get me. They need this thumb drive, and they need my expertise, to launch the cyber attack."

"So why did you come here, to this hotel? This room?"

"Cole overheard a conversation among the *Seises Seises hermanos* about some gringo named Navarro and his bitch, who were staying at this hotel, making noise about looking for me."

"Where did they get that information?"

Cole Keegan spoke up, his ear still pressed to the door. "From a fat lowlife named Dobyns. Ray Dobyns sold them out, led this guy Navarro into a trap. The Mexicans grabbed him so the Chechens could interrogate him. They're holding Navarro at *El Pequeños Pescados*, the brothel I've been holed up in for the past couple of weeks."

"If you were planning to bust out, why didn't you do something earlier, before Fay . . ." Milo's voice trailed off, he swallowed. "Before Tony got captured?"

"I tried to get out of there, warn this Navarro guy—"

"His name's Almeida. Tony Almeida," said Milo, breaking protocol.

"Well, I tried to slip away and warn Agent *Almeida* they were coming for him, but it appears I arrived too late."

Milo glanced back at the bathroom door. "You were too late, all right, Lesser," he said bitterly. "Too late for Fay." Then he turned and met Lesser's eyes. "But we can still get Tony out of there."

Lesser adamantly shook his head. "Are you crazy? I just got away from those crazy Chechens, I'm not about to go back—"

"I'll go with you, Pressman," Cole Keegan spoke up. "I'll help get your guy out."

"Oh, no you don't, Keegan," Lesser protested, rising to his feet. "Don't forget you work for me."

Cole Keegan shrugged. "I do work for you, and I have your best interests in mind, so I'll give it to you straight. If you want to get out of Tijuana and across that border alive, we're gonna need help. And when we get across the border, we're going to need a few bargaining chips or we'll end up in a Federal penitentiary. Returning their agent to CTU would signal our good intentions and a willingness to cooperate. . . . Don't you think?"

Lesser's bony body sagged back down onto the wobbly desk chair. Instead of answering Cole's question, he turned to Milo. "Now you see why I pay this guy a million dollars a year to watch my ass."

9:47:53 A.M. EDT
Admiral House, The Naval Observatory
Washington, D.C.

"Because of a legislative deadlock in the Congress, the Vice President is unable to attend—"

"*Regretfully* unable to attend."

Megan Gleason looked up from the monitor, rolled her gold-flecked green eyes. A resident of the Vice President's home state, she was the very pretty daughter of a very wealthy and generous political contributor with strong ties to the state party.

"I always forget that *regretfully* part," Megan said, her pale, delicate features reddening.

Standing over her, Adam Carlisle smiled patiently.

"That's why you're the intern and I'm the intern-turned-almost-staff member."

"You're the 'almost-staff member' because you graduated in June and can take the job in the fall. I've got another two years before I'm sprung."

"But you can still enjoy the perks."

Megan frowned, curled straight brown hair behind an ear. "Perks? What perks? My pay is nonexistent. I live in a two bedroom Georgetown apartment with three roommates, and I work twelve hours a day."

"Oh, the humanity," said Adam. He removed the blue blazer from his athletic frame, hung it on the back of the chair beside Megan, then sat down and pointed to the document on the screen. "And let's not use the word *deadlock*. It has negative connotations."

"But aren't the President and Vice President having a problem getting their legislation passed?"

"Yes, but we never, ever admit something like that," Adam replied.

"Why not?"

Adam shook his head. "So young, so naïve."

"I'm only two years younger than you, Adam."

"In the ways of the world, you are a mere babe." He pointed to the computer screen. "Let's say 'because of a legislative impasse.' That sounds nice and diplomatic. You can smooth over anything—even gridlock in Congress—with a word like *impasse*."

Megan retyped the line. "It's amazing how much disputation can go into a simple press release."

"Welcome to Washington," said Adam. "Nothing inside the Beltway is ever simple. You cannot just say 'the Vice President is stuck here and can't make the Silver Screen Awards so his wife is going without him,' even though that's exactly what's happening."

"Why not? I mean *really*. I'd like to know."

"There are so many reasons." Adam ticked them off with his fingers. "*One*: by not going, the VP could appear to be snubbing the wife of the Russian President, even though both she and her husband will attend a White House State Dinner in two days' time—which is why we're going to make a little joke about the Russian President's wife and our VP's wife having 'girl time' without their husbands. But just a little joke because we don't want to offend the feminists."

"Why don't we say the two wives can go to Chippendale's together?"

Adam raised an eyebrow. "I know you're being flip, but that joke actually worked at the annual Correspondents Dinner. It's a little too raw for a presidential press release, however. Still, if you come up with more like that, let me know. I'll have someone feed it to the writers over at *The Tonight Show*."

"You're not kidding, are you?"

Adam stared.

"Okay, okay, give me another reason for your release rhetoric," said Megan.

"Reason *two*: we don't want to tell the Hollywood community—which was so generous during the President's campaign—that a stalled farm bill is more important that the Veep showing his face at their annual awards show—"

"But it *is* true!"

Adam shook his head again. "You can never, never tell wealthy people they are not important. Especially wealthy movie stars. That just won't do."

Megan rubbed her tired eyes. Adam checked his watch. "Let's get back to work. We have to finish this in the next hour."

"What's the rush?" Megan asked.

"We have to catch Air Force Two in ninety minutes."

"Ha, ha. Very funny."

"It's true. We're flying with the Vice President's wife, and we have tickets for the awards show tonight. We'll be sitting right behind the Russian contingent."

Megan was gaping. Speechless.

"I told you this job has perks," said Adam with a flirtatious wink.

1 2 3 4 5 6 7 8 **9**
10 11 12 13 14 15 16 17
18 19 20 21 22 23 24

....

THE FOLLOWING TAKES PLACE
BETWEEN THE HOURS OF
1 P.M. AND 2 P.M.
PACIFIC DAYLIGHT TIME

....

1:01:03 P.M. PDT
Palm Drive
Beverly Hills

Jack Bauer had patiently reconnoitered the lushly
manicured grounds around Nareesa al-Bustani's
estate—the carefully tended gardens, the tall stone
fence that completely circled the property—before he
set foot into its perimeter. Jack had found no cameras,
no motion detectors or sound sensors, yet he knew
that many of these affluent homes had invisible motion and sound monitors buried in the ground, or security cameras the size of a plum nestled among the
branches of trees. It would take a specialist and a
brace of high-tech gear to breach that kind of security

without detection, and Jack had no time to summon such help.

After carefully examining the area for tripwires, Jack scaled the fence near an overgrown section of the garden. He came down among a thick tangle of palms trees and razor grass. The vegetation was dry from the prolonged drought and it rustled like crumpled newspaper as he moved through it. He could only hope the swish of the grass in the hot, dry breeze would mask the sound of his footsteps.

Jack emerged from the tangle behind the pool house, where an air conditioning unit hummed. He didn't want to risk crossing the expansive stone patio, so instead he skirted the adobe wall until he was within reach of the sliding glass doors of the main house.

Peering around the wall, Jack saw that one of the glass doors was ajar. Behind the pane, virgin white curtains rippled in the hot wind. Jack's instincts bristled. Everything about this entry was too easy, too convenient—the open door was either an invitation or a trap. Whatever it was, he knew he had no choice. If he'd been discovered already, he would soon be stopped. It would be wiser for him to have the confrontation now.

Jack slipped the USP Tactical from its shoulder holster. Though it was heavier than the 9mm version used by most CTU field agents, Jack had recently come to value the stopping power of the .45-caliber model. Right now, however, Jack drew little comfort from the cold weapon in his grip as he moved silently across the sun-baked stone patio and through the door.

The interior was spartan—steel recliner chairs arranged around a curved glass table, a mirrored wall with a recessed bar, stocked with glass sculptures instead of spirits. Near a standing lamp Jack found another doorway that led deeper into the mansion. He'd just stepped over that threshold when someone moved behind him, shoved the barrel of a gun into his kidney.

"Please sheath your weapon, or my men will be forced to take it from you."

Men emerged from cover, M-16s held shoulder high, trained on Jack Bauer. Their black battle suits were scorched and scuffed, a bloody bandage encircled one man's forearm. Their masks were gone, to reveal close-cropped hair over steely-calm eyes.

Jack slipped the Tactical under his jacket, raised his arms. The weapon pressed into his torso withdrew and the man clutching it moved to face him. He was as tall as Jack, eyes tree-bark brown, hair as black as an imam's robes. A deep scar divided the flesh around his right eye, from hairline to cheekbone.

"You may put your arms down, Special Agent Bauer. We mean you no harm. There's been enough killing today."

"No, no! You fool. What are you doing?"

The outraged voice came from another room. The men around Jack lowered their weapons, stood at attention when a short, middle-aged man burst into the room, fist shaking.

"I told you to kill the intruder, Major Salah, not capture him. Kill! Kill!"

The newcomer was a head shorter than everyone around him, his flesh the color of untreated leather, hair gray-white and cropped in short bangs across a creased forehead. His eyes were dark and flashing with anger. But the one called Major Salah met the older man's rage squarely, refusing to back down.

"I have followed your orders up to now, Deputy Minister. But murdering the Special Agent in Charge of the Los Angeles Counter Terrorist Unit would have dire repercussions not even a man of your political power and wealth could ignore." Major Salah paused, his gaze met Jack's. "And I will not murder a member of an intelligence service our nation is allied with. It is dishonorable, and there has been enough killing this day."

Understanding now that he was not dealing with terrorists but a unit of the Saudi Special Forces Brigade, Jack felt some relief. Because of the unusual structure of the Saudi military, government ministers each controlled a unit of the Special Forces, ensuring no individual or branch of the Saudi government had more power than another. It was a byzantine system that kept the royal family safe from betrayal or mutiny, but it also compelled professional soldiers like Major Salah to take orders from men better suited to banking or economic planning.

Sensing the growing tension, Jack stepped between the Major and the diplomat. "I thank you for sparing my life, Major Ja'far al-Salah. I know that you must obey the orders of the Minister—"

"Omar al Farad is but a Deputy Minister—"

"And the father of Ibn al Farad," Jack added, turning to face Omar. "And as a father, Deputy Minister, you are understandably concerned about the welfare of your son."

Omar al Farad's gaze shifted from Jack to the doorway. A regal, middle-aged woman stood there, her dark, gray-streaked hair just brushing the collar of her ivory silk blouse, her long legs clad in matching silk pants. The woman was striking, with large, dark eyes and high, brown cheekbones damp with tears. To Jack, the family resemblance was noticeable. This woman was related in some way to Omar al Farad.

"What is it, Nereesa?" asked Omar.

Nereesa al-Bustani, Jack realized, the owner of this estate. He watched her glide across the room, seemingly oblivious to the ranks of armed men bickering around her. With a slender hand, she touched Omar's arm. "Ibn is awake now, brother, come," she whispered in flawless English.

As Omar turned to follow his sister out the door, Jack seized his arm—eliciting an alarmed response from the armed men, an angry glare from Major Salah.

"You must let me speak to your son," Jack urged.

"No," Omar al Farad replied, yanking his arm away. "Your nation, your evil culture, has done enough to ruin him. As soon as my son is well enough to travel, he is leaving the house of his aunt and going home."

"Listen to me, for what I am telling you is true," said Jack. "Your son will never reach Saudi Arabia alive. In fact, he will never leave this city."

The Deputy Minister glared. "Is this a threat?"

"No," Jack replied. "When your men attacked our convoy, we were moving your son from a police facility to CTU Headquarters for his own safety. Ibn was in protective custody because we feared those he conspired with now want to silence him forever."

Omar al Farad shook his head. "My son conspired with no one. He is not a terrorist."

"I never called him a terrorist, But your son had committed multiple murder. He must face justice—"

"You see! You speak of justice for crimes that were not Ibn's fault."

"That is exactly right," said Jack, his voice even. "Your son is not responsible for his crimes. I believe he was drugged and brainwashed by a man named Hasan. It is Hasan I seek. If your son can lead me to him, it will do much to prove his innocence."

Again, the man's anger faded as abruptly as it came, replaced by confusion and uncertainty. Beneath the immaculate London-tailored clothing, the passionate outrage, Omar al Farad was a man in crisis, a man on the verge of collapse.

"Talk to me, Deputy Minister," Jack continued. "Tell me what happened to your son. How he became involved with this man Hasan."

Omar al Farad glanced at his sister. She closed her eyes and nodded once.

"Very well," said Omar. "But not here."

Nareesa led the two men to a small library packed with books in English and Arabic. They sat across from one another, a café-sized table between them. A maid appeared, served them tea and honey cakes. When Jack looked up again, he and Omar were alone.

"My first mistake was marrying an American wife," Omar began. "She loved the boy too much, spoiled him until he was seven years old—"

"What changed?"

"She died, Mr. Bauer, at our home in Riyadh. Cancer of the brain. First she was confused, then her madness became violent, finally she succumbed. There was nothing anyone could do. After an appropriate mourning period, I married again—this time someone more suitable, a member of the Saudi royal family."

"I see."

"My second wife did not approve of my first marriage or the product of that marriage. So when Ibn was eleven, I sent him to Andover, the same boarding school I'd attended. I tried to give him a good education, make him wise, but when he was of college age, Ibn demanded to be sent to the University of Southern California. He wished to become a filmmaker."

The man sighed heavily. "He'd been polluted by the filth he'd been exposed to."

"Filth?"

"The rap music, the movies full of wanton harlots and venal men, sin and degradation. Of course, I disapproved of Ibn's choices, but there was little I could say to dissuade him. To my shame, I finally relented."

Omar's features darkened, his fingers clawed at the cup. "In his first year, he met a girl. An American girl. My son, he was not sophisticated in the ways of the world, and he was weak. Because he was robbed of his mother's love early on, he craved the attention of women. This . . . whore . . . She took advantage of him—"

"She hurt him?"

"She *used* him, Mr. Bauer. Like an evil sucking harpy. And what was left was not my son. He stopped going to the mosque, dropped out of school, he took drugs, even drank liquor. Then, six months ago, he vanished. My lawyers could not find him. He did not touch his trust fund for we watched the account. I feared my son was dead—until today, when Major Salah told me Ibn had been found by your police. That he was about to be charged with terrible crimes."

More than anything else, Jack wanted to throttle Major Salah, demand to know what made the rogue officer think he could stage a covert operation inside the United States with impunity. But he was forced by circumstance to hold his tongue. Silently, Jack vowed to bring Major Salah, his men, and even Deputy Minister al Farad to justice for the policemen they maimed and murdered—but only after he'd gotten what he needed. The priority at the moment was interrogating the fugitive. A reckoning would come later.

"Your sister said your son is awake," said Jack. "Let me speak to him."

"Why? What can be gained?"

"Ibn has had contact with Hasan. When I find Hasan I will make him confess to his crimes. What he did to your boy. The faster I find Hasan, the faster I can clear your son's name."

Omar's eyes appeared haunted. Finally he nodded. "Very well, Mr. Bauer. But my son does not leave this house."

1:13:37 P.M. PDT
Valerie Dodge Modeling Agency
Rodeo Drive, Beverly Hills

"If that were me I'd just die! But not the Material Girl. No, that woman is a force of nature."

Valerie Dodge, CEO and founder of Valerie Dodge Modeling Agency, lounged in her contoured leather office chair. She held the silver phone to her ear, tapped the flawless surface of the desk with long, pink enameled fingernails. Her own forty-year-old reflection stared back at her from the polished glass. She had an oval face, framed by long, straight sun-bleached hair. White, perfectly capped teeth flashed against a dark tan. Laugh lines were evident around her light blue eyes and at the edges of her generous mouth. Hardly the same face that had graced the cover of every fashion magazine in the world in the late 1980s.

But not so bad, either, she mused. *A little too old, a little too tanned, and a little too brassy—but just tough enough to parlay a supermodel fame into a lasting career. To conquer the most cutthroat town in America.*

"Yes, darling. Tonight *is* the big night. My girls are ready, the venue's ready. My Katya's handled everything. She's a wonder—I'd just die without her. After all the work she's done these past weeks, Katya will probably want a raise, the ingrate!"

A knock interrupted her laugh. "Here's Katya, now. I'll see you tonight, at the wrap party. Remember, Club 100. Midnight—unless that damn awards show runs overtime."

The office door opened. The woman who entered looked to be in her early thirties. She wore a simple black dress, black leather boots that just touched the bend of her knee. Straw-blond hair in a tight bun, her only jewelry a black choker around her long, graceful, bone-white neck. In her arms she cradled a square box emblazoned with the name of an exclusive Rodeo Drive boutique.

"Come in, darling," said Valerie Dodge. "Where have you been all morning?"

"I went over to the Chamberlain Auditorium to make sure everything was in order, that our models have the privacy they need."

"Good girl. Last year half the stagehands were ogling my girls. All they had were canvas cubicles and Japanese screens for a dressing room."

Katya smiled. "I took care of that, Ms. Dodge. This year they'll have real rooms, backstage."

Valerie smiled. Then her eyes drifted to Katya's desk in the next room. On top of it, a thick red folder stuffed with contracts appeared untouched. Valerie Dodge nearly jumped out of her chair.

"My god, Katya. The models' contracts! They're

still there on your desk where I left them. The girls
can't appear tonight if those contracts are not filed
with the television network, the producers."

"Relax, Ms. Dodge," said Katya, fumbling with the
box in her arm. "The proper paperwork went to the
right people. I made sure of that."

Valerie leaned back and smiled. "Thank god. For a
moment—" She fumbled with a cigarette, a solid gold
lighter. "Well, I knew you were on top of everything.
Believe me, Katya, without you—"

The woman in black dropped the box, squeezed the
trigger. The sound suppressed Walther PBK in her
hand bucked once, twice, three times. Valerie Dodge
jerked as each shot struck her. With a final moan she
sank to the carpeted floor.

Katya lowered the weapon. Ignored the twitching
corpse. "I know, Ms. Dodge. You'd just die without
me."

The woman set the weapon on the glass desk. Then
she grabbed the dead woman by the ankle and
dragged her to the corner of the room, leaving a long
crimson trail on the spotless white rug.

Katya dropped the leg and stepped around the
corpse. Sitting in the chair, she booted up Valerie
Dodge's computer, then slipped a pen drive into a
USB port. It took less than two minutes for the plans,
the schematics, the codes to load. Next Katya typed in
her call sign—ChechenAvenger066—and sent coded
e-mails that activated sleeper agents all over America's
West Coast.

1:19:16 P.M. PDT
Terrence Alton Chamberlain Auditorium
Los Angeles

The loading dock was guarded by the auditorium's
regular security staff, but supervised by Secret Service
Agent Craig Auburn. A twenty-year veteran of the
Currency Fraud Division, Auburn had been
temporarily—and *inconveniently*—pulled from an investigation of a Pakistani funny money ring in San
Diego and dispatched to Los Angeles for the impending visit of the Vice President and his wife.

After he'd already arrived, it was announced that
Number Two—the Vice President—would not make
the trip, so many of the duties were scrambled.
Auburn ended up serving as an entry monitor, which
was not much more than a glorified doorman, but he
made no complaint. Special Agent Auburn took his
job seriously. He also planned to retire in five years
with a full pension and no blots on his exemplary
record.

Things had been quiet until a Middle Eastern man
arrived. He led a parade of carpenters and a half-
dozen mechanical dollies piled high with formed steel
parts partially or completely swathed by crude
wooden crates.

"What's this?" Auburn demanded, stepping in
front of the column.

"Stage prop," said the Middle Eastern man, waving
a manifest. Auburn took the clipboard, scanned it
with one eye on the man who gave it to him.

"Who are you?" Auburn asked, handing the clipboard back to the man.

"I am Haroun. It was my truck that brought these
sculptures in from the fabricator."

"Let me see your identification."

Smiling, Haroun handed Auburn his driver's license, union card, and security pass. Everything seemed in order, but there was something about the man, these crates, that set off Auburn's internal alarms. His colleagues said he could always spot a phony when he saw one, and Haroun felt like a ringer.

Auburn pushed past Haroun, paced down the line of dollies, circling one after the other. The crates were sizable—the smallest taller than a man, the largest nearly the size of an automobile. Finally, the horn honked on one of the mechanical dollies in the rear of the line.

"What's the hold up?" barked its operator.

"Who cares," said another. "We get paid by the hour."

Just then, the auditorium's crew chief arrived. He spied the crates and threw up his hands. "About goddamn time. Get those dollies in here. I got an empty stage up there."

"I am coming," Haroun called back. "As soon as this man lets me pass."

The crew chief shook his head, approached Special Agent Auburn. "*Please* don't tell me you're harassing Haroun just because he's Middle Eastern. He's worked here for a couple of years, right Haroun?"

"That is correct."

"How's the wife, by the way?" asked the crew chief. Haroun grinned. "She baked honey cakes. I am sorry they are all gone. I would have liked to save one for you."

"Maybe next time." The crew chief turned to Auburn. "Come on, guy. We're running late here. Save the double-oh-seven stuff for the bad guys. Unless this really is a case of racial profiling."

Auburn stepped aside. "Go on," he said, waving the men through.

One by one, the dollies began to move. Under Special Agent Auburn's watchful eye, the Chechens carefully maneuvered the mechanical dollies through the tight loading dock and up the ramp to the stage. They were exceedingly careful not to bump the crates, or send them tumbling onto their sides. The men moving the crates knew that those hidden inside were martyrs—armed and highly trained members of the faithful who were willing to die for the cause of Chechen independence, and for jihad.

This was the primary reason the phony union workers moved the props into attack position with reverence and respect. They did not want to disturb such heroes more than necessary on their final day on Earth.

1:34:07 P.M. PDT
Ice House
Tijuana, Mexico

Despite the chemical stench and the cuffs cutting off the circulation to his swollen hands, Tony Almeida had fallen into a fitful sleep. Someone had erected a plastic screen around the corner where he'd been thrown and on the other side of it, men continued to cook pills, separating the deadly and addictive narcotic from its component parts.

Tony had no idea how long he'd slept when two men approached him and hauled him to his feet. They were fair-skinned giants with light hair cropped close to their scalps. Each wore a surgical mask.

"Hey," Tony yelled, the moment they'd touched him, "what the hell do you want with me!"

The men responded with stony silence. They freed his arms, tore away his shirt. Then they slammed Tony against the wire box spring propped upright against the wall. When he realized what was happening, Tony struggled frantically, but his hands were useless, completely numb, and his elbows were poor substitutes for fists. The men easily bound him against the cold metal.

When they finally moved back, another man stepped up. He wore overalls, stained with sweat, thick rolls of fat bulging around a tight collar. His eyes were small and close set, over a flat nose and wet pink lips. While the other two men rolled the friction generator into the room and connected the electrodes to the bedsprings, the fat man watched, arms folded, until they were finished. Then he moved his face within inches of Tony's.

"Mr. Dobyns tells me you pass yourself off as a credit card cheat, a petty criminal. But he believes you are more than that. So do I."

"Who are you? What do you want from me?" Tony was appalled at the note of panic in his voice, but he couldn't control it, or the fear mounting inside him.

"My name is Ordog. What I want from you are answers. If you give them to me, you will be spared much agony. If you do not, you will suffer before you die."

"I don't know anything about Lesser, or what he's doing. Only that he owes me money, and—"

Ordog gripped the handle with a meaty hand, cranked the ancient generator. After a few turns, sparks exploded across the box springs and electric fire burned through Tony's entire body. He jerked helplessly as volts crackled through him. Then the fat man ceased cranking. Tony sagged against his bonds.

"Do not delude yourself, Mr. Navarro, or whatever your name is. You will die in this room. It's up to you to decide if you'll perish after prolonged agony, or mercifully quick."

1:39:54 P.M. PDT
La Hacienda
Tijuana, Mexico

Milo used his cell phone, connected to the secure and scrambled monitor in Fay Hubley's computer, to contact Nina Myers at CTU Los Angeles. He reported Fay Hubley's death and Tony's capture by Chechens working with *Seises Seises*. He also told Nina that he'd located Richard Lesser—who was now fast asleep in the hotel bed—and about the computer virus attack scheduled for midnight—an attack that might or might not have been thwarted by Lesser's defection.

"You're sure Lesser has the only copy of the virus?" Nina asked.

"I'm *not* sure," Milo replied. "But he has a thumb drive with a copy of the virus on it. Working with a sample of the virus, we can find a cure, or work on a way to shield the web servers from its effects."

"Can you trust him?"

"Lesser is an asshole in so many ways," said Milo. "But I believe him now. He's scared of the Chechens, of what they are capable of. He'd rather face charges in the States than let this cyber attack take place."

Nina contemplated his words. "Then it is imperative that you get Lesser and the data on that thumb drive across the border immediately. I'll have an extraction team at the border, and a helicopter waiting at Brown Field Municipal Airport to fly you to L.A."

Milo paused. Nina's command was sane and rational, and he wanted very much to obey her. "No," he said at last. "I have to try to rescue Tony first."

"You're not a field agent and you're not even armed."

"No, but I have someone with me who's ready to help. Cole Keegan, Richard Lesser's bodyguard."

"You can't do this, Milo. It's too important we get Lesser back. Tony knew what he was getting himself into—"

"Tony knew, but Fay didn't. I can't help Fay, but I refuse to give up on Tony while he's alive—"

"Listen, Milo—"

"Me and Cole Keegan worked out a plan that we think will work," said Milo. "It's a pretty solid plan and if it works I won't even need a gun. But I will need two hours. I can grab Tony, and we'll bring out Lesser together. We'll all cross the border and be at the airport by four o'clock."

Another pause. Cole, still guarding the door, pretended to ignore the conversation even as he hung on every word.

"Okay," Nina relented. "Two hours. No more."

Milo thanked his boss and signed off. Then he faced Cole Keegan. "So, do you have a plan? 'Cause I sure don't."

To Milo's surprise, Cole nodded. "There's someone who can help us. A woman at Little Fishes, one of the girls. She knows everything that goes on at the brothel and in the old building behind it."

Cole shot Milo a surprisingly sheepish look. "Her name's Brandy—at least that's what she calls herself. I kind of promised her I'd get her out when Lesser and I made our escape, but everything happened so fast I had to leave her behind."

"And you think she'll still help you?"

"Brandy's pragmatic. She knows the score. If you give her what she wants, she'll cooperate."

Milo was skeptical. "So how do I find this Brandy?"

"Meeting a whore ain't hard in Tijuana. Just go to the brothel and ask to see her."

"But . . . But I can't do that!" sputtered Milo. "Why don't you go? Brandy knows you."

"And everyone there knows *me*, but they don't know you," Cole replied. "If I walk into that brothel, those Chechens are gonna ask me a whole lot of questions I can't answer."

"But I don't look like the kind of guy who goes to a brothel, do I?"

"What kind of guy is that?" Cole asked.

Milo thought it over. "Good point," he said.

"Look," said Cole, "*El Pequeños Pescados* is always crowded at lunchtime—gringo truckers, mostly, coming across the border for a freight pickup and a quickie. Keep your mouth shut and your ears open and they'll just think you're another road rat."

"Come on—"

"When you find Brandy, tell her you know me, and that you're there to help her get out of Mexico, and I guarantee she'll help you find your missing agent—if he's still alive, that is."

1:47:14 P.M. PDT
Palm Drive
Beverly Hills

Major Salah's men bristled. They could not believe the American CTU agent had been given permission to interview Ibn al Farad—and by the boy's own father! The men, members of the elite Saudi Special Forces Brigade, had just fought—and two of them had just died—to prevent the American authorities from capturing the Saudi citizen. Now Jack Bauer was interrogating Ibn al Farad, subjecting the boy to unknown tortures in the back room of his aunt's home.

Sensing the unrest in his men, Major Salah divided them to quell a potential mutiny. He left several behind to guard the house, and dispatched two others to the front gate to watch for any sign of the American authorities. After that, he further divided his forces, sending the wounded men to their beds, and placing two armed men outside the study occupied by Jack Bauer and the rest. With his unit spread all over the mansion, the Major headed outside to check on the gate sentries posted in a gazebo on the other side of the wall from Palm Drive. Not surprisingly, Major Salah found the two men locked in a debate.

"You cannot trust the American authorities," Corporal Hourani was saying. "Their injustices are well known."

"Known by whom?" Sergeant Raschid replied.

"I learned of America's treachery as a boy in the madrassas. And from the Hollywood movies that truly depict this country's evil, its racism. Have you never seen *Mississippi Burning?*"

Sergeant Raschid shook his head. "I only watch James Bond movies. And Jackie Chan."

"I suggest you both keep your eyes on the road," Major Salah interrupted. "There is a vehicle approaching the gate." As the Major stepped into view, his men jerked to attention. "You are supposed to be on sentry duty," he admonished, "not discussing Hollywood movies."

"I beg your forgiveness, Major," Sergeant Raschid said, eyes forward.

"At ease," the Major replied with a hint of a smile. "I only meant to alert you that a vehicle is approaching, in case you had not noticed."

Sergeant Raschid hefted his M-16 as the electronic gate swung open, and a white Dodge van swung into the driveway.

"It is probably a routine delivery," said Major Salah. "But see what they want."

Sergeant Raschid and Corporal Hourani turned their backs on their commander as the van approached the gazebo. Eyes on the approaching vehicle, the soldiers did not see Major Salah slip two six-inch black stilettos out of hidden sheaths. And their deaths were so quick the two men barely felt the simultaneous thrusts that plunged the cold, hard steel blades deep into their brains.

The van rolled to a halt in front of the gazebo a moment later. The passenger door opened. Major Salah stepped over the dead men and climbed into the cab next to the blond-haired, blue-eyed driver. Behind them, a half dozen armed, masked men huddled inside the van's cargo bay.

"I have observed the American intelligence agent and learned that CTU knows nothing. Once Ibn is dead, their only connection to Hasan will be severed."

"So we strike?"

Salah nodded. "The way is open. We will kill the minister, his son, and his sister. And I will take care of Jack Bauer personally."

1 2 3 4 5 6 7 8 9
10 11 12 13 14 15 16 17
18 19 20 21 22 23 24

• •

THE FOLLOWING TAKES PLACE
BETWEEN THE HOURS OF
2 P.M. AND 3 P.M.
PACIFIC DAYLIGHT TIME

• •

2:00:56 P.M. PDT
Free Trade Pavilion
Russia East Europe Trade Alliance
Los Angeles

Sweeping in among the very first wave of reporters to
enter the Free Trade Pavilion since its opening last
month, Christina Hong, KHTV Seattle's twenty-
eight-year-old entertainment reporter, could not help
but be impressed. The Pavilion was designed by
Saudi-American architect Nawaf Sanjore, and featured a vaulted glass ceiling and three lofty steel and
glass ziggurats of various heights, the tallest of which
reached eighteen stories into the Los Angeles skyline.

Christina knew from her extensive research that the Pavilion was just one wing of the Russia East Europe Trade Alliance headquarters on Wilshire Boulevard, a twelve-story office building that housed the international trade organization. REETA had been established to promote mutually beneficial economic and political associations among the members of the former Soviet Union. The governments of these new republics were often at odds with one another, yet REETA had been instrumental in forging trade pacts that revived, modernized or transformed old industries into profitable new ventures.

The area of most interest to Christina Hong—who enjoyed covering the business side of the entertainment industry and harbored dreams of hosting her own cable news show—was the phenomenal resurrection of the Eastern European film industry in the last five years. Thanks to an infusion of capital from REETA, the movie business was alive and thriving in places like Prague, Budapest, Belgrade.

Yet this sea change in the film industry had gone virtually unnoticed by most media types. Christina Hong would not have known herself, except that two months ago her station manager had sent her to do an up-tempo story on American actors and extras who moved to Montreal from California or New York City for better acting jobs. Instead of finding happy and fulfilled character performers, she interviewed people who were suddenly strapped for work. The reason? Because so many so-called Hollywood productions were being shot in Eastern Europe.

The term *outsourcing* sprang immediately to mind and Christina realized that her producer had sent her to cover the wrong story. From long nights spent doing research on the Internet, or with the Lexis/Nexis search engine, Ms. Hong discovered that the Russia East Europe Trade Alliance was the catalyst for the change. She also learned that the organization itself was the brainchild of a single visionary man—financier and internationalist Nikolai Manos, a sometimes controversial figure who earned great wealth and power through his shrewd dealings on the international currency markets.

Suddenly the crowd surged around her, shaking Christina out of her thoughts. She saw people approach a raised stage at the opposite end of the hall and ordered Ben, her cameraman, to stake out a choice position before the press conference began.

"Let me know if you spot Nikolai Manos in this mob," she said. "I'd like to corner him with a few questions if I get the chance."

Ben brushed a tumble of brown bangs away from his face. "What's your fascination with this guy? I'd rather be over at the Chamberlain taking red carpet footage of the stars than watching a bunch of suits pat one another on the back."

"Manos is a billionaire." Christina chuckled. "Every girl is interested in a billionaire."

"You probably know more about this guy than you know about yourself."

"Go. Shoo," Christina commanded.

In her heart-of-hearts, Christina knew Ben was right. She did know an awful lot about Manos—he was born in Prague, the son of a Russian physician and a Greek freight tycoon, and orphaned at an early age. After the death of his parents, Manos inherited the bulk of his father's modest wealth, and multiplied it several times. Then, five years ago at the age of fifty, Nikolai Manos altered his life trajectory, to become something of a philanthropist. He established REETA with a large chunk of his personal fortune, in a seemingly altruistic effort to benefit the overall economy of Eastern Europe. Nikolai Manos's stated goal in creating the organization was peace through prosperity, and Manos was doing his part to bring about a measure of understanding to one of the bitterest political situations in the region—the feud between the Chechen people and Russia, their much resented masters.

All that, Christina knew, could be found in a REETA press release. Digging deeper—much deeper—she had discovered that Nikolai Manos had made enemies in his years of speculation in the money markets.

From the archives of the *Wall Street Journal*, she learned that among his business rivals Nikolai Manos had a ruthless reputation. In an interview with a former high-level employee in Manos's money market fund, it was revealed that the financier had knowingly pushed legal boundaries in his quest for profit.

Some of Nikolai Manos's activities even bordered on the criminal—at least in the view of certain foreign governments. In Singapore he was a wanted criminal because of a scheme he allegedly devised to undermine that nation's currency. Speaking off the record to a government official, Ms. Hong also learned that Manos was the subject of an ongoing Securities and Exchange Commission investigation in the United States.

But today, as she looked around at all the happy faces, the glamorous stars and producers, the media tycoons and business leaders who came out for this event, it was clear to Christina that the tycoon's checkered past and current woes did not seem to trouble the elite in this town. For them, the celebrity they turned out to see was Marina Katerine Novartov, the attractive and popular wife of Russian President Vladimir Novartov. Russia's First Lady was in America to attend the Silver Screen Awards, and meet with America's President and First Lady in Washington later in the week.

Right now the First Lady of Russia, a former principal dancer for the Bolshoi, stood in the middle of a small stage, swathed in a Diane von Furstenburg dress and grinning at the cameras. As the short press conference began, the woman haltingly answered questions, sometimes with the help of her translator.

Standing beside her on stage was the man who had been Christina Hong's obsession for the past month or more—Nikolai Manos. A full head shorter than Marina, Manos preferred to hug the sidelines, offering the popular First Lady as the main course for the hungry media. Christina studied the man, going so far as to snap a few photos with her own digital camera, despite the presence of her camera crew.

Manos wore a talc-white London-tailored suit and coal-black silk shirt. At fifty-five he looked a decade younger—beard iron-gray, close-cropped hair more black than white, his square, Slavic face hardly lined with age. His teeth were even and white behind a modest smile, his close-set gray eyes bright and intense as they gazed out at the crowd. Flanking the billionaire bachelor, a brace of blond, blue-eyed men served as bodyguards. All were said to be former members of various Eastern European security forces.

Because the First Lady of Russia spoke slow and

uncertain English, Christina took the opportunity to shift the topic to the host and yelled out a question.

"Mr. Manos! Mr. Manos! I'm Christina Hong, KHTV Seattle. Is it true you visited the set of Abigail Heyer's last film in Romania?"

Manos seemed shy and reluctant as he stepped up to the standing microphone. Christina waited anxiously for his reply. She already knew the answer, of course, but was wondering how he would choose to respond.

"I was in Romania, Ms. Hong, visiting a new studio complex my trade organization helped build. I did meet Ms. Heyer. I'm a big fan so it was quite a thrill—"

The philanthropist spoke with a low voice, so low some of the reporters in the back strained to catch his words despite the microphone. He seemed uncomfortable in front of the cameras, and was ready to fade into the background again when Christina bellowed out her follow-up question.

"Mr. Manos. Are you the mystery man Abigail Heyer was spending her free time with during the shoot?"

Nikolai Manos blinked at the question, then focused on Christina Hong. He seemed annoyed somehow, yet managed a polite, if dismissive smile.

"You flatter me, Ms. Hong. I could only hope."

The crowd exploded with laughter and Nikolai Manos used the interruption as an opportunity to step off the stage. Behind the raised stage, in full view of Christina Hong and the rest of the national press, Manos approached his security head, began a whispered conversation. Christina Hong, who had studied this man for so many weeks, burned to hear his words, strained to read his lips.

* * *

"Any word?" Nikolai Manos asked, one eye still focused on the persistent reporter from Seattle.

The bodyguard nodded. "Major Salah reports that CTU is flailing. They know nothing. In any case, the hit team has infiltrated the grounds. The men will strike momentarily."

"Make sure no one is left alive. And kill the CTU agent. I don't care what Major Salah believes. CTU is getting too close, too quickly."

2:02:11 P.M. PDT
Palm Drive
Beverly Hills

Forty minutes into the interrogation, Jack Bauer had obtained no useful information. At the start of the session, he'd placed Ibn al Farad in an upright chair in the middle of the study, the youth's back to the glass wall, the sun streaming through curtains that were shrouded in white. As Jack began his gentle questioning, Omar al Farad and his sister Nareesa hovered in the background; Omar fretting, Nareesa in tears.

Soon it was apparent Jack's questions would not be answered. Part of the problem was that his methods of extraction were limited. There was no time for truth serums to be administered, for sleep deprivation techniques or long periods standing in a position of maximum discomfort. And with Ibn al Farad's father and aunt looking on, more radical physical intimidation was out of the question, though Jack doubted it would work in any case. The youth he interrogated was still in the insidious throes of the amphetamine Karma, and rational replies to hard questions were rare.

Jack didn't know how long the effects of the drug would last, or even how much Ibn had absorbed before he'd been captured. Thus far, Ibn had alternated between chanting Muslim prayers and spewing raw, hateful venom at his father. His rational speech came between fits of sobbing, hallucinations, or episodes of trance-like inattention.

Jack began to wonder if shock therapy of some kind would work—either a physical shock, like an electric current or even a dousing in a tub of ice, or perhaps a psychological blow of some kind, one powerful enough to snap the youth back to some semblance of reality. Unfortunately, Jack didn't know Ibn well enough to know his fears or weaknesses, and his options were running out.

As Ibn lapsed into one of his silent trances, a knock came at the door—an odd knock, Jack noted. Three taps, followed by two, then four more. The Deputy Minister did not react to the strange knock, though he seemed troubled by the interruption. His son Ibn, however, lifted his head and grinned when he heard the staccato knocking, a reaction that concerned Jack.

"What is it?" Omar al Farad demanded, crossing the study to the locked door. "I asked not to be disturbed."

"It is Major Salah, Deputy Minister," called Salah through the door. "You have an urgent phone call."

"Hasan comes," Ibn muttered, his dazed expression transforming into naked glee.

Jack heard the young man's words and cried out, "Don't open the door!"

But Omar al Farad had released the lock already. The door burst open, knocking the small man backward, into the wall.

Nareesa al-Bustani jumped to her feet. "What's the meaning of—"

Salah's M-16 shot the elegant woman through the mouth, spraying blood and brains on walls and furniture. Behind the Saudi officer, Jack saw the corpses of two of his guards—obviously killed with a silenced weapon.

Jack drew his Tactical, but had no time to bring the handgun into play before Major Salah leveled the muzzle of his M-16 at Jack's heart. But just as the man squeezed the trigger, Omar al Farad threw himself on the Saudi officer's back. The M-16 discharged a spray of bullets, blasting the glass wall behind Jack to shards, showering him with razor-sharp splinters that sliced his flesh in a half-dozen places. While the Deputy Minister struggled with the Major, Jack cut Ibn al Farad loose, intending to drag the young man out of the house. But Ibn was bleeding profusely— he'd been shot by one or more of the M-16's stray bullets.

With a banshee cry, Major Salah flipped the helpless Saudi minister over his shoulder. Omar landed flat on his back at his son's feet. Ibn opened his eyes in time to see Major Salah furiously reduce his father's face to a splattered goo in a long burst of automatic fire. When Omar was dead, the officer again leveled his weapon at Jack. But when he squeezed the trigger, it clicked on an empty chamber. He'd fired on full automatic mode at the fallen Deputy Minister, emptying his magazine.

Jack raised his own weapon and fired twice—a double-tap that sent the Saudi officer's brains out the back of his head. From another part of the compound, Jack heard smoke grenades pop, more gunfire, and he knew Chet Blackburn and the CTU Tactical Unit had arrived like the cavalry.

Kicking the M-16 out of Salah's death grip, Jack bent over Ibn to check his condition. The young man's lips were white, face pinched with dazed agony. One .22-caliber shot had torn away a chunk of his shoulder muscle, another had entered his left lung and exited through his back. Jack knew the boy didn't have much time. Through the pain and shock, Ibn stared at the puddle that had been his father's face.

"Hasan did this to you," hissed Jack, speaking into the dying man's ear. "Hasan murdered your family. Betrayed you. Who is he? How did you meet Hasan? Tell me."

With pale, trembling lips, Ibn al Farad muttered a name. A moment later, Chet Blackburn burst into the room at the head of his assault team, weapon at the ready. He found a bleeding Jack Bauer in a room full of shattered glass and casualties.

Jack looked up. "I have to get back to CTU right away."

2:11:34 P.M. PDT
El Pequeños Pescados
Tijuana, Mexico

"Carlos says you're lookin' for me."

Milo glanced up from his warm beer. A woman leaned over him, her back to the busy bar, her long, wine-colored fingernails drumming the chipped table. She smiled but the expression on her full, generous mouth, painted the same dark red, did not extend to her eyes. Her complexion was the color of lightly creamed coffee; her long, blue-black hair danced around her naked shoulders. Her belly-baring halter top, pierced navel, and micro-mini faux-satin skirt left little to the imagination.

"Are you Brandy?" Milo asked timidly.

The woman moved her long fingernails from the table to the back of his neck. She lightly stroked his skin. "You must have been talkin' to your gringo friends to hear about me. Hot news travels fast, eh, cowboy?"

"Actually Cole Keegan sent me."

The woman's attitude immediately changed. She looked around cautiously, then slid into the chair across the table from him.

"Where is that son of a bitch?!" the woman whispered.

"I'm here to make good on his promise to get you out of here, across the border," Milo replied. "But first I need your help."

Brandy shot Milo a sidelong glance. "It's about the American dude the Chechens are torturing in the lab, isn't it?"

Milo's eyes went wide. "They're torturing him?"

"They emptied out the lab about an hour ago. I knew they brought someone in earlier. Then, when I saw Ordog, I knew . . ."

"I need to get him out."

"You need to get *me* out," Brandy shot back. "I kicked my drug habit, and I'm ready to split. Only I owe my pimp so much money he'll never let me go. That's why I made a deal with Cole. He promised to get me out, across the border where I'll be safe."

"I need to get you *and* my American friend out, or nobody's going."

Brandy glowered at Milo as if sizing him up. He

steadily met her challenging gaze. For a long moment, neither relented. Finally, the girl slapped the table with the palm of her hand.

"Go to the roof of the brick building behind the bar, Cole knows how to get up there. You find a barred window in the roof near Albino Street. Be ready to come through that window at three o'clock, sharp."

"What are you going to do?" Milo asked.

"Make a lot of noise, empty this place out."

"How?"

Brandy rose, touched Milo's arm. This time her smile was genuine. "I'm gonna burn this fucking shit hole to the ground, that's what I'm gonna do."

2:42:52 p.m. PDT
CTU Headquarters, Los Angeles

Nina Myers felt it was time to bring Ryan Chappelle up to speed on a number of developments, but she wasn't about to face the sure-to-be-irate Regional Director alone. At her command, Jamey Farrell abandoned her work station to participate in a meeting in the conference room. Even Doris Soo Min—a young programming genius who had previously been tapped by CTU Los Angeles because of her impressive skills—interrupted her work on the Lesser Trojan horse to attend.

From the start, the atmosphere in the conference room was tense. "Where's Jack?" Ryan asked, his voice simmering the moment he strode in and saw the Special Agent in Charge was missing.

"I just spoke with him. He's on his way," said Nina.

"From where?" Ryan sat down, adjusted his tightly knotted tie.

Nina took a breath, lowered her eyes. "Beverly Hills."

"I presume he wasn't there to visit the homes of the stars?"

"Jack Bauer followed up a promising lead in the Hasan investigation earlier today, a tip from a former colleague in the Los Angeles Police Department. Jack went to interrogate someone who may have had actual physical contact with the terrorist leader."

Ryan frowned. "Why am I learning about this now, and not three hours ago?"

"Jack felt the lead was questionable, that he was on a wild goose chase. He didn't want to bother you. Then, when things worked out, events happened too fast to keep you apprised. Jack made a major breakthrough once he contacted Omar al Farad—"

"The Saudi Deputy Minister of Finance?"

"The Deputy Minister's son, Ibn al Farad, had met with Hasan, became a disciple, perhaps even a member of his terrorist cell. Jack hoped Ibn might be able to describe the man. Ibn al Farad did give Jack one promising lead before he was murdered—"

"*Murdered*. The Deputy Minister's son was killed?"

"Along with the Deputy Minister and his sister, Nareesa al-Bustani."

Ryan placed his hands on the table. They were shaking. "Please tell me Jack had nothing to do with these deaths. That he was somewhere else."

"Jack was at the al-Bustani home when it was attacked by a team of professional assassins," Nina coolly replied. "CTU's Tactical Unit arrived too late to save them. The assassins were unfortunately killed in the assault, so we have no immediate knowledge of who they were, why they wanted the Saudis dead."

"On whose authority was the Tactical Unit mobilized?"

"Jack's," said Nina. "He felt he would need back up in case of trouble. He was right. CTU was monitoring the woman's home through the mansion's own security cameras. When Chet Blackburn's unit observed the van enter the property, detected the sound of gunfire, they moved immediately. They were inside the house within three minutes, but they were still too late to save the minister and his sister."

Ryan closed his eyes for a moment, fighting down his anger. When calm finally returned, he shifted his attention to Jamey Farrell. "I see you called in Doris Soo Min to help. Doris still has her Level Three security clearance from the Hell Gate incident?"

Jamey flinched when he'd first addressed her. She nodded timidly and Chappelle shifted his gaze to the younger woman. "Welcome back, Doris . . ."

"Er . . . Thank you, Mr. Chappelle."

"I hope you've made some progress isolating Lesser's virus."

Jamey and Doris exchanged nervous glances. "Well—" said Jamey.

"Actually—" said Doris.

"Just give me the facts so I can deal with them," Ryan said, his control slipping again.

"Well, actually this Trojan horse is a tough little bug," said Doris. "It's nearly impossible to separate it from the program it's embedded in—you know, the movie download. Anyway, Frankie—"

"Who's Frankie?"

"Frankenstein. A reverse-engineering program I created," Doris explained. "Frankie's on the job, and he'll sort it all out eventually, but it will take hours, maybe days—"

"We don't have days," Nina said. "Time is running out."

"What now?" Ryan asked.

"Milo Pressman made contact with Richard Lesser, who told Milo that an attack on the computer infrastructure of the world will be launched at midnight. Since Jack's not here, I'll need your permission to activate the Threat Clock—"

"I need to hear more," Chappelle said.

"Richard Lesser has agreed to cooperate with CTU in exchange for protection from Hasan, who is masterminding the attack. Lesser is even providing a copy of the virus that will be launched—"

"That's the first good news I've heard. Where's Lesser now?"

"Milo refused to leave Tijuana without at least trying to rescue Tony Almeida, who's been captured by the Mexican gang *Seises Seises*."

"But Milo's not a field agent," Chappelle cried, losing it now. "He's not even armed!"

"Milo's getting help from a United States citizen named Cole Keegan," said Nina, lifting a file from the stack on the table. "I've run Keegan's name through the Pentagon computers. Cole Randall Keegan was a sergeant in the Army Rangers during the First Gulf War. He hasn't held a job, or paid taxes since he received an honorable discharge from the military in 1992. Keegan's last known associates are the Lords of Hell motorcycle gang out of Oakland, California."

"So Milo and some expatriate biker are going to rescue an experienced field agent from the very people who outsmarted and captured him?" Ryan paused. "People, I am not hopeful. Get Milo on his cell *now*. If he wants to play hero, he can do it on his own time. But he's got to send Lesser and a copy of that virus back with Fay Hubley—"

Nina cleared her throat. "Milo asked for two hours and I gave him the time. Milo feels Tony's life is in danger. You see, Fay Hubley was murdered by the same men who captured Tony. Milo verified her death."

Fay's murder was news to Jamey. Though she remained outwardly calm, her lip trembled, her eyes misted when she heard the news.

"Does the virus embedded in the movie download have any connection to the virus that will be launched at midnight?" asked Chappelle.

"We don't know," said Nina. "Either way, we'll need Richard Lesser's expertise to prevent the imminent attack."

"And he's still down in Mexico—"

"He'll be here in two hours, Ryan. Milo swore he would pull it off and I trust him," said Nina.

Ryan nodded. "Okay, start the Threat Clock. Zero hour, twelve A.M." Next he focused on Doris. "What do you need to isolate that virus. To speed up the process?"

"That's easy," Doris replied. "A copy of the virus program independent of the download. Just the execute file. But—"

"I know," grunted Ryan. "It's still down in Mexico with Milo Pressman."

The room was not much bigger than a walk-in closet.
A bed, a nightstand, a chair and a dresser with a fly-
specked mirror above. In the corner a chipped, rust
stained enameled sink trickled cold running water, the
faucet long broken. There was no window in the air-
less space, the fan above the door only sucked hot air
from the narrow hallway into the cramped room. A
single lamp burned in the corner, offering a constant,
dim glow day and night.

A tall, tattooed man who said he was a married
truck driver from Portland sat on the edge of the bed,
scribbling in a small notebook.

"I figure the CTU operatives will try to cross the
border in the next two hours," said Brandy, "just as
soon as they rescue their agent."

"You're absolutely certain they don't suspect you?"

Brandy nodded. "Positive. Cole Keegan bought my
cover story and sold it to the others. With luck they'll
whisk me across the border, and all the way back to
CTU headquarters."

The man rose, tucked the notebook into his frayed
denim jacket and sauntered to the door. "I'll deliver
your report. Take care of yourself."

Brandy smiled. "Always."

When the man was gone, Brandy crossed the rough
wooden floor to the dresser. She popped the cork on a
fifth of Soberano, poured some of the liqueur into a
lipstick smeared glass, and swallowed it in a single
gulp. The brandy was as warm as the day and burned
her throat.

She glanced at the watch on her wrist. Almost time.

The woman crossed the room, grabbed the bottle of warm brandy. Then she tore the sheets off the bed, piled them up on the mattress. On top of the pile she tore up a box of tissues. Then she sprinkled brandy over the whole mess. In the hot room, the fumes became overpowering—all the better to guarantee a fire.

Finally, Brandy reached under the pillow where she'd stashed her last john's disposable plastic lighter. She grinned before she struck the lighter, realizing that the cowboy with the wedding ring he'd tried to hide and the breath that stank like too many beers was indeed her last john—forever.

She struck the lighter and put the flame against the tissue. The mass ignited immediately, the flames leaping up to the ceiling much faster than she'd anticipated. Brandy slipped into her sandals and crossed the room. When she ran into the hallway, she left the door behind her wide open. Amazingly fast, smoke was filling the second floor of the brothel. Brandy heard alarmed voices from another room. Time to start screaming. So she took a deep breath and opened her mouth.

"¡Vaya! ¡Funcione! ¡El edificio se arde!"

1 2 3 4 5 6 7 8 9
10 **11** 12 13 14 15 16 17
18 19 20 21 22 23 24

••

THE FOLLOWING TAKES PLACE
BETWEEN THE HOURS OF
3 P.M. AND 4 P.M.
PACIFIC DAYLIGHT TIME

••

3:01:07 P.M. PDT
Ice House
Tijuana, Mexico

Cole decided they would climb onto the roof of the old brick building using a vertical fire escape "hidden" in an alley off Albino Street, while Richard Lesser waited in Milo's car a few blocks away. Initially Milo objected to the plan, distrusting Lesser to stick around long enough for them to rescue Tony. Cole eventually pulled Milo aside and smoothed things over.

"Lesser's scared," Keegan said while the computer genius was out of earshot. "I've been with him for a year and he's never been this antsy. He needs protection from this Hasan guy and he knows I ain't enough. As long as CTU can defend him from *Seises Seises*, the Chechens, Hasan, you can trust Lesser to do the right thing."

Cole eventually convinced Milo to trust Lesser, but the plan itself was another matter. Milo looked around nervously as Cole led him into the alley. He felt curious eyes following them down the narrow byway, making Milo very uncomfortable. As it was, the gringo biker stuck out like a neon beer logo in a convent—dirty blond beard and ponytail, leather vest, tattoos, he was at least a head taller than everyone else around him. Even worse, Cole had donned a dun-colored duster to hide the sawed off shotgun strapped with duct tape across his broad back—a fairly obvious ploy to conceal a weapon, especially in near one-hundred-degree weather. Trying to break into the headquarters of a Mexican gang and their Chechen cohorts in broad daylight seemed the height of insanity to Milo.

Yet brazenly, without a backward glance, Keegan walked up to the wrought iron ladder and began to climb. From Albino Street, a crowd of children on their way home from school gathered to point and watch them.

"Jeez, Cole. It's broad daylight. Everyone can see us."

Already four rungs up the ladder, Keegan peered over his big shoulder to reply. "I know, dumb ass. That's why we better look like we belong here, capeesh? Now hurry up and climb."

Milo took hold of the rusty ladder and placed his foot on the first rung. Groaning under their combined weight, the steel ladder rattled with every step they took.

"I hope this thing holds," carped Milo.

"Don't worry, we just have to get to the top. We ain't coming back this way."

Cole reached the roof, three stories above the street. He pulled himself over the low wall, turned and offered Milo a lift to the top. The dusty expanse of roof was flat and covered with black tar paper, peeling in places. There was a single chimney and Milo could see the recessed skylight Brandy told him to find. Beyond the edge of the building he spied the rickety, sloped roof of the wood-framed brothel that abutted the brick structure on Albino Street.

Near the chimney a chemical stench was overpowering—a reek like nail polish remover with an ammonia taint.

"God," gagged Milo, covering his mouth.

"Vapors from the meth lab underneath us," said Cole. "Somebody's been cooking pills."

"For what they're doing to the environment alone, these guys should go to jail."

"We're on a rescue mission, not a campaign to stamp out evil." Cole removed his duster, tore free the shotgun taped to his back. He drew a pair of Colts from his belt, handed one to Milo.

"Can you shoot?"

"I've had training, but I haven't practiced in a long time."

"This ain't no fancy James Bond gun. It kicks like a sonovabitch," Cole warned.

Milo hefted the steel-gray weapon, tucked it into his belt between the two bottles of water he'd brought. Milo glanced at his watch. "Let's go." He took a step toward the barred window; Cole dragged him back by the scruff of his neck.

"Look where you're walking—away from the sun. You're casting a shadow that's gonna fall right across that grill."

Milo bristled. "So?"

"Ever been in a dark room when someone walked past the only source of light?"

Milo's shoulders sagged. There was so much he didn't know about this field agent stuff. "Okay. You do it."

Milo waited near the ladder while Cole Keegan circled the barred window, then got down on his belly and crawled to the edge of the window to peer inside. He backed away a moment later, returned to Milo's side. "All I see is some guy tied to a box spring and a generator. Hispanic, longish black hair, goatee—"

"It must be Tony. He grew the goatee and hair for field work—"

"He's alive, but he isn't in great shape and he ain't alone down there. I heard voices."

Milo grabbed the Cole's arm. "Look!"

From somewhere inside the brothel, wisps of smoke began to rise. A few lazy white puffs, followed by billows of darker smoke. They heard voices—first a woman's hysterical screams, then many excited voices calling out in anxious fear. Smoke rolled across the tarred expanse, choking Milo, burning his eyes.

Cole didn't hesitate. He dragged Milo to the window, kicked the iron bars once, twice. The grill didn't budge. "You gonna help?" Cole asked.

Covering his mouth, Milo stepped forward and slammed his booted foot down on the grill with all his might. To his stunned surprise, the steel grate gave way under his weight and Milo plunged helplessly through the hole, into the dark, smoky interior of the burning building.

3:07:23 P.M. PDT
CTU Headquarters, Los Angeles

The impromptu meeting had broken up already, but Jack Bauer found Nina Myers and Ryan Chappelle in the conference room, still debating the best course of action. The Threat Clock had already been activated, and Jamey Farrell had been ordered to reestablish contact with Milo Pressman in Mexico by Ryan himself, who had taken over the operation.

"Sorry for the delay," said Jack. "I waited for the CTU Autopsy Team to arrive. They're bringing the bodies here."

"Sit down, Jack. You look like hell," said Ryan. He keyed the intercom built into the table. "We need a doctor in the conference room."

"I'm all right, Ryan," Jack protested.

"You're a mess," Chappelle replied, "and the doctor's going to have a look at you."

Jack slumped into a chair and tried to compose his thoughts. He told them what transpired at Nareesa al-Bustani's Beverly Hills home, about Major Salah's treachery, the death of Omar al Farad, the Saudi Deputy Minister, and about the murders of producer Hugh Vetri and his family. The only thing Jack left out was the disk with his CTU personnel file burned on it, found in Hugh Vetri's computer. Jamey was still working on analyzing that disk, and Jack didn't want to mention the data leak until he knew where it came from.

Dr. Darryl Brandeis arrived with a young African-American medical technician. The woman grimaced with concern when she saw Jack.

A former member of the Special Forces, Brandeis was forty-five, completely bald, and in constant need of a shave. He took one look at Jack Bauer's condition and shook his head. Brandeis checked Jack's pupils while the technician worked on the glass cuts on his arms.

Jack spoke to Nina. "Tell Ryan what you learned about the original Hasan."

Nina opened the file in front of her. "Hasan bin Sabah was an eleventh-century Muslim holy man. Taking advantage of the schism in the faith at the time, Hasan created a sect called the Nizari. He soon converted the servants of a prince's castle to his own violent form of Islam, and one morning the prince awoke to find himself dispossessed, his servants faithful to a new master. Hasan renamed the fortress the Eagle's Nest—"

"Eagle's Nest," interrupted Chappelle, "as in Hitler's mountain retreat?"

Nina nodded. "After that Hasan ruled the region like a despot. In 1075, in an effort to increase his political power, Hasan hit upon a brilliant new tactic to strike terror into his enemies. Using hashish, a form of cannabis, Hasan brainwashed disciples by convincing them they had visited Paradise."

"And how did he do that?"

"He built a secret garden inside of his castle, stocked it with willing harem girls who fulfilled the subject's every desire. When the drugs wore off, Hasan told these dupes that if died in his service they would return to Paradise forever."

"That worked?"

"Quite effectively. Hasan's suicidal assassins were the world's first terrorists. For the next two centuries, they struck fear into the rulers of the Muslim world. No king or prince was safe because there was no protection from a killer who didn't care if they lived or died, an assassin who was willing to trade his life for the deaths of others and a promised spot in Paradise."

"Okay, so what happened after Hasan died? Did the terrorism end?"

"No, the violent Nizari sect continued to flourish. Its most public success was the murder of Crusader Conrad of Montferrat in 1192. Scholars believe that the sect continued to brainwash its subjects until its eventual extermination centuries later."

Nina closed the file. Ryan crossed his arms. "So obviously you believe this new Hasan is emulating the methods and tactics of the original?"

"It fits the facts," Jack replied, wincing as the doctor extracted a shard of glass from his forearm. He winced again when Brandeis sprayed on instant skin to stop the bleeding. "Ibn al Farad was hunting for someone he called the Old Man on the Mountain when he was captured in the Angeles National Forest. I believe the youth was brainwashed using the methamphetamine Karma, which he had in his possession when he was captured. And don't forget. I witnessed a loyal member of the Royal Saudi Special Forces Brigade turn on his own soldiers, and then murder the minister he swore an oath to serve."

Ryan shook his head. "But brainwashing? Mind control? It sounds impossible."

"Not so." It was Dr. Brandeis who spoke.

"Enlighten us, Doctor," said Ryan.

Brandeis continued to work on his patient as he spoke.

"While there are several ways to exercise control over another human mind, drugs can be very effective. In the 1950s a CIA black operation called MKULTEA experimented with LSD, psilocybin, scopalamine, sodium pentothal and a combination of barbituates and amphetamines, in an attempt to control the minds of test subjects."

"How successful were they?" Nina asked.

Brandeis shrugged. "Results were mixed. Drugs alone were found to be ineffective. Control was better achieved if certain psychological techniques were also applied."

Jack tested his wounded arm. "Such as?"

"Effective methods of mind control were outlined in the 1960s and codified in what's called the Biderman's chart of coercion. The methods include isolation, threats, degradation. But the chart also lists monopolization of perception, induced debility, and demonstrations of omnipotence by the master controller—"

"I don't follow," said Ryan.

"Well. A subject in isolation only sees one other human—the controller, the interrogator, whatever. The subject becomes dependent on that controller, longs for the contact after long stretches of isolation. A relationship is established—a first step. Threats and degradation follow. If used judiciously—and arbitrarily—the subject slowly accepts his helplessness."

"Sounds like battered wife syndrome," said Nina.

"An abusive spouse instinctively uses these very same methods," Brandeis replied.

"But Hasan's primary lure is spiritual, if Jack is correct."

The doctor nodded. "True, Mr. Chappelle. That's where the other methods come in. If you control a person's perception, you can convince them of any truth—bad guys try to control the media, use propaganda to that end. But drugs can also exert a powerful control over one's perceptions. And drugs can also be used to induce debility and exhaustion, deepen the subject's a sense of isolation. The controller can even demonstrate his omnipotence through the manipulation of the subject's emotions by the use of hallucinogenic drugs."

Ryan scratched his chin. "And once the subject's will is broken?"

"The controller rebuilds it," said Brandeis. "In the case of religious fanaticism, a sense of exclusivity is fostered—the subject is saved, everyone else is damned, that kind of thing."

"Ibn al Farad was searching for Paradise. He believed himself among the elect."

Brandeis nodded. "These are all techniques outlined by Biderman."

"Okay, let's say that Hasan has found a way to control the minds of his subjects. How does this connect to the midnight cyber attack on the World Wide Web's infrastructure, or Richard Lesser's Trojan horse?"

"I didn't say I had all the answers yet," Jack replied. "We need to know how the Trojan horse works, what it does before we know its purpose and intended target. Anyway, I'm not convinced Hasan's only endgame is an attack on the West's computer infrastructure. Those kind of attacks have been defeated before."

Chappelle sighed. He pumped the pen in his hand, tapped it on the conference room table. "Unfortunately we seem to have hit a dead end. With Ibn al Farad murdered, Major Salah and his Chechen hit team dead, we don't know where to turn."

Jack nudged the medical technician aside, leaned forward in his chair. "Ibn al Farad whispered a name to me before he died. He could have been trying to reveal the true identity of Hasan, or perhaps he was naming another disciple. Either way, we have to check out this new lead right away."

Dr. Brandeis interrupted them again. "I'm sorry, Special Agent Bauer. You're not going anywhere without further tests."

"I don't have time for tests."

Brandeis folded his arms. "You probably have a concussion, Jack. You have the symptoms."

"I'm fine."

"You have a constant throbbing headache, don't you? Maybe blurry or double vision . . ."

"No," Jack lied.

Nina turned to her boss. "Give me the name, Jack," she urged, plastic wand poised over a PDA screen. "You go with the doctor down to the infirmary, I'll run the name through the CTU database, see if we come up with a match, an address or phone number."

Jack shook his head. "You won't have to do that, Nina. This man will be easy to find. Architect Nawaf Sanjore is quite well known around the world. His firm has an office in Brentwood, and the man resides in a luxury high-rise he designed and built near Century City."

3:11:57 P.M. PDT
Ice House
Tijuana, Mexico

Milo felt a strong grip on his arm, then a familiar voice. "Get up kid, you did good." He opened his eyes, saw Cole Keegan standing over him. Behind the biker, the iron grill lay on top of a heavyset bald man wearing a sweat-stained leather apron and rubber gloves.

"Jesus, what about Tony!" Milo cried. He tried to stand, nearly toppled. His leg burned with agony.

"Settle down, you probably sprained something in that fall." Cole checked his leg. "Nothing broken. Try to walk it off."

Milo coughed, hobbled over to the man strapped to the rusty box spring. Limp, shirtless, Tony Almeida's wrists were bound with wire, the flesh scorched around the coils. Milo saw the ancient crank generator and knew Tony'd been subjected to electric shock.

"Here." Cole thrust a pair of wire cutters into Milo's hand. "Hurry up. They're putting out the fire. We've got to get out of here."

Tony groaned as soon as the cold metal touched his burned flesh. His eyes fluttered, then opened wide. Milo cut the wires and gently eased Tony to the floor.

"Milo?"

"Don't look so incredulous. You'll hurt my feelings. Drink this." Milo helped Tony to a sitting position and thrust a bottle of water into his numb, shaky hand. Almeida gulped it down, choking once or twice. Tony noticed the fat man crushed under the iron grate. "Did you do that?"

Milo nodded. "Pressman to the rescue."

"His name was Ordog," said Tony.

"Now he's Dead Dog." Keegan grinned.

"He a friend of yours?" Tony asked Milo.

"Meet Cole Keegan. Richard Lesser's bodyguard."

"You found Lesser?" Tony asked, gingerly flexing his arms.

Milo nodded. "Lesser decided to give himself up, come back home," said Milo. "He was looking for you when—"

"When the Chechens found me first." As he spoke, Tony dribbled some water on the burns on his wrists. The sting jolted him. "How's Fay?"

Milo didn't answer. Instead, he used tatters of Tony's shirt to wrap the burns. Cole Keegan kept an eye on the door at the opposite end of the lab. Tony watched Milo work, waited for a reply to his question. Finally Tony caught Milo's eye.

"Milo? *Fay Hubley?*"

"The Chechens found her, Tony . . . she's dead."

Tony closed his eyes, grunted as if punched. He dropped the plastic bottle, stumbled to his feet with Milo's help. "We've got to get out of here. Track them down."

"Now you're talking," said Cole, moving to Almeida's side. "At least that 'let's get out of here' part." He handed Tony his duster. "Put this on."

Tony slipped the long coat over his muscled shoulders.

"Come on," Milo told Tony. "Richard Lesser's waiting for us in a car a couple of blocks from here, and an extraction team is meeting us across the border at Brown Field."

"The exit's over here," called Cole. He clutched his shotgun, cocked and ready.

When they kicked open the door, the alley off Albino Street was deserted save for one. Brandy leaned against the wall, tapping her booted foot impatiently. She wore long black jeans, a Sunday church pink ruffled blouse, and clutched a small cherry-red suitcase in one hand.

Seeing her, Keegan froze in his tracks. "I knew this was too easy," he muttered.

Brandy jerked her head toward the opposite end of the byway, where a crowd had gathered around the still-smoking brothel. The hoot of sirens signaled the not-exactly-timely arrival of the local fire department.

"Don't worry," she told them. "The gang guys went north for some kind of score, and the Chechens are holed up on the other side of town with that slob Ray Dobyns. Something big is up—"

Tony met her eyes. "Dobyns. You're sure?"

"I'm sure," Brandy replied. "I heard all about how Dobyns sold you to the Chechens from Carlos—"

"I see." Tony's voice was tight with barely contained rage. "Who's Carlos?"

It was Keegan who replied. "Her pimp. The guy behind the bar."

Brandy ignored Keegan, stepped up to Tony. "Listen, if you want Dobyns's head I'll tell you where the pig is, but you gotta visit him later. I want to be across that border and on my way to my sister's house in Cleveland before Carlos figures out I'm gone. Otherwise I'm a dead ho' walking."

Tony nodded. "Don't worry. I promise we'll get you across the border. But first we have a stop to make."

"*Samurai*? Samurai, where are you, man? This is Jake. You remember. Jake Gollob? Your boss? Pick up the phone and talk to me. Where the hell are ya? I'm here, with a tape recorder in one hand and my dick in the other. Why? Because I don't have my photographer here, *that's* why. In an hour they're going to seal off the press area and you won't get in. If you're in your apartment, pick up. I'm begging you—"

The message machine cut off after thirty seconds. Lonnie went right back to work, moving the cursor and isolating another section of the photograph, enhanced it to the limit. He studied the disappointing results on his computer monitor, wondering if another photo shop program would do a better job of enhancing the image without pixelation. With the Mohave program all he got was a blurry mess—a silhouette of Abigail Heyer sitting in the back of the limousine, sure—but the details he was looking for were gone, faded into a soft blur.

Lonnie cursed and saved the image. It was just habit, the picture was useless. He moved to the next digital photograph in the sequence he'd snapped earlier that day, at Abigail Heyer's mansion. This picture was taken just a split-second after the previous one. He expanded the picture until it filled the screen, then cropped off the driver's shoulder and head, making the actress the central figure.

Before he tampered further, Lonnie studied the photo for a long time, absorbing every detail. He stared long enough for the phone to startle him out of his cyber trance. He ignored the call and on the third ring the machine answered.

"Nobunaga you son of a bitch! You're fired. That's what you are you bastard. You're fired!"

Lon tried to ignore the stream of obscenities that followed his boss's threat.

Sorry, Jake, thought Lon. *I'll get to the Chamberlain Auditorium tonight, but on my own time. Anyway, I might just have the celebrity photograph of the year right here, and if you want it you're going to have to be much nicer to me in the future.*

The message machine clicked off. In the silence that followed, Lon exited Mohave Photo Shop and activated a similar program from a software rival. To test the resolution, he selected an image from much later in the sequence, the best of which was a shot of Abigail Heyer crossing the stone patio to her front door, looking very pregnant under her voluminous slacks and pink cashmere maternity blouse.

A good photo, Lon decided. Crisp. Clean. Perfect composition. Jake Gollob would be proud to put it on the cover of his rag, with a banner headline announcing the pregnancy, and pondering the identity of the father. A *Midnight Confession* exposé. It would boost the weekly circulation by thirty percent.

But it would be a lie.

Lon went backward, through the photo sequence to the very first picture he'd snapped, a photo of the interior of the limousine taken the moment the driver opened the door. He isolated a section of that image, Abigail Heyer's torso as she leaned forward to exit the vehicle. This time, he reversed the image before he expanded it, so the dark lines would be light, the light sections dark, like a photo negative.

The computer churned and the results appeared on

his screen. Lon contemplated the image without blinking.

There it is. Plain as day.

He saved the enhanced image, printed out several copies. Then he copied all of the digital photo files from the Heyer mansion shoot onto a pen drive dangling from his key chain.

Lon rose, grabbed one of the photos of Abigail Heyer that he'd just printed out and literally ran to his bedroom. He scanned the DVD collection packing his bookshelf, found his copy of Abigail's film, *Bangor, Maine*, and dropped it into the player. He remembered a passage on the DVD extras. After thumbing through the interviews and deleted scenes, he finally found it in the director's commentary.

"It was very hard to get just the right angle, especially in the long shots," said Guy Hawkins, the film's British director. "In several scenes, perfect shots were ruined because the pregnancy harness was clearly visible under Abigail's clothes. Most of the time, when this happened, we used digital effects to clean things up, but this blooper got past us . . ."

Lon froze the image. For a long second the harness she wore was clearly visible under the flannel shirt, just as the director had said. He compared the image on the television screen with the photo in his hand.

"Abigail Heyer is no more pregnant than *I* am," he murmured. "She's wearing a goddamn pregnancy suit!"

Lon gaped at the screen, absolutely certain he'd discovered Abigail Heyer's secret. The international star was pretending to be very pregnant. The only question was—

"Why?"

Tony crossed the inn's deserted lobby, cradling the blanket-wrapped corpse in his arms. He moved through La Hacienda's tiny kitchen in the rear of the building where he found the innkeeper, his wife, and a housekeeper had been herded, and then murdered, by the Chechens.

In the narrow alley behind the inn, Milo stood waiting beside the car. Keegan, Lesser, and Brandy sat inside.

When Milo saw Tony coming, he popped the trunk. Tony placed the body inside, marveling at how light Fay felt in his arms, as if much of her substance had faded away with her life.

Milo gently closed the trunk, faced Tony. "Ready?"

"Take Lesser, Keegan, and Brandy back to the United States. Rendezvous with the extraction team. And make sure forensics gets Fay's body—"

"What about you?"

Tony peered down the alley to the busy street beyond. The white van in which he'd driven across the border was still parked on the street where he'd left it. "I'll be right behind you. I'm going to secure the equipment up in the room, erase all evidence of CTU involvement."

Milo stared hard at Tony. "You're going after this guy Dobyns, aren't you?"

Tony nodded, short and sharp. "The Chechens might have information we need, too—"

"But Tony, you'll be alone. Don't you think—"

Tony's cold, lethal gaze met Milo's anxiety-ridden

eyes. "I'll make sure I ask them a few questions before I finish them off."

Milo sighed, giving it up. "What do I tell Chappelle?"

"Tell him I'll be right behind you. . . . Tell him to send another extraction team. That's all he needs to know until it's finished."

A horn blared. Milo jumped. "Damn!"

"Hurry up," Brandy cried from the passenger seat. "We ain't got all day."

Milo frowned, tried one last time. "Tony. Reconsider. Come back with us. A follow up strike team can take care of this—"

"You know that won't happen." Tony glanced away. "Chappelle doesn't like to make waves . . . he'll consider the international issues, probably balk. This is something I'm going to have to do myself."

"But—"

"*Go*, Milo," Tony snapped. "That's an order." Then his voice softened. "I'll see you back at headquarters in a couple of hours."

· ·

THE FOLLOWING TAKES PLACE
BETWEEN THE HOURS OF
4 P.M. AND 5 P.M.
PACIFIC DAYLIGHT TIME

· ·

4:00:51 P.M. PDT
CTU Headquarters, Los Angeles

Stripped to the waist, lying flat on his back in a hospital bed, Jack Bauer gazed at the bomb-proof concrete ceiling. The CTU's L.A. headquarters more resembled a military bunker than a federal office, and its infirmary reflected the same utilitarian style—windowless concrete walls, exposed ducts snaking along the ceiling or between banks of medical equipment.

Standing steel and glass partitions separated the twelve-bed hospital ward, where Jack waited, from the triage unit and intensive care facility down the hall. Farther along the blast-resistant concrete corridor sat a glass-enclosed surgical theater, a biohazard treatment unit, and a state-of-the-art biological isolation and identification facility.

Dr. Brandeis had brought Jack here, sent him through the CT scanner, then the MRI. Alone now, Jack waited for the test results, and for the painkillers he'd hastily swallowed to knock his raging headache back down to a dull, manageable throb again.

Jack glanced at his watch, grimaced, and reached for the secure telephone on a buffed aluminum nightstand beside his bed. He tapped in his personal code for an outside line, then dialed his home phone. Teri answered on the second ring.

"Teri? It's me."

"Hello, Jack." He could feel the chill in her voice. *Well, she has a good reason to be upset.*

"Look, I'm sorry I didn't call sooner. There's a situation—"

"Another crisis. I thought as much. Don't worry about it."

There was a long silence. "Is Kim home from school yet?"

Teri sighed. "Since I didn't hear from you, I sent her over to my cousin's house. She's going to watch the Silver Screen Awards with Sandy and Melissa."

Jack blanked for a second. "The Silver Screen Awards?"

"Yes, Jack. Her mother is going to be in the audience tonight, remember?"

Their early morning conversation came flooding back: how Teri had received that call from her old boss, got the last-minute invitation to attend the awards show, was excited about seeing some of her old friends.

"Of course, that's why I called," Jack lied. "I

wanted to tell you to have a good time. What did you decide to wear?"

Jack could almost feel Teri melt a little. "My black Versace," she told him. "You know the one . . ."

"I remember," whispered Jack. "And I remember the last time you wore it."

They'd spent a long weekend in Santa Barbara. The first night, she'd worn it to dinner. The second and third nights, dressing was the last thing on their minds. But that was nearly six months ago. They'd had few romantic moments since.

"I'll bet you look great," said Jack.

"You can see for yourself." Now Teri's voice was as soft as Jack's. "Tonight, when I get home. Probably around midnight."

"I'm looking forward to that," Jack replied, but he tensed up the moment he'd said it. Although he hoped his work would be over by midnight, he honestly couldn't be certain. "Look, about tonight, I'm really sorry—"

"Jack, don't apologize. We both know what you do is important . . . more important than I probably realize. . . . It's just that sometimes—"

"Teri, listen—"

"Oh, the limousine is here. I have to go."

Jack checked his watch. "So soon?"

"Yes, it actually starts in an hour. Dennis says they stage it early so they can broadcast it during prime time on the East Coast. Look, the driver's honking. I have to leave. Bye."

"Have a great time," Jack said. "I love you—"

But Teri had already hung up. Jack listened to the electric hum for a moment, then dropped the receiver in its cradle. He lay back in the bed, closed his eyes and massaged his temples. When he opened them again, Dr. Brandeis and Ryan Chappelle were approaching. Jack sat up and slipped his shirt over his head—more to hide the patches, bandages and bruises than out of modesty.

"How are you feeling, Special Agent Bauer?" Dr. Brandeis asked, his eyes scanning, assessing.

"The headache is almost gone," Jack said. "The vision's pretty much cleared up. The rest did me good."

From the doctor's pinched expression, Jack knew the man wasn't buying it. Ryan spoke next.

"Dr. Brandeis tells me you have a concussion. That you've been walking around with it for most of the day."

"The MRI revealed potentially dangerous swelling of the brain," said the doctor, addressing his remarks to Chappelle. "I've given Special Agent Bauer something to treat the pain and swelling already. There's nothing more I can do. He requires rest and time to heal. I'm recommending he be relieved of active duty for five to seven days—"

Jack cut him off. "I can't do that. We're in the middle of a crisis. A terrorist attack may be imminent."

Brandeis refused to meet Jack's gaze. Speaking only to Chappelle, he argued, "Surely there are other agents who can handle this situation—"

Again, Jack cut him off. "I'm going to see this through to the end. No matter what you say."

Ryan Chappelle faced Jack and folded his arms. "Is that how you really feel? Think about it carefully before answering."

Jack opened his mouth to speak, then paused to consider the Regional Director's offer, because that's exactly what it was. Chappelle was giving Jack an out, a chance to dump this operation onto somebody else. Jack could sign himself out of the infirmary, drive over to Teri's cousin's house and pick up Kim. They could watch the awards show, and greet Teri when she got home.

Jack visualized the moment before he banished it from his mind. He could see Kim's happy face. His wife in that killer dress. But then another image interceded: Hugh Vetri and his entire family brutally murdered.

Jack remembered the disk that was in the dead man's possession. The disk that contained his CTU personnel file, home address, the names of his immediate family.

"I can't go, Dr. Brandeis," said Jack. "I have to see this operation through to the end. Who knows how many lives are at stake."

With obvious frustration, Dr. Brandeis turned away from his patient and faced the Regional Director. "It's your call, sir. You can keep this agent on active duty and risk killing him. Or you can order Bauer to stand down, place himself on medical leave under medical supervision."

Ryan Chappelle shook his head. "I understand the dangers, Dr. Brandeis, and I thank you for bringing them to my attention. But there's a crisis looming, one we don't even have a handle on. It's a threat that could have far reaching implications." He turned to look Jack squarely in the eye. "Unfortunately, I need Special Agent Bauer. I don't have time to get another manager up to speed. I have no choice but to return this man to active duty immediately."

4:07:21 P.M. PDT
Outside La Hacienda
Tijuana, Mexico

Before he sent Milo on his way north with Richard
Lesser and the rest, Tony Almeida relieved Cole Keegan of his sawed off shotgun and thirty rounds of am-
munition. After they drove away, he climbed into the
battered white van, unlocked the secret compartment
in the cargo bay and opened the cover.

Tony paused when he saw the empty cradle that
had held one of the two Glocks. He remembered giving Fay that gun so she could protect herself. From the
look of the crime scene, she hadn't used it.

Frowning, Tony tucked the remaining Glock into
Keegan's borrowed duster, dug deeper into the compartment for the eight 17-shot magazines, which he
stuffed into the pockets. Then he placed the shotgun
and shells into the compartment and locked it again.

Tony hefted the unfamiliar weapon in his hand.
The Glock was a Model 18C, a brand-new variation
with a fully automatic mode capable of spitting out
eleven hundred rounds per minute. Restricted and not
available to civilians, the model had a left side, slide-
mounted fire control selector switch; a barrel that extended past the front of the slide; and three horizontal
and diagonal cuts that ran across the top of the barrel
to act as compensators.

With the weapon and the van's first aid kit stuffed
into his coat, Tony went back up to the hotel's second
floor. He entered room six, cleaned and bandaged his
electrical burns, and donned fresh clothes. He spent
the next thirty minutes sweeping the room of all evidence that he and Fay had ever occupied it.

The computers were dismantled and tossed into the

back of the van, along with his and Fay's luggage, the stolen credit cards and card readers. The second CTU handgun was nowhere to be found, but he gathered up the water bottles they'd drunk from and even the empty plastic glasses. Those went into the van too. When the room was empty, he used a cloth to wipe down all the surfaces, hoping to eradicate or smear any usable fingerprints.

Next, Tony sat on the edge of the hotel bed and studied the road map for Tijuana, mentally choosing the best route across town. According to Brandy, Ray Dobyns and the Chechens were hiding out in a house on the Avenue de Dante, on the southern edge of the city.

When he was done, Tony rose, folded the map and stuffed it into his pocket. He loaded his Glock, slipped it into the duster, and without a backward glance left the room where Fay Hubley had died.

On street level again, Tony stepped into the scorching afternoon. The street around him was practically deserted. A hot wind kicked up dust. Squinting against the glare of the sweltering sun, he slipped on his heavy-framed sunglasses.

It was the hottest period of the day and for many traditional Mexicans it was siesta time. They would rest now, when the heat was at its height, then return to work at five or six o'clock, and toil well into the evening.

Tony sighed, unlocked the van. He had a long afternoon ahead of him, and a long night too. But until this was finished, there would be no rest.

4:17:21 P.M. PDT
CTU Headquarters, Los Angeles

"You've cracked the Trojan horse?" Nina asked. She stood in the situation room, watching sequential data scroll across the computer monitor.

From her chair in front of the screen, Doris looked up and nodded. "We're more than halfway there. The clue was in the transcript of Milo's conversation with you. Milo said that Richard Lesser told him this program targets a software accounting program, but he didn't say which one."

"There's more than one?" Nina asked.

"There are dozens, maybe hundreds of accounting programs out there," Jamey explained. She sat next to Doris, her focus remaining on the screen as she spoke. "Many communications industries use a German software program called SAP, customized for their specific needs, of course—"

"But Lesser's Trojan horse didn't affect SAP," said Doris, "the program used by publishers and magazine distributors. The movie studios use something different."

"The program's called CINEFI," said Jamey. "Short for Cinema Finance. It's a film production payroll and financial management program that has been adopted by the accounting department at virtually every studio."

"Lesser's Trojan horse virus is very specific," Doris added. "It infects only systems using CINEFI."

"Okay." Nina pulled an empty chair over to the work station and sat. "Tell me why."

Doris swiveled her chair to face Nina. "By sabotaging that program specifically, terrorists could do damage to multinational corporations in the entertainment industry. Transfer funds or render security codes inoperative."

"So what does this one do? All of the above, or is it just a nuisance virus?"

"That we don't know. Not yet," Jamey replied.

Doris turned her chair again and directed Nina's attention back to the computer monitor. "I loaded the CINEFI program into this isolated server, then infected the program with the Trojan horse. As you can see, something is going on. The virus is searching for some sort of protocol, maybe. Or it's using the CINEFI program as a platform to launch an attack elsewhere."

Nina's expression remained neutral, but her voice cut sharp. "That's not specific enough."

"We did find out there's a code embedded in the Trojan horse," Doris quickly noted, "one that launches the virus at a specific date and time."

"When?"

Doris exchanged an anxious look with Jamey, then said, "Three hours ago."

Nina's posture tensed. "Then we're too late to stop it."

"Yet there's no measurable effect that we can see," Jamey pointed out. "I secured a warrant to monitor the big studio computers with CTU surveillance software. There's no reported problem, no delays, no data dumps or anything to indicate the virus was destructive."

Doris nodded. "The target specificity explains why this virus hasn't done major damage hours after its release. It's just too narrowly focused to worry 99.9 percent of computer users, even if someone downloads the movie *Gates of Heaven*, their system will be infected, but not affected."

"Only the major studios and their computers are in

jeopardy," Jamey said, relief audible in her voice. "But so far, nothing's happened, even to the studio's mainframes. Richard Lesser might be an evil genius when it comes to cracking secure systems, but it looks like his Trojan horse is a bust."

4:38:54 P.M. PDT
Rossum Tower
Century City

Architect Nawaf Sanjore lived on the top five floors of a thirty-five-floor apartment building of his own design on the cusp of Century City.

Formerly the back lot of 20th Century Fox Studios, Century City had been transformed in the 1980s into a compact and crowded high-rise area of banks, insurance companies, financial institutions, blue chip corporations, shops and cinemas, all tucked between Beverly Hills and West Hollywood. The Sanjore-designed Rossum Tower, with its sleek, sterile appearance and glass-enclosed exterior elevators, perfectly fit the ultra-modern aesthetics of this Los Angeles community.

Jack Bauer steered the black CTU motor pool SUV along the boulevard, toward the entrance to the building's underground parking garage. In the passenger seat beside him, Nina Myers pulled out her PDA and began reviewing the information she'd stored on the famous architect.

"Born in Pakistan, Nawaf Sanjore immigrated to Great Britain in 1981. He attended the London School of Design, then graduate school at MIT. He went to work for Ito Masumoto in 1988, left to form his own architectural firm in 1992."

"Is he a Muslim? Devout?" Jack asked.

"He was born a Muslim, and he designed a mosque in Saudi Arabia, but he seems to lead a secular lifestyle. The FBI report cites several long- and short-term affairs with various American and British women."

"Is he political?"

"Not very. He's involved with several charities and nonprofits, including the Red Crescent, the Russia East Europe Trade Alliance, and Abigail Heyer's organization, Orphan Rescue. He's donated to the campaigns of the current mayor and governor."

Jack frowned. "Ibn al Farad was secular, until he met Hasan. What other project has Sanjore worked on?"

Nina called up a new page on the PDA. "Nawaf Sanjore has personally designed sixteen skyscrapers— five here in the United States, the rest scattered across the globe in places like Dubai, Singapore, Kuala Lumpur, Hong Kong, Sydney. There are three buildings here in Los Angeles. The Rossum Tower, the Russia East Europe Trade Pavilion in Santa Monica—"

"I've seen it," said Jack.

"Look at this," said Nina. "The Trade Pavilion was mentioned in today's CIA/CTU security alert. The Vice President's wife was there, along with the wife of the Russian President. The event went off without a hitch. The Secret Service didn't even request CTU assistance."

"Where are the dignitaries now?"

Nina called up the official itinerary. "The wives are having an early dinner at Spago's. Then they're going to attend the Silver Screen Awards."

Nina fell unusually silent and Jack glanced in her direction. Her slender form appeared tense. One hand held the PDA, the other moved to massage her forehead in thought.

"Nina? What you have found?"

"I'm not sure. Maybe it's just a coincidence."

"Tell me."

"The Trade Pavilion event began at the same moment the time code in Lesser's Trojan Horse activated the virus."

Jack chewed on that fact. "But we still don't know what it does, correct?"

"That's right." Nina went back to squinting at the tiny text on her PDA screen. "The biggest project Sanjore worked on was the Summit Studio complex, which was built to revitalize a large section of downtown."

She looked up. "By the way, Summit is the studio that is releasing *Gates of Heaven*. Hugh Vetri had an office on the ninth floor of Tower One."

"Interesting, although it proves nothing."

Jack entered the parking garage and grabbed the paper tag spit out by the automatic dispenser. The gate rose and Jack drove deeper into the bowels of Rossum Tower.

"There's a lot of circumstantial evidence here," said Nina. "But all of it could be discounted as simple coincidence."

"Ibn al Farad whispered Nawaf Sanjore's name to me seconds before he died. It has to mean something."

"Do you think Sanjore could be Hasan?" Nina's tone was skeptical.

Jack guided the SUV into a space and cut the engine. "We'll know soon enough."

An ebony silhouette in Giorgio Armani, Nawaf Sanjore glided through his thirty-fifth-floor office on Bruno Magli shoes. Outside, the skyscrapers of Century City rose around him, the glass walls of his penthouse apartment affording the architect a magnificent view.

But Nawaf Sanjore ignored the vista as he moved from computer to computer, dumping megabytes' worth of data onto micro drives or zip disks. As each storage device became full, Sanjore yanked it out of its drive, its USB port and slipped the item into a fawn-brown attaché case. His intelligent, alert eyes scanned the monitors, checking the contents of each data file before preserving it. He moved with calm, deliberate precision, even white teeth chewing his lower lip in concentration.

Behind the architect, two assistants burned papers, plans and memos in the crackling flames of his central fireplace—a raised circle of gray slate capped by a horn-shaped steel exhaust vent.

On an HDTV monitor at a large workstation, Nawaf Sanjore called up the crucial schematics he'd just loaded onto a micro disk—the blueprints for the Chamberlain Auditorium. He had provided Hasan with these plans while the facility was being built. Under Hasan's orders he'd made secret alterations to the original blueprints, adding a secret land line accessible only by the terrorists once they took control of the auditorium. Now the day had come. Three years of planning and preparation were coming to fruition, yet still Nawaf Sanjore harbored secret doubts.

Could such an audacious plan succeed?

The architect bowed his head, shamed by his lack of faith. Hasan was wiser than he, Sanjore knew, and to lose faith in the man who had brought him enlightenment was worse than a betrayal—it was madness. Before he met Hasan, Nawaf Sanjore did not believe that Paradise was real. Hasan had showed him the light and the way and now he was a believer. All Hasan asked in return was absolute obedience, unquestioning faith. *A small price to pay for eternal bliss.*

"When the hard copies and paper files are destroyed, I want you to purge the mainframe's memory—all of it," Nawaf commanded. "I don't want the authorities to recover anything."

"Yes sir—"

A chime sounded, interrupting them. The architect turned back to the monitor, switched it off. "Sanjore here . . ."

The voice recognition program built into the apartment's elaborate intercom system identified the speaker's location and piped the message through.

"This is Lobby Security, sir. Two CTU agents are here. They wish to speak with you. They say it's an urgent matter of national security."

A large man with a substantial black beard emerged from the living room, his expression alarmed. "What do they want?" he whispered.

Sanjore shot the man a silencing look. "I will meet with these agents," he told the voice on the intercom. Send them up to the thirty-fifth floor, please. I'll have someone greet them there."

"Roger, Mr. Sanjore."

The intercom faded. Saaid spoke. "It is madness to speak to these Americans. They must have learned something. The whole plan might be unraveling. They could be here to arrest us all—"

"Two of them? I doubt it." Sanjore clapped his hands on the other man's shoulders. "Have faith, Saaid! All is not lost. And if it is, then we shall meet again in Paradise."

Nawaf's words calmed his colleague. Still, Saaid

spoke in worried tones. "They suspect something. Why else are they here?"

"It was the youth, Ibn al Farad," said the architect. "He was weak and he was foolish. Most likely it was the Saudi who gave us away. It is good that Hasan moved the evacuation schedule forward. He must have sensed the danger."

Saaid rubbed his hands. "The American intelligence agents are on their way up right now. What are you going to do about them?"

"I'm nearly finished here. These men"—Nawaf gestured to his assistants—"will purge the computers. Go to my room, take the suitcase and my PDA and go to the roof. Tell the pilot to start the engines. I will join you momentarily."

"You must hurry! The Americans are coming—"

Sanjore raised a manicured hand. "Do not fear, my friend. We will leave this place together. Yasmina will deal with the Americans."

The view through the glass elevators was spectacular, but Jack hardly noticed. He kept his eyes on the quickly ascending digital numbers above the door. The car began to slow on the thirty-first floor. On the thirty-fifth, the burnished steel doors opened.

The woman who greeted Jack and Nina was so petite Jack thought for a moment she was a child. A second glance revealed her age to be at least twenty-five. Slim, with a dark complexion and wide, black eyes, her tiny, perfectly proportioned frame was wrapped in a tight, sky-blue sari. Her small feet were encased in jeweled slippers. Her dark hair, piled high on her head and held in place with ornamental silver daggers, added inches to her height.

Still, she barely topped four feet. Jack doubted the young woman weighed more than ninety pounds.

Graciously, she dipped her head. "Shall I announce you? My name is Yasmina." Her smile was warm, her voice light and melodious as wind chimes.

"I'm Special Agent Jack Bauer of the Counter Terrorist Unit. This is Nina Myers, my partner."

"Mr. Sanjore is eager to help you if he can. Please follow me."

The woman turned and walked in short, measured steps down the carpeted corridor.

After he spoke with the helicopter pilot, Saaid realized he had not retrieved his master's things from the master bedroom, as commanded. He hurried down the spiral staircase, terrified he'd meet armed American agents around the next corner—or Nawaf, who would realize Saaid's mistake.

He reached his master's bedroom, found the Louis Vuitton suitcase on the bed, the PDA on the dresser. Relieved the task was so simple, he grabbed the items and hurried out the door. In the hallway he heard voices, froze.

The Americans.

Saaid stared down the corridor. Someone approached, their shadows dancing on the walls. He had to get out of there! Heart racing, he hurried across the hall to the spiral staircase. On the way he crashed the suitcase against a stone pedestal, tumbling a pre-Columbian sculpture onto the concrete floor. The shattering sound was like an explosion.

Jack and Nina were walking down a hallway when they heard the noise. Jack turned his head toward the

sound, but Nina Myers faced the woman Yasmina—
and that was what saved them.

As Yasmina whirled, her dainty hand plucked the
ornamental daggers out of her thick hair. She hurled
one at Jack's exposed throat.

"Jack!" Nina cried, pushing him against the wall.
Her movement put Nina in the path of the dagger.
The silver blade sank deep into her shoulder, and
Nina cried out.

In an agile and graceful movement, Yasmina spun
through the air and landed, legs braced, in front of Jack
while he was still regaining his balance. A second dagger slashed his forearm. But the blade caught the bandages already under his shirt, and with a reflexive strike
from Jack, the weapon flew out of the woman's hands.

A heavyset man burst past them and down the hall,
barreling like an out-of-control train toward a spiral
staircase. He clutched a suitcase in one hand, what
looked like a silver revolver in the other. For a split-
second, Jack thought it might be Nawaf Sanjore.

Yasmina took advantage of the momentary distrac-
tion, aimed a sharp kick at Jack's knee, slammed his
jaw with the palm of her hand, then reached for another pair of daggers secreted in her clothing. She
pulled both blades, poised to impale Jack, when a
sliver dagger plunged into one side of her throat and
ripped out the other. A fountain of blood gushed as
Nina tugged the weapon free, cutting through veins,
arteries and cartilage.

Yasmina lurched forward, eye glazed, red lips curled
back. The daggers dropped from her hands. Then her
head lolled backward and she pitched forward.

At the end of the corridor, the heavy man thun-
dered up the spiral staircase. Jack's head swiveled
wildly. "Nina are you all right?"

Clutching her wounded shoulder, Nina stepped over Yasmina's corpse. "I'll be okay, but you've got to stop him."

Jack was up and running for the stairs before she'd finished her sentence. He grasped the handrail with one hand, drew the Tactical with the other. Before he reached the top he thumbed the safety off. The stairs led to a narrow catwalk and a steel door. He slammed his shoulder against it, and pushed it open. Dust and hot wind battered him as a helicopter rose from the flat roof, twisted in the air and soared away.

Jack ran across the roof, aiming his Tactical at the fleeing chopper. He almost squeezed the trigger when he saw the heavyset man. The man was poised on the edge of the roof, the Louis Vuitton suitcase sitting beside him, as he watched the helicopter fade into the bright horizon.

"Do not move!" Jack commanded. "Step away from the edge of the building and turn around."

The man raised his hands in surrender, but he did not face Jack.

"Step back and turn around!" Jack repeated. In the large man's hand, he saw the object that he'd thought was a silver revolver. It was actually a PDA, an item that might have belonged to Nawaf Sanjore. Jack knew he had to get it.

"Face me!" Jack commanded, moving forward.

At the sound of Jack's approaching footsteps, the man lowered his arms, then jumped off the edge of the high-rise.

"*Allah Akbar!*"

The diminishing volume of the suicidal scream reached Jack's ears as the big man disappeared from view.

1 2 3 4 5 6 7 8 9
10 11 12 **13** 14 15 16 17
18 19 20 21 22 23 24

• •

THE FOLLOWING TAKES PLACE
BETWEEN THE HOURS OF
5 P.M. AND 6 P.M.
PACIFIC DAYLIGHT TIME

• •

5:01:55 P.M. PDT
Rossum Tower
Century City

Jack returned to the corridor where the fatal confrontation had begun. He found the body of Yasmina,
but Nina was gone. He dropped the Louis Vuitton
suitcase he'd found on the roof, drew his weapon and
held it in ready position with both hands.

"Nina! Nina, can you hear me?"

Her reply emerged through hidden speakers. "Jack!
There's a staircase at the end of the corridor. I'm two
floors below you, in Sanjore's office. I think I found
something."

Jack made his way downstairs, found Nina hunched

over a computer keyboard. She had dressed her shoulder wound with century-old cognac, wrapped it with shreds from a white, Egyptian cotton towel. The puncture wound was deep. Already her bandage was stained with seeping blood.

"I've called in the forensics team," he informed her, snapping shut his cell phone. "They'll be here any minute. Nawaf Sanjore got away in a helicopter. CTU had the aircraft on radar, but lost it in the ground clutter over Los Angeles. He could be headed anywhere, by now. We've lost him."

Jack secured his weapon. "I managed to corner one of Sanjore's aides, but the man threw himself from the tower rather than face capture. He had a PDA in his hand, I doubt it survived the fall . . ."

"The computers have been wiped clean, too," said Nina, her voice rock-steady despite the stab wound. "But look at this! I found it when I turned on the monitor."

It was the largest screen in a room filled with them. Jack stared at the color schematic—some kind of plans for a building. But there was nothing to identify the structure.

"Someone forgot to close the program when they wiped the memory. The file is gone, but the contents of this screen can be downloaded into the printer's memory," said Nina. "At least I hope so."

She tapped a few keys. A large printer in the corner fired up and spit out an oversized spread sheet of the plans. Nina and Jack both released breaths they didn't know they were holding.

"That's something, at least," said Nina.

"Good work," Jack replied. He touched her arm. "And thanks for saving my ass."

"Jack! You're bleeding."

Jack raised an eyebrow as he rolled up his sleeve. "So are you."

Nina glanced down at the blood staining the strip of towel she'd used to wrap her puncture wound. "But I dressed it already," she told him.

She indicated the shredded towel on the desk. Jack reached for it. "Yasmina caught me where I had been cut before, at the al-Bustani mansion," he told her, wrapping a strip of Egyptian cotton around his seeping arm. "I think the blade got tangled with the bandage. It saved me." He smiled at his second in command. "Neat trick, Nina. Killing her with her own blade."

Nina smirked. "Well, she stuck the damn thing in my shoulder. The least I could do was return it to her."

Jack chuckled, but in that brief moment he saw a cruel glint in Nina's eyes he'd never seen before. It was gone in a flash—so quickly he thought he'd imagined it.

5:07:45 P.M. PDT
Terrence Alton Chamberlain Auditorium
Los Angeles

Secret Service Agent Craig Auburn accompanied two private security consultants for a final electronic sweep of the entire auditorium. Both men were experts at special event security and brought along their own equipment. One man, about forty with peppered hair, carried a high-speed gas chromatography unit over his shoulder. A younger man, not even thirty, had a silver-gray micro-differential ion mobility spectrometer strapped to his back. The trio started in the wings, climbed high into the catwalks above the stage, through the entire upper stage area, then down again.

Auburn, a fifty-five-year-old veteran of a Currency Fraud Division desk job, was huffing and puffing by the time they reached the massive main stage. Briefly he wondered if he'd make retirement, or if his deteriorating heart would kill him before he ever saw his pension.

Concerned, the older rent-a-snoop powered down his unit. "Hey, buddy. You okay? Need a rest or something?"

Auburn rasped a reply. "No, no. Just jet lag."

The men crossed the stage, which seemed shiny smooth from a distance. Close up, Auburn saw blocking marks, hatches, electric plugs covered by metal hoods dotting the empty expanse.

Dominating center stage was a huge mock up of a Silver Screen Award, modeled after an old-fashioned box camera mounted on a tripod. This stage prop was massive, soaring thirty feet into the air. The box camera itself was the size of a minibus and fabricated from sheets of metal insulated with some type of synthetic construction material. The structure was mounted on a motorized dolly wrapped with burnished aluminum to reflect the footlights. It loomed over the stage, its shadow stretching beyond the orchestra pit to the front row seats.

As the men approached the prop, the ion spectrometer chirped urgently. The operator froze in his tracks, tapped the keypad to recalibrate the detector, but the chirping just became more insistent.

"What have you got?" the older man asked.

"Traces of nitrates, tetryl."

The older man shook his head. "I have nothing, and your ion sniffer has a lousy false reading rate."

Auburn studied the stage decoration and realized the huge Silver Screen Award prop was the final, assembled version of the parts the union men had brought in earlier—the team led by the Middle Eastern man.

"Are you sure it's a false reading?" Craig Auburn pressed, ready to tear the prop apart if either man gave him reason.

The older specialist touched the base of a tripod leg. His hand came up stained with paint. "They just put this stuff together. There's wet paint, traces of acetylene, fruit in somebody's lunchbox. Anything like that can set this equipment off."

"These traces are pretty weak," the younger men said in agreement.

"Sure they're weak," the older man said. "If there was a bomb anywhere around here, this spectrometer would be ringing its head off. My bet. The culprit is wet paint."

The specialists wandered off to scan another part of the stage. Auburn took one last look at the prop. Something about the prop still bothered him, but he knew very well that a hunch in the face of hard forensic proof was pretty much regarded as a crock of shit by anyone who had a career or cared about keeping it.

"Whatever you say. You guys are the experts."

5:13:45 P.M. PDT
Terrence Alton Chamberlain Auditorium
Los Angeles

"Whatever you say. You guys are the experts."

The words of the Americans were faint. Softer still

were the footsteps moving away. But Bastian Grost had heard enough to feel great relief. He removed the stethoscope from the wall of the container, exchanged a glance and a nod with his brothers in arms.

Hasan was right.

The part of the stage prop they occupied was airtight. Above their heads, an air scrubber silently refreshed the atmosphere inside the chamber. Hasan had provided the materials, of course. Everyone had been pleased with the look of the large sculpture on the outside, the roominess within. But there was some skepticism among his men about the lining. Lead had always been the best shield against explosive detectors. But a lead-lined stage prop, combined with the weight of the men, would have been far too heavy.

None of them knew whether the specially treated polymer lining would do the job. Clearly, it had. Seven of his men sat around him now in the large box with twenty-five guns and sixty pounds of plastique—and the stupid Americans had failed to detect a thing.

Grost was confident they would also fail to detect the additional weapons inside a much smaller version of the Silver Screen prop he and his men now occupied. That smaller prop was positioned as a decoration at the back of the auditorium. When the time was right, their accomplices would shed their disguises among the audience, grab those hidden weapons, and guard the theater's exits.

Grost checked the illuminated dial of his watch. Everything had been planned to the smallest detail. In less than two hours it would all come together. In less than two hours, he and his men would begin their journey to Paradise.

5:16:12 P.M. PDT
Avenue de Dante
Tijuana, Mexico

Ray Dobyns was holed up in an unexpected place—a modest split-level brick and wood-framed house in a quiet upper-middle-class suburb. To Tony, the streets, the houses seemed no different than the sitcom neighborhoods where Beaver Cleaver or the Brady Bunch grew up. The house was nestled in a shallow dip in the landscape, isolated from the other houses on the block by an expansive yard. The building itself was surrounded by shrubbery, now thin and brown and not worth much as cover. There was a large bay window and a garage in the front of the house and plenty of lawn around it, though little grass was green due to the prolonged drought that scorched both sides of the Cal/Mex border.

Tony noticed a large satellite dish on the roof, a microwave transmitter in the back and another dish mounted in a tall tree farther from the house. With all that state-of-the-art communications technology, Tony knew that more than chocolate chip cookies were being baked inside this particular house.

When Tony first arrived and saw the residence, he did a double-take, figuring that hooker Brandy had played him for a fool. But after he drove around the neighborhood a few times, and past the house once or twice, Tony finally spied Dobyns waddling into the backyard like some suburban fat cat. The man was wearing shorts, his bulk settling into a lounge chair next to a small built-in pool while he sipped tequila and puffed on a thick cigar. Now that he knew he'd found the right place Tony parked the van across the street and watched the house.

After twenty minutes Tony determined that the Chechens were probably somewhere else, and Dobyns was alone. Tony's fists crushed the steering wheel. *That just won't do,* he mused. *I want everyone to be here for the party I have planned.*

5:20:47 P.M. PDT
Rossum Tower
Century City

The data mining team had arrived and Nawaf Sanjore's office was a high-traffic area. The noise was so thick Jack could not hear his cell phone when it rang, only felt its tremble.

"Bauer."

"Jack? Jack . . . Is that you?" The voice was Frank Castalano's. "You're going to have to speak up, my ears still aren't so good."

Jack remembered the RPG hitting Castalano's vehicle, knew the man had been lucky to walk away with only diminished hearing. "It's me, Frank," Jack loudly replied, eliciting stares. "How's your partner?"

"What?"

"How's Jerry Alder?"

"Still in surgery. His wife's at the hospital now . . . What a mess."

"How are *you?*"

"Cuts and bruises. The docs say my hearing will improve in a couple of days. Meanwhile, I've got the bells of Notre Dame Cathedral ringing in my head." A pause. "Jack, about an hour ago we found a cell phone Hugh Vetri hid under some papers in his desk. Turns out he bought it with a fake ID just eight days ago—"

"Vetri must have thought he was being watched.

Wiretaps, maybe. Any sign of unauthorized surveillance?"

"Not yet. But we did find out that Vetri made three calls with that phone. All of them on the night of his murder, all to the same number—the office of Valerie Dodge, CEO of the Dodge Modeling Agency."

5:22:42 P.M. PDT
Highway 39
Angeles National Forest

The helicopter swooped low over the San Gabriels, skimming a section of thick forest until it located a particular stretch of deserted roadway that had once been part of Highway 39. The aircraft descended to the road's cracked pavement in a cloud of dust, fallen leaves, and parched pine needles. The wheels had hardly touched down when a door opened and Nawaf Sanjore jumped out. Crouching to avoid the whirling blades, the architect hurried across the concrete to the narrow shoulder of the road.

Shielding his face from the aircraft's hot blast, Nawaf watched the helicopter lift off and soar away, the sound of its beating blades quickly fading. With mounting trepidation, Nawaf Sanjore scanned the empty road and the thick curtain of foliage on either side. Wind rustled the trees. A raptor cried out in the distance. Surrounded by wilderness, he felt quite vulnerable. He nearly cried out when he heard the sound of rock scraping against rock. He turned toward the sound and saw what appeared to be a section of ground opening up. Revealed in the gap was a narrow set of concrete stairs leading underground.

Nawaf heard footsteps. A bearded man in the black robes of an imam climbed the stairs to greet him.

"Please follow me."

Inside the tunnel, the air was cool and scented. The robed man led Nawaf down the long corridor, into an underground maze of natural caves that led ultimately to a huge chamber deep inside the mountain. The hollow in the center of the earth had been transformed into a kind of paradise. Recessed electric lighting illuminated the breezy chamber with the colors of a fairyland. Hidden speakers filled the space with the gentle sound of wind chimes. Nawaf Sanjore estimated the cave's ceiling was seventy or eighty feet above his head. It dripped with delicate icicles of stone—stalactites bathed in a rainbow of shifting lights.

On one end of the massive cave, a tumble of chilled mountain water plunged over a rocky ledge, into a rippling pool with underwater lights that glowed phosphorescent blue. On the other side of the cave, perhaps three hundred yards away, a three-tiered glass and stone structure had been constructed against the cave wall. Lights gleamed behind glass walls, where Nawaf Sanjore saw luxurious rooms filled with modern furnishings. The uneven stone floor under his feet glistened with bits of quartz, sparkling granite, crystals shards embedded in the stone.

At each turn, a different aroma touched his senses—jasmine, rose, honeysuckle. The placid calm of the mystical location was broken only by the rustle of the imam's robes as they passed through a stone garden of tall, serrated stalagmites sprouting out of the cave's floor like bizarre cacti. Crossing a crystal bridge over a small stream, they entered a pathway to the house fashioned from inlaid black quartz illuminated from behind by buried lights.

The otherworldly beauty and aesthetic perfection of the underground lair awed the architect. As they approached the entrance to the structure, the doors opened with a whispered hiss.

The robed man halted. "Please go inside. Servants will minister to your needs. Hasan has not yet arrived, but he is expected shortly."

5:30:02 P.M. PDT
Terrence Alton Chamberlain Auditorium
Los Angeles

Thirty minutes before the curtain rose for the Annual Silver Screen Awards, Teri could not even get to her seat. Dozens of people were bunched up in the lobby, crowding around the arched entrance to the auditorium, where a handful of ushers tried to deal with the mob.

Teri was about to snake her way to the front of the line when she heard a familiar voice. "Tereeee! Teri Bauer!"

"Nancy!"

The women embraced. "You look fantastic! What a great look for you," Teri cried.

Nancy Colburn wore a bright red flapper dress, complete with layers of fringe. Her black hair was pressed, pre-Depression era style, and she wore a tiny hat. She'd gained a few pounds, but was happier than Teri had ever seen her.

"And aren't you elegant," cooed Nancy. "Is that Versace?"

Terri nodded. "Where is everyone? Why won't they let us in?"

A male voice spoke up. "The Vice President's wife and the First Lady of Russia's coming through here, ma'am. She's due any minute."

Teri faced the police officer, a handsome, tanned Hispanic man with broad shoulders. She read the name under the badge. "Thanks for the heads up, Officer Besario."

He smiled. "My pleasure, miss."

"Over here, Teri. Come on!" Nancy called. She was standing with Chandra and Carla.

"Hey!" Teri cried.

She hugged her old colleagues. When they'd first worked together, Chandra was barely out of her teens, a gawky African-American garage animator who lived in oversized shirts and clunky glasses. Now she was a confident and successful filmmaker. The glasses were gone and the garage look was replaced with a svelte figure wrapped in blue-violet silk. But it was Carla who turned out to be the biggest surprise.

"Dennis tells me you're engaged," said Teri.

"And you can see why," Carla said, rubbing her protruding belly. "Eight months and counting. Here's the joke. Gary asked me to marry him three hours before the strip turned pink! Dennis said that means it's true love."

Teri laughed.

"Honestly," said Carla. "I'm due to have this little bundle in seven days. I wouldn't even be here except Gary insisted I come. Told me I'd worked on the movie, and I'd only have myself to blame if Dennis won a Silver Screen Award and I wasn't here to share in the glory."

"Speak of the devil. Where is the elusive Dennis Winthrop?" Teri asked, trying to hide her eagerness.

"He's a producer. He gets to walk the red carpet," said Nancy.

"You're kidding?" Carla laughed. "I hope he's wearing something besides those sweat pants of his. Otherwise Joan Rivers is going to tear him a new one."

"Here come the VIPs," said Chandra.

The woman watched as the First Lady of Russia and the Vice President's wife entered the auditorium. Flanked by grave-faced men wearing dark suits and headsets, the ladies swept through the crowd, which parted like a body of water in a Cecil B. DeMille biblical epic.

Teri noted how much older the Vice President's wife looked in person, and how tall Russia's First Lady was—the tallest woman ever accepted to the Bolshoi, she had read somewhere. The dazzling women and their entourage were whisked through the archway and gone in a flash.

A moment later, a brace of uniformed ushers appeared in the doorway and began escorting singles and groups to their assigned seats inside the auditorium.

"God," groaned Carla. "I hope they seat me near a bathroom. This close to the big day, I have to go all the time."

"You know award shows," said Nancy. "If this thing goes into double overtime, you might just have your baby right here."

5:46:58 P.M. PDT
CTU Headquarters, Los Angeles

Alerted to their arrival, Ryan Chappelle intercepted Milo Pressman at the security desk. Flanked by four

CTU agents who'd met them at the airport, the fugitives were hustled into a waiting area. On the way, a gurney rolled by carrying the shrouded figure of Fay Hubley to CTU's morgue.

"Where's Tony?" Chappelle demanded.

Milo cleared his throat. "He's still down in Tijuana, following up some leads on Hasan."

"Don't bullshit a bullshitter. Tony's down there playing John Wayne." Ryan eyed the gurney rumbling down the corridor. "What he's doing is fine with me, as long as I don't have to read about it in the morning papers—or get a call from the State Department."

"I'm sure he'll be discreet," said Milo.

Ryan's gaze shifted to the newcomers. "Introduce me to your friends."

"This is Richard Lesser—"

"You're Chappelle, right? Milo's told me all about you." Lesser offered his hand. Ryan ignored it.

"This is Cole Keegan, Lesser's bodyguard. And this young woman is Brandy—"

The woman stepped forward, offered Ryan her hand. "Pleased to meet you Regional Director Chappelle. My name is Special Agent Renata Hernandez, of the Federal Bureau of Investigation. I was on an undercover mission in cooperation with the Mexican government, investigating a string of kidnappings of young girls in Texas and California, when I met up with your agents."

Milo blinked in shock. Cole Keegan's jaw went slack. Even Richard Lesser's typically confident demeanor appeared stunned by the revelation.

"I told my contact down in Mexico that I'd be crossing the border this afternoon. I'll like to contact my superiors in the San Diego office," the woman continued.

"Of course," said Chappelle, examining her identification.

"My compliments on the quality of your personnel," Agent Hernandez continued. "Though obviously not a field agent, Mr. Pressman did what he had to do to rescue his colleague. I could not have acted alone and I frankly didn't trust Cole Keegan here to get the job done."

"Hey! That's cold," Cole whined.

"Thank you, Special Agent Hernandez. You can contact the FBI from my office." Ryan faced the guards. "Take Mr. Keegan to the interrogation room for debriefing. He's to remain here incognito until further notice."

"Damn! That just ain't right!" cried Cole.

"No, Mr. Keegan, but that's how it is." Ryan faced Milo next. "A Threat Clock is already running. I want you to take Mr. Lesser down to Jamey Farrell's work station. She and Doris Soo Min are eager to ask this man some questions about his Trojan horse."

Lesser smirked. "Government workers?" he muttered with disdain. "I'm not surprised they're baffled."

"We're also eager to get a first-hand look at the second virus in your possession. We would appreciate it if you would help us find a cure for it before it is launched."

Lesser nodded, smirk still in place. "Consider it done . . . as part of my immunity agreement, of course."

Ryan matched Richard Lesser's wry expression with one of his own. "We'll talk terms later, Mr. Lesser . . . Or, if you prefer, I can turn you over to the CTU Behavioral Unit for extensive interrogation. You'll find their methods are quite effective—for 'government workers.' "

1 2 3 4 5 6 7 8 9
10 11 12 13 **14** 15 16 17
18 19 20 21 22 23 24

....

**THE FOLLOWING TAKES PLACE
BETWEEN THE HOURS OF
6 P.M. AND 7 P.M.
PACIFIC DAYLIGHT TIME**

....

*6:01:01 P.M. PDT
Avenue de Dante
Tijuana, Mexico*

The Chechens finally arrived. Three big men in a black Ford Explorer. They swung into the driveway, but not the garage. Dobyns, dozing in his lounge chair near the pool, heard them coming. He got up and disappeared from view, presumably to go through the house to let them in the front door.

From his vantage point in the van, Tony could see Dobyns in the back yard, the Chechens in front. Watching the men through microbinoculars, he wondered which one of them molested Fay Hubley, who cut her throat. Fair skin, blond or brown hair, blue or green eyes, the men were interchangeable as they laughed, traded jibes in their native tongue. Two of them carried cases of beer. A third clutched an open bottle in his fist, drank deep—Miller time.

Tony's eyes narrowed when he saw a gun tucked into one man's belt. It was the Glock he'd given to Fay for protection. Tony watched the man until the front door opened and they went inside. They entered without bothering to check their surroundings. If they had, they might have spotted the CTU van. The Chechens were already sloppy, but Tony decided to give them a few more minutes of hard drinking before he started the party—it would make things go down that much easier.

While he waited, the heat seemed to abate a little as the sun dipped toward the horizon. Shadows stretched across the lawns, lights went on and curtains closed in the tidy houses up the block. Appetizing smells, familiar to Tony from his youth, saturated the air from the neighborhood kitchens.

After twenty minutes, Tony slipped the duster over his shoulders, the shotgun under his coat. With the Glock tucked in his belt, a universal key tucked between the fingers of his right hand, Tony climbed out of the van and crossed the empty street. As he approached the house, he heard slurred voices, peals of laughter, some kind of sports programming playing on a television. He walked up to the door and slipped the serrated metal prod into the lock, quietly jiggled it a few times, heard the tumblers click.

Tony left the key in the door, turned the knob and stepped inside. The foyer had desert-pink walls, a large bullfighting poster. A flight of polished hardwood stairs led to the second level, the arched doorway to his right opened into the living room. It was there the Chechens laughed and talked, oblivious to the arrival of their uninvited guest.

Tony felt no fear, only cold, calculating calm. Cautiously he approached the doorway, saw the men sitting in a circle around a large-screen television, watching a European soccer match. Dobyns was not in sight, but Tony knew he was the least dangerous of the bunch.

Tony quietly slipped the shotgun out from under his arm and gripped it in his right hand. With his left he pulled the Glock out of his belt. Then he stepped into the room.

The men looked up at once, but only one of them moved. The man's fingers actually closed on the handle of Fay's Glock before the shotgun blast did a Kurt Cobain to his head. *The nice thing about a shotgun at close range,* thought Tony, *no second shot needed.*

Gore spattered the other men, rattling them. With his left hand Tony aimed the Glock and fired six times—methodically assassinating the drunken men where they sat with a shot to the heart, two to the head.

The near-silence that followed was eerie because Tony knew it wasn't real. The soundlessness was an illusion induced by temporary deafness from the noise of the shots. In reality, there were always sounds in the aftermath of violence. Cries of shock or surprise, moans of pain, blood splattering on the floor.

Tony dropped the shotgun, empty now, and shifted the half-empty Glock to his right hand. It was time to find Ray Dobyns. A quick check of the rest of the floor turned up nothing. The kitchen was empty save for beers in the refrigerator, the garage was full of stolen goods—mostly electronics, factory sealed, with some luxury items like furs and leather coats hanging on a rack in the corner.

Tony found Dobyns on the second floor. The man

was cowering in the upper portion of the split-level ranch, which had been transformed into one large room filled with computers. There was so much equipment, the place resembled a miniature version of CTU's command center. Dobyns had tried to dial someone on his cell, but his hands were shaking too hard to manage it. Now the phone slipped from his grasp, bounced off the carpeted floor.

"They don't have 911 down here," Tony calmly informed him.

"Don't kill me, Navarro! Please, please don't," Dobyns whined. His fat pink knees were shaking.

"What is all this?" Tony asked, waving his free hand at the network of computers.

"I don't know," Dobyns sobbed. "Your friend Lesser set it up for Hasan. Me and the Chechens were supposed to guard it. In a couple of hours some technicians are gonna take over. Honest. I don't know what they're up to!"

Tony waved the Glock. "Speaking of set ups, why did you sell me out to the Chechens?"

"I . . . I knew that story about Lesser you told was a lie," said Dobyns. "I knew you were some kind of Federal agent, too. Within days of your last disappearance, the cops swooped down on everyone who ever worked with you. I just put two and two together—"

"You know Richard Lesser's flipped. He wants immunity."

Dobyns shook his head. "It's an act. He's still working for Hasan."

"How do you know?"

"Nobody crosses Hasan and lives. There's no 'protection' from him. If Hasan wanted Lesser dead, he'd be dead. You couldn't do anything about it, and Lesser knows it."

Tony contemplated Dobyns's claims. The man was unreliable at best and likely to say just about anything to save his own life. Glancing around, Tony figured the answers to a lot of questions were probably right here in this room—including evidence of Dobyns's veracity where Lesser was concerned.

"Please don't kill me, Tony. I can help you. I can get you out of here, across the border. You'd be crazy to off the only guy who can help you. You know you don't want to kill me . . ."

Dobyns kept talking, but Tony had stopped listening. There were a lot of reasons to shoot the man. His betrayal. Fay's brutal murder. Turning Tony over to be tortured at the hands of the Chechens. His part in whatever scheme of terror was about to go down.

Yeah, Tony had a lot of reasons to kill Ray Dobyns. But in the end, the reason he finally pulled the trigger was to shut him the hell up.

6:29:53 P.M. PDT
Valerie Dodge Modeling Agency
Rodeo Drive, Beverly Hills

Rush hour traffic was heavy on Tinsel Town's glorified strip mall for obscenely expensive shopping. If you wanted a fifteen hundred dollar pair of shoes or a ten million dollar necklace, Rodeo Drive was the street for you. It was also the address for the lead Frank Castalano had given him.

Six blocks from the Valerie Dodge Modeling Agency, Jack dialed a number. The phone was answered on the first ring.

"Hello," said Jack. "I need to speak with Ms. Valerie Dodge. It's a matter of some importance. My name is—"

"Ms. Dodge is unavailable. Please call during business hours."

The line went dead. The next call Jack made was to Jamey Farrell. "I need to you to check the IRS records for a Valerie Dodge Modeling Agency, CEO Valerie Dodge."

"What are you looking for?"

"I need to know the name of a supplier. Someone Valerie Dodge's agency works with often. Maybe the name of a company she uses as a major deduction."

Jamey paused. "How much time can you give me? Ryan's on my back. We're about to run a diagnostic on Lesser's virus program."

"I need the information, Jamey, and I need it now."

"Wait!" she cried. "I can use Fay Hubley's bloodhound program. With Lesser here, all those megabits are going to waste. Let me just change the search parameters . . ."

A minute later, Jamey had the files Jack needed. "This program is amazing. . . . Okay, I have an A.J. Milne Fashions, on Sepulveda."

"Can you possibly cross check that company's records with the overnight carriers, Federal Delivery, that kind of thing?"

"With Fay's program I can . . ." After a moment's pause, she said, "Okay, I have a match. Federal Delivery had nine priority packages in Valerie Dodge's name, all of them delivered today to the Chamberlain Auditorium."

"Today?"

"Yeah, Jack."

"That will do. I'll get back to you."

Jack pulled up and parked in front of Valerie Dodge Modeling. The woman's office occupied the first floor of a faux-adobe building. There were no windows in the front of the building and the door was locked. Jack saw the intercom and pressed the bell. He buzzed three times before a voice crackled from the speaker. Jack recognized the woman's voice. It was the same person he'd just spoken with on the phone.

"We're closed," she said.

"This is Federal Delivery. A delivery to the Chamberlain Auditorium was refused. We're returning the package to the sender."

"I'll be right there."

Jack moved close to the door, drew his Tactical. A woman walking her poodle saw the gun and moved quickly from the scene. Jack heard the lock click. The knob turned and the door opened a crack. There was no chain in place and Jack kicked open the door. It crashed against a blond woman and she flew backward, striking her head against the wall. Jack moved through the doorway, weapon ready as he scanned the office for threats.

There were two people in the whole place: the blond woman he'd knocked senseless, and a female corpse that had been unceremoniously dumped in a corner. The blond woman was lying still. Jack leveled his weapon at her, kicked the gun out of her hand.

He searched the office, saw a handbag on a chair. He rifled through it, found a wallet, and ID. The picture of Valerie Dodge matched the face of the corpse.

He noticed the computer on the desk, print outs stacked up around it. On the monitor he saw a schematic similar to the one they'd printed out at architect Nawaf Sanjore's home. He caught movement out of the corner of his eye, saw the woman on the floor shifting, heard her groan.

"What are these plans on the screen?" he called to her. "What are you up to?"

The woman wiped a trickle of blood off her cheek, saw her gun was gone. She seemed to realize she was helpless, trapped.

"Why did you murder Valerie Dodge? What are these plans for?" Jack repeated.

The woman moved to sit up, adjust her clothing.

"Answer me," barked Jack. He moved toward her, pointing the Tactical.

The woman simply smirked. "You can kill me, but you're too late to stop us."

Her smile turned radiant, eyes bright. Suddenly she looked away, bit down on something. Jack saw her jaw move, heard the crunch of the capsule in her mouth. With a gasp, the blond woman began jerking spastically, legs kicking wildly, foam flecking her mouth.

"No!" Jack shouted. He leaped toward her, reached into her mouth to pull out the poison. He found bits of glass on her bloody tongue. The woman's eyes went wide and she gurgled. With a final spasm, she died. Jack checked for a pulse, found none.

He gazed at her young, lovely face, and the smile of pure ecstasy that remained after all life had fled.

Then Jack stood up, crossed the room. He slumped down in the office chair and studied the computer screen. Within a few seconds, he found the text box that identified the plans he was looking at. Heart racing, he called Ryan Chappelle.

"Ryan. Valerie Dodge is dead—murdered. Someone was in her office, using her computer. There are

schematics on the monitor, part of the same plans
Nina found—"

"We've already got a situation here, Jack. Can't this
wait?"

"Ryan. You have to listen to me. These plans.
They're blueprints for the Terrence Alton Chamberlain Auditorium. Whatever is happening there is already in motion. Our time may have already run
out."

6:42:07 P.M. PDT
CTU Headquarters, Los Angeles

Richard Lesser leaned back in an office chair. He sat
at a vacant computer station, behind Jamey, Milo, and
Doris Soo Min, observing their activity with detach-
ment.

The three CTU analysts were busy isolating a computer, physically disconnecting it from the mainframe
and all other networks so Lesser's virus could not escape. Ryan Chappelle stood behind them, watching
them work. When the team was sure the single server
was secure, Doris plugged Lesser's thumb drive into a
USB port.

"It's loaded," she said after a few minutes.

The group was about to take their first look at the
virus when Ryan's cell phone chirped. The Regional
Director checked the identity of the caller, then answered. He stepped away from the group to talk in
private.

Doris decided not to wait for Ryan and punched up
the diagnostic analysis program she'd built into
Frankie.

"Looks like a pretty straightforward start and stop protocol here," she said as data popped up on the monitor. "That kind of thing is annoying, but most servers can deal with them."

"This virus is complex, though. A real mother," Milo observed as more data appeared.

"Good thing we have a copy," said Doris. "In the next five hours, I'm sure we can create some kind of firewall. That way the major ISPs will be shielded, at least . . ."

While the others were busy watching the screen, Lesser turned toward the computer at the vacant workstation—a computer still hooked into CTU's mainframe. He quietly established a quick link to the CIA's system in D.C., then smiled to himself.

The more chaos, the better.

He took one last glance around. Chappelle was still on the phone, talking intently. The others were hypnotized by the data unspooling on the monitor.

Reaching into his boot, he found the hidden pen drive. He pulled it out and plugged it into the computer's USB port. He called up the execute file stored inside the drive and launched it.

With a satisfied grin, he unplugged the drive and tucked it back into his boot. Then Lesser faced the others again. The blind idiots hadn't noticed a thing.

6:55:01 P.M. PDT
Terrence Alton Chamberlain Auditorium
Los Angeles

Comedian Willy Diamond finished a hilarious monologue, the highlight of the evening. Special Agent Ron

Birchwood hadn't laughed or even smiled. In fact, he had barely uttered ten words since the Silver Screen Awards had begun.

Sitting in the Presidential Box directly behind the Vice President's wife, he could see she was getting along well with Marina Katerine Novartov, whose English was better in a private conversation than in a public forum. The First Lady of Russia had discussed many topics with the Second Lady of the United States during the long, boring lags in the awards show.

At Birchwood's side sat his counterpart, Russian security chief Vladimir Borodin. Like Birchwood, he hadn't laughed at a single joke since the awards ceremony began—and he'd uttered even fewer words. Language wasn't the issue. Borodin spoke excellent English. Both men were absorbed in their jobs, watching the crowd, listening to the chatter in their earbuds, all channels open.

On stage, Willy Diamond bowed to thunderous applause. Then the orchestra struck up a reprise of the night's ubiquitous Silver Screen Awards theme, and the event's broadcast cut to a commercial.

As the audience buzzed with gossip, stagehands guided the giant camera prop to center stage on a motorized platform—the signal that another award was about to be presented after the commercial break.

Birchwood noticed a well-known movie star step out on stage for a moment to check the prompter's position before returning to the wings. He couldn't remember the actor's name—Chad or Chip? That was it, he thought, Chip Manning. His preteen daughter had a poster of the handsome actor on her bedroom wall, next to a popular boy band group and a half-dozen photographs of rainbows.

She'd been so excited to hear that her dad would be at the famous awards show, taking care of security for the Vice President's wife. He knew she was watching at home in Maryland, right now, with her mother and baby brother. He could just picture them, trying to spot him in the split-second shots of the awards show crowd. For the first time that evening, Ron Birchwood smiled.

The orchestra struck up again. As the broadcast came back from commercial, one of Birchwood's detail, standing behind him in the Presidential Box, touched his shoulder. "Channel one, sir."

An outside line? Birchwood thumbed the transmitter, turned up the volume in his headset.

"Special Agent Birchwood? This is Ryan Chappelle, Regional Director, Counter Terrorist Unit, Los Angeles."

To prove his identity, Chappelle gave the Secret Service agent his authorization code, which Birchwood confirmed on his PDA.

"What can I do for you, Director?"

"We have a credible threat that an attempt is about to be made on the life of the Vice President, or on the wife of the Russian President. Probably both."

"How credible?"

"In the last hour, a CTU agent killed a terrorist who was in possession of elaborate blueprints of the auditorium you're in. We have reason to believe the strike is imminent."

Birchwood turned to Vladimir Borodin. "Sir, I—"

"Yes, I heard," the Russian said, frowning. "I suggest we move now."

Birchwood stood up, addressed the agent behind him. Borodin did the same.

"Get the women out of here now," Birchwood

commanded. "Orderly evacuation. No panic. Quick as you can."

For nearly an hour, Tony had been investigating the evidence in the room where he'd silenced Ray Dobyns.

He finally managed to crack the security protocol that guarded the system. He couldn't go very deep into the files—too many of them had secondary security—but a few were not secured and Tony perused them.

He learned Richard Lesser had created the virus he claimed Hasan had given him. He'd done it right here at this console; the set up at the brothel had been a ruse, or a back up system. From some unsecured notebook files Tony found Lesser's notes. Most of them made no sense, but one file's title grabbed Tony's attention: ACTIVE CTU.

Amazingly the file was not locked. Someone had used it recently, and burned this data onto a disk, which was missing—the system was already asking if the user wanted a second disk burned. Tony opened the file and found a comprehensive dossier on Jack Bauer, taken right out of the CIA's database.

"Son of a bitch."

Another file, called TROJAN HORSE PART TWO, was also unsecured. Tony scanned the file, and his blood turned to ice.

This was it, the evidence that confirmed Dobyns's

claim was true. He snatched up the cell phone Dobyns had dropped on the carpet, punched in Ryan Chappelle's number, and got Nina Myers.

"Nina, where's Ryan?"

"He's with the Crisis Management Team. I was on my way there when your call was forwarded to me—"

"Richard Lesser is a traitor. I've got hard evidence here. He's only pretending to flip. He's about to take down CTU's computers, phones, and electronic communications. Everything. You've got to—"

The line went dead. Tony punched redial and got a busy signal. He punched in CTU's emergency number. It was also busy—which was never supposed to happen.

Tony cursed, realizing his warning had come too late. CTU's computer system was down. Lesser had unleashed his virus.

$$1 \quad 2 \quad 3 \quad 4 \quad 5 \quad 6 \quad 7 \quad 8 \quad 9$$
$$10 \quad 11 \quad 12 \quad 13 \quad 14 \quad \mathbf{15} \quad 16 \quad 17$$
$$18 \quad 19 \quad 20 \quad 21 \quad 22 \quad 23 \quad 24$$

....

THE FOLLOWING TAKES PLACE
BETWEEN THE HOURS OF
7 P.M. AND 8 P.M.
PACIFIC DAYLIGHT TIME

....

7:03:00 P.M. PDT
Television Control Booth
Chamberlain Auditorium

"Cue camera three, pull back camera one. Get ready for a close up, camera five. On three, on two, one . . ."

From his cushioned chair, director Hal Green watched the main monitor that displayed the feed as it was going out to the network and millions of viewers. He ignored the huge picture windows a few feet in front of him, though they offered a vista of center stage and almost the entire auditorium. He wanted to see what everyone else was seeing on their TV screens.

At the moment, the camera was focused on Chip Manning as he strode into view from stage left and moved toward the main podium. Manning was a popular actor, tall and muscular with dime-a-dozen cover-boy model features capped with hair in a Caesar cut. He'd paired his exquisitely tailored Helmut Lang suit with a white shirt, open at the collar, ostrich-skin cowboy boots and a salon-trimmed five o'clock shadow. The entire look had been carefully calculated by his stylist to accent Manning's "casually-aloof-yet-elegant tough guy" persona.

"Cue camera five. Two, one . . ."

The camera focused on Ava Stanton, a long-limbed beauty in a daring fuchsia gown. The eyes of every technician in the control room remained fixed on Ava's strapless décolleté, riding low on her ample cleavage. As the glammed-up actress teetered on her high heels in a shaky journey from stage right to center stage, the crew braced for a "costume malfunction" with a combination of FCC fear and hopeful anticipation.

"Cue camera one on the podium . . ."

Hal Green lowered one hand and rested it on the control board. With the other he sipped coffee from a thermal cup. Under bushy gray brows, his alert hazel eyes almost never left the main screen. When they did, it was only to check the view from another camera in one of six secondary monitors.

Ben Solomon, at the next console, groaned. "It's going to get dicey here. Ava never gets it in one. And she flubbed her lines at both rehearsals. And look who she's paired with. Chip Manning—"

Hal smiled at the remarks of his sixty-year-old assistant director. He'd heard several like it in the past ninety minutes. But that was Ben. After hiring the man for this job consistently for the past nine shows, Hal knew what to expect.

"It's a crying shame what this business has come to," Ben muttered. "Chip Manning teaches a couple of government trainees a few karate chops at a Sunset Strip dojo and his press agent calls him 'a career martial artist who advises members of America's intelligence community.' And Ava Stanton is nothing more than a glorified supermodel. She's no Elizabeth Taylor, that's for sure."

"She's no Elizabeth *Berkeley*," Green replied, suppressing a laugh. "But that's what we've got now, Ben. Ava Stanton wiggles her assets on a prime time soap and she's a star."

"Please," Ben muttered in genuine horror. "Don't use that term with me. I remember the real stars— Bogart, Jimmy Stewart, Bette Davis, Bergman—"

"What the hell is that?" Hal suddenly cried.

Rising to his feet, he lifted his gaze from the monitors to stare through the immense windows overlooking the auditorium. Ben tried to rise but got tangled in his headset. He heard confused cries, shouts, even nervous laughter from the audience.

Chip Manning and Ava Stanton had just launched into their scripted "off-the-cuff-sounding witty banter" when they'd been upstaged by a prop. Behind their backs, the top of the huge Silver Screen Awards sculpture had opened up and eight armed men wearing black masks had slid down short ropes to the stage.

This absurd, ridiculous, almost surreal scene had been greeted by nervous titters of laughter mingled with cries of surprise and alarm. *Is this all a part of the show?* the audience collectively wondered. *Maybe a publicity stunt for Chip Manning's new movie?*

"Clear the stage!" Hal Green shouted into his headset. "Security, get them off, *now*—"

Obeying the director, several security men rushed onto the stage to intercept the masked invaders. Armed only with nightsticks and electronic stunners, they'd never had a chance. Every trained assassin had dropped to one knee, raised his weapon, and fired into the uniformed ranks.

The explosion of weapons, then the red tracers warbling across the stage to rip through flesh, muscle, and bone had ended any notion that this was some sort of prearranged stunt. People in the audience stumbled into the aisles, trampled over each other, trying to flee the auditorium, only to be turned back at the doors by the handsome ushers and seat escorts provided by the Dodge Modeling Agency. These young men, who'd already donned black headscarves and green armbands, waved submachine guns, firing into the air in an effort to throw back the panicked mob.

Meanwhile, on stage, Chip Manning and his tough-guy five o'clock shadow were giving the world a demonstration of his martial arts skills. With lightning quick evasive maneuvers, he'd managed to flee the attacking gunmen faster than his lovely co-presenter who, hobbled by her high heels, was easily brought down by the butt of an assassin's gun.

Up in the control booth, the director heard a crash, turned to find a trio of armed men breaking in. Black headscarves covered all but their eyes, and each carried some kind of machine gun with a banana clip and a big ring under its barrel.

The single security guard inside the booth aimed his sidearm. The chatter of a machine gun stopped him, eliciting cries of horror from everyone in the small space.

"Put your hands up!" One of the masked men was aiming his short, stubby machine gun at the control booth crew. The invader slapped a gloved hand on Hal's shoulder and roughly yanked him off his chair, to the floor.

"Bastard," Ben Solomon spat. He tried to strike back, but the terrorist threw the older man off, hitting him with the butt of his gun.

"Ben!" Hal cried.

Now both men were cowed and down on the floor. The masked man herded them into a corner. The second gunmen pushed the soundman and the rest of the staff into the opposite corner.

The third masked man strode to the center of the control booth, machine gun resting on his elbow. He scanned the room, then spoke.

"This auditorium, this event is now in the control of the United Liberation Front for a Free Chechnya. Cooperate and you may live. Resist and you will most surely die."

7:05:09 P.M. PDT
Security Booth
Chamberlain Auditorium

"LAPD respond! Respond!" cried the uniformed dispatcher over the radio. "This is an emergency, the Chamberlain Auditorium is under attack. There's gunfire, officers down. Repeat. We are under assault."

Static was the only answer.

Security Chief Tomas Morales squeezed the dispatcher's shoulder. "The system's down. Or the signal's jammed. We can't talk to the outside. I hope the cops figure out what's going on. Until then, let's open up the arsenal."

Nodding, the young dispatcher stood and hurried to the next room.

"The goddamn phones are out too," said a woman at the next desk, a bank of security monitors in front of her. Heavyset, with short red hair, Cynthia Richel slammed the receiver into hits cradle. Today was her forty-fifth birthday.

Cynthia turned to the security chief. "I could have predicted this, Tomas. In fact, I *did* predict this. I told them land lines. *Land lines*. But the architect ignored me and went wireless. He put control of everything through that goddamn computer. 'Sanjore's vision of the future,' claimed the papers." Cynthia snorted. "Well guess what? When the shit hits the fan, the future doesn't work!"

Morales shifted his gaze to the dozens of monitors in front of Cynthia, all displaying scenes of terror and chaos, save one.

"The network has gone to commercials," noted Morales.

"Someone's thinking."

The dispatcher returned, handed out weapons. Cynthia dangled the barrel of a handgun between thumb and forefinger. "What am I supposed to do with this. I'm a computer programmer."

That wasn't entirely true and Tomas Morales knew it. Before joining Summit Studios, of which the Chamberlain Auditorium was a part, she'd been an intelligence officer in the U.S. Air Force.

Morales checked his weapon, removed the safety. "Then tell me what's wrong with the computers."

Cynthia Richel set the gun onto the desk. "Five

minutes ago some kind of overlord program took control of our security protocols—"

A succession of strange noises interrupted her. Over the sounds of shots, screams, and thundering feet, the entire auditorium shook from an eerie, rhythmic booming, like dozens of gongs sounding off one after the other.

Cynthia's full face went pale.

"What's wrong?" asked the dispatcher.

Morales already knew. "That was the sound of the steel doors closing all over the auditorium. Those doors are meant to be activated in case of fire—after the building has been evacuated—to isolate the damage to one section of the structure."

"Now they're obviously being used as jail house doors," said Cynthia, "to trap all of us inside."

Morales scanned Cynthia's computer screen. "Can't you do something?"

"Sure." Cynthia Richel picked up the weapon again, this time by the handle. She checked the magazine like a professional, flicked off the safety. "Tell me where to aim."

Special Agent Craig Auburn had memorized the evacuation route the old-fashioned way, by walking it ten times.

When the evacuation order had come through his earbud, the Secret Service agent had been at his post in the lobby. He'd followed standard operating procedures and immediately moved to a set of utility stairs that led directly to the evacuation route—in this case a long, avocado-green corridor running beneath the theater, which led to a pair of glass doors that opened onto a loading dock.

Earlier that day, Auburn had walked the route with

the bomb detection team. A service elevator was located near the loading dock exit and he personally locked it into an open position to maintain the security of the route.

Now that he'd arrived at the end of the corridor, Auburn was surprised to see that he was the first agent on the scene—and nearly six minutes after the flight order had been given. He moved through the glass doors, weapon drawn, to make sure the exit was clear of threats.

Something's wrong, he thought immediately. No other agents were outside, or any of their vehicles.

While it was possible they'd gotten the two wives out by another route, no one had communicated a successful evacuation—or anything else for that matter. Auburn's earbud had been quiet. He'd assumed the detail was maintaining radio silence, but now he suspected something else was happening and he couldn't hear it.

He walked back into the corridor, tried to hail his boss, Ron Birchwood, but got no response. Then he heard a loud clanging boom right behind him and realized with a shock that a pair of steel fire doors had just closed off the only exit on this end of the corridor. He searched for some way to open the doors or override their lock, but could see no key pads or control panels. Nothing.

The sound of approaching gunfire came next. Auburn drew his weapon and ran toward the noise. Four people were entering the far end of the hallway through the open stairwell door. He immediately recognized the Vice President's wife and the Russian First Lady. Marina Novartov was limping, trailing blood, from a wound in her calf. Assisting her were a young man in a blue blazer and a pretty, young woman with straight brown hair. Auburn knew they were two low-level members of the Vice President's staff, but he couldn't recall their names.

Behind the foursome, Auburn saw Special Agent Ron Birchwood, and the head of Russian security, Borodin. They had their weapons drawn and were pumping off shots while retreating. A red tracer burned down the hall and tore through the Russian's chest. A crimson explosion, and Borodin's arms flew out as he fell backward.

A masked man appeared in the stairwell doorway. Birchwood pumped off a shot, then two more. When the man vanished again, Birchwood glanced over his shoulder.

"Auburn! There's a whole hit team behind me. Caught us right outside the Presidential Box. The others are down . . . they're gone. Communications are jammed. I'll try to hold them off, buy you time while you evacuate the women."

The foursome moved past Auburn. "The exit's cut off!" he cried to them, stepping behind them to guard their back. "Get into the elevator."

When they were all inside, Auburn plugged the key into the elevator panel and called to his boss. "Come on, Ron! It's clear."

Before he could even turn around, the hail of gunfire tore Special Agent Ron Birchwood to pieces. Auburn turned the key. The doors closed and the elevator moved down the shaft.

7:38:12 P.M. PDT
Downtown Los Angeles

Jack Bauer raced through the streets, running traffic lights without a siren. For the twentieth time, he auto-dialed Teri's cell phone. Once again, he reached her voice mail.

It was obvious she'd turned off her phone for the duration of the Silver Screen televised broadcast. The show had probably requested it of its audience, so he wasn't surprised, but he was damned frustrated. With the Chamberlain Auditorium compromised, he wanted her out of there.

By now Jack had realized that CTU had become non-operational. He'd come to that conclusion back in Valerie Dodge's office when he'd tried to summon forensics and cyber-unit teams to the site.

From what he'd seen of the schematics on Dodge's computer screen, Jack had suspected more informa- tion was locked in the hard drive. He could be sitting on a gold mine of intelligence, but he couldn't safely access it without a cyber-unit's help. And with CTU in operational chaos, he knew he wouldn't be able to get that help anytime soon. So he'd powered down the PC, yanked its connections, and dumped it into the back of his vehicle.

Knowing CTU channels would be dead, he'd tuned his car radio to the Los Angeles Police band. That's when he'd learned that the attack at the Chamberlain Auditorium had already begun.

Slaloming around slower vehicles, he flew through the streets with one hand on the wheel, one hand on the speed dial of his cell, trying to reach his wife. He hit the first police barrier five blocks from the audito- rium.

"I'm Special Agent Jack Bauer, Counter Terrorist Unit," he told the uniformed officer who'd asked for his ID. "I need to speak with your superior, immediately."

The man spoke softly into a shoulder radio. Listened to a response in his headset, nodded.

"Okay, Special Agent Bauer. Captain Stone wants to speak with you. Park your car and follow me, sir."

Escorted by the uniformed officer, Jack walked two blocks along eerily deserted streets in the middle of downtown Los Angeles. A hot wind blew in from the desert, only to be scattered by the beating blades of helicopters circling the theater. Columns of white, beaming down from their belly-mounted searchlights, crawled along the pavement, across roofs, down walls.

Around the next corner, Jack was still three blocks away from the brilliantly lit facade of the Chamberlain. Hugging the walls of buildings, a line of black armored vehicles were positioned to remain invisible from the auditorium's view. Jack realized they belonged to his old outfit, the Los Angeles Special Weapons and Tactics unit.

Captain Gavin Garrett Stone was inside the mobile command center armored-up and loaded for bear. As tall as Jack and at least fifty pounds heavier, his physical presence had nothing on his personality. He was a hardened police officer who'd distinguished himself many times over on the job. As forces of nature went, the man was a Category Five.

Around the Captain, other members of the SWAT team were preparing for a physical assault of the complex. Jack approached Stone, hand extended. The man gave Jack a cold, don't-piss-on-my-parade stare.

"We've been trying to contact CTU, Bauer. Finally sent a squad car out to your headquarters. Some kind of computer attack, they said. Your Tac Team leader, Chet Blackburn, checked in with us over LAPD radio."

"Good," said Jack.

Stone made a show of checking his watch. "Blackburn claimed he'd be here. But he and his team are obviously having trouble getting out of the gate—or through traffic—or both."

"Homeland Security?" asked Jack.

"The Director's already spoken to the Governor. The California National Guard has been activated to help us secure the perimeter. With CTU offline—or, for all we know, sabotaged from within—Homeland Security is advising that LAPD take point."

Jack jaw tightened. "What are you planning, Captain?"

"What's it look like?"

"Have the terrorists identified themselves or made any demands? Have they executed any of the hostages? Released anyone? Have you even made contact with them, opened a line of communication?"

Stone brushed past Jack, gestured to a television monitor. A single camera displayed a long shot of the stage. Men in black masks were gesturing, waving Agram 2000s, a compact Croatian-manufactured submachine gun, easily recognizable by the unique ring grip under the front of the barrel.

"There are three men on the stage," Stone said. "We figure maybe a dozen more among the audience. They've sealed the fire doors. They think we're screwed. But we have an override ready to go on two doors—" Stone showed Jack a blueprint. It looked eerily familiar. "The doors are here . . . and here."

The attack points were on opposite ends of the auditorium. It looked good on paper, but Jack shook his head. "It's too neat, too tidy. It could be a trap."

Stone sneered. "I won't let this siege go on. The longer these guys have control of the situation, the worse it's going to get."

"Listen," said Jack, holding the man's gaze, "what you probably have here is a reprise of the Moscow Opera House scenario. That means there may be dozens of terrorists in there, strapped with bombs. If you charge into that auditorium, they'll set off those bombs and hundreds will die. You've got to wait for a better plan—"

Another voice interrupted. "We're out of time, Special Agent Bauer. The Vice President's wife and the wife of the Russian President are both inside that building—"

Jack turned. "And you are?"

The man stepped closer. The dim light of the monitor illuminated his face. His skin was dry parchment, eyes hard behind lines and creases. "Evans, Secret Service. One of ours, an agent named Auburn, managed to get the two women down a service elevator to a sub-basement. He's holed up there now with them and a pair of White House interns. The terrorists haven't gotten to them yet. Auburn has the elevator locked. But it's only a matter of time. FBI's with us on this. We can't wait."

"How are you communicating with Auburn?" Jack asked.

"Crank phone, connected to a temporary land line. It was left there with tools and equipment by a crew working on the air conditioning system. Good thing, too. Cell phone and radio transmissions are being jammed."

Jack noticed one of the command center monitors was tuned to the television station that had been carrying the Silver Screen Awards show. A commercial was running. Jack pointed to the screen. "What does the public know?"

"Nothing yet," said Evans. "The network put a twenty-second delay on the broadcast feed. Someone at the network hit the panic button as soon as the bad guys showed up on stage. All Mr. and Mrs. America saw was the screen going dark for twenty seconds, then a commercial. Now they're playing a rerun of a show that usually appears in the same time slot, but their news people want to know what's happening."

"What are you telling them?"

The Secret Service agent paused. "You have a suggestion?"

Jack nodded. "Cut the power grid in the downtown area. A blackout is a visible event and television news can show it to the world. The public becomes convinced it's a technical glitch, and if the men inside that auditorium insist on making some kind of broadcast statement to the world, we can tell them the power's out, tough shit."

Captain Stone and the Secret Service agent exchanged glances. Evans nodded, and Stone motioned another SWAT officer over.

"Talk to the power company," Stone said. "See that the power is cut in a ten-block radius around the Chamberlain as soon as possible."

Relieved he'd gotten the proverbial inch, Jack tried for the yard. "Captain, you have to rethink this assault. Lives could be lost unnecessarily—"

Stone cut him off. "I've spoken with the Mayor and the Governor. It's my call to make and I've made it—"

"But—"

"Enough," Stone said. "You guys at CTU are supposed to prevent this type of attack. You didn't. Once my assault team's ready, I'm going to see this is finished before it gets worse."

1 2 3 4 5 6 7 8 9
10 11 12 13 14 15 **16** 17
18 19 20 21 22 23 24

••

THE FOLLOWING TAKES PLACE
BETWEEN THE HOURS OF
8 P.M. AND 9 P.M.
PACIFIC DAYLIGHT TIME

••

8:01:01 P.M. PDT
CTU Headquarters, Los Angeles

Almost as soon as the computers went down, Nina
Myers arrived at the Cyber-Unit with a security team
in tow, and took Lesser into custody. He didn't resist.
A crooked smile broke over his face as they led him
off to a cell.

For an hour after that, Milo, Doris, and Jamey
worked frantically to restore CTU's computers. No
matter what they tried, the servers seemed to be stuck
in a loop. Reboots and restarts, flushing and washing
all failed to purge the system. Calendar rollback
programs—which should have restored the system to

the point where it was before the attack—simply wouldn't function. There was no help coming from outside, either. The CIA's computers had caught the bug and were down, too.

After half an hour, Jamey began to panic. The LAPD had shown up and delivered the news of the hostage situation down at the Chamberlain; and CTU couldn't even get its satellite televisions on line to see the events unfold like the rest of the world. The situation, and pent up emotion over Fay Hubley's murder, sent Jamey over the edge.

"I'm a programmer, not security expert!" she cried, her voice rising in volume. "That's your job, Milo. Why don't you do it?!"

Jamey threw up her hands as she watched countless files vanish into cyberspace.

Then Milo hit on an idea. He rebooted one computer, the very one they'd isolated and intentionally infected with Lesser's midnight virus. Milo used the rollback program to purge the non-executed virus string, then washed the memory. Now he had a clean computer. With Doris's help he tried to use it to hack into the infected mainframes and put Humpty Dumpty back together again.

8:12:54 P.M. PDT
Interrogation Block
CTU Headquarters

Ryan Chappelle entered the cell and sat down at the small table opposite Richard Lesser. The computer whiz had been searched, his hidden thumb drive taken from him. Now the two men silently eyeballed one another. The unspoken challenge? Who would talk first.

Chappelle, a master of bureaucratic silence, won the match.

"Why are you bothering me, pinhead?"

Ryan didn't reply.

"What?" continued Lesser. "Is this some kind of silent torture? Sitting across from you, looking at your sorry, earthbound face."

"Earthbound," said Ryan. "That's an interesting choice of adjective."

"Yeah, earthbound. You'll never know the ecstasy I felt when I was touched by God."

"Don't you mean *Allah*? What's a nice Jewish boy like you going to say when he meets his new Muslim pals. *Shalom*?"

"You wouldn't understand. God. *Allah*. It's all the same. I've been to Paradise. I know."

"Paradise? You mean that place in the mountains?"

Lesser's eyes narrowed. He pointed his finger. "Now you're trying to trick me. But you can't." He leaned forward, lowered his voice. "You don't understand how I've been changed. Transformed. Only one man understands."

"Hasan?"

Lesser sat back in his chair, fingered a button on his shirt. "Even you've heard of him. All of you people in your government cubicles, your marble matrixes, your subversive multinational corporate castles—Hasan already has you quaking in your military-industrial complex boots. He's the real deal, the prophet, the savior, he's—"

"The Messiah? Is that why you're working for him?"

Lesser smirked. "I don't work for Hasan. I serve

him. Just like you're all going to serve him. Like
everyone is going to serve him. All of this you serve
now, it's nothing, vacant and pointless. All of human
life, all of it, is a blink in cosmic time. You, me, everyone, we live in the past, the constant, continual past.
Hasan is the future—"

"Whereas you don't have a future, Mr. Lesser."
Chappelle leaned back, causally folded his arms.
"You'll be seventy before you walk out of a federal
penitentiary, unless we drop you in the general popu-
lation with cartel members, mob assassins and the
like. You may last a week, but it won't be a pleasant
seven days."

Lesser's smirk vanished. His face clouded, brow
furrowed in thought. Chappelle waited, hoping Lesser
would bargain for a shorter sentence in exchange for
cooperation. Finally, Lesser spoke.

"I guess I have no choice."

Chappelle nodded, pleased he'd broken through.

"Goodbye, Mr. Chappelle," said Lesser. In one
fluid motion, he ripped the top button from his shirt,
slipped it into his mouth, and bit down.

8:16:03 P.M. PDT
Terrence Alton Chamberlain Auditorium
Los Angeles

Teri Bauer winced. Carla Adair was squeezing her
hand so tightly her fingers were turning purple. Between moans, Carla took deep, noisy breaths through
her mouth, just as she'd been taught to do in her
Lamaze classes. Finally, she released Teri's hand.

Carla's labor pains began shortly after the auditorium was taken over. Nancy Colburn, in her fringed flapper dress, who had given birth herself just two years before, had helped Teri lift the armrests of the plush blue seats for Carla to lie across them. Their old boss, British producer Dennis Winthrop, had covered the pregnant woman's gown with his formal evening jacket.

"It's the adrenaline," whispered Nancy. "The fear she's feeling is inducing labor."

"Christ," hissed Dennis.

Now Carla was propped on her elbows, face flushed, brow sweaty. Chandra Washington was about to tear off a section of her violet wrap dress, then spied a white silk scarf someone had left on his seat. She picked it up and used it to mop Carla's brow.

Pieces of elegant outfits were strewn all over the theater. During the crowd's vain race for the exits, stiletto mules and strappy sandals had been kicked off, satin wraps and beaded handbags had been dropped, jewelry had been ripped away. Teri noticed a single diamond earring with a platinum setting, a broken necklace of rose gold.

Are the owners of these items even still alive? Teri couldn't help wondering. At least two dozen people had been shot during the initial mad rush for the exit doors. Then the terrorists demanded everyone drop to the floor wherever they stood. Now clusters of people were sitting in the aisles and by the theater's back doors.

Teri closed her eyes and tried to calm down by picturing Kim at her cousin's. But then the inevitable questions came. How much had her daughter seen of the awards show? Were the terrorists broadcasting scenes from inside? Was Kim watching now? Was she scared?

Carla moaned again.

Teri opened her eyes and glanced at her slim, jeweled watch. "The pains are coming closer together," she told Chandra.

"We need a doctor," whispered the young woman.

Carla heard the exchange, her face was twisted with pain. "I don't want to lose my baby," she rasped.

"You won't," Teri assured her. "I won't let that happen."

Carla laid back again, her shoulder-length auburn hair fanning out against the blue velvet theater seats.

"Gary and I cleared out the second room last month," she murmured, meeting Teri's eyes, "we got it all ready . . . you should see the wallpaper. It's this beautiful sunrise yellow . . . and the baby furniture . . . it was delayed so long we thought maybe the baby would come before the furniture . . . but it came two days ago." Sweating and tearful, she sobbed in a tiny voice, "I want to go home."

So do I, thought Teri, scanning the crowd. Most of the audience was quiet now. Like her, they'd all given up trying to use their cell phones. Teri couldn't get a signal and neither could anyone else. She could only assume the terrorists had activated jamming equipment.

She watched silently as ten armed men with black headscarves wrapped around their faces moved around the auditorium, lapping the aisles in slow circles. The rest of the terrorists—and Teri had counted over twenty of them during the initial assault—were nowhere to be seen.

When the terrorists had first taken over the auditorium, they'd emptied the mezzanine, forcing everyone down to the ground floor where they could be guarded with a single perimeter sweep. Soon after, the masked men had led four women into the room. Teri had recognized one as the beautiful young usher who'd escorted their party to their theater seats.

All of the women had changed out of their evening gowns and swathed themselves from head to toe in black robes. Members of the audience had gasped when they'd seen what else the women now wore— bricks of plastic explosives strapped to belts around their waists. With beatific smiles on their faces and push-button detonators clutched in their hands, the women had moved into position, one in each corner of the room.

When the audience first realized that suicide bombers had been placed among them, a second burst of panic had ensued, put down with more shots fired into the air, more pistol whippings.

After that, Teri had witnessed dozens of brutalities and strange little dramas. Cowards tried to broker deals for their own lives. Heroes tried to protect those near them without regard for their own safety. But the most memorable act of courage was still to come.

"I'm so thirsty," Carla murmured, her eyes closed. Teri could see the woman's lips were dry and she was having difficulty swallowing.

Dennis Winthrop stood up. "There's a pregnant woman here!" he cried. "She's going into labor. She needs a doctor!"

Two masked men immediately confronted him. One man slapped him across the face, but his British pluck remained. He refused to back down, just stood in front of them, waiting for an answer. Finally, he told them, "If you can't get this woman help, at least get her some water."

One of the men had replied to his demand in perfect English. "If you want water, come with me. The rest of you remain here and make no trouble."

That's when Nancy jumped to her feet. "I'm going too," she declared, a crusader in flapper fringe. "I can bring back water for everyone."

The masked men said nothing, simply pushed the pair forward with the barrel of their submachine guns. With worry, Teri and Chandra had watched them go, until they were lost in the crowd.

Ten minutes went by, then twenty, but Dennis and Nancy had not returned. Not for the first time Teri began to ask herself where Jack was. She checked her watch again, wondering whether he knew what was happening in the auditorium and what he and his CTU team would do once they found out.

"Where's Nancy? And Dennis?" Chandra fretted. "When are they going to come back with the water?"

Teri's heart nearly stopped when she heard muffled but clearly audible sounds of gunfire from somewhere behind the stage. There were two short bursts from an automatic weapon, then nothing more.

"Teri?" rasped Chandra, her eyes wide with fear.

Willing her hands to stop shaking, Teri checked her watch again. "They'll be here soon," she assured the young woman. "Soon."

A ring of shadows now surrounded the brilliantly lit auditorium. The power had been cut in a twenty-two-block radius, but the Chamberlain didn't need the grid to continuing glowing like a torch in the night. Its own generators supplied electricity for lights, water pumps, and the air circulation and cooling system.

Over twelve hundred people were trapped inside the sealed structure, according to the seating chart. A hundred more counting the Chamberlain's service staff, stagehands, and broadcast technicians. No attempt would be made to shut down the Chamberlain's generators. Without air conditioning, lights, and water, the situation would go from bad to worse for the hostages.

Jack Bauer was well aware his wife, Teri, was among them.

While preparations for the assault were finalized, Jack continued to argue against the attack. "You have to give us more time to formulate a rational response," he badgered Stone. "We can't just blunder in there, guns blazing."

"We have two of the most important women in the free world trapped inside that building," Stone replied, his patience obviously wearing thin. "We have limited communication with the single agent protecting them through a temporary land line that might be cut at any moment. There's no time for negotiation."

A member of Stone's team interrupted them. "Deputy Chief Vetters and the men from the fire department are here, sir."

Three firemen swathed in heavy gear and helmets,

stepped forward. Captain Stone faced the oldest of them, a ruddy-faced man with a gray moustache.

"I understand you've performed fire drills with the Chamberlain's management, that you can open these steel fire doors." He gestured to the schematic on a monitor.

Chief Vetters nodded. "We have the codes to open those doors. They're both designated fire department entry points. But there are twenty-four other steel fire doors we can't open."

"Doesn't matter," Stone replied. "We only need two doors. Your men are coming with us to work the locks. Then my SWAT teams are going in."

Vetters did not appear happy with the plan, but he said nothing. The Fire Chief huddled with his men, then all three firemen moved toward a pair of armored assault vehicles outside. Jack followed Vetters to the vehicles, pulled him aside.

"Chief, you have doubts about this, like I do," said Jack by way of introduction.

The Chief looked over Bauer, as if sizing him up. "As a rule, I don't like armchair quarterbacks, and I have the Mayor telling me to obey Stone's orders."

"But?" Jack sensed there was one in there.

"But I was a Ranger in the First Gulf War, and this smells like a trap to me."

Rather than return to the crowded command center. Jack stood side-by-side with Vetters, waiting for the operation to begin. When the black armored assault vehicles rolled down a dark, deserted four-lane avenue toward the luminous auditorium, Jack pulled out his mini-binoculars to better observe the action.

One vehicle circled around the Chamberlain and out of sight. The second rolled right up to the glass-fronted facade, crashed through it a moment later to reach the fire door and the theater entrance behind it.

"There they go," Jack informed the Chief. "Your man is out, flanked by the SWAT team. He's at the fire door . . . It's opening."

The chatter of automatic weapons reached their ears before Jack realized what had happened. "Dammit!" Jack cried. "The SWAT team's getting slaughtered. Your man is down. Wounded. Not dead. A cop's grabbing him, pulling him clear. No, the cop's down too."

"Christ," muttered Vetters.

Jack was about to lower the binoculars when he saw two civilians moving through the chaos, dodging bullets. A man and a woman. The man wore a dark suit, the woman was clad in an ivory evening gown. They raced out of the auditorium, hand in hand, using the armored vehicle for cover. But as soon as they reached the rear of the assault vehicle, the pair was pinned down by the hail of gunfire that poured out of the auditorium.

"Two people just escaped. They're trapped out there," Jack told the Chief. Scanning the street, Jack spied a third armored assault vehicle parked behind the command center.

"Come on, let's go." Chief Vetters was right behind him. As they crawled into the vehicle, Vetters placed himself behind the wheel.

"I commanded a Bradley fighting vehicle in Desert Storm. Same damn thing," said Vetters by way of explanation.

The engine roared to life and they were off. The vehicle rolled on giant puncture-proof tires which gave it a much smoother ride than the tracked fighting vehicles both men were accustomed to. And it was fast. They reached the auditorium in under a minute.

Vetters stopped the assault vehicle behind the shot up one near the fire door. Jack popped the side hatch, saw the formally dressed man and woman crouched behind the meager cover. Sporadic gunfire still erupted, but Jack could see the fight was over—everyone from the assault team had been massacred.

"Come on!" screamed Jack. The pair didn't hesitate. They bolted the five feet to the hatch, the woman making good time on high heels, the man rushing her along. They leaped through the door and Jack slammed the hatch with a clang.

Vetters swung the vehicle around as bullets pinged off the armor. Jack faced the newcomers—a young, attractive Chinese-American woman, and a Japanese-American youth with a digital camera dangling around his neck.

"Who are you?" Jack asked.

"Christina Hong, entertainment reporter for KHTV, Seattle. This is—"

"Lon Nobunaga. I'm a photographer."

"You were both inside the auditorium," Jack prompted.

The pair nodded. "I got there late," the man replied. "I was sneaking in through a side entrance when everything started to go bad. I tried to get out, got trapped in the lobby when the fire doors came down, so did Christina—"

"We both hid inside a storeroom. We watched the terrorists line up at the fire doors, waiting to fire on the police. They *knew* the cops were coming. It was an ambush!"

The man nodded, wiped sweat from his brow with the sleeve of his evening coat. "In the middle of the firefight, I saw a path through the mess and grabbed Christina. We made our move, got outside." Nobunaga paused, shook his head. "We were lucky. Those terrorists, or whoever they are—they're crazy and they don't care about anything or anyone. I saw them shoot people, beat women in the head with guns. Unless they're stopped, they're going to kill everyone in that place!"

1 2 3 4 5 6 7 8 9
10 11 12 13 14 15 16 **17**
18 19 20 21 22 23 24

····································

THE FOLLOWING TAKES PLACE
BETWEEN THE HOURS OF
9 P.M. AND 10 P.M.
PACIFIC DAYLIGHT TIME

····································

9:02:06 P.M. PDT
Terrence Alton Chamberlain Auditorium
Los Angeles

In the rows nearest the stage, where the celebrity presenters had been instructed to sit, Hollywood publicist Sol Gunther shifted nervously in his seat. He opened his cell phone, saw there was *still* no signal. He tucked the phone away, whispered to his star client.

"What do you think they'll do?"

"Like everybody in this town, they'll make a deal," Chip Manning replied. "You don't think they're nuts enough to kill themselves, do you?"

Sol shrugged. "Maybe they are, maybe they aren't.

But if they aren't, then you don't have a career unless the network cut away before you bolted off that stage and let your co-presenter take one to the head. It's not exactly heroic to leave a woman behind."

"Listen, Sol," Chip whispered, propping his ostrich-skin boots on the back of the seat in front of him. "I'm not gonna die because some over-hyped bim can't run on high heels."

Sol rubbed his chin and sighed. "Why don't the damn cell phones work?" He checked for a signal again. "I want to call my wife. I want to talk to her."

Chip Manning didn't respond to his publicist. The man had been chanting the same mantra since the hostage situation had begun. Bored, Chip's gaze skipped around the nearby seats and settled on Abigail Heyer's stunning profile—a far more interesting vision than the sight of documentary filmmaker Kevin Krock blubbering hysterically into the arms of his agent. The actress sat quietly, only a few seats away, her face expressionless, her manicured hands resting on her bulging stomach.

"She's a cool one, eh?" Manning whispered to Sol. "I mean, look at her. Not even fazed. I wonder who knocked her up? Lucky bastard, that's for sure."

"If you're feeling so damn rambunctious, why don't you use those martial arts skills of yours to take out a couple of these guys?"

Manning snorted. "Don't fall for your own hype, buddy. Breaking boards in a dojo is a far cry from facing down a bunch of armed men."

"But you could do something," Sol pointed out. "You have more skills than the rest of us. Act like a man."

"Please, Sol. Let the fascists take these bums down.

Better the LAPD break out their guns here than in some oppressed neighborhood like South Central."

Milo Pressman continued struggling with the CTU's infected mainframe, using the only isolated computer. He'd restored a modicum of functionality by running various virus dump protocols. The work was slow, inefficient, and minimally effective. To top it off, his focus was off. Thoughts of Richard Lesser continuously overran his concentration.

Chappelle had told Milo what had happened less than an hour before: "Lesser said he'd tasted Paradise. He didn't care what he we did to him. He'd found religion and said he was ready to die. Then he committed suicide."

Milo's jaw had gone slack at Chappelle's words. "You're saying Lesser's . . . *dead*?"

Chappelle had nodded. "A button on his shirt was actually a cyanide capsule."

"But Lesser's a secular, agnostic iconoclast, not some kind of religious fanatic."

"Hasan managed to turn him into a believer. Used drugs to dull Lesser's mind, broke down his will. Call it mind control. Brainwashing. A coerced religious delusion." Ryan shrugged, "I didn't believe it was possible either, until I saw it for myself."

Ever since that conversation, memories of Lesser had crashed over Milo in waves—the arguments, the insults, the struggle for one pretty classmate's attention that neither ended up getting. Even back in grad school Lesser had displayed a vicious anti-social streak. Twice he'd sabotaged the Stanford University computer labs, reveling in the chaos he'd caused for others. Just when students were sure their projects were ruined beyond repair, Lesser would sweep in, tap a few keys, restore everything.

Just then, Milo's fingers paused over the keyboard. "Wait a minute."

"What?" asked Doris.

"Is the mainframe still up?"

"It's up, but it's ignoring all commands."

Milo spun in his chair, rolled across the floor and muscled Doris out of the way at her station.

"What are you doing?" Doris cried. "If you shut it down, it will take me twenty minutes to get it up again!"

"I have a hunch," said Milo.

"A hunch! This is no time for a hunch!"

Milo ignored her, entered a series of commands.

"What commands are you issuing?" Doris asked, afraid to look.

"It's something Lesser used back in grad school."

Doris was aghast. "And you actually think that will work?"

Milo launched his hunch and held his breath.

For a moment nothing happened. Then every system, every monitor came back on line—fully functional—as if it had never gone down in the first place. Cries of surprise, joy, relief and scattered applause exploded all over the situation room.

Milo heard the sound of pounding feet. Ryan Chappelle rounded the corner at a run. He stopped so quickly he skidded on his Oxfords.

"How?" he asked.

Doris pointed to Milo. "Ask him."

"Pressman, you know what? It doesn't matter how. You're a genius!"

Milo sighed. "Good enough for government work."

9:41:22 P.M. PDT
Avenue de Dante
Tijuana, Mexico

Minutes after Tony Almeida lost all contact with CTU, two Chechen technicians pulled up in front of the house in a late-model Ford. The men climbed out of their car, chatting in their native tongue as they walked to the front door.

Tony waited for them to enter the house, then finished them off with the Glock he'd given Fay for protection—rough justice, but earned in Tony's estimation.

The last of the wet work wrapped up, Tony had spent the next two hours scanning the contents of the computer database. Fortunately for Tony, the Chechens had been careless—they'd left the system running, the security protocols bypassed, allowing Tony full access to the mainframe and all of its contents.

Using the computer's log, Tony opened the active files in reverse order, one at a time. Occasionally he would cross-reference a name or address, to uncover another rich cache of intelligence. After an hour of fitting together seemingly unconnected data, Tony began to grasp the bigger picture.

He learned that Richard Lesser had created the Trojan horse in this very house. After burying the virus inside the movie, he'd sent it into cyberspace using the server ticking in the corner. Inside that *Gates of Heaven* download, Lesser had hidden an overlord virus that took control of a program called CINEFI. Hugh Vetri, who had an office in the Summit Studios complex, found the pirated version of his yet-to-be-released film on the Web and downloaded it—releasing the Trojan horse into the studio's computers, where it lay dormant until a couple of hours ago. At that time the virus woke up, took control of Chamberlain Auditorium. Fire doors were closed, the telephone system was shut down, the hostages locked inside.

But that was only phase one. Richard Lesser had not been lying about the midnight virus or its potential to wipe out the World Wide Web's infrastructure. That virus was to be released from this facility by the two Chechens who were currently staring at the ceiling with dead eyes.

Tony sighed with relief. *At least he'd thwarted that part of Hasan's plan.*

Clearly, Lesser had never intended to hand that virus over to CTU as he'd claimed—he'd been a living Trojan horse, sent to wreck CTU's computer system. Judging by the agency's silence, Tony assumed Lesser had accomplished his mission.

Continuing to mine data, Tony came up with the names of people who were either accomplices or dupes of Hasan—Nawaf Sanjore, Valerie Dodge, Hugh Vetri.

It was architect Sanjore, or someone in his firm, who had provided Hasan with plans for the auditorium. It was ex-supermodel Valerie Dodge, or someone inside her modeling agency, who placed Hasan's assassins at Silver Screen Awards in the guise of ushers.

From the files in the computer Tony learned about Hugh Vetri. The producer had accidentally stumbled onto part of Hasan's plot—not much, but enough to recognize a threat. So Vetri and his family had to be silenced before Hugh went to the authorities.

After two headache-inducing hours there were still dozens of files unopened, but Tony's time had run out. Before he left, he decided to fill every blank disk, pen drive, and removable memory chip he could find with data culled from the system.

In the middle of the process, his cell chirped. It was Jamey Farrell. "Tony? Is everything okay?"

"Yeah. What happened?"

"Lesser infected the mainframe," Jamey replied. "But the problem's been corrected."

"What about Lesser?"

"That problem's been solved, too. He's dead."

Tony didn't ask how. He didn't care. "Listen, I think the Chamberlain Auditorium is a target for terror—"

"Too late, Tony," Jamey interrupted. "The place has already been seized. There are hundreds of hostages."

Tony cursed. "Look, I want to send you the contents of Lesser's computer. There are dozens of files."

"Fine, I'll open a secure line, you transfer the data. Dump it all in Cache 224QD." Tony and Jamey worked together and Tony quickly dispatched the files.

"I've got them," Jamey said a moment later. "Ryan wants to know when you're coming back."

"I have one more job to do," Tony replied.

He ended the conversation, went downstairs to the kitchen, shoved the stove away from the wall, exposing the natural gas pipe, which he broke open with several kicks of his booted foot.

When he heard the hiss of leaking gas, Tony grabbed a cloth sack full of computer disks, paper files—any piece of intelligence he thought might be useful—and headed for the front door. He paused in the living room just long enough to set a paper fire in front of the television.

Tony Almeida was behind the wheel of his van and halfway down the block when the place blew, shattering the quiet evening. His rearview reflected tongues of crimson vainly trying to burn the sky.

10:00:04 P.M. PDT
LAPD Mobile Command Center

The command was Jack's now. After Captain Stone's disastrous assault, and after word reached the Mayor, Governor, and Director of Homeland Security that CTU's computer capabilities had been fully restored, the Captain was quietly relieved.

Jack's first act as operations commander was to make things right with Stone. He vowed to utilize the man's resources as soon as a new plan was finalized. Until that time, he positioned the Captain and the rest of his SWAT team to a forward position, where they could assist the National Guard in securing the perimeter.

Before Jack contacted CTU, he called Teri's cousin.

He was relieved to hear that Kim had fallen asleep waiting for the Silver Screen Awards show to resume. Like the rest of the nation, Teri's cousin believed the downtown blackout had caused the cancellation of the rest of the show. Jack didn't enlighten her. He simply explained that Teri would be delayed and asked if Kim could spend the night. He thanked the woman, ended the call, then it was back to business.

He phoned Ryan Chappelle. Chet Blackburn's tactical team had arrived at the staging area, but Jack requested that one of CTU's own mobile command units be dispatched to the scene as well.

Chappelle agreed. "I'll send one immediately. Milo will join the team coming out to you. I'll keep Jamey here to coordinate things."

"Have Milo pick up a computer from my car. The vehicle's a few blocks from here. I've activated the GPS chip so he'll have no trouble finding it."

"What computer?" Chappelle asked. "Where did it come from?"

"The Valerie Dodge Modeling Agency. Ms. Dodge was responsible for staffing the auditorium with ushers, seat fillers, celebrity escorts. I have reason to believe she was duped by an employee into sending terrorists to the auditorium instead. There are plans and schematics of the Chamberlain Auditorium in the computer hard drive. I want Milo to review all the data as soon as possible."

At the communications console, a young police technician clutched his headset, looked up.

"Special Agent Bauer!" he called. "I have someone on the outside line. He claims to be the leader of the hostage takers. He demands to speak to the person in charge."

"Put him on speakerphone. Record the call for digital analysis," Jack commanded. The technician activated the recorder, switched lines, nodded.

"This is Jack Bauer, Special Agent in Charge of the Counter Terrorist Unit, Los Angeles. You wanted to speak to me."

"You have seen what we can do. Your dead litter the street. Another attempt to assault this place will result in the deaths of a hundred hostages." The voice was flat, emotionless.

"Who do you represent? What are your demands?"

"For now, our demands are simple. Restoration of broadcast capabilities in the next fifteen minutes—"

"That might be difficult," Jack interrupted. "There's a blackout in progress. We have no power in the downtown area—"

"Find a way. If we are not permitted to make a statement to the world in the next thirty minutes, we will begin to kill the hostages. One life will be taken every five minutes until you comply."

"Wait—"

But the line was dead. Jack faced the communications technician. "Send the recording to CTU for voice analysis."

Evans spoke up. "We can't let them use America's airwaves as a soapbox."

"No. we can't," said Jack. "But if we look like we're acceding to his demand, it will buy us some time to formulate a new plan of attack." Jack massaged his forehead. His headache was returning with a vengeance. "There must be a way we can fool them into believing they *are* getting their message out."

10:29:09 P.M. PDT
Outside the Chamberlain Auditorium

Everything was ready, thanks to the work of broadcast technicians culled from rival networks on the scene to cover the Silver Screen Awards.

At Jack Bauer's request they had cooperated to accomplish the impossible. In under twenty-five minutes, these experts in their fields had managed to locate the fiber optic cables under the street and tap into them—the first step toward controlling the images the terrorists saw on their television screens inside the auditorium.

CTU knew there were dozens of monitors hooked up to cable inside the Chamberlain. The terrorists would surely be watching to see their own broadcast on the local channels, or perhaps on the 24-hour cable news nets. That meant those channels and only those channels would have to be jammed and replaced with bogus broadcasts. It seemed an impossible task, but the technicians assured Jack they could accomplish it.

"Trust us," said one producer. "We're in the illusion business. We can make the audience believe anything, for a little while at least."

"I hope a little while is all we'll need," Jack replied.

Now the cameras were in position. The brilliantly lit auditorium had been carefully framed as a backdrop. As Christina Hong awaited her cue, her makeup was perfected by a feature film stylist, her hair was sprayed stiff by a famous anchorwoman's personal assistant. Her entire segment had been put together by an Emmy Award-winning producer. It was about to be directed by a veteran of one of the national networks. The whole thing was something of a dream come true for a girl seen three times a week on a local station in Seattle.

"I'm about to give the performance of my television career," she muttered, "and no one but a bunch of psycho terrorists will ever see it." Half-exhilarated and half-terrified of the consequences should she fail to pull it off, Christina cleared her throat and squared her shoulders.

The makeup artist and personal assistant stepped back as the director loudly counted down. On the final three seconds, his voice disappeared. Three fingers were up, then two. He pointed—

"This is Christina Hong, broadcasting live from the Chamberlain Auditorium in Los Angeles. We're interrupting your regularly scheduled programming with this breaking news. Unknown terrorists have taken control of the annual Silver Screen Awards ceremony and are holding hundreds of people hostage, among them many well known celebrities . . ."

Inside the command center, Jack watched a monitor. Ms. Hong was certainly convincing enough. From the logo on the lower right hand corner of his screen, Jack appeared to be watching Los Angeles News Channel One. He changed the channel. On Fox News he saw the same image of Christina Hong—now framed by the familiar Fox News logo.

"Officials of the United States government currently on the scene say they are awaiting an imminent statement from the unknown terrorist group, scheduled to begin in under a minute."

Christina Hong's image vanished, replaced by a man swathed head to toe in black, an ebony headscarf obscuring his features. Only his eyes were visible. He clutched an Agram 2000 in the crook of his elbow. Jack winced when he recognized the green and black flag of the United Liberation Front for a Free Chechnya, an ultra violent splinter group of indeterminate size.

Though it was a menace to peace and stability within the region it operated, Jack Bauer had never regarded the United Liberation Front as a threat to national security, nor did he believe they had the intelligence or the resources to pull off a masterful takeover like this one—not without help.

Meanwhile Christina Hong's impromptu voiceover continued. "Perhaps we will learn what these people want, and what cause they represent, and what drove them to such a desperate act. Here is their statement, coming to you live . . ."

After a pause, the masked man began to speak. He issued a long list of impossible demands—Russia was to end its presence in Chechnya, release all political prisoners, pay restitution to the victims of its occupation.

Jack noted that the masked terrorist claimed to be holding Russian First Lady and the U.S. Vice President's wife hostage—lies, and Jack knew it. He'd briefly spoken with Craig Auburn in the sub-basement under the Chamberlain before the broadcast began, and they were still secure in their hiding place. This told Jack that he was facing a man willing to bluff his way through a difficult position.

10:51:39 P.M. PDT
LAPD Mobile Command Center

Near the end of the masked Chechen's twenty-minute tirade, Jack's cell rang. It was Nina Myers.

"Jack, we have a positive voice match on the terror-ist leader."

"Great!"

"The first phone conversation you sent us was in-conclusive, but this broadcast provided us with all the voice samples the audio lab needed to make a positive match—"

"How positive?"

"Our audio people and the voice analysts are ninety-eight percent sure the man speaking right now is Bastian Grost, forty-four years old, a former associ-ate of Victor Drazen and a member of his secret police force the Black Dogs."

"Damn," muttered Jack. "Drazen again."

"You know Drazen?"

"I've . . . read a few files," Jack replied.

"Bastian Grost is wanted by the United Nations War Crimes Tribunal," Nina continued. "He fled ar-rest, vanished. Interpol suspected he'd been hired to train terrorist groups in Chechnya."

"I can believe Grost is training terrorists," said Jack. "But this type of suicide assault, it doesn't fit his profile. Drazen's legions were made up of political op-portunists. They're survivors not suicidal fanatics willing to die for a cause."

"Unless Grost was brainwashed," Nina replied, "like Ibn al Farad and Richard Lesser."

Jack nodded. "Brainwashed by Hasan."

1 2 3 4 5 6 7 8 9
10 11 12 13 14 15 16 17
18 **19** 20 21 22 23 24

••

THE FOLLOWING TAKES PLACE
BETWEEN THE HOURS OF
11 P.M. AND 12 A.M.
PACIFIC DAYLIGHT TIME

••

11:01:01 P.M. PDT
Chamberlain Auditorium
Sub-Level Three

White House intern Adam Carlisle was worried. Secret Service Agent Craig Auburn had been sweating more than normal. Even in the recessed emergency lights dimly glowing in the walls, Adam could see the man's face was gray. He didn't look good.

For the past four hours Craig Auburn had been crouched in a dark corner, huddled with the battered portable phone, black plastic receiver in hand. Every few minutes he would speak in whispered words with someone on the other end of the line. Another Secret Service agent? The FBI? CTU? Adam didn't know. All he knew was that there were probably hundreds of people working feverishly to rescue them from this sub-basement—*well, the First Lady Novartov and the Vice President's wife, anyway.*

The two political wives sat at a card table in two folding chairs, the only furniture in the dank, dark sub-basement. They'd kept pretty much to themselves, keeping stiff upper lips.

In the first hour, after they'd left the service elevator, Adam had found a steel lunchbox. Among its contents was an empty thermos. He cleaned it at a spigot mounted in the wall on the opposite end of the sub-basement, the water draining through a circular hole in the inclined floor. He brought the ladies water and asked them to please let him know if they needed anything else. After that, he and fellow intern Megan Gleason had kept pretty much to themselves.

About an hour before, Megan, exhausted from the adrenaline spike of fear followed by inaction, had drifted off to sleep. Now she began to stir. Suddenly she opened her eyes wide. They were filled with panic.

"It's okay," Adam whispered, worried she'd scream or something—Special Agent Auburn had cautioned them early and often to keep quiet. At one point, they'd heard crashing sounds and voices echoing through the vents from above, and they knew the terrorists were hunting them.

"What time is it?" Megan asked, sitting up and brushing back her straight brown hair.

"After eleven," Adam replied.

"I can't believe I fell asleep," she whispered.

"You were close to shock. We all were. But the phone still works, and the Special Agent vows they're coming for us."

The concrete floor was cold. Megan had lost her

heels in the chase and her stockings were shredded, her feet bare. Clad only in a filmy black dress, she began to shiver. Adam took off his evening jacket and wrapped her in it.

"Thanks," she said, teeth chattering. "God, I'm starved. I didn't have time to eat anything since this morning."

Adam smiled. "Look at this," he whispered conspiratorially. From his jacket's pocket he pulled a cellophane-wrapped Ho Ho he'd found in that battered lunchbox. "It's only a day or two past the freshness date, I checked. Frankly I think these things contain so many chemicals they're eatable after a decade."

Megan reached for the cake with a shaky hand, then paused. "Shouldn't we offer the Ho Ho to First Lady Novartov, as a point of protocol?"

Adam glanced over his shoulder. "Don't you remember, while we were helping the VP's personal assistant coordinate post-show party appearances, they were stuffing themselves with a gourmet dinner at Spago's. I think they can wait a little longer . . . and the VP's wife doesn't look like she's in any danger of starving."

Megan gaped at her fellow intern, then shook her head. "I can't believe you said that."

"Eat," Adam commanded. "I told you this job had perks."

"Adam."

Special Agent Auburn waved him over. It took only one glance to see why. The man was having trouble breathing. His features were twisted. He was obviously in pain.

"Sir, are you all right?" Adam whispered in alarm.

He leaned close. "I think it's my heart."

"Sir, what can I do for you?"

"Don't tell the others." He reached into his jacket,

pulled something out and thrust it into Adam's hands.

The intern looked down. He saw two pounds of black metal.

"I'm going to instruct you how to use it," whispered the agent, "just in case anything happens to me. Okay? You with me?"

Adam nodded.

"This weapon is a forty-five caliber USP Tactical— a Universal Self-loading Pistol," Craig Auburn whispered. "It's hard-hitting, but it's got a good recoil-reduction system, so when you fire, the kick will be dampened. Are you following me, son? Don't be afraid."

Actually Adam wasn't afraid. After seeing who the terrorists had hurt and killed, knowing who they intended to hurt and kill . . . mostly what Adam felt was anger.

"Yes, sir. Go on."

11:23:46 P.M. PDT
Terrence Alton Chamberlain Auditorium
Los Angeles

"It's been over three hours since Dennis and Nancy were taken away," Chandra said, frowning. "Where did they take them? What did they do to them?"

Teri Bauer ignored the questions, checked on Carla. Her contractions seemed to have stopped. The woman's eyes were open and she was pale, sweating.

"Carla?" Teri whispered. "Talk to me."

"I don't know what's worse," Carla replied. "When the contractions come, I think I'm going to die. Now that they've stopped, I'm terrified that something bad is happening to my baby."

"Try not to worry," Teri replied. "I was in labor with Kimberly for over twenty-two hours. My contractions stopped and started many times. My cousin's stopped altogether and had to be induced."

"I don't know, I don't know . . . I'm so scared."

"You have to think positively, Carla. It's the only way to get through something like this. For the sake of your baby, you have to keep your spirits up, believe things will turn out all right."

Carla nodded, swallowed with difficulty, forced a smile.

"Hey, watch it there!" an angry voice suddenly cried.

Teri looked up to see two masked men approaching, machine guns slung over their shoulders. They were dragging the limp form of an older man between them. In the row in front of Teri, there was a line of empty seats, and the terrorists tossed the injured man into one of them.

"Nazi bastards," the man muttered, spitting blood. Crimson rivulets poured down his face and onto his white shirt, open at the collar, the bow tie undone. One eye was swollen shut and there was a bloody gap in his jaw where a tooth used to be.

Another older man, still wearing his evening jacket, hurried up the aisle. He moved toward the injured man's side, only to be yanked back and cuffed by one of the masked men. The man tore the Rolex off his own wrist and held it out to the masked men. Brushing the offering aside, the two walked away, laughing.

"Ben, Ben," said the newcomer to the injured man. "Why did you have to shoot your mouth off?"

"Lousy Nazis. I should spit at them again." Then Ben's bloodied mouth grinned. "I sure pissed them off, didn't I, Hal?"

"And look what it got you, you putz!"

Teri leaned forward. "Here, clean him up with this," she said, handing Hal a discarded satin wrap.

"Thank you," he said and went to work on his bleeding friend.

"I'm Teri Bauer."

"Please to meet you. I'm Hal Green, the director of this miserable turkey." He pointed to his friend. "And this big mouth here is my AD, Ben Solomon. We were in the control booth when everything went down. Tomas Morales and his security people tried to stage an attack but the terrorists gunned them all down. Then, after these nuts took over, they forced me to set up a camera in the booth and teach one of them how to operate it. Then they dumped us down here."

Hal Green scanned the auditorium. "How are things down here? We've been out of touch upstairs."

"They're giving us bathroom breaks now. Ten people at a time. Abigail Heyer and her entourage got first dibs—"

"No surprise there." Chandra snorted. "Once Hollywood royalty, always Hollywood royalty."

"Still no food or water for the rest of us," Teri added. Then she glanced up at the glass booth high over their heads and leaned in close to Hal so Carla wouldn't hear. "You said they wanted to use a camera up there?" she whispered.

"That's right."

"They must be preparing to issue demands then. And if their demands aren't met, they'll start killing hostages."

Hal Green eyed Teri. "What are you, doll, an FBI agent? CIA?"

"Close," she replied.

11:38:46 P.M. PDT
LAPD Mobile Command Center

Jack Bauer, Chet Blackburn, and a group of hastily assembled consulting engineers had been reviewing the blueprints for the Chamberlain Auditorium for over an hour. As one of only two people who'd escaped the terrorists, Lonnie Nobunaga was among them. Jack thought that since the photographer had actually been inside the auditorium, he might offer some insight.

The group deduced that the terrorists were unaware of a new air conditioning and filtration system being retrofitted to the auditorium to meet new state government standards for indoor air quality. The ducts being assembled were large and extensive enough to move armed snipers through the building unseen. But they would have to get into the building's basement to reach the duct ports.

They studied the city's water and storm drain system, but ran into another dead end. Nothing larger than a twenty-inch pipe ran into or out of the auditorium—too narrow for a human to pass through. The only building close to the auditorium was the Summit Studios offices, which actually abutted the theater. But the offices shared the same fire door system as the auditorium itself and was just as impenetrable.

"The walls of that auditorium are three feet thick in places," said Jon Francis, a portly engineer in a rumpled Hawaiian shirt with a bald head shaved clean as a billiard ball. By day a professor of engineering at a local college, Francis freelanced as a CTU advisor. "It would take a construction team an hour to break through—maybe more," he warned.

"And the terrorists would detonate their bombs as soon as they heard the first jackhammer," Jack added.

Evans spoke up. "What makes you so sure they have bombs?"

"The Chechens were responsible for the siege at the Moscow Opera House," Jack replied, "and you know how that went down. The terrorists seized the theater, used Chechen war widows with bombs under their clothing to cow the authorities into inaction. Eventually President Putin authorized the Russian police to use sedative gas to knock out everyone—that option isn't available to us in this situation."

"Why not?" asked Lonnie Nobunaga. "We have non-lethal gases in our arsenal, don't we?"

"Unfortunately there's no such thing as a non-lethal chemical attack, no matter what the experts say," Jack replied. "Fentanyl or other calmative gases are deadly in large enough concentrations, and massive amounts would be needed to fill up the Chamberlain. That would mean death to a large number of people in the crowd. Children would be most susceptible, but everyone under a certain weight will overdose. Those who are allergic will have adverse, possibly fatal reactions. People with prior medical conditions could die from complications, and pregnant women will most surely miscarry. Over a hundred hostages lost their lives in the Moscow siege—most because of the gas, not the terrorists."

Lonnie's face fell. "I see your point."

Evans frowned at the schematics on the monitor. "This place is impenetrable. With the fire doors closed, it's like a fortress."

A police technician approached the group. "Special Agent Bauer? Nina Myers is on the horn for you."

Jack Bauer accepted the headset, slipped the earbud

into place. "Nina. What have you learned about the terrorists?"

"The United Liberation Front for a Free Chechnya has been around for about eight years. The organization began small, but has tripled in size and power very quickly. It's violent—sort of Chechen version of the Hezbollah. The group has become so influential that two years ago Nikolai Manos, the head of the Russia East Europe Trade Alliance, assisted the State Department in secret negotiates with its rebel leaders."

"Nikolai Manos. Can we reach him?" Jack asked.

"I tried," Nina replied. "Unfortunately Mr. Manos is unavailable. He was in the Los Angeles headquarters of his organization for a press event early this afternoon, but his aides tell me he's left the city on a secret trade mission."

"A bit too convenient. Find out all you can about Manos and his organization."

"I'm already on it," Nina replied.

Jack ended the call, looked at the monitor where Christina Hong continued her bogus broadcast in the likely event the terrorists were still tuning in.

12:10:59 A.M. PDT
CTU Mobile Command Center

Edgar Stiles needed no mirror to tell him he was a short, dumpy man. He was not handsome, nor was he a slave to fashion—his khaki pants seemed to wrinkle as soon as he put them on, and he wore shirts buttoned all the way up to his thick neck. But Edgar was not stupid. He grasped the tactical dilemma facing Jack Bauer almost immediately.

Sitting in the eight-wheeled CTU mobile command and control unit within sight of the Chamberlain Auditorium, Edgar could glance out the door and see the LAPD mobile command center parked just across the street. Only a few yards separated the two massive vehicles; for Edgar, however, they might as well have been parked on opposite sides of the planet.

Less than six weeks on the job at CTU, Stiles had not been happy to be torn from his familiar workstation and assigned to a glorified mobile home sitting only a few blocks from a terrorist crisis. When he'd arrived on the scene, Milo Pressman, his immediate supervisor for the evening, had assigned him the mind-numbing task of scanning and digitizing blueprints. The schematics came from all over—the Los Angeles Department of Water and Sewage, the Pacific Power and Light Company, LA Cablevision, and the California Department of Highways.

It didn't take long for Edgar to deduce that Special Agent Bauer and Tactical Unit Chief Chet Blackburn were trying to find a way inside the Chamberlain Auditorium without alerting the hostage-takers to their presence.

Though Edgar's first instinct was to devalue his own self-worth, he knew very well that in this situation he possessed information that might possibly help his superiors and save lives. Still, Edgar vacillated, wondering whom he should approach with the information. For fifteen minutes he mulled over this dilemma. Finally, he decided to speak with Milo—although he wasn't particularly at ease with the idea. It wasn't that he didn't like Milo. Edgar just didn't feel comfortable with him.

"E-excuse me," Edgar said, so nervous he was already flustered. "I need to speak with someone—"

"If you need help, talk to Dan Hastings," Milo said. "Dan knows this command center like the back of his hand. I'm kind of swamped right now."

"Oh, sure . . . S-sorry," Edgar replied. "I won't bother you again, sir."

Deflated, Edgar returned to his workstation. He labored to deplete the pile on his desk, then he took a break, stepping outside for a breath of fresh air. Through an open hatch in the LAPD command center, Edgar could see Jack Bauer in quiet consultation with Blackburn and the others.

"You have to say something," Edgar muttered to himself.

Twice he took halting steps toward the vehicle's doorway, only to turn back, or pace nervously in the dark street. More minutes passed, and Edgar realized he'd better return to his workstation in case more files came in for him to scan. But as Edgar turned to go, he heard raised voices coming through the hatch.

"It's like Masada!" exclaimed Chet Blackburn in a frustrated voice.

"No fortress is impenetrable. The Chamberlain Auditorium must have some weakness we can exploit. We just have to find it."

The second speaker was Jack Bauer himself, and just hearing the man close up made Edgar want to bolt in the opposite direction.

This guy's killed people. He's been in every kind of dangerous situation imaginable. How can a slob like me help someone like him?

Yet the longer Edgar eavesdropped on the conversation, the more he became convinced that the information in his brain—trivia, really—*could* actually help. And if he could help, then didn't he owe it to the innocent lives at stake to do all he could?

Summoning his courage, Edgar took a deep breath

and walked into the operational command center. As he moved through the busy control hub, crowded with monitors, communications gear and high-tech workstations, Edgar fully expected to be challenged and summarily tossed out on his ear. Instead, no one paid attention to him. Obviously they were too wrapped up in their tasks to notice a newcomer.

Edgar approached Jack Bauer. The man's face was lit by the digital image displayed on a horizontal screen of the map table. The harsh light made the man's already pale face seem almost white as bone.

"Mr. Bauer, sir?" Edgar cringed inwardly when he heard his own voice, strained by nervousness and too loud. "Can I have a word with you?"

Jack, jolted out of his thoughts, faced Edgar. "Excuse me?"

Face-to-face with the Special Agent in Charge of CTU, Edgar fought the urge to flee. Instead, he cleared his throat and spoke up. "I wanted to speak with you, sir. I think I have information that could help."

Now Jack's sharp eyes were fixed on Edgar, and the lowly computer technician shrunk under his intense, expectant gaze.

Edgar continued. "Do . . . Do you know anything about the building the Chamberlain Auditorium replaced?"

Chet Blackburn was listening now, and so were the engineers.

"No, we don't," Jack replied. "What's your name again?"

"Stiles, Mr. Bauer, sir. Edgar Stiles. I work in the computer services division—"

"Under Dan Hastings?"

"Yes, sir, and for tonight also Milo Pressman."

"So what were you saying about the Chamberlain Auditorium?"

"Actually, sir, I was talking about the site where the auditorium was built."

One of the engineers remarked, "As I recall, this part of downtown was pretty depressed."

"Yeah," said Edgar. "But it had one of the greatest old movie palaces in the city. They tore the place down to build the Chamberlain."

"How does this information help us?" Jack asked.

"The Crystal Palace was built in the 1930s, before the Great Depression," Edgar replied. "It was one of those huge old theaters with balconies and everything. A real showplace."

"I recall reading about that theater," Blackburn remarked. "But I thought it was farther west."

"No!" Edgar cried, again too loudly. "It was right here, at this intersection."

"Really," said Chet, suppressing a chuckle.

"My mother worked in that theater in the 1960s and '70s, during the Cold War. She told me there were four or five sub-basements under the theater. The two lowest levels were used as air raid shelters by Civil Defense. They stocked the place with water cans, radiation detectors, the works."

The engineers were the first to react. "That would explain that notation on one of the blueprints," said Jon Francis. "Something about an existing underground structure, a wall or something."

"You're sure about this, Edgar?" Bauer asked.

Edgar nodded. "My mom saw *Fail-Safe* on television and had a lot of nightmares after that. She told me that if a nuclear war ever broke out, she would head right down to the Crystal Palace, where the basements were so deep she knew she'd be safe from radiation."

"Jesus," grunted Jon Francis. "If this guy's right, those sub-basements may still exist. And even if they don't, the air shafts that fed them may still be buried beneath the facility even if the basements are gone."

"But what good does that do us?" Chet asked. "We don't know where the shafts are, or the basements for that matter.

"No, but *somebody* does," Francis replied. "The plans for the Crystal Palace are on file somewhere, probably with the County of Los Angeles House of Records, or maybe City Hall."

"What about the old Civil Defense files?" Special Agent Evans asked. "There's got to be blueprints for those air raid shelters filed with the Federal government."

"We've got to locate all the information we can gather about this, ASAP," said Bauer. "If these tunnels, those basements still exist, *that's* our way in."

Jack spun around. "Where's the Mayor's liaison?"

"Right here, sir," replied a young woman in an immaculate pinstriped suit.

"I need you to locate some records, as soon as possible."

Meanwhile the engineers spooled the digital schematics back several pages, trying to locate the existing wall one of them spied on the blueprints. Activity was now swirling all around Edgar Stiles, but he was not a part of it. He watched the men scramble for a few minutes, then assumed they didn't need him anymore.

Knowing that a new batch of paper files were probably already piled high on his desk, Edgar Stiles left the command center and returned to his workstation, unnoticed.

1 2 3 4 5 6 7 8 9
10 11 12 13 14 15 16 17
18 19 20 **21** 22 23 24

• •

THE FOLLOWING TAKES PLACE
BETWEEN THE HOURS OF
1 A.M. AND 2 A.M.
PACIFIC DAYLIGHT TIME

• •

1:01:56 A.M. PDT
CTU Mobile Command Center

Milo thought it was a total waste of time to mine the late Valerie Dodge's computer. He couldn't have been more wrong.

Inside the PC there were lots of files about the modeling agency, but only one file that was secure. It took Milo only a few minutes to bypass the password system and open the file—a large multimedia affair full of bells and whistles.

"W00t," he cried.

Milo quickly located a schematic of the Chamberlain, then found photos and profiles of female suicide bombers—Chechen women whose husbands had died or simply disappeared during the ongoing insurgency against the Russians. Next he found the photos and profiles of twenty Chechen gunmen smuggled into the United States by a company called MG Enterprises, then hired on as ushers for the Silver Screen Awards show.

As he moved through the file Milo found that it was all in here—the timing for the raid, the entry and exit points—most importantly, the position of the suicide bombers inside the auditorium.

Everything was here, a gold mine of intelligence.

1:07:19 A.M. PDT
LAPD Mobile Command Center

Milo had just delivered the good news to Jack, when the engineers returned, all smiles.

"We've got something for you, Jack, and you're going to like it," said Jon Francis. He plugged a pen drive into the digital map table and called up a file.

"That little guy was right," Francis began. "The old Crystal Palace movie theater was located on the site currently occupied by the Chamberlain, and that old theater had five—count 'em, five sub-basements. If you look hard enough, some of the old walls appear in the Chamberlain's blueprints."

"But can we get inside the auditorium through those basements?" Jack asked.

"We can cut a hole into the old sub-basement through this storm drain, right here," a man from the Department of Water and Sewage explained. "That will put you under the Chamberlain. You'll probably have to cut a hole somewhere else, but you'll be inside."

"It's all completely underground," Jon Francis interrupted. "The security cameras outside the auditorium, the ones the terrorists are using to watch us, they won't see a goddamn thing."

"The noise will be a problem, though," another engineer cautioned. "We'll need to use a jackhammer for five minutes or so to get through this wall—it's over two feet thick. Normally we'd blast something this stout, but in this case . . ."

"That's okay," said Jack. "We'll set up loudspeakers around the Chamberlain, blast music. It will drown out the sound of the jackhammer."

"What will the terrorists think?" Francis asked.

"They'll think we're practicing psychological warfare techniques," Jack informed them.

"Techniques that aren't effective, and everyone knows it," Secret Service Agent Evans interjected. "Won't that make us look foolish?"

In the harsh white light of the map table, Jack held Evans's eyes. "Let the terrorists think we're helpless. If they underestimate us they'll get careless, make a mistake. Then we'll take the bastards down."

1:18:06 A.M. PDT
In the storm drains

Jon Francis brought in a digging team from Pacific Power and Light. Armed with picks, shovels, flashlights, and a portable electric jackhammer, they entered the sewer system three blocks away from the auditorium.

Led by a team of inspectors from the Department of Water and Sewage, they moved efficiently through the murky, ankle deep water that flowed through a maze of seven-by-ten-foot concrete tunnels. Bringing up the rear, two technicians from the telephone company unspooled a long telephone wire—a land line that connected the construction team to Jack Bauer in the LAPD command center.

The inspectors led the team to what seemed like a dead end.

"Yep, this is the place," grunted Jon Francis, shining a mini Maglite on a paper map—he never used digital versions in the field. "There's eight inches of poured concrete right here. Behind it two feet of solid brick. Think you can break through without dynamite?"

"Stand back," said the man with the jackhammer.

Using the land line they laid on the way in, Jon Francis contacted the command center. "Cue the music," he declared.

1:25:50 A.M. PDT
Terrence Alton Chamberlain Auditorium
Los Angeles

From his throne-like chair in the center of the massive stage, Bastian Grost maintained a confident facade in front of his men, and in front of the hostages. His headscarf dangled around his neck—he did not care who among this crowd saw his face, for they would all be dead soon. Casually but authoritatively, he clutched his Agram 2000 in the crook of his arm in a gesture that suggested power and confidence.

So far his strategy had worked. Even the high and mighty members of the Hollywood elite averted their eyes when he fixed his glacial gaze on them. Despite his cool exterior, however, inside Sebastian Grost was boiling with rage. As an operational mastermind, he cursed his men's missteps and missed opportunities, their inability to follow even the simplest order without indulging in violence of every sort, including the violation of some of the female hostages. Indeed, everything had gone wrong from the start.

After the successful seizure of the awards show, his trained strike team had failed to capture Russia's First Lady, Marina Novartov, or even the wife of America's Vice President. Most of Grost's team had been shot during their firefight with the American and Russian security teams, and none of his men had witnessed exactly where the women had fled. It was possible the women had gotten out before the fire doors had slammed shut. It was also possible the two had escaped into a service elevator.

That elevator, Grost subsequently discovered, had not been in the auditorium's original blueprints, nor was it controlled by the facility's computer. Grost could find no way to unlock and reactivate the elevator, but he didn't waste much time on that effort. He knew from his study of the blueprints provided to him that this structure had only four floors to search: the mezzanine, the theater floor, the ground floor, and the basement.

Hours had passed now, and the few men Grost could spare from guard duty had failed to locate the women. He would have to accept that he could not show the women on camera. He could only bluff that he had them in his custody.

The second problem arose at 11 P.M., when Hasan had failed to contact them through a secure and secret landline that connected the Chamberlain Auditorium to the computer center in Tijuana, even though Hasan had promised he would make "a final statement to the martyrs," as he put it.

Then, at midnight came the final blow. The destructive virus that was supposed to destroy the West's computer infrastructure had not been launched as scheduled. Grost knew that was true because he dispatched men to the auditorium's roof, to watch the Los Angeles skyline beyond the blacked-out area around them. They reported that city lights still blazed, traffic lights functioned, and there were even passenger airliners lining up in the sky overhead as a prelude to landing at LAX.

At that point, Grost could no longer deny what he knew to be true.

The computer center at Tijuana must have been compromised, perhaps destroyed, which means that we are truly on our own—

Bastian Grost's thoughts were interrupted by a curious sound—the throbbing beat of American hip-hop music. The sound was muffled, but still loud enough to be heard throughout the auditorium. He listened stonefaced for a minute, then he began to chuckle, inviting a curious stare from a lieutenant on stage with him.

One of the foot soldiers arrived on stage a moment later. "They have set up loudspeakers in the street outside," he reported. "What does it mean?"

"It's a tactic right out of the Americans' counterterrorism text book," Grost replied with a sneer. "They mean to drive us out of this place with bad music. A ridiculous tactic that has no chance of success."

Bastian Grost shouldered his machine gun. He wrapped his head with the long, night-black scarf hanging at his neck. It pleased him to think that his enemies were so helpless.

If this is the best CTU can come up with, then the final phase of Hasan's plan—the mass murder of

*everyone in this auditorium during L.A.'s morning
rush hour, in front of a million eyewitnesses—is in no
danger at all.*

1:33:09 A.M. PDT
LAPD Mobile Command Center

The pre-mission briefing was so populated it packed
the vehicle from one end to the other. Every chair
was occupied, and many stood, including Lonnie
Nobunaga, who managed to hang around long after
his active role in the proceedings had ended. Even
Christina Hong was there, after being spelled by a
well-known network journalist who was doing a masterful job of bogus reporting for his audience of terrorists.

Despite the air conditioner laboring overtime, it was
sweltering inside the command center. The hatches
and doors had been shut tightly to guarantee security,
and block out the music blasting around the auditorium.

Most of the men who occupied the room were
snipers, ten of them, culled from Chet Blackburn's Tactical Unit, the FBI, and Captain Stone's SWAT team.

Jack began the briefing without preamble. "The auditorium and over a thousand hostages are being held
by twenty Chechen gunman, all well-trained, all
armed with 9mm Agram 2000 submachine guns.
Their leader is this man—"

A face appeared on the wall-mounted flat screen
monitor.

"Bastian Grost. He's not a Chechen by birth, but
he is, as far as we can determine, fanatically dedicated
to their cause."

The image on the screen changed again. Portraits of four women appeared, some in headscarves.

"More dangerous than the twenty gunmen are five suicide bombers placed in the audience—"

The women were replaced by the seating chart of the auditorium.

"—From the plans in Valerie Dodge's computer, we know that the bombers have been positioned to do maximum damage to the structure's five support columns when the explosives are detonated. You see from this chart that they are planted here and here, and two in the back of the auditorium. There is also a bomber close to the stage, seated among the celebrities."

Jack paused. "The plan is simple. Five of our operatives—all female, all dressed in evening clothes, take out the female bombers. At the same instant, the snipers each take out two gunmen in quick succession. Our timing has to be perfect, and because the terrorists are jamming all radio signals, individual groups will be out of contact once we enter the auditorium and separate."

"Jesus," muttered an FBI sniper.

"The takedown has to be timed perfectly. We'll prearrange a time for the strike, and everyone will have to act at the same split second."

Groans and sighs greeted the news.

"Unfortunately, timing's not the worst of our problems." Jack paused until everyone quieted down. "While we have photos and names for four of the bombers, the identity of the fifth bomber is unknown—"

Outcry greeted this news.

"That means one bomb will most likely go off," an FBI sniper shouted.

"Not necessarily," said Jack, raising his voice to be heard over the mounting commotion. "We know where this bomber is located—down among the celebrities. We're going to send the female strike team in ahead of the sniper attack. If we're lucky, Nina Myers and her fellow operatives will locate and neutralize this unknown bomber along with the other four."

"Wait a minute," Lonnie Nobunaga cried. "You said the unknown bomber is in the celebrity seating area?"

"Yes," Jack replied. "She has to be. That's what the terrorists' plans indicate and that's also where the fifth support beam is located. If they miss just one support beam, the structure may not collapse even after the blasts."

"And you're sure it's a woman?"

"That's how the Chechens have done things up to now," Jack replied. "Your point?"

Nobunaga took a deep breath. "Listen. This may have nothing to do with the terrorists—"

"Get to the point. We're running out of time here."

"Abigail Heyer rolled into Hollywood for the award's show very pregnant—"

"No surprise," said Christina Hong. "Gossip is she and Nikolai Manos are an item."

Jack blinked. "Did you say Manos?"

Christina nodded. "It's in all the tabloids, including that low-rent rag Lonnie works for."

Nobunaga smirked. "I'm wounded."

Jack fixed his gaze on Lonnie. "So you're telling me Abigail Heyer is pregnant with Manos's child?"

Lonnie shook his head. "I'm telling you that she's been faking her pregnancy the whole time. Wearing a harness, just like she did in the movie *Bangor, Maine*. I have the photo to prove it. Shot it this morning on the woman's estate." He dangled the thumb drive from his key ring.

One of the snipers spoke up. "That's crazy. How could Abigail Heyer get a belly full of explosives past auditorium security?"

Even Lonnie knew the answer to that one. "The celebrities walk the red carpet. They don't pass through security. It would be like wanding the President and First Lady. You don't screen the people you're supposed to protect."

$$1\ 2\ 3\ 4\ 5\ 6\ 7\ 8\ 9$$
$$10\ 11\ 12\ 13\ 14\ 15\ 16\ 17$$
$$18\ 19\ 20\ 21\ \mathbf{22}\ 23\ 24$$

••

**THE FOLLOWING TAKES PLACE
BETWEEN THE HOURS OF
2 A.M. AND 3 A.M.
PACIFIC DAYLIGHT TIME**

••

2:09:03 A.M. PDT
Chamberlain Auditorium
Sub-Level Three

White House intern Adam Carlisle awoke with a
start. He began to stir, but his back was stiff from
sleeping on the cold concrete. His movements awoke
Megan Gleason, who had been using his thigh for a
pillow.

"What's wrong?" she whispered.

"I heard a noise," said Adam, rising quickly.

Though the two wives had been dozing in their
chairs, they were awake now too, and whispering nervously. In the sub-basement's gloom, Adam spied
Craig Auburn close to the crank phone, where he'd

collapsed. He was lying on the ground now, his right hand still holding his left arm. His eyes were closed, his breathing shallow.

A terrible crash boomed, as loud as a landslide.

"Jesus," Megan whispered. "What's that?"

Adam informed her, "From what Special Agent Auburn said before he passed out, that's the calvary. . . . I hope."

Megan blanched. "You *hope*?"

At the far end of a long corridor, Adam saw flashlights stabbing through the darkness. Dark silhouettes appeared a moment later.

Raising the USP Tactical that Special Agent Auburn had given him, Adam walked resolutely toward the flashlights, the weapon leveled at the man on point.

"Who are you?" Adam loudly demanded.

"Special Agent Jack Bauer, Counter Terrorist Unit," Jack replied.

With an audible exhale, Adam lowered the weapon. A moment later the sub-basement was filling with armed men. One of them approached the two ladies.

"I'm Special Agent Evans, Secret Service," he told them.

"Thank god," said the VP's wife.

More men emerged from the gloom, flanking the two ladies and helping Marina Novartov stand on her injured leg. Adam told Evans about Auburn's serious condition. A medic and another man were summoned to help.

"We're walking out of here, right now," he told the ladies and the interns. "Follow these two agents and stick close. We're not out of danger yet."

The group walked the length of the dark basement, until they came to an open steel hatch set in the concrete wall. Adam had found the hatch earlier and tried to open it, but it had been locked from the other side.

Just then, five women in fashionable evening gowns and high-heeled shoes emerged from the hatch. Megan shot Adam a curious look. He shrugged, shook his head. *Don't ask me.*

Evans stepped up to them. "Let's go. Through that hatch, to the sewers."

Megan shuddered. "The sewers?"

Adam smiled and put his arm around her shoulders. "Didn't I tell you when I first welcomed you to Washington—"

"I know, I know," she said, "this job has its perks."

2:13:32 A.M. PDT
Chamberlain Auditorium
Sub-Level Three

Jack checked the digital map display strapped to his forearm. It glowed green in the dimly lit sub-basement. He assembled everyone in front of a large metal grill set into the wall. Using a universal key, Jack picked the lock. The grill swung wide like a door.

Behind the steel mesh grill an aluminum shaft climbed straight up to the Chamberlain's roof. Steel rungs were embedded in the walls of the shaft, leading upward and out of sight. Jack could see light shining into the shaft from grills on the upper levels—the occupied floors.

"Okay, women first," Jack whispered. Nina stepped forward, wearing a black spangled dress. The other four women were similarly attired. Jack addressed them all.

"Climb until you pass four more grills, then exit

through the fifth. You'll come out in a corridor right next to the women's rest rooms on the main floor. Presumably the terrorists are allowing people to take bathroom breaks. I want you to mingle with the women returning to the auditorium, then get as close as you can to your respective targets. Understand?"

The women nodded, their faces tense.

"Take them down as soon as you hear the first shot. We'll fire at exactly 2:45 A.M.—not a second sooner."

Jack paused. "Remember, the success of the entire mission rests on your actions. Do not hesitate to do what is necessary to save lives. If you fail, hundreds may die."

Jack and the snipers watched the women enter the shaft. When they climbed out of sight, Jack closed the grill behind them.

"Let's go," he said, leading his snipers to the next air shaft, where they would make their own climb.

2:32:27 A.M. PDT
Chamberlain Auditorium
Mezzanine

Jack peered through the ornate brass grill of the auditorium's deserted mezzanine. He'd climbed the air shaft with his team of snipers following behind. Now Jack carefully scanned the darkened area, using night vision goggles to determine that every seat was empty. Listening intently, Jack heard the murmur of the crowd on the main floor below.

Silently he slipped his universal key into the slot on the grill and jiggled it. The rattle of metal sounded like an explosion, but the simple lock mechanism was easily tripped. With the squeak of metal on metal, Jack opened the ornamental grill and squirmed through the opening.

He crawled forward on his belly, moving down the aisle between rows of seats. The glass control booth was behind and above him, but it overhung the mezzanine, and even if the booth was occupied, no one would be able to see him.

As he crawled down a carpeted aisle to the mezzanine's edge, snipers silently emerged from the shaft behind him. Jack used hand signals to position the shooters at various points until they had a complete field of fire.

Finally, Jack peered over the edge of the balcony. Below him he saw hundreds of people, in seats or sprawled on the floor. Debris was scattered on the carpet, clothing draped over seat backs. Circling the hostages along the perimeter of the auditorium, Jack counted sixteen masked men, another two on the stage. There were still two shooters unaccounted for and Jack hoped they were escorting hostages to the rest rooms. As he watched, the missing pair appeared. They began chatting with the man seated on an ornate, throne-like chair in the middle of the expansive stage.

With hand signals, Jack issued the command for the shooters to assemble their weapons. Then he assembled his own.

Jack opened the soft cloth bags he'd slung over his back during the long climb up the shaft. Carefully he unwrapped the barrel, the magazines, the sniper scope and the two receivers and stuffed the cotton packing cloths back into the bag. Quickly and efficiently, Jack assembled the 7.62mm Mark 11 Mod 0 Type Sniper Rifle System.

The Mark 11 was a highly accurate precision semiautomatic rifle. Men who used it in the field dubbed it "an M16 on steroids." Light, versatile and portable, the rifle could be broken down into two main sections, which made it perfect for an operation like this one.

When Jack completed assembly, he shoved a magazine in place and flipped the control switch to semiautomatic. He had to hit at least two targets in rapid succession and wanted the fastest rate of fire possible.

Near one of the auditorium's rest rooms, Nina had just closed the brass grill behind her and smoothed her dress when a masked man appeared at the end of the marble-lined corridor. He spied the knot of women and hurried forward.

"Hey, what for you do?" he bellowed in fractured English. The man slipped the black submachine gun off his shoulder, waved it menacingly.

"Bathroom," Nina cried, throwing up her hands. "We just went to the bathroom, that's all."

The other women followed Nina's lead, threw up their hands, started to babble.

"Shuddup! Shuddup!" the gunman commanded. "Go back now. Back!"

The masked man gestured them forward, down the long marble lined corridor toward the auditorium.

As they approached the audience, Nina could hear the quiet murmur of the crowd. Another gunman who'd been guarding the doors stepped aside to allow Nina and the other women to enter the vast space. "In, in!" the armed man barked.

"Okay, we're going," Nina replied.

Immediately, Nina's senses were assaulted. The interior of the auditorium reeked—an unsavory combination of stale air, fear sweat, and spilled blood. To move down the aisle, Nina had to walk past a pile of elegantly attired corpses, stacked like cordwood against a wall, rivulets of blood staining the lush carpeting. The muted roar of a thousand people talking, crying, sighing, whispering filled her ears.

Once inside the auditorium, the women quickly dispersed, each subtly maneuvering to move as close to their respective targets as they could get. Nina had the farthest to go—from the back of the auditorium to the front row seats where international film star Abigail Heyer waited to blow herself and a thousand of her closest Hollywood friends to Kingdom Come.

Not only did she have a long way to go, Nina had the toughest job. The other women only had to kill their targets, knocking the detonators from their hands and slitting their throats with hidden knives before the suicide bombers had a chance to set off the explosives. Nina had to stop Abigail Heyer from setting off her bomb without killing her. Nina was tasked with taking the movie star alive.

2:43:16 A.M. PDT
Chamberlain Auditorium
Main Floor

Carla bit down on the pink satin handbag. Her face was flushed, her skin coated with a thin sheen of perspiration. A whimper escaped her lips, which were pale and white. Dark shadows hollowed her eyes, her gaze seemed far away and lost in jets of agony.

"Oh, Jesus. Oh, God," Carla wailed.

Teri Bauer knelt on the floor, both hands grasping Carla's arms to steady the woman. The contractions had started up again. Now they were less than three minutes apart. The baby was on its way.

"You! American bitch. Keep her quiet!"

Teri looked up. A masked man watched her from the aisle, just two empty seats away. He clutched a machine gun, the strap draped over his shoulder.

Teri bit her lip. Carla howled again, louder.

"Shut her up!" barked the gunman.

Carla cried out just then, oblivious to the danger.

Angrily, the man stepped forward. "I shut her up," he grunted.

Teri Bauer jumped to her feet, blocked the assassin's way. Her knees trembled, but her veins were suddenly filled with burning ice and she refused to back down.

2:44:06 A.M. PDT
Chamberlain Auditorium
Mezzanine

Peering over the edge of the balcony, Jack had already taken aim at the masked man seated center stage. The way the others deferred to him, and the way the man clutched his Agram 2000 in the crook of his arm—"Palestinian style"—told Jack this was their leader, Bastian Grost. Though the Serbian fugitive might prove to be a valuable prisoner, Jack decided he would not take the man alive. Victor Drazen's killers had a knack for eluding justice. But Bastian Grost wouldn't get away with anything. Not this time.

Jack checked the digital clock inside his sniper scope. It was less than a minute before the strike. His grip tightened on the pressed Kevlar handle, his finger rested on the grooved steel trigger. As he prepared to fire, Jack's attention was drawn to a commotion in the aisles. A gunman was gesturing wildly at a woman.

Even from this distance he recognized his wife. Jack tensed when he realized it was Teri. He swung the Mark 11 away from his target, to level the barrel at this new threat.

Squinting through the scope, he placed the crosshairs over the masked man's forehead. As the seconds ticked down, Jack steadied his hand and held his breath.

Five seconds—

The gunman stepped into the aisle. Teri jumped to her feet to block him.

Four seconds—

"Leave her alone," Teri shouted.

The man raised an arm, poised to strike her down, possibly kill her with a blow from the butt of his machine gun.

Three seconds—

Jack pulled the trigger. The man's head exploded.

2:45:00 A.M. PDT
Chamberlain Auditorium
Main Floor

Rifles seemed to pop all over the auditorium at roughly the same time, followed by supersonic cracks as the bullets warbled toward their targets.

Everywhere armed men in black jerked wildly, or spun around, or threw their arms wide as 7.62mm rounds tore bloody holes through their flesh, bones and organs.

One masked man, his skull shattered by a single round, flopped onto the lap of Chip Manning, still seated beside his agent. The dead man's brains spilled out on the star's Helmut Lang jacket.

Tough guy Manning squealed like a little girl.

Abigail Heyer jumped to her feet when she heard the supersonic crack. She'd been watching Bastian Grost, who suddenly flew backward as two bullets blew a massive hole through his chest, and the back of his chair.

When the Heyer woman stood up, Nina Myers spied a plunger in her hand. It was black, about the size of a large hypodermic needle, and trailed two thin wires that flowed into her clothing.

Nina leaped over a seat, grabbed the woman's arm and twisted it backward until she heard the satisfying snap of bone. The actress howled, the plunger dropped from her limp hand. But Nina didn't relent. She jerked the broken wrist upward, forcing Abigail Heyer to bend double. Then Nina brought her forearm down on the back of the woman's neck, smashing her to the ground.

Nina dragged the still struggling woman into the aisle, flipped her over and cut the dress away with the Gerber Guardian II double-edged knife she'd tucked into her garter. Under the shreds of designer clothing, Nina saw the white harness. She sliced the straps and yanked the prosthetic loose. The inside of the fake belly was stuffed with explosives.

"Clear!" Nina cried at the top of her lungs.

From other parts of the auditorium, she heard her words echoed several times. What she didn't hear told the real story. There was no deafening thunder of a detonating bomb, and Nina knew CTU had won this round.

* * *

"Go, go, go!"

Captain Stone screamed the words into his headset. Not even a second passed before dozens of LAPD squad cars, armored vehicles, ambulances, fire trucks and emergency vehicles rolled out of cover and across the pavement to converge on the Chamberlain Auditorium. Sirens blared and dozens of emergency lights flickered like tiny red beacons.

There was no way for Stone to know if Jack and his team had met with success or failure but it didn't matter anyway. His orders were to move his officers in to surround the building at precisely 2:45 A.M., to open the fire doors they'd opened before, and enter the auditorium with maximum force, and that's exactly what he did.

Stone watched through binoculars as firemen opened the steel doors, then police and SWAT team units poured through the opening. He listened for a long time, waiting for an explosion, the sounds of a fire fight. Instead, a voice crackled over his headset.

"Area secure. Repeat, area secure. The hostages are safe . . ."

2:59:09 A.M. PDT
Terrence Alton Chamberlain Auditorium
Los Angeles

Jack found his wife in the lobby. An emergency rescue team was wheeling Carla out on a gurney, with Chandra and Teri following close behind. As she rushed past him, Jack touched his wife's arm and their eyes met.

"Jack, Jack," Teri cried, throwing herself at him. "I knew you'd come. I just knew it."

"It's okay," Jack whispered, holding her close. "You're safe now."

For a long time they embraced, an island in a sea of swirling activity. Then Teri pulled back, tears dewing her face.

"Is it over, Jack? Is it really over?"

"Almost," he replied.

1 2 3 4 5 6 7 8 9
10 11 12 13 14 15 16 17
18 19 20 21 22 **23** 24

• •

THE FOLLOWING TAKES PLACE
BETWEEN THE HOURS OF
3 A.M. AND 4 A.M.
PACIFIC DAYLIGHT TIME

• •

3:09:10 A.M. PDT
CTU Headquarters, Los Angeles

Jamey, Milo and Doris had taken control of the Cyber-Unit. It took all three of them to enter all the search parameters into Fay Hubley's bloodhound program. Along with the names of the victims and players in the hostage drama—Bastian Grost, Nawaf Sanjore, Valerie Dodge, Hugh Vetri, Nikolai Manos—the names of their firms, companies, and institutes such as the Russia East Europe Trade Alliance, were also added to expand the search exponentially.

Once the program was launched, there would be so much information to correlate, so many places for the computer to search, that virtually every other computer function at CTU had to be shut down or curtailed.

"Ready?" Jamey asked when the programming was complete.

"Go," Ryan commanded.

Jamey punched "execute" and they waited.

Jack and Nina observed the search from Jack's glass-enclosed office on CTU's mezzanine while they waited for a security team to process their prisoner, Abigail Heyer. Nina had expressed skepticism that the process would yield results, but Jack was willing to try anything. Milo, Jamey, and Doris all believed it was *possible* that the computer, augmented by CTU's random sequencer, would come up with some clues— perhaps even answers—but none of them would state categorically that the program would work.

Only Tony Almeida, boots propped on a desk while he silently watched the process, truly believed Fay's creation would find her killer. He remained cool when five minutes went by with no results.

The single screen that should have displayed promising leads remained dark.

Then, twenty-one minutes and six seconds into the process, the monitor abruptly lit up and the screen was filled with hundreds of possible clues. The operation was moving so fast Jamey had to step in and slow things down. In a steady stream, pertinent facts continued to emerge.

The single link that united all the disparate threads was Nikolai Manos. The program revealed that one of Manos's shell companies hired a very expensive mapping firm to survey public land in the Angeles National Forest.

MG Enterprises, a Nikolai Manos-controlled shell

company, paid for a series of deliveries of construction material to an area along Route 39—a road through the San Gabriel Mountains that had been closed to traffic for over a decade.

Pacific Power and Light recorded two years of mysterious power surges and incidents of voltage theft from high-tension wires running through the same region of the San Gabriel peaks where the survey had been conducted.

Three hikers and a pair of campers in an area near the spot where Ibn al Farad had been captured vanished without a trace over a fourteen-month period.

Rangers in the Angeles National Forest reported strange lights at night.

Unauthorized helicopter takeoffs and landings were reported to the FAA. A near miss between a light plane and an unauthorized aircraft was reported over that same area six months ago.

A 1977 article from the National Spelunking Institute—now posted on its website—featured an unconfirmed report of a large network of caverns discovered in the San Gabriels. Subsequent expeditions failed to locate the caves. The last one mounted just eighteen months ago ended tragically. The team's vehicle was found at the bottom of a ravine, everyone dead inside. The incident was judged an accident, at the time.

Jamey Farrell kept narrowing the search until, at precisely 3:33 A.M., the program spit out a longitude and latitude in the San Gabriel Mountains, a three-square-mile area just four miles from where Ibn al Farad was caught searching for his master.

Fay Hubley's program had nailed the Old Man on the Mountain.

3:46:17 A.M. PDT
CTU Headquarters, Los Angeles

Abigail Heyer was seated in an aluminum interrogation chair. Both hands were strapped to the armrest, the woman's broken right wrist, swollen and purple, had been treated with no more care than her left. The woman had been strip searched, had endured a thorough cavity check, and all of her clothes, jewelry and personal items had been taken from her. She would not get the opportunity to swallow poison, like Katya or Richard Lesser.

The international star wore an orange prison jumpsuit and nothing else. She stared straight ahead, unblinking, but Jack believed she knew he was right there, on the other side of the one-way mirror.

"Break her, Jack. Get her to confess." Tony Almeida still wore his undercover clothing—black jeans, sweatshirt stained with blood, steel-tipped cowboy boots. His unshaven face was ravaged by fatigue, his eyes haunted. Jack knew Tony blamed himself for Fay Hubley's death. Jack knew because he'd been in Tony's situation himself, more than once.

Nina, still wearing the spangled dress, gazed impassively at the woman in the chair. It was Nina who'd brought Ms. Heyer back to CTU for interrogation. The woman had demanded her lawyers—plural, she had a team of them—and was denied. The actress went silent after that, not even answering Dr. Brandeis's queries about her condition.

The doctor requested time to set her broken wrist—Jack vetoed that. Then Dr. Brandeis asked permission to administer a painkiller. Jack nixed that too. Brandeis did not ask to witness the interrogation. He already knew the answer.

Jack studied Abigail Heyer through the glass, his jaw moving. Nina touched his arm, leaned close and whispered, "The crisis has passed, Jack. Let the doctor take care of her. Hold her here until she's willing to talk."

Jack gently shook off Nina. "This ends now." He swiped the keycard that dangled from a strap around his neck and entering the soundproofed interrogation chamber.

The woman refused to acknowledge his presence. Jack placed a metal chair in front of her, sat down. Still she resisted his gaze.

There were a number of ways to extract information, Jack knew—torture, drugs, sleep deprivation, the threat of death.

But such techniques wore the prisoner's will down over time, and Jack was nearly out of it. Hasan had to be stopped. Now. They were never closer to the man than at this moment, and might never get this close again. He had to extract the confirmation he needed from his prisoner as quickly as possible.

Yet Jack knew in this case physical threats would also fail because Abigail Heyer was willing to blow herself up for Hasan, so she was not afraid of death. Which meant that he had to hit her fast and hard—with something she *did* fear.

"Hasan is dead," Jack began. Despite herself, the woman winced.

"We knew about his hideaway—that place in the mountains. Five minutes ago we blew it up. Everyone inside perished. We're assessing the damage now. I can show you the man's corpse, when we find it."

"Hasan will never die," Abigail Heyer said, a half-smile brushing her full lips.

"You may be right." Jack nodded. Now was the time to take the chance, make the leap. "Hasan, as a symbol, an ideal, might never die. But Nikolai Manos, the man who called himself Hasan, is dead. I killed him."

Jack studied the woman's face. He watched her calm, controlled demeanor crack into a thousand tiny splinters. He saw a black void open up inside of her and swallow the woman whole.

Jack watched Abigail Heyer's reaction, and he *knew*.

....

**THE FOLLOWING TAKES PLACE
BETWEEN THE HOURS OF
4 A.M. AND 5 A.M.
PACIFIC DAYLIGHT TIME**

....

4:55:01 A.M. PDT
Over the Angeles National Forest

Jack had called in every resource he could find for this raid. Chet Blackburn's overworked Tactical Unit would lead the strike, but elements of the FBI, Captain Stone's LAPD SWAT team, the California National Guard—even State Troopers under the command of Captain Lang—had been tapped.

Now a dozen helicopters circled the mountain, while CTU specialists used deep ground imaging to locate the hidden entrances to Hasan's no longer secret underground lair.

"We found two exits, both covered now," Chet Blackburn told Jack, shouting to be heard over the noise of the beating blades. "All the elements are in place. We're ready to go once you give the word."

Jack Bauer nodded, activated his headset. "Begin the assault . . ."

4:59:17 A.M. PDT
Under the Angeles National Forest

Hasan's anger was a physical force that battered everyone and everything around him.

Nawaf Sanjore followed a trail of smashed furniture and broken glass, to the deepest region of his master's underground headquarters. He found several acolytes cowering in front of a steel door.

"Is he inside?" the architect asked.

The robed men nodded. "The master does not wish to be disturbed."

Sanjore ignored the warning, pushed the heavy door inward. The chamber beyond was small, and crowded with computers and satellite communications equipment. Hasan sat in his command chair, his back to the door. He stared straight ahead, at a darkened monitor.

"Hasan?"

"Leave me."

"Master. Such behavior is unseemly. This is a setback, not a defeat."

The chair spun on its axis. Hasan faced the architect. "I have just learned that the communications center in Tijuana was destroyed hours before the virus was to be unleashed. The authorities have rescued the hostages, and CTU has captured Abigail Heyer—alive."

"She knows nothing—"

"She knows enough. But I do not care about the

woman, only the movement. We have been wounded—"

"We will survive," Sanjore cried. "No one knows your true identity. No one could possibly know of this place. Even if that foolish actress implicates Nikolai Manos, who will believe her? The Old Man on the Mountain will endure."

Hasan seemed mollified by Sanjore's words, but a shadow of doubt crossed his face. "We have lost assets. Irreplaceable assets . . ."

"A mere setback. We can rebuild. The vision has not died."

"But if I am exposed?"

"Then you shall continue your operations in secret, from this very base of operations. Do not forget that a great portion of your wealth is intact, unreachable in a Swiss account."

"But we have lost so much."

"But not all, never all. You are still alive, Hasan. And alive, you can still fight. The Americans, the Russians, they cannot harm you as long as you remain hidden in this impenetrable fortress. In time, from this secret place, we will again launch an attack."

Hasan pondered the man's words. "You restore my faith, Nawaf. Truly you are the most loyal and valuable of my followers."

Nawaf Sanjore's heart soared at his master's compliment, rarely given. He bowed deeply.

"I live to serve you—"

The architect was interrupted by explosions, screams, gunshots. Then an amplified voice boomed throughout the underground cavern.

"This is CTU. Lay down your weapons. You are surrounded and cannot escape. Surrender now or you will be shot."

Richard Walsh turned off the recorder, sat back in his chair. Jack Bauer stifled a yawn, fought back the throbbing pain behind his eyes. His black battle suit was scorched and he still smelled of cordite hours after the raid had been successfully concluded.

Walsh opened a file on the table in front of him. He leafed through it, shook his head. "There's evidence that Manos had contact with Hugh Vetri, the murdered producer. They worked together on a number of charities, and last year Vetri accompanied Manos to Eastern Europe to tour some of the refurbished film studios."

Jack nodded. "I think Manos tried to brainwash Hugh Vetri, but it didn't take. Maybe because Vetri had a wife and a family, something to live for beyond himself. In that sense Vetri was different than Ibn al Farad, Richard Lesser, Nawaf Sanjore, Abigail Heyer, maybe more grounded in reality. I think Vetri resisted Hasan, and he was murdered."

"The LAPD found hundreds of personal files in Vetri's computers," said Walsh. "At his Summit Studio offices and his home. He was big on investigating the people with whom he intended to do business. That's most likely why he had that file on you, Jack— he was trying to find someone he could trust to tell the things he'd learned about Manos, about Hasan. Lesser somehow supplied Vetri with the data disk as a way to lure CTU into the case."

"That makes as much sense as anything," Jack replied.

"I'm going to debrief Tony Almeida next," said Walsh. "Chappelle tells me I should reprimand him for disobeying a direct order, staying behind in Mexico for no other purpose than revenge."

"Chappelle's got it wrong," said Jack. "Lesser was sent to us by Hasan to divert our attention away from his operation in Mexico. His plan would have worked if Tony had listened to Chappelle. The midnight virus would have been unleashed from the command center in Tijuana, and Hasan would have been able to coordinate and direct continued assaults against the country from his secret base on the Avenue de Dante."

Walsh slipped another file from the bottom of his stack. "I have something else here you might find interesting. Washington has run an extensive background check on Nikolai Manos and came up with a dossier. Are you curious about their opinion, Jack?"

Bauer did not reply so Walsh pressed on.

"According to Langley, Nikolai Manos was born somewhere in Eastern Europe, probably Chechnya, but no one really knows. In the chaos following the first Chechen insurgency, Manos was orphaned and became a refugee. At the age of nine, he was discovered by a wealthy Greek family who adopted him. While our knowledge of his adopted family is extensive, we don't know much about his real parents, except that they were murdered by the Soviets when he was still very young. The analyst who reviewed the data believes Manos was seeking revenge against the Russian people for their crimes against the Chechens. That's why he wanted their First Lady—to humiliate and intimidate the hated Russians. What do you think?"

"I think the analyst missed the boat."

"Excuse me?"

"Manos . . . Hasan. He'd gone beyond mere revenge. He was setting himself up as a religious leader, a living god. He found his model in the medieval Islamic leader, but he was no Muslim either. Hasan was building a brand new religion, a faith he hoped would outlive him."

Walsh stroked his moustache. "Did he succeed?"

"Manos refused to surrender—killed himself in the bunker along with Nawaf Sanjore—so I think we stopped him in time. But maybe not. If his disciples survived . . . if there is even a single follower left, then his religion lives on as well."

Walsh shifted, uneasy with this idea. "Well, there were a lot of deaths in that auditorium but CTU saved the lives of most of the hostages, not to mention some of the country's most beloved stars."

"There's only one star on my mind now," Jack replied.

Walsh understood his meaning. On the wall in the lobby of CIA headquarters at Langley, Virginia, there hung more than seventy stars—all of them anonymous—one for each of the CIA operatives who died while serving their country. Behind a glass case, the Book of Honor held some of their names. Other identities were still classified. Though Fay Hubley's name and her service would probably not be revealed for decades, Walsh had no doubt her star would shine continually in the minds of her colleagues.

Jack yawned, massaged his forehead.

"You know, Jack. It sounds simplistic but I always felt that family was the only thing in this world that kept me grounded in reality, that kept me sane, and this operation certainly doesn't dissuade me from that notion."

"Sir?" asked Jack, the endless day finally catching up to him.

Walsh closed the file. "Go home, Jack. Kiss your wife and hug your daughter. Have a nice dinner with your family and play chess with Kim."

"Thank you sir, I think I will." Jack rose from the table.

"And Special Agent Bauer . . ."

"Yes, sir?"

"Take tomorrow off."